CALL THE SHOTS

CALL THE SHOTS

DON CALAME

CANDLEWICK PRESS

Copyright © 2012 by Don Calame

First paperback edition 2013

Library of Congress Catalog Card Number 2012938812
ISBN 978-0-7636-5556-3 (hardcover)
ISBN 978-0-7636-6454-1 (paperback)

13 14 15 16 17 18 BVG 10 9 8 7 6 5 4 3 2 1

Printed in Berryville, VA, U.S.A.

This book was typeset in Melior.

Candlewick Press
99 Dover Street
Somerville, Massachusetts 02144

visit us at www.candlewick.com

To my wife, my everything

I KNOW WHAT YOU DID LAST SUMMER

It's my best idea yet." Coop's got a huge grin on his face as he wrestles his ice skate onto his left foot. "It came to me last night while I was launching a mud missile."

"Oh, God, here we go again." Matt rolls his eyes as he pulls the blue plastic skate guards off his blades. "It's like a recurring nightmare."

"No, listen," Coop insists. "This is the *one.* I'm telling you. It's going to make us all obscenely rich."

"Seeing a live naked girl last summer was 'the *one.*'" I dig around in my backpack, searching for a pair of wool socks. "Playing in the Battle of the Bands was 'the *one.*'" Instead of socks, I find one of Buttons's fossilized hair-balls, which I quickly huck under the bench. "Every one is 'the *one.*' Except that they never are."

"How can you live with yourself, being so wrong

all the time, dawg?" Coop says. "All of my plans have turned out for the best. Think about it for a second. When we saw a live naked girl, Matt got a girlfriend. When we played in the Battle of the Bands, I got a girlfriend. If you play your cards right, Sean-o, this could be the thing that finally gets *you* a girlfriend."

The muscles in my jaw twitch. "I've *had* a girlfriend."

"You know what I mean," Coop says. "One who doesn't look like a hobbit and who sticks around for more than a week."

I flip him off. "Remind me again why we're friends."

Coop claps me hard on the shoulder and beams. "Because I'm always thinking about how to make your life sweeter."

I finally find the wadded-up socks at the bottom of my bag. I give them a quick sniff and recoil at the damp, woolly urinal-cake stench of them.

Matt laughs at me. "Why do you always do that? You think this time they're gonna smell like cinnamon?"

"I don't know," I say, my ears getting hot. "I smell things. It's how I experience my world. Maybe I was a dog in a past life."

As soon as the words spill from my mouth, I realize I've just set myself up. I brace myself for the barrage of butt-sniffing jokes from Coop but nothing comes. Which is totally uncharacteristic. And can only mean that he must be über-focused on his new plan. Used to be that him being so excited about his ideas would get me going too, but I don't know. As we've gotten older—and everyone but me has benefitted from his insane schemes—I've found it harder and harder to take him seriously.

Of course, if I thought there was even the tiniest chance that this plan of Coop's, whatever it might be, could actually make us rich, I would be on it like a parrot on a peanut. Because, as much as I hate to admit it, he's right about my girlfriend situation. I *am* a lost cause. After Tianna broke up with me at the end of last summer, I've been on a starvation diet where girls are concerned. I could use any advantage I can get—and if that extra boost came from being a millionaire, I'd take it, despite what my mom says about the kinds of girls who like you for the size of your bank account instead of the size of your heart.

But it's stupid to get hopeful, because all we ever get out of Coop's schemes are headaches and heartbreaks. And that's when things actually go well.

So life will just continue on as it has, with everyone else paired off.

Coop and Helen.

Matt and Val.

And me and my urinal-cake wool socks.

On the plus side, at least I don't have to spend the night with only our pack of foster animals for company. Love them as I do, they're a little boring in the conversation department.

"A movie," Coop announces, like me and Matt have been begging him to spill the beans. "That's the sitch this semest. We're going to make a cheap-ass horror film like *Psychopathic Anxiety*. Or *The Jersey Devil Assignment*. They shot those things for a few thousand bills and then sold them for megabucks. There's no reason we can't do exactly the same thing."

"I can think of a few thousand reasons right off the bat," I say, my feet feeling claustrophobic in my old stiff hockey skates. "I mean, seriously. If there were awards for your dumb ideas, this one would win Best . . . Most . . . Dumbest."

"Ouch," Coop says flatly. "That stings, Sean. Too bad you don't know what the hell you're talking about. Because it's a *genius* idea. Case in point. Your favorite movie of all time. A little film called *El Mariachi*. Made for seven grand. Turned over two mil. And that was just in theaters. That's not even counting the five trillion copies of the DVD you bought."

I blow a lip fart. "Wha*tever*. Even if we knew the first thing about making a movie—which we don't—where the hell are we going to find seven grand? Or *any* grand, for that matter? We might as well conjure up a million dollars and be done with it."

"It's not like I'm springing this on you uninformed," Coop says. "I researched filmmaking on the Internet for almost an hour last night."

"A whole hour?" Matt says, sounding fake-impressed. "Why didn't you say so? This plan is obviously fool-proof."

"Look." Coop starts pacing around, a little wobbly on his skates. "There are a ton of ways we can raise the cash. We get a bit here. A bit there. Family. Friends. Local businessmen. It'll be simp. You'll see."

The DJ turns on the music in the rink. It's a Justin Bieber ballad that's been everywhere lately. It's actually not a bad song. The lyrics are sort of catchy, really.

Coop turns on me, his eyes narrow. "You're tuggin' me, right? You don't actually know the words to this crap, do you?"

I clamp my mouth shut, suddenly aware that I've been singing along. "Uh . . . no. I just . . . no."

"Sean-o likes the Biebs!" Coop cracks up. "Now I totally understand why your sister's convinced you're gay."

I glare at him. "First of all, munch my left one, okay? And B, Cathy isn't *convinced* I'm gay. She *wants* me to be gay. Because she thinks it'd be cool. There's a big difference."

"Okay, sure, fine. Whatever you say." Coop sighs and runs his hand through his hair, doing nothing to fix the hat head he's been rocking all day. "*Anyway,* as I was saying. We can raise the money for the movie. I mean, Christ, B&M Deli sponsors Little League baseball teams all the time. And what do they get for *that*? Their name spanked across the back of a uniform? A cheap-ass plastic trophy every few years? Big whoop. If our movie rakes in even one-quarter of the coin that that puddle of spooge *Psychopathic Anxiety* made, they'd never have to sell another pastrami on rye with a flaccid pickle spear ever again."

Matt shakes his head, tugging his pant leg down over his skate boot. "Please, count me out on this one, okay? I just want to have a normal, boring school semester for once."

Coop sighs. "I don't get you guys sometimes. This is the kind of thing that can separate us from the miserable masses. Don't you dawgs want to be in charge of your own destinies?"

"Tell me," I say, carefully untying the dog-chewed laces on my skates and pulling the tongue up and out to try and give my feet a little more breathing space. "What's Helen think of this 'genius plan'? She on board?"

Coop glances toward the rink, where the Zamboni is finishing up resurfacing the ice. "I haven't told her yet. *Because,*" he adds before Matt or I can interrupt, "I wanted to tell you guys first. But I'm sure she'll be all over it. She loves the movies. Why wouldn't she want to help make one?"

"And what about Val?" I ask Matt. "Think she'll go for it?"

Matt holds up his hands in surrender. "Like I said, I just want to have a nice, normal semester. I'm sure Val does too."

I flash a grin at Coop. "See?"

"Fine." Coop smashes his knit cap on his head. "But don't you two come squalling to me when I pull up to the car wash you're slaving at in my bitch-red Gullwing, blowing my schnoz with fifty-dollar bills and wiping my ass with hundreds."

"Why would you be wiping your butt at a car wash?" I ask.

Coop shakes his head. "I was being metaphorical."

Just then, I look up from adjusting my skates to see Val and Helen entering the arena.

"Okay," Coop says when he sees the girls. "Let's keep our movie plan on the q.t. for now. Until we have a few more details hammered out."

"Yeah, well." Matt shrugs. "Seeing as we're not doing it, I don't see what there is to keep quiet about."

"I'm just saying." Coop keeps his voice low. "If the girls learn about it before we know exactly what kind of film we're going to make, they might have . . . *opinions*. And we don't want to have to make some gay-ass lovey-dovey chick flick. No offense, Sean."

"Just because I liked *Mamma Mia!* doesn't mean I like all chick flicks. And it certainly doesn't make me ga—"

"Hey, whatever." Coop shoots me with a finger pistol and winks. "We accept you for who you are, dude."

I look skyward as the girls approach.

"What's up?" Helen says, her white figure skates tied together and slung over her shoulder.

"Nothing much," Coop leaps in. "Just discussing how lame it is that we have to go back to school on Monday."

Helen's looking pretty cute in her powder-blue mittens and matching pom-pom hat. It used to be that she would only wear bulky clothes in various shades of gray. But ever since the Battle of the Bands, Helen's been trotting out the pastels in a big way. I just can't believe she and Coop are going out. After all he did so he wouldn't have to be her partner in Health class. Beefing her out of the library. Stealing her combination so Prudence could ransack her locker. Filling out an application to try and get her to change schools. I don't get it. But that's Coop for you. Always landing on his feet.

"Yeah. Vacations always go so fast," Valerie says. "Hi, you." She leans over and gives Matt a kiss. Lucky jerk. I've had a crush on Val—with her long red hair, full lips, and sexy French accent—ever since she moved here in seventh grade. I would have been totally pissed at Matt for dating her if I hadn't been going out with Tianna at the time.

As it is now, I'm just insanely envious.

"Have you guys been here long?" Helen asks, sliding her arm around Coop's waist.

"Not really. Maybe fifteen." On skates, Coop is several inches taller than Helen. He leans down, and the two of them start making out.

There's a twinge of something inside me as I watch them go at each other. Jealousy, for sure, but also . . . oh, gross. I quickly shift on the bench to try and stanch the rapid swelling in my pants. Jeez Louise. That is *not* cool. I really wish my body was a bit more selective sometimes.

I turn my head before anyone notices the flush in my cheeks. Pretend I'm looking to see if the gates to the ice are opened yet.

The rink guards have just finished putting out the orange traffic cones to cordon off the center oval for people who want to practice their figure-skating moves.

A deep breath and I manage to regain control over my careening hormones. I yank hard on my skate laces, and just like that, they snap in unison, causing both my clenched fists to punch me right in the mouth.

Coop sputters with laughter. "Dude, no need to beat yourself up. Things'll turn around for you eventually."

Perfect. This just gets better and better.

"Are you okay, Sean?" Helen says.

"Yeah. Sure. Fine." I feel my throbbing lip with my tongue. There's no taste of blood, so that's one good thing. But the way this night is headed, I'm sure it'll swell up to the size of a bratwurst.

I do some quick repair work, knotting up the broken

laces, then stand and do a few deep knee bends to limber up.

"You guys want to go get something to eat first?" Valerie lifts her chin toward the warm glow of the Wigwam's doors.

Matt, Coop, and Helen say they're up for some food, but I beg off using the pork chops I had for dinner as an excuse. But really, I'd rather chew my own arm off right now than sit through half an hour of my friends making googly eyes at their girlfriends while they feed each other French fries. Besides, the smooth ice beckons.

Nobody puts up any arguments. No "Come on, Sean." Or "Hang with us. You don't have to eat anything." Just a thumbs-up from Coop and a "Catch you later" from the others, before the four of them turn and head off without me. At least no one's there to see me lip-synch the last few lines of the Justin Bieber song.

☛ CHAPTER TWO ☚

THE FUNHOUSE

THE CIRCULATION HAS been completely cut off from my feet, but who cares? It feels right to be gliding over the ice at top speed. The electronic fizzing tweet of the music buzzing and pounding over the arena sound system is like my own personal soundtrack.

The cold air feels good on my face. That frosty bite on the cheeks and nose. A chilly sting in the lungs. I've got my arms pumping and my legs working overtime as the acid builds up in my calves and thighs. I can usually get three or four good fast laps in before the rink crowds up and it's all dodging and weaving around bodies.

I do a sloppy crossover as I round my first lap. I can't tell you how many times I've tripped over my own feet attempting to cross one over the other. But even though I'm going full tilt now, I don't really care if I take a spill.

When we were kids, Coop, Matt, and me would fall on purpose. Seriously. It was sweet. Especially on a newly cleaned ice surface. We'd take off as soon as the gates opened and then we'd drop like we'd been shot, sliding and spinning until we slammed hard into the boards. We could only get away with it twice a night— once at the start of the session and again at the midpoint just after the Zamboni resurfaced—because that's when the ice was slickest and there were the fewest people skating.

I'm tempted to hit the ground right now—even though it's probably too crowded at this point to avoid a collision. Still, a part of me is craving that loss of control. Those few moments when you're slipping this way and that. Trying to right yourself. Bracing for the impact of the boards. The heavy thud against the body.

Then, as I head into another turn, crossing the blue line, I see an opening. A nice stretch of clear ice heading straight over the far right face-off circle. And before I can talk myself out of it, I dig out a few extra strides to get my speed up and take the plunge.

I'm not on the ice half a second—my jeans absorbing the wet like a ShamWow—when I realize that I didn't exactly think this through. Sure, there *was* a clear path to the boards when I went down, but the fact that everyone is moving in a circular motion around the rink didn't get factored in to my snap decision. Neither did the fact that I'm not quite as small as I was five or six years ago.

I clip the first person—a little boy in a white Michelin Man coat—causing him to do several wobbly Bambi-esque pirouettes before he grabs a hold of someone's arm.

The red-jacketed rink guard is my next victim. I only catch one of her legs, but she isn't expecting it, and so she goes ass over teakettle, her right skate barely missing my face.

If I hadn't taken those extra strides before I dove to the ice, that might have been the end of it. As it is, I'm still moving pretty fast heading toward the boards. Lucky for me, the word seems to be out, because people are leaping to the side, clearing a path.

Not so much the pretzel-thin girl who's clinging to the wall as though this is the first time she's ever strapped on skates. She's much too focused on not falling to notice the guy who's hurtling wildly toward her.

She looks sort of familiar, but I can't really place her. I try to shift my position in an attempt to avoid her, but the beauty and the curse of freshly cleaned ice is just how slick and smooth it is.

And so I take her out like a bowling pin as I plow into the boards.

There's a loud *thunk,* followed by a high-pitched scream, which, if I'm being totally honest, I think came from me.

"I'm sorry, I'm sorry," the girl says as she lands on top of me. "I told them I didn't know how to skate."

She's all bony elbows and knees, and smells a lot like Swiss cheese.

"It was my fault," I say, scrambling to get out from under her.

It shouldn't take this long to extricate ourselves from each other, but we're slipping around on the ice like a couple of hot-oil wrestlers.

Two rink guards skate over to help us up and out of the gates. Thankfully, everyone is treating this like an accident and not something I stupidly did on purpose.

We get to the benches, and a quick inspection reveals we're both okay. Just a little bruised up. Nothing major.

"Evelyn," the girl says to me when the rink guards finally take off. "Evelyn Moss."

"Sean," I reply, since we seem to be introducing ourselves. "Hance."

"I know." Evelyn smiles shyly, her eyes cast down to her doe-brown rental skates. "You were in my computer class last semester."

"Oh, yeah. That's right. Computer class." I nod like it's all coming back to me. She must have been one of the ninth-graders we tended to ignore.

"You don't remember me. It's okay." She glances over at me. "The only reason I remember you is because I used to eavesdrop on you and your friend Matt. You guys were pretty funny."

"Thanks," I say, trying to wiggle some life back into my strangled toes. I should probably take off my skates, but if I do that, I'll never get them back on. And I'd still like to take a few more laps before I call it a night.

"Are you taking any computer classes next semester?" she asks, picking at the fuzz BBs on her avocado-colored sweater.

"Web Design. Maybe. I don't know if I'll get in; I handed in my forms late."

"Me too," she says. "Web Design, I mean, not the late part. I always get my schedule in way before the deadline. Hey, maybe we'll get lucky and be in it together."

"Yeah. That'd be cool."

Okay, let me get this out of the way right off the bat. I am *not* attracted to Evelyn Moss.

At all.

Sure, she has reddish hair, but it's stringy and dull. Not long and lush like Valerie's. And she's got a raccoon mask of freckles, which isn't a good look for a girl with the sort of pinched-thin nose that she has. Also, her voice is all nasal and shrill. Like a crow with a cold.

And then there's that cheese smell. It's weird. It's not like it's so awful as much as just really *there.* Like maybe she works in a deli or something and is exclusively in charge of slicing the Swiss. Don't get me wrong, I actually like Swiss cheese. Just not wafting off a girl's body.

"Are you here with anybody?" Evelyn asks.

"Just some friends. Matt and Coop," I specify, reminding myself that she was in our computer class. "You?"

"My Girl Scout troop. We took a vote for our winter break outing. Needless to say, this was *not* my choice." She snort-laughs like an excited piglet.

"Girl Scouts? Really? Do people still do that?"

"Sure. I'm a Senior Scout. I'm also a Counselor-in-Training. It's cool."

"Oh, I don't know about that."

"Shut up." Evelyn giggles as she punches me in the shoulder. Hard. "Is too. We go on all sorts of cool trips. Plus it'll look great when I apply to college. It shows I'm committed."

"Like, to a mental institution?"

"Oh, funny, funny. *No.* But once I finish the Counselor-in-Training program, I *can* get a job at a summer camp."

"I sure hope you can swim better than you skate."

"Okay, Mr. Graceful." She whales me in the arm again. Jesus. "Or *maybe* you slid into me on purpose so you could start talking to me?"

"Um, no. I definitely did not mean to run into you. I'm actually a pretty good skater."

"Good." And before I know what's going on, Evelyn grabs my hand, stands, and yanks me up. "Then you can teach me how to skate better. To make up for knocking me over."

God, she's strong *and* pushy.

I glance around and don't see my so-called friends anywhere. So, fine. I'll be the nice guy and show Swiss-cheesey how to balance on her skates. What could it hurt?

✸ CHAPTER THREE ✸

REPULSION

OH, MAN, HER PALM is super clammy. Ick.

I didn't notice at first because I was so shocked by her bossiness. And her superhuman strength. But now that we're skating around the rink, hand in hand, it's like I'm holding a warm soggy dinner roll.

"How's this?" Evelyn says, shuffling clumsily along on her skates. "Pretty good, huh?"

I nod. "Yeah, you're doing great."

She's gripping my hand tight, cutting off all the feeling in my fingers. I'd really like to let go of her, but she's using me for balance, and if I pull away right now, she'll do a face-plant onto the ice for sure.

Evelyn looks over at me and smiles. "You're a good teacher, Sean." She stumbles and nearly falls. I have to use all my strength to keep her on her feet.

"Eyes ahead," I instruct. "We've got to get you so you can do this on your own." Like, now.

"I don't know," Evelyn says, staring forward again. "I kind of like skating like this."

It's strange, but she's much more attractive from the side. Not like a "Yeah, I've got to tap that" kind of attractive. But certainly an improvement over how she appears face-to-face. I guess that's what people mean by having a "best side." Evelyn's is definitely her left one by a good margin.

I wonder if I should mention this to her. So when she gets her picture taken, she can always pretend she's looking off at something over to her right.

As I debate this with myself, the lights are suddenly dimmed and some slow, sappy love song starts playing over the loudspeakers. A disco ball is lowered from the center of the ceiling and casts little squares of light all over the place.

"Couples skate," a guy announces in a deep Darth Vader-ish voice. "Couples only."

"Hey, we can stay on," Evelyn caws, crushing my hand. "Because there's two of us."

"Yeah." I look around at all the other couples joining us on the ice and feel like someone just dumped a fistful of itching powder down my boxers. People are going to think I actually asked her to skate. "Great."

I sigh quietly. But then I think, *So what?* So what if people think I asked Evelyn to skate with me? It's not like she's *so* hideous. And it's certainly not like I have any other prospects. Besides, Evelyn seems to really be enjoying herself. Let her have her fun. Maybe I'll bank some karma points with the girlfriend gods.

See, he's a nice guy. Let's send him someone really special.

"I *love* this song!" Evelyn sways in time to the beat as the female singer bellows on about how people wait their whole lives for a moment like this.

"Careful now," I shout over the music. "Focus on your balance. Don't get too carried away."

"I'm already carried away." She looks over at me as the song swells, her eyes wide and wet like a love-starved puppy.

Oh, crap. I think I might have boarded a runaway train here. Not good.

I flip through the possible excuses in my head. Food. Bathroom. Leg cramp. They all sound so made-up. And nowhere near good enough to make her release the death grip she's got on my hand.

Still, it's not fair to lead her on.

I'm about to throw myself to the ice under the guise that I've lost an edge on my skate blade when Coop and Helen glide up next to us, the flickering fairy lights of the disco ball dancing across their faces. Helen gives me a big smile. Coop shoots me a way-to-go wink and thumbs-up combo.

I glance over at Evelyn again. The muted lights make the left side of her face that much more appealing. Cute, even.

Could I overlook all that other stuff—the voice, the whiff of cheese, the sweaty palms—for a girl with a moderately pleasant profile?

Yeah, I think I probably could. I mean, I'm not looking for someone to marry. I just want a girlfriend. Someone to go to the movies with. And watch TV with. And to hang out along with my friends.

Besides, everyone says you should play the field before you settle down. This would just be like that. Who knows? Maybe we'd really get along.

And then, out of the blue, I get a pang of uncertainty. Like, what if I read the signs wrong? What if I imagined that look of longing in her eyes? What if I make a move and she smacks me down? Rejected by a sort-of-homely ninth-grader. That would *not* look good on the dating résumé.

Suddenly, just as the cornball song reaches a crescendo, Evelyn's skate blade catches a rut and she trips.

I grasp her hand tightly and pull her up before she hits the ice.

"Oh, my God." Evelyn gazes into my eyes, her arms somehow having wound up around my neck. "Did you hear that?"

"Hear what?" I ask, wondering if she popped her shoulder or something.

We're standing in the middle of the rink, all the other couples streaming past us like a river around a rock.

"The lyrics to the song," Evelyn says breathlessly.

"She was singing about how she wants someone to catch her when she falls. And then you caught me just as I was falling! It's a sign, don't you think?"

"I don't know. I wasn't really listen—"

Evelyn leaps up and smashes her mouth against mine. Her tongue pries open my lips and she's exploring the inside of my mouth like a spelunker searching for cave treasure. There's a moment when I think she's actually playing tetherball with my uvula.

Part of me wants to detach Evelyn from my face, but another part—a *lower* part—is enjoying the kiss too much, however ferocious it might be. My eyes dart around like crazy as I try to guide the two of us out of traffic and toward the boards.

When I finally get us to safety, she pulls away with a loud wet smack, biting my lower lip like a wild animal.

Evelyn's out of breath. She's staring at me with this strange hungry look in her eyes. Like if she could, she would actually eat my entire head.

She grabs me in a powerful hug, pressing her cheek to my chest and squeezing the air from my lungs. "I guess this means we're going out now, huh?"

"Uhhh." I choke. "I . . . um . . ." My brain is short-circuiting. Can't focus. Though the throbbing in my boxers is unmistakable.

And that's when I see Val and Matt, smiling and waving from the other side of the glass.

Something about how they're beaming at me, and the

swirl of the song coming to an end, and how I don't want to wind up being the guy at college who dated only one girl in high school, clears the fog from my head.

Well, that, and the uprising going on downstairs.

"Yeah," I say. "I guess so."

Evelyn laughs and hugs me harder, if that's even possible. "Ohmygod, my very first boyfriend! I can't even believe it!" She leans back, her dead-serious stare boring into me. "Don't *ever* break up with me, okay?" Her eyes start to fill up at just the thought of it. "I mean it. I don't think . . . I don't think I could take it. Promise me, okay?"

"Uh . . . okay," I croak. "Sure."

"Thank you." Evelyn buries her face in my coat and sniffles. "I believe you."

I pat her back awkwardly.

I should be happy here, right? I mean, I'm finally dating someone again. Someone fairly cute. Sort of. From the side. So why do I feel a nauseous sourness in my stomach? Like I just ate three Big Macs with way too much special sauce?

Like, I maybe just made one of the biggest mistakes of my life?

☙ CHAPTER FOUR ☙

DARKNESS FALLS

I'VE GOT BROCK LESNAR down on the mat—ready to take my rightful place as the Ultimate Fighting Champion—when I hear the family-room door open and footsteps coming up behind me.

"Off the TV, scrotum. I'm watching a movie." It's Cathy, Queen of Darkness.

"Clearly you're not," I say, waving my Xbox controller.

"I will be once you turn off your idiot games." She gestures at the cold pack I've got wrapped around my neck. "What's up with the ice? Get a little too vigorous with the wanking?"

"Ha, ha. You should be a clown, Cath. You've already got the white face makeup."

"Is that right?" Cathy snatches the ice pack from my neck and dangles it in the air. "Who's laughing now, little boy?"

"Give it back, jerk!" I pause my game and leap off the couch.

Her dark-shadowed eyes go wide when she sees my neck. "Holy crap, Sean. Where'd you get all those welts? Were you attacked by bats or something?"

"Yeah, that's right. Some of your vampire buds ambushed me last night." I lunge for the cold pack, but she swings it behind her.

"If I didn't know better, I'd say those were some major hickeys." Cathy laughs. "Tell me who gave them to you, and I'll give you back your ice."

"Eat it," I say, glaring at her. It looks like she's got a new brow piercing, which makes two over each eye now. Mom's going to flip.

Cathy shrugs. "Fine. But secrets just lead to speculation." She taps the silver stud in her lip. "Let me guess: Johnny Weir showed up at the rink last night and the two of you spent the entire evening doing some serious neck sucking."

"Johnny Weir would never skate at the Salisbury Park Ice Rink," I say, making a grab for her arm that she easily dodges. "He trains at the Ice Vault Arena in Wayne, New Jersey."

Cathy's jaw drops.

"Well, well, well," she says. "Someone knows quite a lot about a certain flamboyant figure skater."

"Just give me the freakin' ice pack, will ya? I have to get rid of these things before school on Monday."

"It's a simple barter system, baby brother." Cathy dangles the cold pack in the air. "Goods for information. Now come on. Tell your big sister who's been gnawing on your neck."

Cathy was born nine minutes before me, which she loves to rub in any chance she gets.

"Don't you have a cemetery to haunt or something?" I say.

"Listen, Sean." Cathy gives me her I'm-so-compassionate look. "I could be your biggest champion if you let me." She reaches out and grabs my shoulder. "All you have to do is be honest. I'd be totally support-ive, I swear. Now tell me, do I know him?"

"I'm *not* gay." I step back from her. "What about that don't you understand?"

She cocks her head. "*Please.* It's so obvious. I mean, besides your stalker-like knowledge of Johnny Weir's whereabouts, there's also the little matter of your iTunes library. Lady Gaga? Justin Bieber? The *Sweeney Todd* soundtrack? The signs are everywhere, sweetie. You dress up in women's clothing. You're a mama's boy. You play homoerotic video games. Should I go on?"

"One time! I dressed up in girls' clothes one time! And it was to see a naked *girl,* which you seem to have conveniently forgotten."

"So you claim. But what about this?" Cathy gestures at the television, where Brock Lesnar and Heath Herring are lying frozen on the mat in a bare-torsoed grasp. "Tell me there's nothing gay about two barely clothed men embracing each other on the floor."

I point at the screen. "That's a rear naked choke."

Cathy raises her eyebrows. "I rest my case."

"They're beating the pus out of each other."

She shrugs. "If you say so. But it looks like man-love to me. And it's totally cool. Some of the most influential people in the world have been gay. Leonardo da Vinci. Alexander the Great. Oscar Wilde. Isaac Newton. It's nothing to be ashamed of."

"I'm *not* ashamed." A vein in my left temple pulses. "If I was gay, I'd admit it."

"Really? I'm not so sure. Or maybe you just don't realize what's so clear to the rest of us."

"You know what? Keep the stupid ice pack." I grab the remote control, shut off the television, and storm out of the family room.

The second I'm through the door, I am engulfed by our panting, whining dogs. I make my way through the living room, trying to pretend that I can't hear Cathy hot on my heels.

Ingrid, our African gray parrot, squawks from her cage in the corner of the room. "I'm hung like a horse!"

"You're a *girl,* Ingrid," I snap. "You're not even hung like a bird."

"Take the pecker!" She jabs her beak at the air.

Two years ago, Ingrid was found in the home of some dead old guy who must have had nothing better to do with his time than teach her how to curse at people. Strangely enough, we haven't been able to adopt her out.

"You like it birdie style!" she caws, grabbing the side of her cage with her claws and doing little thrusting motions with her body.

"You see?" Cathy laughs. "Even Ingrid knows."

I ignore both of them and go to the kitchen. Yank open the freezer door and look inside to see if we have anything I can use as a substitute cold pack. Peas. A box of Fudgsicles. A whole salmon.

"I mean, Mom and Dad probably won't understand," I hear Cathy say from the doorway. "Being as uptight as they are. But they'd have to accept it eventually. With some counseling, they'd learn to love you again. And think about how much more interesting you'd be."

"Blah, blah, blah." I stare into the freezer, not wanting to give her the satisfaction of my full attention, even if it means I have to shout for her to hear me. "You can talk and talk all you want. It doesn't matter. There is nothing you can say that is ever going to convince me to change how I feel about guys, okay? I know who I like and who I don't. And frankly, what Mom and Dad think about my sexual tendencies doesn't even enter the picture."

Someone clears their throat behind me and I can tell immediately that it's not Cathy.

I whip around to see my parents standing there, shopping bags dangling from their hands, their eyes wide. I scan the kitchen for my sister, but she's nowhere to be found.

I shut the freezer door and clap my hand on my hickey-peppered neck. "Hi, guys."

Mom's eyes start to tear up. She glances at Dad, then back to me. "Is there . . . ? Is there something you'd like to tell us, hon?"

I blink, confused. Then it finally hits me. "Oh! No. No, there's nothing. Cathy was just . . . She was trying to . . . Never mind. It doesn't matter."

Mom takes a deep breath, sniffling. "It's okay, sweetie." She uses her placating, everything's-fine-here voice. The one she uses whenever Dixie—our lactose-intolerant beagle—accidentally soft-serves on the living-room carpet. She plops her bags on the kitchen table, then looks at Dad. "Believe it or not, your father and I have actually discussed this. We had a . . . a hunch that you might be . . . you know . . . and we are . . ." She swallows the jagged little pill. "We are okay with it. Aren't we, honey?" She looks over at Dad again.

"Yes," Dad says, sounding like his shorts just shrank three sizes. "As long as you're absolutely sure. And you don't want to, you know, maybe talk to Father Hurley about it first."

"What? No! I don't—"

"I'm sure there's no need for that," Mom says, coming to my rescue. "If he knows, he knows. It's not going to make a difference."

"Okay, this is ridiculous," I say. "What you heard me say was . . . I was talking to Cathy and . . . Look, the point is, I like girls, okay? End of story. I've had a girlfriend. Tianna, remember? You met her."

"You mean"—Mom scrunches up her face—"the girl who sort of looked like a boy?"

"*What?* She did not!"

Dad grimaces. "She kind of did, Sean. Like that actor. What's his name? The one who played the hobbit."

I smack my forehead. "Holy crap, are you serious?"

"Sean," Mom scolds. "Language. Please. My goodness. And here I was under the impression that the gays were more refined."

"You know what? Forget it. I'm just going to pretend we never had this discussion." I storm out of the kitchen, the excited dogs swarming around me.

Mom calls after me, "We love you, Sean! All we want is for you to be happy. Whatever that means for you!"

As if this moment weren't awful enough, just then my cell phone vibrates against my thigh. I don't have to look at it to know who's texting me. Evelyn's been cell-stalking me from the moment I left the ice rink last night. Thirty-six texts and counting. I never should have given her my real number.

I reach into my pocket and blindly dismiss the text

because I'm "at my grandmother's today" and we don't get any cell-phone service in the mountains.

Speaking of mountains, I wouldn't mind escaping to them right now. Or to the 7-Eleven at the very least. I wade my way through the dog pack and head toward the front door. Just as I go for the doorknob, someone knocks.

The dogs erupt into a chorus of barks and I freeze, convinced that it's Evelyn trying to catch me in a lie. I duck below the peephole, picturing her standing on the other side of the door, her weepy eye pressed against the circle of glass, looking for a teeny, tiny Sean.

Evelyn knocks again. "Hello?"

My heart hammers in my chest as the dogs leap against the door, some of them howling now. There's nothing they love more than visitors—though shouldn't their animal senses alert them to the danger that awaits on the other side?

A third thump, this one so heavy that it reverberates through my body, which is trying to melt into the wood of the door. "Open up, jackass. I know you're in there. I just saw you walk by the window."

Jackass? That doesn't sound like Evelyn. The dogs are now dancing in circles. Sure, they get excited for visitors—any visitors—but there's only one person who makes them dance like this.

I let out a relieved breath and pull open our creaky front door, boxing out the snuffling dogs, to see Nessa—Cathy's best friend and partner in Gothworld—standing on the stoop, her squid-ink-black hair hanging in her ghost-white face.

"Jeez, took you long enough," Nessa says. "What the hell were you doing, tweeting about your doll collection again?"

"They're not dolls. They're action figures. And I don't tweet about them," I say, and step aside to let her in. "She's upstairs."

"Cool." Nessa enters and brushes past me. I get a whiff of her heavy makeup as she goes by. The smell brings back memories of spirit gum and Halloween costumes.

"Oh, hey." She turns back and smiles. "I never got to tell you. You guys were totally savage at the Battle of the Bands. I didn't expect you to be that good."

"Thanks," I say, completely caught off-guard by the compliment.

"Okay, well. See ya." Nessa flashes another smile, then makes her way into the living room. The dogs attach themselves to her like iron filings to a magnet, wagging their tails, squeaking and whimpering, leaping this way and that. You'd think they were starved for affection the way they crawl all over her.

A brief flash of *me* crawling all over Nessa blindsides me, and I shake my head like a golden retriever, trying to dislodge the unsettling image.

CHAPTER FIVE

THE BROOD

ROAST BEEF, POPOVERS, potatoes au gratin, creamed spinach, creamed corn, and vanilla shakes.

This is the fattening feast that has been laid out in front of us tonight. Which, if we were a normal family, who ate normal food all the time, might seem completely . . . normal, if a bit excessive. But since Mom is a total health freak who swallows fistfuls of vitamins and runs five miles a day, every day, rain or shine, it's more than a little weird to see this kind of food on our table. Weirder still, this is the third time in five days that Mom's prepared some kind of ginormous spread.

"Okay, what the hell's going on?" Cathy stares at the food on the table. "Are you guys getting a divorce, or what?" She plops herself down in her chair and ushers several of the curled-up dogs out from under the table with her stocking feet.

"Don't be rude," Dad says, tucking his napkin into the collar of his sweater with one hand and scooping a pile of potatoes onto his plate with the other.

"I'm not being rude," Cathy says. "I'm just concerned about my pants size. I've gained, like, ten pounds in the last week."

Mom shrugs. "So I've relaxed my dietary restrictions a bit. Big deal. If you ever turned off your computer and exercised a little, maybe you wouldn't be gaining so much."

"Is that so?" Cathy says, staring at Mom's rounding belly. "Then what's your excuse?"

Dad points a serving spoon at her. "That's enough out of you, young lady."

"What?" Cathy shrugs. "It's not like I'm saying anything we all haven't noticed. Right, Sean?"

"I don't . . . know." I avert my eyes, not wanting to get involved.

"Oh, come on. You *know*. Mom's packed on a few lately. And she's cooking like she expects Paula Deen to show up and join us for dinner. If Mom's depressed or something, are we just supposed to ignore it?"

"I'm not depressed," Mom says, her eyes getting moist.

"Just eat your food, Cathy," Dad says.

"I'm a vegetarian," she announces, staring at her empty plate.

"Oh, really?" Mom asks, snuffling back her tears. "Since when?"

"Since right now. I just decided."

"Not me." My mouth is watering as I serve myself some roast beef. "I love me some meat."

Cathy smirks. "So I've heard."

I glare at her. "I didn't think vampires *could* be vegetarians."

"And I didn't think little mama's boys could think for themselves."

"That'll be quite enough," Dad says.

"Ignore your sister, Sean." Mom pats my hand. "She's probably just having her period."

Cathy narrows her eyes. "Just because I don't want to have a heart attack at eighteen doesn't mean I'm PMSing."

"Look, if you don't want to eat, don't eat," Mom snaps as she serves herself a puddle of creamed corn. "I'll bring the leftovers down to the shelter, where I'm sure the starving homeless children would appreciate a nice home-cooked meal."

"Fine." Cathy crosses her arms tightly across her chest. "Can I be excused then?"

"No, you cannot." Dad lowers his gaze at her. "You're a vegetarian now, okay, fine. Potatoes, spinach, corn. Last

I heard, those were all vegetables. And just a little factoid for you: there is no substantial proof that being a vegetarian prolongs a person's life span."

My shoulders start to shake as I try to hold back my laughter.

Cathy stares lasers at me, then angrily slings a spoonful of creamed spinach onto her plate with a wet *splat.*

We eat in uncomfortable silence until Mom makes a loud slurping sound with her straw as she attempts to get the last of her vanilla shake from the bottom of her glass.

"Heaven," she says, slapping her cup down on the table. "Shakes should be illegal. Or at least there should be a hefty fine. They're just too good. I can't believe I've denied myself for so many years." She forces a smile. "So, what's the latest and greatest? Who wants to share? Sean?"

I shrug. "I don't know. School starts tomorrow. Not looking forward to that."

Mom looks at me sideways. "Anything . . . *else*?"

"Uh, no. Not that I can think of. Why?"

Mom's eyes slide to the side. "No reason. I just thought, you know . . . maybe there were some *other* things you might want to talk about. You know. *Other* things."

Oh, Christ. Here we go again with the gay thing. There's no way I'm taking this bait. "Sorry. No *other* things to discuss." I lift my utensils and resume slicing up my food.

"Okay." Dad gestures toward Cathy. "How about you, Cath? What's the news?"

"I just announced I'm a vegetarian. That's not interesting enough for you?"

"All right, you two want to be stingy?" Mom shakes her head. "That's fine. Don't share your lives with us. We're only your parents. The people who gave you life. Why should we know anything about anything that's going on with you?"

Mom looks at Dad across the table.

Their eyes meet, and he gives her a little nod and a small smile. Some sort of silent answer to a psychic question she's just asked him.

"Well, then," Mom says, "your father and I will start the ball rolling with some news of our own."

I put my silverware down, eyeing my roast beef suspiciously. Suddenly the food seems like a trap or a bribe.

"Something very exciting has happened," Mom continues. "Something that's going to have an enormous impact on all of our lives. For the *rest* of our lives."

☛ CHAPTER SIX ☚

ROSEMARY'S BABY

Y OU'RE *WHAT?*" CATHY SAYS, blinking furiously.

"But . . . how?" My voice sounds a thousand miles away.

I realize that Mom has just told us she's going to have a baby but my brain seems unable to fully process it. Like a computer with too little RAM and too many open programs.

And so I sit here at the table, my hands tucked under my legs, my feet resting on the warm furry body of our chocolate Lab, Bronson, and the spinning beach ball of death rotating uselessly in my mind.

"I don't get it," Cathy says. "I thought you were fixed."

"I had a tubal ligation, yes," Mom explains. "But sometimes—it's rare—but apparently, according to Dr. Halpern, your tubes can grow back together. What can I say? All that running and vitamins and healthy eating for so many years. I guess I'm a strong healer." She shrugs. "That's why we only just figured it out. Your father put it together after I started having my cheesy-creamy food cravings. So, anyway, it looks like I'm around five months." She grabs her rounding belly. "And here I was thinking I was just giving your father a bit more of me to love."

"So, wait." Cathy screws up her face. "Are you telling us that you guys . . . still do it?"

Mom laughs. "Uh, yes, Cathy. As difficult as that is for you to believe, your father and I have a very vigorous, active, and healthy sex life."

"Eww," I blurt. And just like that, my brain has been smacked back into functioning again, offering up a seriously disturbing image of my pasty parents rolling around in the nude.

"That's totally gross." Cathy shudders.

I rub at my eyes, trying to lock this image away in the never-to-be-thought-of-again file of my mind—right alongside Ms. Luntz on the nude beach and the foot-long snot rope Coop stretched from his nose in third grade.

Unfortunately, my brain doesn't want to cooperate and so I need to change the subject.

"Do you know if it's a boy or a girl?" I say, the idea of a sweet little pink-or-blue-bundled baby thankfully trumping the freak show of my parents' sweaty bedroom antics.

"Not yet," Mom says. "But I'm scheduled for an ultrasound in a few weeks. We should know after that what color we're going to have to paint the bedroom. Although we're thinking of leaving it as a surprise and maybe just painting the room green or yellow."

And with that, a terrible realization hits me.

We only have three bedrooms in our house. Mom and Dad's. Cathy's. And mine.

"The baby's going to sleep in your room, right?" I say.

"Well." Dad steeples his fingers and takes a deep breath. "That's the other thing we need to discuss with you."

"We're moving?" A panicky flutter dances in my chest.

Mom flashes a quick tight-lipped smile. "No. We're not moving."

"Funds . . . are going to be a little tight for a while," Dad says. "Especially since we want your mother to be able to stay home with the baby for the first few months."

My head swivels from Dad to Mom to Dad to Mom. "So it *is* going to sleep with you?"

"I'm afraid that won't work out," Mom explains. "I'm going to be up and down all night with feedings. It'd be too disruptive with your father having to get up so early for work."

"Well, it's not sleeping in my room," Cathy declares. "I'll tell you that right now."

"That's not fair," I say. "I've already got the smallest bedroom."

"Too bad." Cathy shrugs. "I'm the oldest. And I called it."

"The baby's not going to be sleeping with either one of you," Mom says.

An incredible wave of relief washes over me.

"That's right." Dad picks up his knife and fork and begins sawing off a piece of his popover. "We've discussed the situation extensively, and the only reasonable solution we could come up with"—he pops the gravy-drenched dough into his mouth and starts chewing—"is that the two of you will have to share Cathy's bedroom."

Cathy whips her head in Dad's direction. "I don't *think* so."

"Think again, young lady," Mom says, with just a hint of satisfaction in her voice. "We're going to make Sean's room into the nursery, and that only leaves one place left."

"Forget it," I say. "I'll sleep in the family room."

"No, you will not." Dad takes a sip of his shake. "There is only a limited amount of common space in this house. We're not going to have your games and computer paraphernalia strewn everywhere. I'm sorry, but we're all going to have to make some sacrifices."

"Fine, then." My shoulders slump in defeat. "I'll share my room with the baby."

"Aw, sweetheart." Mom gives me a sympathetic look. "That's just not going to work. You wouldn't get any sleep."

"I don't care. I'd rather not sleep than share a room with *her*."

"This is not up for debate," Dad says. "The decision's been made. We knew you two weren't going to be happy about it, but that's life. I shared a bedroom with three of my brothers growing up. You should consider yourself lucky."

"Lucky?" Cathy huffs. "Right. I'm so sure. Why can't we just get rid of all the stupid pets? Then we'd have more money and we could move to a bigger house."

My stomach drops, but I don't say anything. Cathy'll just rail into me. Instead, I give Bronson a little consoling cuddle with my feet.

"We're not getting rid of the animals, Cathy." Mom stares at her in disbelief. "Honestly. The amount of money we would save casting out our little furry friends here"—Mom scoops up one of the kittens and works his paws like he's a marionette—"wouldn't even come close to offsetting the cost of a new home."

"Whatever." Cathy turns away so she doesn't have to look at the adorable kitty puppet.

"What about building an extension?" I say. "To add another room. That'd be cheaper than buying a brand-new house."

"We already looked into it." Dad pulls the napkin

from his collar. "It's still too much. It would cost twenty to thirty thousand dollars. And that's *if* a contractor could stay on budget. I'm sorry, but this is our only option."

"And who knows?" Mom adds. "You might even enjoy it after a while. I mean, you shared my womb, right? Now you'll share a room." She laughs like this is the funniest thing in the world. "Who knows, maybe this is the thing that brings you two closer together."

"What about Uncle Doug?" I say, the tightness in my chest getting even tighter. "He's rich. Maybe he can lend us the money to build an extension."

"Your uncle Doug is not rich," Mom says. "He's got some money, yes, but he's got his . . . habits, and he needs all the money he makes to live on. I don't understand why you kids are trying to turn this into something bad. This is very exciting news. Sure, we're all going to have to pitch in a little, but this is a miracle from God we're talking about here. Dr. Halpern said I'm the first patient he's ever had get pregnant after having her tubes tied. We should be celebrating. This baby obviously wants to be born into our family. There's going to be another Hance in this world." Mom grabs her empty shake glass and hoists it in the air. "Let's have a toast. To the baby."

Dad is the first to pick up his glass. I raise mine because you can't *not* toast to a baby. And Cathy is the last one to lift her untouched shake, hefting it like it weighs a thousand pounds.

My sister and I glare at each other across the table. I don't think I've ever seen her look so angry before. And believe me, I've seen her *royally* pissed. I'm not sure if it's directed at me or if it's just an overall loathing of the world in general.

But I do know one thing.

Whatever it takes, even if I have to sell part of my liver, I will *not* be sharing a room with my sister.

CHAPTER SEVEN

DEAD ALIVE

I'M PEDALING MY BIKE through the wet streets of our neighborhood, flanked by Coop and Matt. Usually we have the ride to school timed out perfectly—so that we step through the doors right at first bell—but I was running late this morning and so we're having to make up some time.

It's a cold, miserable morning, and the roads are lined with mounds of old snow that don't seem to want to melt. I don't know if it's the protective coating of car exhaust soot that's thwarting the natural water cycle or what, but everything looks really dank and depressing.

Or maybe it's just the mood I'm in.

There was a split second at dinner—right after the baby announcement and before the disturbing realization that our parents are still having sex—when I was actually thinking it might be cool to be an older brother.

You know, reading bedtime stories, giving bike-riding lessons, having someone in the house who still believes in Santa Claus.

But anything good that could have possibly come out of it has been smashed on the rocky shores of having to share a bedroom with my stupid sister.

All I can think about now is how there will be less of everything once the baby's born. Less privacy, less TV time, less crispy beef when we go out for Chinese.

I can't believe how much I dislike this dumb baby already, and it's not even here yet.

Which makes me feel like an enormous tool. Because how can you hate a baby? I don't want to be that guy. The douche bag who's all mean and nasty to his younger brother or sister.

I've got to figure out a way to get enough money so that we can build an extension.

And fast.

You know what they say about desperate times. . . .

"All right," I say, glancing at Coop. "Tell me more about this movie idea of yours."

Coop's sweatshirt-hooded head snaps toward me. "Ha! Knew it! They always come back begging."

"Sean, you can't be serious," Matt says, looking at me like I've totally lost it. Which maybe I have.

"I don't know," I say. "I'm just gathering info." I look at Coop again. "How easy do you think it'd be to sell a movie?"

Coop laughs like I've just asked him if he thinks it might be fun to see two smokin' babes hot-fudge wrestling in a giant bowl of ice cream. "Are you kidding? As long as it's halfway deece, someone will snatch it up. I mean, have you seen some of the crap-o-latte they trot out? There's no reason we shouldn't be able to perpetrate the same kind of fraud and rake in the mega-chips."

"So, you don't even want to make a *good* movie?" Matt snickers. "Well, at least that seems like a realistic goal."

"You're obviously missing the point, Matthew," Coop says. "The idea is to make something that will *sell*. Quality is secondary. And maybe not even *that* important."

"But do you know *how* to sell it?" I ask. "Once we've got the thing made?"

Matt stares at me. "Sean, why are you encouraging him? We killed this idea Saturday night."

"Yeah, well, my situation has drastically changed since Saturday. I need a whole load of cash, and I need it PDQ." I look back over at Coop. "How long do you think a movie would take to film? And don't say more than four months."

Coop sits up and rides no-handed. "Depends on how fast we can raise the chedda to fund it. Once we've got the greenage, it'll be cake. We just come up with a basic idea—demon possession, coven of warlocks, vampire cats, whatever—dash off a script, and then roll camera.

That's how all these cheap-ass horror films are done. It'll take a week. Two at the most."

"Okay, I'm in," I say. "When can we start?"

"Whoa, whoa, whoa." Matt's shaking his head like he's being attacked by hornets. "What's going on here, Sean? Why do you need money all of a sudden?"

I feel my shoulders tense up. I was hoping I could hold off telling them, but I suppose it doesn't really matter. They're going to find out eventually.

I take a deep breath and let it out slowly.

"My mother's having a baby," I say.

"Is it your dad's?" Coop asks.

I scowl at him. "Yes, it's my dad's, doink."

"I wasn't asking about your dad's doink. And just so you know, if it isn't his baby, then it wasn't his doink that was involved."

"It *is* his baby, you nerf herder. Why would you even ask that?"

"I don't know. You said you needed money. I thought maybe your dad took off when he found out your mom got preggers by some other dude."

"Well, you thought wrong. It's *both* my parents' baby."

I hop the curb to take the shortcut through Snyder's Field, pedaling fast to try and put some distance between me and my so-called friends.

"Hey, Sean," Coop says when he and Matt catch up

to me. "You do realize that this means your mom and dad are still grinding the guinea pigs, right?"

"Yeah, thanks for that. I wasn't traumatized enough the first time it occurred to me." My wheel skids out on a patch of snow but I keep my balance and ride on.

"No offense." Matt stifles a laugh. "But your mom and dad are like the *last* people I want to think about doing the nasty."

"So let's *not* think about it," I snap.

"I know, but you kind of have to, right?" Coop says. "I mean, you're mom's got the bun in the oven as proof positive they're doing the grumble rumble."

"I'm serious, dude," I warn.

"Oh, come on," Coop cajoles. "Tell me you're not wondering how they do it. I bet it's not missionary. Because your dad's got that bloated physics-teacher belly going on. Which would just get in the way. Unless he's got, like, a blue whale schlong."

"Can you stop?" I say. "We're talking about how we're going to film this movie."

"Actually," Matt corrects, "we're talking about your parents having sex. Which is infinitely more interesting."

"It's not like we get off on it, Sean," Coop reassures me. "It's more of a let's-go-look-at-the-bearded-lady type thing."

"Or flipping through *Ripley's Believe It or Not!*" Matt adds.

Coop reaches over and swats my arm. "Be honest now. You can't tell us you're not just a little bit curious?"

"Yes, I can. I *can* tell you that." My voice flutters as we ride over the uneven frozen dirt of the field that backs this lane of houses. "I *am* telling you. I'm not the least bit curious."

"Oh, I just had a thought." Coop waggles his eyebrows. "What if your parents are into doing really freaky stuff? Like the Rhode Island Rabbit's Foot. Or the Delaware Deep Dish."

"Or the North Dakota Meat Balloon." Matt sputters with laughter.

"Enough," I say, covering one ear with one hand because I can't ride no-handed when I'm not on flat pavement. "You can shut your pie traps right now."

"All right, all right, fine. Jeez." Coop shifts gears on his bike as we get to the end of the field and turn onto Market Road. "So what if your mom likes to dress up like a mime and eat canned peach slices from your dad's hairy belly folds? Doesn't concern us, does it, Matt?"

"No, of course not." Matt's laughing so hard his bike's zigzagging through the street like he's drunk. "They could be riding each other around the bedroom like wild naked ponies for all we care."

"Go to hell." I stand and pedal hard to try and get away from them, but Coop and Matt have no trouble keeping pace. Finally, I just give up and sit back on my bike seat. "You guys are total dicks, you know that?"

"Aw, don't pout, Sean-o," Coop says. "We're just bustin' your chops a little. Did you actually expect us to let something like that just slide on by?"

"Yeah, if you had any class, you would," I say.

He grins and thrusts his hand out for me to shake. "Hi, Cooper Redmond. Nice to meet you."

I swat his hand away, but it's hard to keep a straight face. Coop's a d-bag, but he's a funny d-bag, which makes it really difficult to stay pissed at him.

"Okay," Matt says. "If you don't need the money for the baby, what do you need it for?"

"Right. Like I'm going to tell you. You assbaskets will just make fun of me."

"I'm not going to lie to you, dawg," Coop says. "There's a very good possibility of that happening. But once we get it out of our system, you know we'll have your back."

I let out a long weary sigh because I know he's right. You couldn't ask for two more loyal friends. "I need the money to build an extension on my house, okay?"

"What?" Matt asks. "Why?"

"Because. My parents can't afford to do it. And if I don't come up with the money"—I shake my head, still unable to believe this—"I'm going to have to share a bedroom with Cathy."

Coop grabs his chest like he's been speared by an arrow. *"Daaamn!"* he howls. "Are you twisting me? Bunking with Count Skankula? That's egregious, dude."

"Tell me about it." I check my cell and see that— even with the shortcut—we are still in serious danger of missing first bell.

"Do you have to move in with her right away?" Matt asks.

"I don't know. My parents said the baby's going to be born in May. I'm guessing it'll be around then. Which is why I've got about four months to figure something out."

"That is harsh, dawg," Coop says. "How are you supposed to do any plug and play with the new lady friend when your Gothed-out sister's sitting there gawking at you?"

Oh, God. Evelyn. I completely forgot about her! Perfect. Now I'm going to have to deal with the neck suckler today on top of everything else.

"And that's just the start of the nightmare," Matt announces. "What about everything else you need privacy for?"

"Right," Coop says. "No more punchin' the munchkin into the wee hours of the morning. And you might as well unbookmark all of those *Bridezillas* videos you like to watch."

I shake my head. "You see? This is why I didn't want to tell you."

"No." Coop points at me. "This is why you *did* want

to tell us. Because we feel for you. Which is why we're going to help you out by making and selling this movie for a chock of cha-ching. Isn't that right, Matt?"

Matt nods. "Of course. We're here for you, buddy. One for all, and all for leaping back into the fiery pits of humiliation."

I look over at Coop and Matt and feel myself getting a little choked up. It's a pretty good feeling to know that I always have my buds in my corner when all the chips are crumbling to pieces.

And who knows? Maybe we can actually pull this thing off. Make a movie and sell it—if not for millions, then at least enough to get a nice big new room—*my* big new room—added onto our house.

Stranger things have happened.

☛ CHAPTER EIGHT ☚

THE CHANGELING

I STROLL DOWN THE HALL with this semester's schedule in hand. I've got a big smile on my face and a bit of a bounce in my step as I head toward our lockers. What started off as a really crummy day seems to be turning around big-time. Not only are my best friends going to help me out with this baby situation, but I also managed to switch out of Web Design and into Drama.

It's two birds with one bush. First, I don't have to be in a class with overbearing Evelyn, and two—perhaps even more important—I can scout out the local talent for our film. Maybe even befriend some of the better actors and get them to work for free.

"What about doing a remake?" Coop says as I step up to our lockers. "Something that's crying out for a gritty reboot. Like *Reservoir Dogs*. Or *Fight Club*."

"Or *Pokémon*!" I exclaim.

Coop levels his gaze at me. "Right, Sean. A gritty reboot of *Pokémon*. That's just what the world has been clamoring for."

"We can't do a remake anyway," Matt says. "You have to get the rights to things like that. We have to do something original."

"Okay, fine, whatever." Coop spins the dial on his combination lock. "But we should definitely film it in 3-D."

"Right, and where the hell are we supposed to get a 3-D camera?" Matt asks.

"Where there's a me, there's a means, Mattington."

"I don't know," I say. "I think 3-D's been a little overdone."

"Pfff, *wrong*." Coop yanks down on his lock and opens his locker door. "What's been overdone are *boring* 3-D movies. Ones that don't take full advantage of the technology."

Matt looks at Coop like he's just spoken Klingon. "What the hell are you talking about?"

"Bountiful babes, dawg. Wouldn't you like to see more jiggling jahoobies in 3-D? You know . . ." Coop lunges at me with two cupped hands. "Comin' at ya!"

I jerk back as Matt busts up laughing.

"Anyway," I say, "I seriously doubt we'll have enough money to film in 3-D." I shut the door to my locker and suddenly catch sight of Evelyn coming up the stairs at the end of the hall.

Oh, crap.

My heart vaults into my throat as I duck my head and try to hide behind Matt and Coop.

"Hey! Bad touch!" Coop shoves me away from his locker.

"Don't let her see me. Please." I shrink into myself and make another attempt to take cover behind my friends.

Matt glances over his shoulder to see Evelyn coming down the hallway. "What's the deal? I thought you guys were going out."

"It was a mistake."

"Why?" Coop grins. "Does she have callused hands or something?"

"I wish. No. She's just . . . a little nuts."

"I don't get it." Matt clicks open the rings on his binder and puts in some paper. "You guys were all over each other Saturday night."

"Correction. She was all over *me*. Like a succubus. I swear she was trying to draw blood. I had to ice my neck all weekend long to get rid of the bazillion hickeys she gave me. And she's texted me *eighty-two times* already! You guys have to do me a solid and break up with her for me."

"Do you a *solid*?" Coop laughs, clicking his lock

shut. "I don't think so. You asked the girl out; you break up with her."

"I *didn't* ask her out. Not really. She just assumed. That's what I'm trying to—"

"Hey there, polar bear," Evelyn says, stepping up beside me.

I brace myself for a rabid face gobbling, but she just lays a gentle kiss on my cheek.

"Hi," I respond warily.

She gives a little cautious smile to Matt and Coop, then looks back at me. "You okay?"

"Yeah, why? Are *you* okay?"

"I'm a little embarrassed, I guess."

"Embarrassed? Why?"

Evelyn's gaze drops to the floor, her stringy red hair falling in front of her face. "I think I came on a little strong on Saturday. And all those text messages yesterday. God." She laughs, shaking her head. "I'm really sorry about that. I was just . . . I guess I'm just a little overeager is all. My brother's always on me about how excited I get about things." She shrugs, then looks at me with this sort of sad, apologetic hangdog expression. "I didn't . . . scare you off, did I?"

All of a sudden I feel like a royal tool for wanting to break up with her.

Of course she was excited. I'm her first boyfriend. It's a big deal for her. I probably acted exactly the same way with Tianna. Okay, well, maybe not *exactly* the same. But it's possible I was a little overzealous. Which is maybe why she ended things with me so quickly. Maybe if she'd just given me a chance, we could have had something kinda special.

"No." I smile at Evelyn. "You didn't scare me off."

I catch Coop rolling his eyes behind Evelyn's back.

"Phew." Evelyn's whole body relaxes. "I thought for sure I blew it with you."

Coop sputters. "No, no. Sean definitely would have mentioned that."

I shoot him a death glare at the same time that Matt smacks him on the shoulder.

Evelyn smiles the vacant smile of someone who doesn't get the joke. "Well, good. I'd really hate myself if that was the case. Can we start over, please?"

I nod. "Sure. Yeah. Okay."

"Oh, thank goodness." She breathes a heavy sigh of relief, then unfolds her school schedule, which I notice is decorated with a multitude of lavish SEAN-PLUS-EVELYN-filled hearts. "So, did you get in to Web Design?"

"Oh . . . uh . . . actually . . . um . . . No, actually."

Evelyn's face falls. "Aw, dang it."

"Yeah." A nervous laugh escapes my lips. I glance down at my own schedule. "Looks like they switched me into . . ." I look up and meet Evelyn's big brown eyes. Oh, God, she knows I'm lying. "I mean, they *put* me in Drama instead."

Evelyn pouts. "I was really hoping we'd get to be in a class together."

"Yeah. Me too."

"Hey!" Evelyn perks up. "Maybe I should switch into Drama."

"No," I blurt. "I mean . . . You don't want to do that, because . . ." Because you'll find out I was lying to you when I hand the drama teacher my transfer slip. "Web Design is . . . it's going to be a great class. I *so* wanted to learn about that. You don't want to miss out because of me."

"Yeah, I guess," Evelyn says. "Oh, hey, wait a minute. I have a good idea. Why don't I be your private tutor?" She beams at me. "You could come over after school and I could teach you the stuff we learn in Web Design. Then it'd be almost like we were taking the class together. How's that sound?"

"Uh, yeah." I nod. "That sounds . . . good. Definitely. For sure."

"Great." She leans over and gives me another soft kiss on the cheek. "It's a deal. Well, I better get to class. Later, gators." Evelyn gives us all a little wave and then strolls off down the hall.

"I thought you said she was a nutcase," Matt says, snapping his lock shut.

I blink once hard, watching Evelyn go, looking as normal as can be. "She *was*. I mean, she was *acting* like one at the rink."

Matt shrugs. "Seems pretty normal to me."

"Yeah." I nod. "I guess it's like she said. She was just overeager."

Coop grins. "That's one of best qualities to have in a girlfriend, dawg. Right after being a gymnast."

☞ CHAPTER NINE ☞

CHILD'S PLAY

Oᴋᴀʏ, ᴇᴠᴇʀʏᴏɴᴇ," ᴍʀ. ɴᴇsᴛᴍᴀɴ, the drama teacher, says, walking with long purposeful strides toward the door. "I think we can get started." He kicks away the wooden doorstop and lets the door swing shut. "Let's all sit in a circle on the floor." He makes a circular motion with his finger as if he's not entirely convinced we know what shape he means. "Girl-boy if we can manage it."

There are no chairs in the room, and so the twenty of us arrange ourselves—alternating guys and girls where possible—on the scuffed-up black-and-white tiles. By the time we're through, we've formed something resembling a sloppy oval.

My body is here in this cold classroom, but my brain is only half-present. The other half is still back at the lockers, replaying the Evelyn thing over and over. Trying to reconcile the girl who nearly chewed off my neck on

Saturday night with the girl who I just met in the hallway. Something doesn't compute.

Mr. Nestman moves to the front of the room by the tiny stage and presses his hands together like he's about to pray. "Welcome to Drama," he says with a little bow of the head. He's got this wispy white-blond hair that looks like a dandelion gone to seed. "I hope you've left all your inhibitions and insecurities out in the hall, because they will not serve you well in my class."

He's wearing these saggy-kneed jeans and a rumpled, tucked-in blue flannel shirt. It's not a great look for him, to be perfectly honest. It really accentuates his dangly limbs and short torso.

"We start this morning with a name game." He gives us a fleeting closed-mouth grin. "Each person will state their name along with something they wish to bring to our very own desert island. But there are a few catches. And they are as follows: Your item must be useful, must be portable, and must start with the same letter as your name. Oh, and you also must remember all of the names and items previously mentioned. Any questions? No. Good. I'll begin. I am Mr. Nestman." He strokes his lumpy pockmarked chin with his right hand, his eyes searching the ceiling. "And I will be bringing to our desert island . . . some nail clippers."

Mr. Nestman gestures to the well-padded eggplant-breasted brunette on his left.

"Okay." The girl adjusts herself and sits up tall, her legs crossed. "Hi. I'm Victoria." A little wave to the class. "And I'll be bringing Vaseline—"

A couple of meathead-type dudes shout, "Yeah!"

"All right, bring it down a notch," Mr. Nestman says. "Vaseline along with what, Victoria?"

Victoria's cheeks have gone rosy. "Along with," she continues, "Mr. Nestman's nail clippers." She turns her head to Mister-Handsome-Guy beside her.

"Me?" The kid smirks. "I'm Ryan and I'll be bringing a rectal thermometer."

The entire class breaks up with laughter.

"I'll allow it," Mr. Nestman says reluctantly. "But only because it is, technically, useful. But keep it clean from here on out, kiddies." He motions for Ryan to continue.

"And also"—Ryan clenches his eyes shut— "Vanessa's Vaseline."

"Victoria," a girl across the oval calls out.

"Yeah. Sorry." Ryan shakes his head. "Her Vaseline. And Mr. Nestman's nail polish."

More laughter.

"Clippers," someone else corrects.

"Yes." Ryan points double finger guns in the direction of the voice. "What *you* said."

I quickly count the people in between me and Mr. Nestman and realize that I am going to have to remember twelve names and twelve desert-island items. Not something I am very confident I can do. My scalp tightens, and I am chewing my tongue like crazy before I know it.

I have to put the Evelyn business aside and concentrate here. I don't want to look like a big old dorkus on the very first day. Especially in a class where I don't even know most of the students. Mainly, though, I don't want to go pissing off any of my potential movie stars by screwing up their names.

I decide to try an old trick Mrs. Ostesheaver taught me in second grade when I couldn't remember who anybody was in our class: matching the names and their items with something very specific about each individual.

Mr. Nestman has a nest on his head and looks like he manicures his nails. Mr. *Nest* Man and his nail clippers.

Victoria is voluptuous and uses vast amounts of Vaseline on her voluminous volcanoes.

Ryan sounds like the name of a soap-opera star, which is also what he looks like. He seems like a bit of a butthole. Rectal thermometer.

So far, so good.

I cup my hand over my nose and sniff my palm. Something about it calms me and focuses me at the same time. Which is exactly what I need right now.

Calm and focus.

Here's Mackenzie and she's bringing a magnifying glass. Mackenzie has a long name that could easily fit on her equally long schnozzola. A nose that would look even bigger through a magnifying glass.

Hunter is a buff chiseled-face dude with a buzz cut who is bringing hand grenades. I love how you get tossed an easy one every once in a while.

Fortney has an un*fortunately* large forehead, and since she is bringing face cream, she makes my life that much simpler.

Daniel Duncan is a douche bag who was in my English class last year, and I'm sure whatever he is bringing will reinforce his douchebaggery.

"*Dollahs,*" he says with a big stupid grin, rubbing his forefingers together.

As I was saying.

Dollars on a desert island? Super douchebaggish. But Mr. Nestman doesn't call him on it, probably because he's relieved it's nothing gross or sexual.

Everything is going great guns, my memory plan working like a charm, until my eyes catch sight of the girl who is sitting three doors down from D-bag Dan.

Blunt spiky bob-cut blond hair. Moist full lips. Red shutter shades hiding her eyes. And a tight crimson sweater contouring her amazingly toned arms. Holy cow! It's like she stepped right out of *Final Fantasy*. How wicked hot would she look wielding a Blazefire Saber?

I am so completely hypnotized by this incredible vision of enchantedness that I totally miss what the next two kids say. Their names. Their items. What they look like.

As if they even matter.

As if anything matters anymore.

And when at last my goddess speaks, it's like the most beautiful sound to ever reach human ears in the entire history of human ears. Soft and sweet and melodious.

"Hi. My name is Leyna and I am going to bring"—she pops the top off a tube of Burt's Bees—"lip balm." Leyna giggles, then applies the balm in a wonderfully smooth motion across her perfectly pouted pucker. I could watch her perform this very act a million times over and I would never get bored. "Gotta keep them protected," she says, pressing her glossy lips together.

Oh.

My.

Gandalf.

CHAPTER TEN

BRAINDEAD

WHERE DID THIS GIRL COME FROM? And how have I never seen her before? She must be a freshman. I *hope* she's a freshman. A junior or senior I'd never have a shot at.

Right. A girl that glorious I don't stand a chance with no matter what grade she's in.

But sheeshkabob. What I wouldn't give to have Princess Leyna plant those silky balmed lips on me. I'd hand over my Xbox 360, all of my video games, all of my *World of Warcraft* gold, every single Star Wars and Star Trek novel I own, my Antonio Banderas DVDs . . . Everything.

I'd even donate my entire replica sword and dagger collection to the homeless.

You think I'm joking, but it's true. Because this girl is not only beautiful; she's got that something extra. It's like you get this warm feeling all over when you look at her.

And once you've seen her, you just want to keep seeing her. You can't peel your eyes away—

A loud clap rouses me from my trance.

"Hellooooo?" It's Mr. Nestman, and he sounds annoyed. "Are we still on this planet?"

The class busts up with laughter. And that's when I notice that everyone is staring at me.

"Oh." I shake my head, blinking hard. "I'm sorry . . . I was—"

"Staring at Leyna." Mr. Nestman nods. "Yes, we all saw you. It *is* considered polite to be a bit more discreet about one's ogling."

More laughter from the circle.

"No. I wasn't . . . That's not . . ." I blink hard again, my cheeks burning up. "Is it . . . ? Is it my turn?"

Mr. Nestman forces a smile. "It is indeed."

Shit shit shit. Okay. Gotta think. Gotta think.

"Right." I swallow. "I'm . . . uh . . . I'm Sean and I'll be bringing . . . to our desert island . . ." Jesus, think, man. Anything that starts with *S*. It doesn't matter. Something useful. Something cool. A weapon. A . . . A . . . "A shillelagh," I announce before I can snatch it back.

The class explodes in whoops of laughter.

Shillelagh? Seriously? Jeez. How about a sword, dinklet? Switchblade not cool enough? Saber, slingshot, submachine gun? No? None of those? *God.* I hate my late-to-the-party brain.

"What the hell is a shileelee?" Ryan calls out. "Is that

like one of those rubber bags you strap to your leg so you can walk and whizz at the same time?"

This gets another nice round of sniggers.

"It's pronounced *shuh-LAY-lee,* Ryan," Mr. Nestman corrects. "And no, it's not a urine collector. It's Irish. A thick wooden staff generally used as a cudgel."

"Wait," D-bag Dan says. "I want to bring *my* thick staff, too."

Mr. Nestman smirks. "Sorry, Daniel. One item per person. Perhaps if you ask nicely, Sean will let you use his staff."

Jeers and howls and hoots ricochet off the walls and ceiling.

The entire upper portion of my body is on fire. All I can do is stare at a piece of fluff that gently scoots across the floor in front of me, probably being propelled by the gales of laughter.

"Okay, okay." Mr. Nestman does a bring-down-the-volume gesture with his hands. "Sean, you've got your shillelagh. Now, why don't you tell us what everyone else is bringing?"

I fake a smile. "I can't remember," my voice squeaks. "I didn't get a lot of sleep last night. My brain is blanking. Sorry. I just—"

"How about you give it a try?" Mr. Nestman says. "We'll help you out if you get stuck. That's what this is all about. We're building community here."

Right, by making me look like a meat sack.

"Okay." I clench my eyes shut, attempting to clear my mind. Have to try and remember all the clues I came up with. "Can I start from the beginning instead of going backward?"

"Whatever works for you, Sean," Mr. Nestman says.

"All right." I breathe. Nest on his head Nestman. "Obviously, you're Mr. Nestman. And you're bringing nail clippers."

Mr. Nestman tips his head. "Excellent."

Okay. Okay. Voluptuous, voluptuous. "Victoria," I say, "is bringing her volcanoes." I wince. "I mean her Vaseline. And . . ." Handsome soap star . . . "Ryan. You're a butthole, so . . ."

"What did you say?" Ryan glares at me, his head jutting forward. "I'm a *what*?"

Oh, shit. Did that just come out of my mouth?

"I said . . . *in* your butthole. Because that's where . . . a rectal thermometer goes. And that's what you're bringing." I press my palms into my eye sockets. Must concentrate. Get this over as fast as possible. I remove my hands from my face and look over at . . . "Mackenzie. Is next. And Mackenzie is bringing . . . a magnifying glass. And Hunter is bringing a, uh, hunting knife? No. Hand grenades. Hand grenades. That's right. And Fortney. She's bringing forehead cream."

"*Face* cream," Fortney says, her fingers gingerly touching her extra-wide forehead.

"Sorry. Right. That's what I meant." Jesus. I am sweating all over. None of these people are ever going to want to be in my film. Not after this idiotic display.

"Continuing," Mr. Nestman calls out. "Let's pick up the pace."

"Yes. Right. Okay, okay. There's D-bag Dan, who's bringing . . . I mean *Daniel.* He's bringing douche bags. *No.* No, he's not." I give my head a smack. "He's bringing dollars. And then, after him . . ." I stare at the girl with the long blond hair and the retainer in her mouth. "I can't . . . um . . . I don't . . ."

"Kelsey," Mr. Nestman offers.

"Kelsey." I point at her, pretending it's just come to me. "Correct. And Kelsey is bringing a"—something that begins with k—"*keyboard!*" It's the only thing I can think of.

"Kerosene lamp." Kelsey huffs.

"Yes. That's what I meant. Kerosene lamp. And next to Kelsey is a guy by the name of . . . Don't tell me—it's on the tip of my tongue. Wait for it. It's, like, right there. Just give me—"

"Jake," somebody barks.

"Jake. It would have come to me. Except . . . I have no idea what Jake's bringing."

"A *jacket,*" the same somebody groans.

"Thank you. Wouldn't have gotten that one." I nod, then gesture toward Leyna. "And next is Princess Leyna and her luscious lip balm." I clench my eyes and my fists simultaneously. "I mean . . . just regular Leyna . . . and just plain old regular lip balm. Nothing else."

I drop my head, wishing that someone would just kill me right now.

☛ CHAPTER ELEVEN ☛

VIDEODROME

Come on, guys." I'm pacing around my room with Judy, one of our foster ferrets, draped around my neck like a stole. "We're supposed to be trying to come up with ideas for our movie."

"Okay, but wait. You have to watch this first." Coop laughs as he points at my laptop. "It's elephant porn, dawgs. Can you believe this is YouTube sanctioned? I mean, look at that ginormous whang. It's bigger than his trunk."

Matt moves over to my desk. "Jesus. He's just flopping it around for everyone to see."

"You don't want to watch this, Judy." I take the ferret from around my neck and put her on the floor. "Go on, get me my socks."

Judy scurries off and disappears into my closet.

Matt watches her go, then turns back to the computer. "I guess elephants don't get embarrassed."

Coop laughs. "Dude, if your schnoodle was that big, you wouldn't be shy about waving it around, either. His porn star name should be Packin' Dermis."

"Can we *please* get back to looking for horror clips?" I say.

Coop cracks up. "What? This isn't horrifying enough for you? Hold on, let me find the one where the dog nurtles the cat. It's set to seventies porn music." He hunches over the keyboard and starts typing just as Judy returns with a Mr. Spock action figure in her mouth.

Matt gestures at the ferret. "Hey, that's a pretty cool trick, Sean."

I sigh. "It would have been cooler if she'd actually brought me what I'd asked for."

"Maybe she heard *Spock* instead of *sock,*" Matt says, laughing.

"You think you're being funny but that's actually a good point. I did teach Judy the names of everyone on the *Enterprise* a few years ago."

Matt knits his brow. "Do I even want to ask?"

"Here it is," Coop interjects. He spins the computer toward us and taps up the sound. "Watch this. It's freakin' brill."

Porn music blasts over my tiny laptop speakers as we watch a dog going to town on a cat.

"You teach your pets to do *these* kinds of tricks," Coop says, "and you'll have my dollar."

"I don't *think* so."

"Jesus." Matt's eyes bug. "That's so wrong." He snorts with laughter. "That poor kitty."

"I don't know." Coop shrugs. "The cat only seems mildly inconvenienced."

Matt laughs. "Yeah, probably because it happens on a regular basis. The cat's all, like, 'Oh, great, here we go again. Just get it over with already.'"

Coop punches Matt in the arm. "Kind of like what Val says to you, huh?"

"More like what your mama said to me last night." Matt swats Coop's head. "After, like, the twelfth round."

"That's funny, because even after a marathon session, your mama likes me to take my time. But I guess that's because I've got the mad skills."

"Are you guys finished?" I ask, grabbing the back of my tensed-up neck. "Because I've only got a few months before my life turns into a total nightmare."

"Really?" Coop picks up my laptop and shows me the dog-on-cat video. "I would think you'd be grateful. I mean, at least you're not being accosted by Rover every night." Coop head-gestures toward the dog sleeping in the corner of my room. "Unless, of course, you are."

Just then, the door to my bedroom is bumped open and in walk Mom and Dad, each carrying parts of a crib.

"Sorry," Mom says. "We would have knocked, but our hands are full."

Dad squints at the laptop screen as he rests the head- and footboards against my dresser. "What are you boys watching?"

"Nothing," I blurt, stepping in front of Coop.

"Oh," Mom says, laying the crib slats on the floor. "Is that the one where the dog and cat are wrestling and then fall off the couch? Angie sent me that. It's so cute."

Dad peeks around me. "Whoa!" He jerks his head back. "That's not wrestling."

Mom looks confused. "What?"

Coop snaps the laptop shut. "It's for biology class," he says. "We're doing a report on animal reproduction."

"Reproduction?" Mom screws up her face. "What are you talking about?"

Dad holds up his hand. "It's okay, Barbara. I've got this one." He cants his head as he looks at us. "You boys *do* realize that animals of different species usually can't reproduce?"

"Yeah," Matt says, his eyes veering off to the side. "That's what we were trying to find examples of. Animals that *can't* have babies together. Because . . . not everyone knows that."

"Although," Dad says, emptying a bag of nuts and bolts onto my rug, "interesting factoid: Certain dissimilar species actually *can* generate offspring. *If* they're closely related. Usually within the same genus and within the same family. Have you ever heard of a zonkey?"

"No," Matt says.

Dad fits the headboard and one of the slatted sides together. "That would be a cross between a zebra and a donkey. And while they're very rare in the wild, they have been successfully bred in zoos. In fact, the first zoo to breed one was—"

"That's fascinating," I say. "Why are you guys bringing this baby stuff into my room?"

"Mrs. Goldstein gave this to us," Mom replies, all sprightly. "Wasn't that nice of her?"

"Yeah, real generous." I stare at the partially assembled crib, my jaw clenched tight. "I thought you said the baby wasn't going be born until May."

"Babies sometimes come early." Dad continues with the assembly. "We can't wait until the last minute to make up the room. Besides, it's going to end up in here eventually, so—"

"But this isn't a baby's room," I argue. "It's not even safe for a baby. There are swords on the walls." I motion to my mounted replica samurai swords. "And glass-framed posters that could fall down and kill it." I point to the Lord of the Rings poster over my bed.

"Aw, sweetie." Mom forces a smile. "We're going to have to take all that stuff down, of course. You'll see. We're going to paint it powder blue with some fluffy clouds on the ceiling." There's a wistful look in her eyes, like she's picturing the whole thing already finished. "We might even paint a nice big rainbow over there." She points to the wall where my Death Star clock hangs.

"And a flutter of butterflies flying up to the ceiling over there." Where my World War II figures are displayed. Then she shakes herself out of her reverie. "But we don't have to do it all right now. I mean"—she glances at Dad—"there's still some time. Right, Gary?"

Dad shrugs, tightening a nut. "I'm not sure I see the point in postponing the inevitable."

"Whatever," I say, catching Matt and Coop's "yikes" expressions. "Can you guys just please leave now? We've got a really tight deadline, and we need to get back to work."

Dad looks down at the half-erected crib. "Okay, okay. Got it. I can finish putting this together later. But if you want some help with your biology project—"

"No, thanks." I usher my parents from my bedroom and shut the door behind them.

"Holy crap," Coop says, staring at the crib. "This is way more desperate than I thought. They're squeezing you out, dawg. Forget four months. You're lucky if you have four weeks."

"It sucks." I kick the stupid headboard. "I'm completely screwed."

"No." Coop points at me. "Not completely. Worst-case scenario you'll have to share a room with your sister for a few months. But we're going to do this thing. We're going to make this movie. And we're going to sell it. The three of us. Together. Don't you worry."

"That's right," Matt adds. "We'll figure something out."

"Forget it." I collapse into my Jabba the Hutt beanbag chair. "It's hopeless. Who are we trying to kid? We don't know anything about making movies. We don't have any money. We don't even have a story, for Kirk's sake."

"That's where you're wrong, dawg," Coop says. "Because I just came up with a killer idea. Full of gross-outs, gore, and cheap scares. I even have a title."

"Oh, really?" I look at him. "And what's that?"

Coop stares at me and Matt. His eyes dead serious. "We're going to call it . . . *Zonkey!*"

CHAPTER TWELVE

FRANKENSTEIN

ZONKEY!?" MATT'S EYES scrunch up with skepticism.

"That's right," Coop says. "Some crazy zoo-doctor dude who's in charge of making the zonkeys comes up with this whacked idea to crossbreed human DNA with chimpanzee DNA. But he doesn't just make a human-monkey *baby.* No. He develops some kind of human-chimpanzee *virus* that he can infect people with, making them into these half-man, half-monkey drones that he can control." The ideas are pouring out of Coop like he's possessed or something while Matt and I just stare at him, mesmerized. "What this doctor *doesn't* count on is the virus mutating and turning people into hairy uncontrollable zombie-monsters with a thirst for human blood. That way we hit all of the hot bases." Coop counts off on his fingers. "We've got technology, we've got zombies, we've got a potential apocalypse, and we've got vampirism. It's a beautiful thing." He crosses his arms and leans back in the chair, a smug self-satisfied smile on his face. "Tell me that's not totally genius."

"Are you kidding?" I say. "That's like the *least* genius thing I've ever heard. And I've heard you say some really ungenius things before."

"Actually." Matt taps his lip. "It's not so bad. I mean . . . at least it's kind of fun."

"Seriously?" I grimace. "I don't know. Half-man, half-monkey vampire-zombies?"

"Zombie-vampires," Coop corrects me.

"I think we can make it work," Matt says. "With a little tweaking."

"Really?" I sit up in the beanbag chair, feeling the fog of anger and frustration starting to lift a little. "All right. Maybe it *could* be okay. If we do it right. But shouldn't we call it *Chuman*? I mean, the guy's not making zonkeys. He's making chimpanzee humans."

"Or what about *Humanzee*?" Matt pipes in. "That sounds even better."

"No." Coop shakes his head. "Those sound made-up. Besides, the dude gets the idea because he's making zonkeys. And a zonkey is a real thing. What's so scary about this idea is that it's something that could actually happen."

"No, it isn't," Matt says.

Coop shrugs. "Let's Wiki it." He spins around and

types something into the computer. "Aha. Right there in black and white on the most trusted source on the Internet." He reads, " 'It's hypothetically possible that chimps and humans could produce a living offspring.' "

"That's good, that's good," I say, getting to my feet. "That just adds to the credibility." All of a sudden, I've got an excited thrumming in my chest.

"Ha!" Matt bellows, pointing at the screen. "And what's the title of the article? 'Humanzee.' So, see? I didn't make it up."

"Which just proves you're not an original thinker," Coop says. "Anyway, *Zonkey!* is a way better title. It's more mysterious."

"Okay, okay." I start to pace. "But I'm starting to worry that this might get really complicated with special effects. Maybe instead of turning them into zombie-vampires, the virus kills the people but also makes them ghosts. You don't ever have to show a ghost. They just moves things around the room. We could do that by attaching invisible thread to stuff."

"Boooo*ring!*" Coop says. "Ghosts are so three years ago."

"Oh, really?" Matt smirks. "And vampires are cutting-edge?"

"These *aren't* vampires, dude." Coop reaches under my desk and grabs a can of Mountain Dew from my minifridge. "These are zombie-vampire hybrids that also happen to be human chimpanzee half-breeds. That's what makes them so cool and different. It's the whole package. Zonkeys are interesting. Humanzees are freaky. And zombie-vampire humanzees are the freakiest of all. Besides, we won't have to show that much of them. A hairy hand here. A close-up of a monkey mouth biting a neck. It's totally doable, dawg. The less you show, the scarier it is."

"All right." I nod. "I'm down with it. I vote for *Zonkey!* What do we do next?"

"We put the plan into action. And as the producer and director of *Zonkey!*, it's up to me to start delegating." Coop wheels the desk chair over to my bookcase. He snaps up my copy of *Leonard Maltin's Movie Guide* and tosses it to me. "Sean, you're our screenwriter."

"Wait a second." I stare down at the book. "It's my butt on the line here. I think maybe I should be the one to direct."

"'I think maybe' ain't gonna cut it when we're out in the field trying to shoot this thing," Coop says. "A director needs to be fast and decisive. Boom, boom, boom." He slaps the back of his left hand repetitively into the palm of his right. "That's me. Not you. No offense, but your talents lie elsewhere. You're more . . . contemplative. Which is why you'll be good at writing this thing."

"I don't know." I blink hard. "I've never written anything longer than a three-page English essay."

"You're gonna be brill, trust me," Coop assures. "Just find your favorite horror films and mark the pages. You'll watch a whole whack of flicks and then you can jack the scariest scenes to use in your screenplay." He rolls back to the desk and opens the laptop. "Matt, since you're the most organized of the three of us, you get to be in charge of all the organizational shit."

"Oh, lucky me." Matt laughs.

"It's vital, dawg. We don't have someone who can coordinate things, we don't have a movie. You're going to have to figure out where we can get the equipment, special effects, and music and everything. Grab some paper and make a list of all the things we're going to need. Video camera, makeup, lights—"

"Whoa, whoa, whoa. Hold on." Matt scrambles around, looking for a pad and pen.

"Here," I say, leaning over and snagging my backpack. I unzip the bag, reach inside, and blindly grab a still-moist hairball. "Goddamn it. Not again." I fling the soggy globule of cat hair into my trash can and wipe my palm on the rug.

"Dude, little advice," Coop says. "If you want to land the luscious ladies, keep the kittens from yurking in your backpack."

"It's just Buttons." I glance over at the white-and-gray cat curled up on my bed. "She throws up if she eats too fast. Air bubbles get trapped in her esophagus. I'm the same way, actually. The problem is that she gets embarrassed when she's sick and then hides in my bag. I probably should just get another backpack."

"No," Coop says. "What you *should* get is a bigger pair of balls. It's a cat, dude. It doesn't have feelings. Just ban the puking puss from your room."

I shake my head. "I can't do it. I feel bad for her. And she does too have feelings." I reach into my backpack again and find the notebook and pen I was looking for. I hold them out to Matt. "Here you go."

He looks at me warily.

"Go on. They're cat puke–free. Don't worry."

"They better be." Matt reaches out and takes them cautiously. "All right. Give me all that again, Coop." Matt starts writing. "Video camera? What else?"

Coop rattles off the items, adding costumes, lights, actors, and editing software to the list.

"Uhhh . . ." Matt looks up from the paper. "I don't want to be the one who craps on the cupcake here, but how are we going to afford all of this?"

"Don't worry. We'll figure it out. Most of the stuff we can cobble together for next to nothing." Coop scrolls down what looks like a horror movie–themed Web page on my laptop. "But there are three things we absolutely need some casheesh for. One is a supreme camera, because it's got to look professional. Two is special effects, for the same reason as one. And three is"—he smiles and clicks on something—"our entry fee."

"Entry fee?" I ask. "For what?"

"For this." He spins the laptop around for me to read.

I squint, trying to read the title. "What the heck is . . . TerrorFest?"

"It's a film festival in NYC, baby. It's where *Psychopathic Anxiety* was discovered. They have an amateur filmmaking contest. Anyone can enter a flick to be screened for two hundred bills. The top three films win fifty grand each. And *Zonkey!,*" Coop says, making a marquee in the air with his hands, "is going to be one of those films. But we've only got two months to get this puppy filmed, cut, and ready to show. So, who do you know who you can beg some coin off of?"

I laugh. "If I knew who we could get money from, we wouldn't have to make this movie."

"It doesn't have to be a lot. Five grand would do. Don't you have a college fund you can raid?"

"Pfff, right." I snort. "As if my parents would ever let me touch that money."

"Desperate times, dawg," Coop says.

"I thought we were going to get someone to sponsor us. Like B&M Deli," Matt says.

Coop shakes his head. "We don't have time to canvas the neighborhood for suckers. If we want to get this bad boy up and running, then we need some scratch and we need it fast."

"Okay, let me think." I put down the *Movie Guide* and scrub at my eyes with the palms of my hands, like if I rub hard enough my brain will pop out an idea.

And then it comes to me. It's not the best solution, for sure, but it's the only one I've got. I open my eyes to see Coop and Matt staring at me hopefully.

"All right," I say. "I guess there is *someone* I could ask."

☞ CHAPTER THIRTEEN ☞

THE THING FROM
ANOTHER WORLD

OKAY, SO, JUST TO WARN YOU," I say to Matt and Coop, "my uncle's a little weird."

Matt's eyes narrow. "Weird, how?"

"I don't know." I shrug. "He's just kind of odd. You'll see." I lift my fist to knock on Uncle Doug's door when Coop grabs my wrist.

"Whoa, hold the phone," he says, looking at me sideways. "We're not going to black out and wake up tomorrow morning feeling like we've been bull-riding all night, are we?"

"Nice." I shake my head. "Leap right in with the sickest thing imaginable."

"What?" he says, feigning total innocence. "Someone tells you they've got a weird uncle, what are you supposed to think?"

"He's just reclusive, is all. He's not a perv." I raise my fist again and rap on the door. "He happens to be a really chill guy. Just sometimes he comes across as a little . . . perma-fried."

I wiggle my numb toes inside my frozen boots as we wait for Uncle Doug to answer the door. I have to admit, I'm a little on edge here. I have no idea what his reaction will be when I ask him for the money. Either he could be totally sympathetic to my plight—I mean, he *does* know Cathy, after all—or he could go ballistic, ranting about how he's not the local bank.

Just then, the inside door swings open and there's Uncle Doug. All six foot, two hundred and fifty pounds of him, wearing an XXL tomato-sauce-stained Buffalo Sabres hockey jersey and smoking a carrot-size joint. His hunormous bushy black beard hangs from his chin like a giant hairy lobster bib.

He's got a big grin on his face and a happy twinkle in his eyes, like us coming to visit him is a welcome surprise. Which only heightens the guilt I'm already feeling.

"Good-morrow," Uncle Doug says, raising his joint in a sort of smoky salute. "Your mom send you over here to shovel my driveway?"

"No." I look over my shoulder at the foot of snow that blanketed all of Lower Rockville this morning. "But we'll do it for you if you need to get your car out."

He shrugs. "Only traveling I'm doing today is on my magic broomstick." He smiles and takes a deep drag on his mega-joint. "These your buds?"

"Coop and Matt," I say, "this is my uncle Doug."

"A pleasure and a privilege," Uncle Doug says, blowing out a plume of smoke. "Come in. It's cold as a witch's tit out there." He takes another toke, turns, and tromps down the hall.

Coop and Matt arch their eyebrows, looking a little worried as we enter the house.

"Take off your boots," Uncle Doug calls from the other room. "And shut that fucking door. You think I'm made of money?" He cackles like this is the best joke ever.

We make our way down the hallway and step into the messy kitchen. Uncle Doug is already planted at the table, a cigarette-butt-and-roach-mounded ashtray on one side of him, a Diet Coke on the other, and a ratty old barely breathing laptop—with a game of Texas Hold'em up on the screen—directly in front of him.

"So, to what do I owe this impromptu sojourn? You come to pay me back for my amplifier you totaled?" He raises his eyebrows and takes a glug of his soda.

"Uh, no," I say. Crap, I forgot all about the amp we wasted during the Battle of the Bands. I take a furtive whiff of my palm. "We just thought . . . we'd stop by. I haven't seen you in a while."

"Is that so?" Uncle Doug gently places his joint down in the ashtray, then lunges out and grabs me in a headlock. "Come by to visit your crazy uncle Doug?" He cackles loudly as he gives me a hair-tearing noogie.

"Ow, ow, ow." Damn it! I should have known this was coming. I just didn't expect his standard reception with my friends around. I struggle to get free, but he's way stronger than me. I can see Matt and Coop—upside-down—pointing and laughing hysterically.

"Say 'uncle,'" Uncle Doug says.

"Uncle!" I shout.

"Say 'Uncle *Doug.*'" He grinds his knuckle into my scalp.

"Uncle Doug, Uncle Doug, Uncle Doug!"

Finally he lets me go and I stumble backward, trying to catch my breath.

Uncle Doug laughs maniacally. He snatches up his joint and takes a deep hit. "It's good to see you, Seanie. You always were my favorite nephew."

"I'm your only nephew," I say, rubbing my sore head.

"That too." He chuckles. "You boys want a drink? Diet Coke? Beer? Whiskey?"

"No, thank you," Matt says.

"A sniff of this?" Doug waves the smoldering joint in the air.

Coop holds up his hand. "That's okay. Thanks, though."

"Good man," Uncle Doug says. "Say no to drugs. I approve." He takes another puff. "If I could go back and do it all again, well . . . ahh, who the hell am I kidding? I'd do it exactly the same way." A giant plume of smoke escapes from his lips as he chuckles. "I mean, look at me. Successful businessman at fifty. Not a care in the world. Living the life of Riley."

My gaze slides over to the stacks of takeout contain-
ers on the kitchen counter, the dirty dishes and empty
soda cans piled in the sink, the towers of magazines and
newspapers in the corner, and I can't help but think he's
not being completely objective about things.

"Still," Doug continues, "I respect your decision.
Even if I don't hold myself up to the same lofty standards
as you kids. Although, Seanie my boy, I'm afraid you will
not be getting off completely scot-free where drugs are
concerned."

I look from Matt to Coop, like maybe I've missed
something. "I'm sorry, what?"

"When I meet my maker," Doug says. "It's in the
will. I'm to be cremated and then the ashes are to be
rolled up, passed around, and smoked by the whole family. No exceptions. If you want your inheritance, you
take a toke. I've got so much THC in my bones, everyone
should get a pretty heady buzz." He howls with laughter
before licking his fingertips and carefully squeezing out
the glowing tip of the joint. "Would you guys take a seat?
You're making me nervous."

Coop leaps in first, spinning one of the empty chairs
around and sitting on it backward.

"So, what kind of business are you in, Mr. Burrows?"
Coop asks.

Matt and me pull out the other two chairs and take
our seats.

"Uncle Doug, please," he says. "If I'm Uncle Doug to

the ladies at the bank, and to the guys at the 7-Eleven, and to my dope dealer, then I'm *definitely* Uncle Doug to Sean's pals."

"Okay. Uncle Doug." Coop suppresses a smile, like the words don't feel natural on his lips. "So, are you, like, a stockbroker or something?"

"Rugs," Uncle Doug says. "You've seen the Doug's Rugs commercials on TV?"

"Oh, my God," Matt says. *"Fit it tight, Fit it snug. A rug from Doug's is a big warm hug."*

"I'll give you one guess as to who Doug is." Uncle Doug winks at us, then busts up laughing as he takes a slurp on his soda.

"That's cool," Coop says. "It must be sweet to be your own boss."

"It's a situation I highly recommend." He taps a cigarette from a blue pack of American Spirits and lights it with a Sabres Zippo. "All right, enough with the niceties. I know you didn't come all the way out here on the shittiest day of the year to talk to Uncle Doug about what he does for a living. So, what the hell do you want?" He takes a drag on his cigarette and releases the smoke. "Are we changing your amplifier repayment schedule or what? Ten bucks a week for the next two years too much of a burden on your allowance? Come on, spit it out."

All of sudden, I don't want to ask him for the money anymore. It feels wrong. Like I'm taking advantage or something.

"Well?" Doug says. "Let's have it. The cat got your tongue or what?" He flicks the ash off his cigarette, and it tumbles down the mountain of butts piled in the ashtray.

"Nothing," I say. "We don't want anything. We just—"

I feel Coop kick my ankle under the table.

I take a deep breath. "Okay, that's not completely true." My voice comes out a little squeaky. "I mean, we did want to see you but . . . there's something else we needed to ask you."

"I'm all ears." He takes another drag on his cigarette.

I press my sweaty palms into my thighs. "Okay, so, you know how Mom's pregnant?"

"What?" Doug reels backward. "My sister's *pregnant*? Are you shitting me? When the hell did *that* happen? And why is Uncle Doug the last one to hear about this?"

Every inch of my skin prickles with heat. "I—I thought," I stammer. "I just assumed . . . I mean . . . You really didn't know?"

"Ha!" Doug points at me with the two fingers that hold his cigarette. "Gotcha! You always were a little too easy to screw with, Seanie." He cocks his head. "Come on, now. You really think your mother wouldn't tell Uncle Doug that she was having a baby?"

I breathe a supreme sigh of relief. "No. Yeah." I force a smile. "You got me for sure."

"That was damn good." Coop laughs. "Even *I* was

convinced. And that's from the baron of bull. Forget about rugs—you should have been an actor."

"Funny you should mention that," Uncle Doug says. "I did contemplate that once upon a time. Way back in the days of my youth."

"Well, count me in as being fooled," Matt adds, shooting me a meaningful look. "That was a brilliant performance."

"Yeah, yeah, yeah." Doug glances up at the Buffalo Bills clock over the sink. "Consider Uncle Doug sufficiently lubed up. Let's get on with the reaming."

I look at my friends, then back at Uncle Doug. Screw it. There's no subtle way to do this.

"Okay." I shake my head. "I'm just going to say this because . . . well . . . I sort of feel bad about it, but I'm desperate and there's no one else I can turn to."

"Uh-oh, here it comes. The International Bank of Doug." Uncle Doug leans back in his chair and takes a long pull on his cigarette. He blows the smoke out and smirks. "Come on, already. Let's have it. How much do you need, and what do you need it for?"

☛ CHAPTER FOURTEEN ☚

CANDYMAN

UNCLE DOUG IS DEAD SILENT after I explain the whole situation. He strokes his long bristly beard and regards us with his piercing, bloodshot eyes. His neck is stained an angry red, highlighting every little bump, mole, and broken capillary.

I can't tell if he's getting ready to blow his stack or if he's just thinking really hard. The thick scent of smoke and stale pizza and uncomfortable silence chokes the oxygen out of the kitchen.

Uncle Doug crushes out his cigarette. He sniffs, then clears his throat. "Okay," he finally says. "Let's do a little role reversal here. If you were *me,* and I came to *you* with this request, what would you do? Be honest, now. Uncle Doug's got a finely calibrated bullshit meter."

"He'd give you the five K," Coop answers. "Because he could see the upside of the whole sitch. The exposure. The advertising. The Doug's Rugs product placement.

The community goodwill. Not to mention the chance to turn a small investment into a mega-fortune."

Uncle Doug smirks at Coop. "Thanks for the sales pitch, P. T. Barnum." He turns back to me. "But I want to hear it from Seanie. Would you lend me the money or not?"

"I don't know." My gaze drops to the scratched-up wooden kitchen table. "I might."

"Might? Or *would*?" He leans to the side. "Come on, now. Meet my eyes like you've got some huevos rancheros. I want a firm yes or no. Do you lend me the cash?"

"It would depend, I guess."

"On what?"

"On if I thought you could pull it off."

"Fair enough." Uncle Doug nods. "So, now I need you to look me square in the face and tell me if you honestly think that you'll be able to produce a motion picture decent enough to generate enough money for you to pay me back."

My eyes slide over to Coop and Matt, who look like they want to bolt.

"Uh-uh." Uncle Doug beans me with an empty pack of cigarettes. "The answer's not over there." He reaches over and pokes my belly. "What's your gut say? Can you do it or not?"

I want to look over at my friends again, but I force myself to focus on my uncle. "Yes," I say. "I think we can do it."

"Wrong!" Uncle Doug roars, slapping the table, which causes a thin cloud of tobacco-scented dust to rise in the air. "You *want* to think you can do it. But you don't really believe it. Not deep down in your scrotum, where it counts. I can read you like a hockey stats chart, Seanie."

"So . . ." My stomach winces. "You won't help us out, then?"

"I didn't say that." Uncle Doug grabs the extinguished joint from his ashtray, straightens it out, and relights it. He takes an epically long toke, then blows the smoke in my face. "*Yet.* I'd like to see your business plan before I make my decision."

"Business plan?" I blink, my eyes dry and stinging from the smoke. I use it as an excuse to cup my palm over my nose and take a reassuring whiff.

"No business plan, huh?" Uncle Doug says. "How about a list of expenditures?"

"A what?" I ask, sinking down in my chair.

"A budget, *dummkopf.*" Uncle Doug reaches over and swats the side of my head. "The spreadsheet that lays out exactly how you intend to spend my money."

"Oh. Um." I look at Matt and Coop, who just stare back at me. "We . . . We know we need at least two hundred dollars for the film festival entrance fee. And then any extra will be used—"

"Right. No budget. Okay, then, what *do* you have for

me? Some comparative box-office analysis? A marketing strategy? A film trailer? A script, perchance? *Anything?*"

"Yes, we have the idea," I say, sitting up. "It's the story of this guy—"

"All right, just so I'm clear on this." Uncle Doug hoists himself off the chair and starts to pace the room. "Am I to understand that you would like me to be an investor in your film project? One that has *no* budget? *No* business plan? *No* marketing strategy? *No* script? To be produced by people who have absolutely *no* moviemaking experience?" He bobs his head in the affirmative. "Is that the general gist of things here?"

"Yeah." I pull my cupped hand away from my nose, the smoky stench of the kitchen having permeated my skin. "I guess so."

"You *guess* so?" Uncle Doug roars with laughter. "Okay, well, notch a point for stupid honesty." He makes an imaginary check mark in the air with his smoldering roach. "Right, so. Here we go." Uncle Doug clears his throat and starts pacing again. "Obviously, investing in your film would be an idiotic colossal gamble. I suppose it could be likened to shoving a fistful of cash up your asshole and expecting you to shit out gold coins."

"I'm sorry," I mutter. "I never should have ask—"

"Uhp." Uncle Doug cuts me off with a traffic cop hand. "Let me finish. You *did* ask the question, Seanie boy, and now you're getting your answer. So sit back and take this like a man."

I do as I'm told, crossing my arms over my chest to avoid the urge to sniff my palm—unlike a man.

"All right, now," Uncle Doug continues, "let me just say this right off the bat. There's no way in hell I'm giving you kids five thousand dollars to piss away on a movie."

My shoulders slump. My head drops. "Okay, well, I guess we better—"

"As I was *saying*. Five grand is out of the question. *But*. Uncle Doug happens to be a gambler. And he bets on cards. He bet on horses. He once even bet that his tongue was longer than every other guy's at his Monday night poker game. Which it was. By around half an inch, in case you were wondering." He brushes this out of the air. "Anyway, back to the terms of our deal."

I shake my head, not sure if I've heard him correctly. "Our deal? Does that mean—?"

"Yes, that *does* mean." His eyes bug out as he grins. "Crazy Uncle Doug is going to help you out with your movie. With *one* thousand dollars. Are you surprised? Well, you should be. Because it's one of the stupidest things I think I've ever done. But hey, could the odds of me getting rich off your movie be much worse than Powerball? At two hundred million to one, I doubt it. And if I can lay a hundred bucks on that every week, why not bet a cool grand on my bozo nephew?"

"A thousand dollars?" I glance at Coop, who shrugs like it's better than nothing. "That's . . . great."

"You bet your sweet ass it's great." Uncle Doug throws back his head, cackling insanely.

"Thank you," I say.

"Don't go slickin' your slacks just yet, mister." He plops himself back down into his chair and taps out another cigarette. "You boys are going to want to hear the conditions before you agree to the contract." Uncle Doug grabs his Zippo and lights up his American Spirit.

"Conditions?" Matt asks. "What kind of conditions?"

"First and foremost." He holds up one chubby tobacco-tanned finger. "If you actually *do* manage a miracle and win this contest, Uncle Doug wants twenty-five percent of the prize money *plus* fifty percent of any subsequent profits thereafter."

Coop leans forward. "Okay, wait a second—"

"Condition *numero dos.*" Doug holds up his fingers in a pudgy peace sign. "If you do *not* win the contest, you are going to return my initial investment. Somehow. Someway. We can work out the details later, but that cash will end up back in my pocket when this is all over."

I nod. "Got it."

"Three. As your new executive producer and partner, I am now going to be intimately involved in all aspects of this production. I want to have full script approval, of course."

"What?" I grimace. "Why?"

Uncle Doug shrugs. "I'm not about to have my good name associated with a piece-of-crap movie. I have a reputation to uphold."

"In rugs," Coop says. "Not in films."

"This kind of thing could have major repercussions on my business. What if you say something racist in your script? Or sexist? Or just something really, really stupid? I could lose customers that way. Nope. I want to see each and every scene before it's filmed."

"All right," I concede. "Is that everything?"

"Hardly. I also want casting approval, and in-movie advertising for my store." He nods and smiles at Coop. "*And* . . . a prominent role in the film."

"Okay," I say. "I'm sure there's some part we can use you for."

"The villain." He points at me. "I want to play the lead villain."

I meet Coop's eyes. He gives me a reluctant nod. And he's right. What other choice do we really have?

"Sure," I say. "Why not?"

"All right, then." Uncle Doug rubs his hands together. "I'm glad we're all so amenable. Now, onto my final stipulation." He grins. "This one you're *really* not going to like."

☛ CHAPTER FIFTEEN ☚

DR. JEKYLL AND MR. HYDE

I SIT BY MYSELF IN THE CAFETERIA, waiting for the happy couples to arrive, breathing in the rising sweet fumes of my barbecue riblette on festival rice. I poke at my overnuked food with a plastic fork as I attempt to jot down script notes on a yellow legal pad.

I scribble ZONKEY! at the top of the page. Now what? How should the movie start? With our two main characters, Jack and Stacy, hanging out at school? Or maybe at the zoo. With the mad scientist coming up with his humanzee plan—Dr. . . . Somebody-or-other.

A hand suddenly claps me on the shoulder, causing me to jump.

"That better be the script you're working on there," Coop says.

I look up and see him and Matt plopping their trays on the opposite side of the table.

"Starting to, yeah." I put my pen down. "Where's Helen and Val? I thought we were telling them about the movie today."

"They'll be here," Matt says. "They had to have a girl meeting in the bathroom."

Coop chin-gestures at my pad. "How much you got so far?"

"Not much," I say. "I'm just wondering: are we going to be able to pull this off with only a thousand bucks?"

"Have a little faith, dawg," Coop reassures me. "Didn't you ever see *Field of Dreams*? 'If you build it, they will come.'" He swats Matt's arm. "Go on. Tell Sean what you told me. About the budget."

Matt teeter-totters his head. "Well, I did a little number crunching, and it looks like our biggest expense is going to be the equipment. A movie-quality camera costs around three grand. So, obviously, we can forget about that. And renting one—assuming we could even get someone with a credit card to do that for us—can run five hundred bucks a week. Which would use up our entire budget fast."

"Exactly," Coop says. "So, the linchpin is figuring out the camera sitch. We do that, and we're golden. But don't worry, I've got a few ideas percolating. What we need to be discussing right now, though, is casting." As Coop mixes his turkey tetrazzini, the sweaty-clothes smell wafts over and makes me gag.

"What about it?" I ask.

"We have to get on it. Asap. Which is why I put a notice on Craigslist last night. And on the school's online bulletin board. So, we should have a pretty nice turnout this Saturday."

"This *Saturday*?" I sputter. "That's in two days. I can't have a script by then!"

"Don't sweat it, boss," Coop says. "We just need the first few scenes for the auditions. I want to get our main actors set so we can start shooting this pup the second we're ready to roll."

I look down at my meager scrawlings. "Okay. I guess I can have *something* by then. Where are we doing it?"

"Your place," Coop announces.

"*My* place." I cough. "You didn't tell me anything about that."

"I'm the producer here. I have to make a thousand decisions a day. I can't be expected to run every single one by you. Besides, I mean, I wasn't about to have a bunch of weirdo actors tromping through *my* house. And Matt's horny grandpa would just scare away all the hot babes."

"It's true." Matt nods, taking a bite of his sandwich.

"So, really," Coop continues, "it was a process of elimination."

"Fine." My right knee starts jackhammering. "I'll clear the house somehow."

"*Quoi de neuf?*" Valerie says, her French doing what

her French always does to me. She and Helen set their plates of food down and take seats next to their respective boyfriends.

"Casting actors," Coop says as if he understands what she's talking about. "We've decided we're going to make a movie. A low-budget horror film. You guys want to help out?"

"A movie?" Helen perks up. "You mean, like, for a school project? That'd be cool."

Coop shakes his head slowly. "No. Not for school. For reals. A *feature* film."

"Right." Valerie chuckles. "What'd they slip into the turkey tetrazzini today?"

Coop ignores Val and turns to Helen. "We've already come up with a killer story idea, and we've lined up some serious financing. Matt's been sketching out the business plan, I'm researching potential shooting locations, and Sean's, like, halfway done with the script." He gestures toward my legal pad, which I surreptitiously cover with my hand.

"What we don't have," Matt adds, "is someone to do the music, the editing, and the special effects. Would you girls maybe want to be in charge of those things?"

"Wait a second," Helen says. "You're really serious about this?"

"One hundred percent," Coop says.

"Oublie ça!" Valerie laughs. "Sorry. Thanks, but no thanks."

"Why not?" Coop asks.

"I just . . ." Val sighs. "Look, no offense or anything, but I'm well aware of your crazy plots and
schemes, Cooper, and, quite honestly, I'd prefer not to be
included."

"This is no plot," Coop insists. "This is a *mission.* A
supreme act of kindness. We're making this film to help
out our friend here." He motions across the table at me.
"Sean's family is in crisis. As I'm sure you're aware of,
his mother is expecting a baby any day now and—"

"Actually, it's a few months," I correct him.

"And," Coop continues, giving me the stink eye,
"they have nowhere for this brand-new bundle of joy to
lay its down-covered head." He turns to address Valerie.
"The money we make from this movie is going to help
the Hance family expand their home so that they can
welcome their new family member with open arms and
a room of his—or her—own. Now, if you don't want to
help out a poor innocent baby, well, then, your soul is
blacker than I thought."

With that, Coop averts his gaze, like he can't bear
to look at someone so coldhearted. But by the tell-me-
another-one look on Valerie's face, I don't think she's
buying it.

Val can barely contain her laughter. "So this is a completely selfless act, then?"

Coop places his hand on his chest. "Did I say that?
No, I did not. As it happens, there might be something in

it for *all* of us. Namely, fame and fortune and millions of dollars. But that's beside the point. The chief *main* reason we're doing this is for Sean-o's family."

"We really need you guys," I plead. "I mean, if we're actually going to get this thing done before the baby's born, we're gonna need all the help we can get."

Valerie looks over at Helen, who shrugs and smiles.

"I'm game," Helen says. "What could it hurt?"

Val rolls her eyes. "Okay, *fine.* But I want to do the costumes too. If by some miracle this ever *does* see the light of day, I wouldn't mind having that credit to put on my premed application. They love to see applicants with diverse interests."

Coop shrugs. "Knock yourself out. You did a great job with Helen's outfit at the Battle of the Bands, that's for sure." He waggles his eyebrows at Helen. And get this, she actually *giggles.* Girls. Jeez.

"Hey, what's up, buttercup?"

I do a double take before realizing it's Evelyn who's sliding in next to me on the bench.

"Hi," I say, my stomach gripping up. "What . . . what are you doing here?"

"Guess who has study hall fourth period?" Evelyn squeals. "And guess who got her study-hall teacher to excuse her to go have some lunch today?"

"Wow." I blink. "That's . . . great."

I don't know why I'm feeling so uneasy. It's not like

Evelyn hasn't been mostly normal lately. She was totally chill when I told her I couldn't hang out yesterday after school because I had to visit my uncle. Granted, I may have added that he was dying of emphysema, but there's a chance that's not actually a lie. Still, I've been bracing myself this whole week, like someone's squeezing a balloon right next to my ear.

"So." Evelyn grins across the table. "What are we gabbing about?"

"The guys are making a movie," Helen blabs. "We're helping out. You should too."

"Ohmygod, I definitely want to help." She looks at me. "I mean, if you want me to."

"No. Yeah," I lie. "Sure. Of course."

"Cool. So, what can I do?" She's practically vibrating.

"You wouldn't have access to a professional video camera, would you?" Coop asks.

Evelyn frowns thoughtfully. "What do you mean by professional?"

Coop cants his head, suddenly hopeful. "Something high-def. Why? Do you have one?"

"Is there, like, a particular brand you wanted?" Evelyn asks.

"Any brand is fine," Matt replies. "As long as it shoots really high-quality video."

Evelyn shrugs. "I *might* be able to get my hands on something."

I stare at her in disbelief. "Really? Seriously? Are you kidding?"

"I'll have to ask around," she says. "It could take a few days. When do you need it by?"

Coop's got an excited gleam in his eyes. "We still have a few things to iron out." He wipes his mouth with his napkin. "We have to cast, of course. And Sean needs to finish writing the script but . . . Maybe two weeks?"

Evelyn nods slowly, pensively. "Yeah. Okay. I can't make any promises, but I think I can work something out by then. I'll let you know. Anything else you need?"

"Sure. Some lighting would be nice. Microphones. A DSLR for publicity stills." Coop laughs. "Seriously, though, if you can get the camera, you'd be a hero."

"Awesome, possum," Evelyn says, bouncing in her seat. "This is going to be a blast."

We spend the rest of the lunch period discussing the film. Coop lays out the basic plot for the girls so that they can get a sense of the outfits, and songs, and props we'll need. Honestly, I expected them to treat this like a bit of a joke. But they actually seem pretty into it. And seeing their excitement makes me think that maybe, just maybe, Coop may actually have hit the jackpot here.

When the bell rings, everyone gets up from the table, grabbing their trays as they go.

I start to stand when Evelyn grasps my arm.

"One sec," she says. "I need to talk to you about something."

"Sure." I settle back down and lift my chin toward my friends. "Catch you guys later."

"Adios, muchachos," Coop says with a point of his finger gun.

"Bye." Evelyn smiles and waves. Then she turns on me with this intense look in her eyes. "Why didn't you tell me you were making a movie?" Her fingers grip my wrists like handcuffs.

"What?" I try to pull my hands away but she's not letting go. "We *did* tell you."

"No, *you* didn't. *Helen* told me. So she obviously knew before me."

"We only just told them. Before you came in. Could you . . . let go of my wrists, please?"

Evelyn glances down at her clenched hands. "Oh, sorry." She laughs and releases me. "I'm just . . . It was embarrassing, that's all. You know, in front of everyone like that. I mean, I *am* your girlfriend, right? So, I should kinda know when you're doing something so big."

"We only decided on doing it a little while ago." I rub my reddened wrists. "I would have told you eventually. I don't see what the big deal is."

Evelyn's right eye squints up like someone squirted her with grapefruit juice. "I just . . . I just . . . Uh-uh . . . No . . . This is not . . . *No!*" She lets out this low growling sound. Like she's a constipated Rottweiler or something.

I glance around the nearly empty cafeteria to see if anyone else is catching this. But the few stragglers who are left are all self-involved. I look back at Evelyn, who appears to be going purple.

"Are . . . are you okay?" I ask.

All of a sudden, her face completely relaxes, her skin returning to its natural pink color. She takes a deep breath and wrenches a smile from her lips. "I'm fine. You're right. I'm overreacting. I'm sorry." Evelyn laughs, like what just happened was not the freaky thing it really was. "It's all good. Seriously." She pats my leg. "I'm going to get you your camera, Sean. You'll see. Don't you worry."

"Uhhh, yeah." I feel myself leaning away, like maybe her madness is catching. "Sure. Okay. Sounds good."

Evelyn stands, brushing something—the wackies?— from her jeans. "We're still on for tomorrow night, right?" She stares at me, a trace of the evil spirit still lingering in her watery brown eyes. "For our Web Design tutoring?"

"Oh." God, I forgot all about that. I had to reschedule due to Uncle Doug. But I kind of assumed she wouldn't hold me to it. I mean, I'm probably still reeling from visiting my dying uncle and everything, right? But there's no way in hell I'm canceling on her right now, not when she still looks like her head could start spinning around. "Yeah. Of course. Tomorrow. Right. What time did we say?"

"Six o'clock." She grins. "You're in for a big surprise, mister."

"Great," I say, a puddle of acid pooling in my stomach. "I . . . I can't wait."

"Me, either." She lunges toward me and grabs my head, squashing her face into mine as she administers a gaping-mouthed saliva-soaked kiss to my lips, chin, and the bottom half of my nose. There's a loud slurping-up-spaghetti sound as she pulls away. *"Boyfriend!"* she squeals. "I *love* that we found each other, don't you?"

"Mmm," I say, trying to casually wipe off my upper lip with my lower one.

Evelyn gives me a little four-finger wave. "See you soon, raccoon!"

She turns and bounces out of the cafeteria.

CHAPTER SIXTEEN

STORM OF THE CENTURY

NOW IT'S RAIN!" Mr. Nestman calls out, his hands cupped around his mouth. This is the fourth improv "event" he's had us react to today. So far we've had to deal with an imaginary blizzard, a thick fog, and phantom falling trees.

We're in our socks, gliding around the room, acting as if we're ice-skating outside on a pond. Pretty strange how just over a week ago I was skating with the girl of my nightmares and today I'm pretending to do the same thing with the girl of my gamer dreams.

Of course, I'd be infinitely happier if Leyna and me could take up our Blazefire Sabers, hop aboard an Eidolon, and ride off to fulfill our Final Fantasy. Which isn't very likely at this point, seeing as I haven't had the guts to actually speak to her yet.

"Now it's a torrential downpour!" Mr. Nestman hollers.

I hunch my shoulders and hold my hands over my head, pretending to be into this exercise but really just "skating" behind Leyna the whole time. Instead of hiding from the rain, she simply opens an "umbrella" and continues to coast light-footedly over the pond.

God, she's amazing. So smooth and graceful and elegant. If I had any balls, I'd coast up beside her and start chatting. Instead, I pull back. Convince myself that I should watch the other kids. See who's doing the best improv here. I mean, casting *is* this Saturday, and I still need to decide who to invite.

So I shift my gaze from Princess Leyna to Hunter, who's taking cover under one of the still-standing "trees." He wipes the rain from his face and arms pretty convincingly.

Then there's Kelsey, clutching herself as she crouches in the corner. Her retainered teeth chattering is fairly realistic. Definitely someone to consider.

And here's Douchebag Dan. Hamming it up, pretending to have fallen through the ice. Though nobody's rushing to his aid, which only goes to show how we all feel about him.

"Hurricane!" Mr. Nestman shouts.

All of a sudden, everyone in the class is stumbling around, struggling against the gale-force winds. It's the perfect opportunity to stagger toward Leyna and possibly make some incidental contact. Maybe then I could apologize to her, which would of course lead to a witty and flirtatious conversation. Or something.

But just as I reel in her direction, I hear someone holler, "Look out!" Before I can alter my course, Voluptuous Victoria blindsides me. I bounce off her soft fleshy buxomness, whip around, and trip over my own feet. A second later and I'm timbering right toward a flailing hurricane-buffeted Douchebag Dan.

My hands shoot out to brace my fall, and I end up grabbing Dan right in the crotch. He howls in pain as he shoves me away, screaming something about keeping my mitts off his shillelagh.

I turn and look up to see Leyna cupping her hand over her mouth, laughing hysterically. Not exactly the way I wanted to get her to notice me. I scramble to my feet, hoping the flaming red disappears from my face by the time I'm "blown" into her. But before I can stumble more than a few steps, the bell rings.

"That's a wrap!" Mr. Nestman claps his hands above his head again. "Nice work, everyone. Really great. Now, get your shoes on and get the hell out of my classroom."

I head over to the corner and grab my beat-up Nikes, which I strategically kicked off next to Leyna's baby-blue Keds in the hope that I might be able to muster up some casual conversation when it was time to put our shoes back on. But now that I see her approaching, my mind is a blank.

"Excuse me," she says, sliding past me to grab her Keds and red shutter shades off the stage steps.

I watch Leyna out of the corner of my eye. She's sitting on the steps, trying to work a knot out of one of her laces. Any other guy would take full advantage of this lucky turn, maybe make a crack about how they don't make shoelaces like they used to and then gallantly offer to untangle them for her. But I'm not any other guy. My body's response to finding itself alone with a hot girl is to turn into a deaf-mute. Evolution fail.

She's making quick progress with her knot, and before I can even replenish my suddenly depleted saliva supply, Leyna has slipped on her Keds and is standing up, ready to go.

"Wait!" I cry, leaping to my feet. Desperation made my voice much louder than I would have liked—more like a shout, really—and the entire class has turned to stare at me. Sweat prickles my underarms as my sluggish brain scrambles to save itself.

"Uh, hello," I say weakly. Excellent start, Sean. "Before everybody leaves I just . . . I wanted to let you all know . . ." That I'm in love with Princess Leyna. That we're destined to travel the universe together. That you are all witness to the start of a beautiful romance. Shit. Shit. Shit.

Then it hits me: I know exactly what to say. This is actually kind of perfect. My whole body relaxes. "My friends and I are making a low-budget horror movie to enter in a film festival. We're casting this Saturday at my house. If anyone's interested in trying out . . ." I grab my notebook, tear out a sheet of paper, and place it on the edge of the stage. "Just write down your e-mail and I'll get you all the info."

You'd think I was giving away free batarangs at Comic-Con the way the crowd of students mobs the sign-up sheet. I look to see if Leyna is among them, but it's impossible to spot her in the horde.

"A film festival?" I feel a hand grab my arm.

I turn around to see Mr. Nestman knitting his brow. "Oh. I'm sorry . . ." I point over my shoulder. "I should have . . . asked you if I could make that announcement in class."

"Well, it's not a school project, is it?"

"No . . ." I take a step back. "I guess, I just figured—"

"But we can make it one, yes?" He grins. "I mean, if you'd like. I don't want to step on any toes here, but I can certainly whip these kids into shape for you. Use our class periods to rehearse. Lord knows I've been doing the same goddamn curriculum for the last twenty years. I could use a change. What do you think? I like it. Do you like it? We can utilize school time *and* school funds to shoot this movie of ours."

It all sounds so great—unbelievably great, really— that it takes me a second to process that last word. "Wait. *Our* movie?"

"Listen, I'm an artist first and foremost, Sean." He

places a hand on my shoulder. "I may have missed my time. Shot my load, so to speak. But that doesn't mean I don't want to help foster my students' artistic endeavors. *That's* my dream now." He glances at his watch. "Look, I've got a staff meeting to get to." He takes a business card from his wallet and hands it to me. "E-mail me your script, and we'll talk more next week. This is going to be great. It'll be fun to have a concrete project to work on in class."

Before I can protest, Mr. Nestman disappears out the door.

I turn back to grab my stuff and see Leyna standing there, looking at me. Everyone else is gone. This should seem like a gift from the gamer gods, but after what just happened with Mr. Nestman, I can't help feeling a little uneasy.

"That's cool that Mr. Nestman's willing to help you out," she says. "He was really great directing me in *The Miracle Worker* last year. Did you see it?"

"Did I see *The Miracle Worker*?" I say, trying to buy some time here. "Of course I saw *The Miracle Worker*!" I exclaim, and am rewarded by a megawatt Leyna smile. "Yeah, wow. You were awesome in it. Really, truly brilliant." I realize I'm laying it on pretty thick, but I can't seem to stop myself. "Wow," I repeat dumbly.

"Thanks." Leyna's still beaming. Phew. "I'm thinking of going to acting school after I graduate."

"Really? Sweet. Me too," I blurt. Half a second later, I realize what I just said. Acting school? Really, Sean?

"Cool!" Leyna says. "Are you going to be acting in your movie, then?"

"Oh. I don't know," I splutter. "I mean, I'm writing the screenplay, so I have to focus on that right now. But maybe. I might do a scene or two."

At least that *could* be true. But what I really want to know is will *Leyna* be acting in my movie? Did she add her name to the sign-up sheet? I want to ask but the words won't come.

"I think you definitely should," Leyna says encouragingly. The sweetest smile I've ever seen in my life tugs at the right corner of her mouth. "I've watched you during improv. You're really good."

Leyna's been watching *me*? My cheeks flush and my palms start to sweat. "No way," I croak. "Nowhere near as good as you."

"We just have different acting styles," Leyna says. "You have this intense emotional thing going on. Even when you're not acting. Like there are all these feelings and thoughts going on behind your eyes."

Oh, Christmas, is it that obvious?

"Thanks," I say, trying to harness my intense emotional thing into something resembling confidence. Because it's now or never, Hance. "So, does that mean you'll be coming to the audition?"

My heart jackhammers in my chest, so loud that I'm afraid I'll miss her response when it finally comes.

"Are you kidding?" She reaches out and gives my arm a gentle squeeze, sending an excited current right through my body. Then, loud and clear: "I wouldn't miss it for the world."

Oh, my God, I can't believe this is happening. Leyna thinks I'm intense. And she's coming to the audition. And she just gave me the I'm-into-you arm squeeze.

The signs couldn't be more clear.

And I now know exactly what I have to do.

☛ CHAPTER SEVENTEEN ☛

THE INNOCENTS

"YOU GUYS ARE GIRLS, RIGHT?" I look over at Valerie and Helen as the five of us walk through the back parking lot of the school.

"Uh, yeah." Valerie laughs. "Last time I checked."

Coop smirks. "And when was that? Can you describe the whole 'checking' proc—"

Matt punches him in the shoulder to shut him up.

"What?" Coop exclaims. "I'm just curious."

"*Anyway,*" I interject. "I need some girl advice. What's the nicest way I can break up with Evelyn?"

Coop makes a face. "You can't break up with her. She's getting us a camera. That's key, dawg. It frees up our entire budget for everything else."

I shake my head. "She's not getting us a camera. Where the heck would she get a professional video camera from? She's just saying that because she's a whackadoodle."

"Evelyn?" Helen's tone is pure disbelief. "She's one of the sweetest girls I've ever met."

"That's what she *wants* you to think," I say. "She had me fooled too. At first. Actually, no, that's not true. At first I thought she was mental. And then, all of sudden, she wasn't. But now she is again. Probably tomorrow she'll be fine. Who can tell? All I know is that she turns the crazy on and off like a faucet." Plus, if Leyna finds out I'm seeing someone, my chances with her are shot.

Matt arches an eyebrow. "Sounds like *someone's* a bit nutty."

"You don't understand. It's like I was telling you on Monday. Evelyn's got this switch in her head. A *loony* switch. And you never know when it's going to get thrown."

"Okay, so what did she do that was so insane?" Valerie asks.

"She grabbed my wrists. Hard. And she glared at me. And then . . . I don't know . . . She was basically pissed off that she had to find out about the movie from Helen instead of me."

"*And?*" Helen asks as we reach the bike racks.

"Look, it's not *what* she said. It's *how* she said it." I turn toward Valerie and Helen. "It's sort of like she was fighting off a demon possession or something. Her face changed color, and she was all twitchy, and then she started making this weird guttural sound."

Matt laughs. "That sounds like maybe she's a were-wolf."

"More like a Dr. Jekyll and Mrs. Hyde," I counter.

"Listen," Helen says. "Just because a girl gets upset with you doesn't make her crazy."

"We're just more emotional than you guys," Valerie adds. "If you're going to be in a relationship, that's something you're going to have to understand."

"Yeah, I get that but . . ." I sigh as I reach down and tug the yellow coil lock from my front wheel. "This wasn't how a normal person gets upset. It was like . . . like she was thinking of doing a lot worse and was just barely able to stop herself from doing it. It was scary."

Helen shrugs. "I've felt like that lots of times. You should be thankful she can keep her emotions in check. There are lots of people who don't have that much self-control." She eyes Coop meaningfully, but he just gives her his smarmy Cooper grin.

"All we're saying," Valerie explains, "is don't do anything rash. Just give it a bit more time. You're her first boyfriend, Sean. She's figuring things out as she goes along."

"I don't know," I say doubtfully. "I'm going over to her house tomorrow, so I guess I'll just see how things go then." I'm wrapping the coil lock around my seat post when I get a thought. "But, okay, let's say she starts acting all unstable again and I *do* want to end things. I'm not saying I'm going to"—I rush to add this as both

Helen and Val open their mouths to rebuke me—"but what would be the best way to break up with her without having her go ballistic and want to kill me?"

Helen laughs. "There is no best way. *Any* way is going to upset her."

"Yeah." I feel my ears get hot. "Okay, forget it. I'll figure something out."

"All right, look." Valerie places her hand on my back. "If you actually *do* decide you're going to break up with her, you have to do it right. Gentlemanly and gently." Valerie motions to the curb. "Come on. Let's sit down and we'll go over the dos and don'ts."

Matt and Coop exchange a look.

"Uh," Matt says, smiling with only half his face. "Should we be concerned that you both seem to be so knowledgeable about breakups?"

"Girls just know girls, sweetie," Valerie responds. "Nothing to fret over."

The five of us take a seat, Helen and Valerie flanking me.

"First things first," Helen says. "*Don't* chicken out and do it over the phone. That's the worst possible thing you could do. Anyone would flip out if they got dumped like that."

Valerie nods. "That's right. No phone, no text, no e-mail. If you're going to do it, do it in person. And do it somewhere private. Not in her house where her family can hear."

"Yes, good, okay," I say, perhaps a little too enthusiastically. I try to control my growing excitement, but it's difficult when I think about how this is all going to free me up to be with Leyna.

"Ask her to go for a walk," Matt offers. "That's how I'd do it."

"Oh, *now* who's the breakup expert?" Helen laughs.

Valerie arches an eyebrow at Matt. "So I guess I should worry now any time you ask me to go for a walk."

"No, I—I was just saying," Matt stammers. "For Sean . . . If I was Sean . . . Not . . . That's not how . . . I mean . . ."

Val smiles and puts her hand on Matt's knee. "Just kidding, *mon amour.* You can relax." She turns back to me, suddenly all business. "A walk is a good idea. And make sure to choose your words carefully. Don't go blaming her or pointing out her faults. Even if she asks you what she could have done better. It's a trap. Avoid it like the plague. Let her friends be the ones to give her advice."

My mouth's drying out. This is a lot to keep track of.

"It's sort of lame," Helen adds, "and completely transparent, but saying that it's *you,* not her, is the best way to go. It's good to be honest and truthful if you're trying to make the relationship work, but if you're absolutely sure you want to end things, there's no point in hurting her any more than you're already going to. Just shoulder the blame and tell her she's great. Doesn't matter if she sees right through it—it'll soften the blow."

"And then get ready for anything," Valerie says. "You might get silence, tears, anger, a tantrum. Whatever it is, let her have her moment. Take what she gives you and don't fight back."

"What if she attacks me?" My throat starts to close up. I can see the whole thing playing out in my mind: Evelyn springing at me like a feral cat, scratching my eyes out, biting hunks of flesh from my neck. "Am I not supposed to defend myself?"

"You can't hit a girl, dude," Coop says. "That's an epic code violation. Just wear some shin guards. And a chest protector. And a cup. Definitely wear a cup."

Sheeshkabob. I chew on my tongue like a rabid dog as I try to remember where my old Little League equipment is. "I don't know if I even have a cup anymore."

Helen laughs. "I seriously doubt it'll come to that. She'll probably just cry."

Valerie pats my arm. "It'll be fine. Just know that if you *do* break up with her, there's no going back. Even if you decide later that you made a mistake. So make sure it's what you really want before you go down that road."

I look at Val's hand on me and think of Leyna touching my arm in Drama.

Oh, it is what I want.

No question in my mind.

☛ CHAPTER EIGHTEEN ☛

BRIDE OF FRANKENSTEIN

INT. ROCKVILLE ZOO LABORATORY — DAY

All sorts of animals — dogs, cats, ferrets, a parrot — are in cages on the shelves in the background.

DR. SCHMALOOGAN, a mad scientist with crazy eyes, works with test tubes and beakers on a lab table. He mutters to himself as he mixes this with that.

> DR. SCHMALOOGAN
> Just need to get the right combination. If this
> works, then I'll be the most famous zoologist
> in the world!

Two MEN IN GRAY SUITS storm into the lab. Dr. Schmaloogan looks up from his work.

DR. SCHMALOOGAN

How dare you come into my lab? Who are you?
What are you doing here?

MAN IN GRAY #1

Are you Dr. Schmaloogan?

DR. SCHMALOOGAN

Who's asking?

Man in Gray #2 flashes a badge shaped like a jungle cat.

MAN IN GRAY #2

We're from PUMA: Protective Union of Most
Animals.

MAN IN GRAY #1

It's come to our attention that you have been
performing immoral acts on the zoo animals
under your care.

DR. SCHMALOOGAN

That's a bald-faced lie. I've only been
conducting board-approved experiments.

MAN IN GRAY #2

Is that so? Did the board approve of you
attempting to graft an elephant penis onto a
hippopotamus?

DR. SCHMALOOGAN

For your information, that hippo was in
a tragic pool-filter accident. I was simply
attempting to —

MAN IN GRAY #1

Were you not also involved in the creation of
a virus meant to increase the intelligence of
chimpanzees?

Dr. Schmaloogan casually slides his beakers behind a large test-
tube shaker.

DR. SCHMALOOGAN

I have no idea what you're talking about. I'm
afraid I'm going to have to ask you to leave.

MAN IN GRAY #2

I'm afraid it's you who will be leaving,
Dr. Schmaloogan.

Man in Gray #1 pulls out a pink piece of paper and hands it to
Dr. Schmaloogan.

DR. SCHMALOOGAN

What is this?

MAN IN GRAY #1

You are no longer an employee of the
Rockville Zoo. Just be thankful that no

charges are being filed. Please collect your
things and leave the premises.

EXT. ROCKVILLE HIGH SCHOOL — DAY

JACK HARRINGTON and STACY PETERS hang out on the bleachers
at the football field.

> JACK
> Don't you wish that something exciting would
> happen for once in our life?

> STACY
> I thought last night was pretty ex —

Suddenly there's a knock on my bedroom door. I stop typing.

"I'm busy." I clench my eyes, trying to remember the next thing I was going to write.

"It's Nessa," a girl's voice says from the other side of the door.

"Cathy's not home," I say. "I think she's working today." I glance at the Death Star clock over my bookcase. Only an hour before I have to leave for Evelyn's.

"I know," Nessa says. "That's why I'm here. Open the door. I want to talk to you."

Ugh. I don't need this right now. I have to get this script written.

"One sec." I save my Word file, then cross the room

to open the door, and there's Nessa—in full ghoul makeup—standing in the hallway. "What's up?"

She cocks her head. "Aren't you going to invite me in?"

"I'm kind of in the middle of someth—"

Nessa brushes past me and steps into my bedroom. She looks down at the floor, surveying all of the donated baby stuff. "I don't think I've ever actually been in your bedroom before." She turns her head and shoots me a coy smile. "At least not while you were home."

"You think I don't know that you and Cathy go through my stuff when I'm not around?"

Nessa laughs, running a finger along the partially built crib. "Just a few times. Let me tell you, we got bored pretty fast, Sean. No porn magazines under the mattress. No pot or cigarettes tucked in any of your jacket pockets. Not even a journal with angry diatribes about how your sister and her best friend sneak into your room and look at all your shit. What's up with that?"

"Sorry to disappoint. So, what do you want?"

She slinks over and stops just a few inches from me. "Do you mean right now or in the grand scheme of things?" Her breath is warm and smells like Good & Plenty.

I take a step back. "You said you wanted to talk to me? What about?"

"Here's the thing." Nessa reaches out and casually

closes my bedroom door. "I guess . . . I've always just thought of you as Cathy's little brother."

"Except that we're twins, remember? Same age."

"Yeah, no, I know." She smiles, her eyes cast down. "It's weird, I just . . . seeing you in your band . . . It was like . . . I don't know. I saw you differently is all. I can't really explain it."

I glance over at the door. "Why'd you shut that?"

"Your mom's home." She laughs. "I told her I needed to talk to you about Chemistry."

I give her an are-you-serious look. "You and Cathy are in AP everything. My mom knows I'm not in AP anything."

Nessa shrugs. "She didn't seem to notice." She takes a step toward me, closing the gap again. Her licorice breath is warm on my face. "Look, why are we talking about your mom? That's kind of a mood killer, don'tcha think?"

I take another step back and find I'm up against the wall, pinned between the closed door and the footboard of my bed. "What mood?" Jeez Louise, she's acting bizarre. More bizarre than usual. Whatever this is, I bet Cathy's behind it.

Of course, that doesn't change the fact that I've got a wizard's staff trying to make its presence known in my boxers right now.

"Okay, look." Nessa shakes her head. "I'm not saying

this the right way. I think what it is . . . Seeing you playing the keyboards so confidently . . . It was the first time I sort of considered you . . . *separate* from Cathy. Does that make sense?"

"Sure. All right. Sounds good." I turn my head, plotting an escape route over the bed. "Look, I've got to get back to work, so—"

Then, out of the blue, Nessa puts her hands on my face, turns my head toward her, and leans in to kiss me.

"Whoa, whoa, whoa!" I wiggle free from Nessa's grasp, leap onto my bed, scramble across the covers, and roll off the other side. "What the hell's going on?"

Once upon a time, way back in seventh grade, I would have offered up my first-edition Star Wars comics for the chance to get a kiss from Nessa. But that was a long, long time ago. In a galaxy far, far away. Before Nessa and all of her friends were assimilated by the Borg.

Right now the only person I want a kiss from is Leyna, despite what the fully extended lightsaber in my jeans might be saying.

"Sorry," she says, shaking her head. "I just . . . I couldn't help myself. I don't know what came over me. Please don't tell Cathy, okay? She wouldn't understand."

"Oh, so I'm supposed to believe Cathy knows nothing about this?"

"You think your sister would be cool with me wanting to make out with you?" Nessa laughs. "Doubtful."

She points to one of the daggers hanging on my wall. "Cool *main gauche*. I don't remember seeing *that* last time I was in here."

"I got it for Christmas." I look at her suspiciously. "How do you know what that is?"

"A Renaissance parrying dagger. I'm a big fan of sharp objects. I've got a few knives myself. So." She spins around and makes her way toward my desk. "What were you so busy with that you didn't want to answer your door?"

"Nothing. It's not—" I reach out to stop her but it's too late.

"I didn't know you wrote, Sean." She's bent over and peering at my laptop screen.

I don't know if she's giving me this view of her butt on purpose, but either way the stretched-tight pockets on her black jeans have me mesmerized.

"A horror movie. Cool." Nessa glances over her shoulder. "Are you taking Mr. Coozman's creative-writing class?"

"It's not for school," I say, my voice an octave higher than normal. I clear my throat and force my tone deeper. "It's just something I'm fooling with."

"Okay, well." Nessa glances back at the computer. "Would you mind if I offered a little constructive criticism?"

"I know, it sucks." I walk over to the desk and shut my laptop screen.

Nessa places her hand on top of mine. My knees buckle, but I catch myself.

"The first thing any writer will tell you," she says, "is that self-flagellation is no way to get the juices flowing."

"What?" I pull my hand away, feeling my face go hot. "No, I don't . . . I don't . . . do . . . that."

Nessa grins. "Beating yourself *up.* Not beating yourself *off,* silly boy. And on both counts you're lying." She lifts the laptop screen up and slides into the chair. "You mind?" She gestures at my script on the screen. "I'm an expert on all things horror."

I step back and shrug. "Sure. Go ahead." It'll give me time to cool off and remind myself that she's not actually a girl-girl, just Cathy's annoying other half.

"Okay, let's start with your evil doctor." Nessa puts her fingers on the keyboard and starts to type. "At least, I assume that's who he is, yes?" Nessa looks up at me and I nod. "Good, okay, well, right now he's coming across as a bit of a dork. You don't want that. You want him to be charismatic. Maybe even a bit misunderstood. So that you're almost rooting for him. Think Count Dracula. Hannibal Lecter. Or even Mr. Freeze."

"You root for the bad guys?"

Nessa flashes a quick grin. "You're not *ultimately* rooting for them. But if you can add that level of enigmatic complexity to your villain, then your audience gets that much more invested. Of course you still want him to be menacing, but with an undercurrent of allure."

Nessa's talking and typing at the same time. Amazing. I can't even read a book and eat at the same time. And what she's saying sounds pretty impressive, too, even if I'm not entirely sure what it means. I lean in close and watch her transform my script.

A half hour later, she's rewritten the entire beginning of the movie—along with the two audition scenes I've been struggling with—and it's all a billion times better than what I had.

"Okay, I get that you know your horror movies," I say, flipping through the printed script pages. "But how do you know how to write so well?"

Nessa shrugs. "I've always liked writing. As long as it isn't for school." She laughs at this. "Back in sixth grade, me and Michelle Audette almost got held back because we had this contest to see who could write the longest story by the end of the year. We hardly did any of our schoolwork. Just wrote like crazy and then read our stories aloud to each other at lunch. I think hers was called 'The Witch Trials.' And mine was 'SPPS.'"

"What's that?"

"The Secret Psychic Princess Society, of course," Nessa deadpans. "It was such a blast. Well, until our parents got called in for an 'urgent' conference with Mr. Provost. Anyway." She pushes the desk chair back and stands. "I should probably get going. Remember now, not a word to Cathy about . . . you know."

"Yeah, okay."

"Kewl." She flashes a smile and heads toward the door. "See you around."

I look down at the script in my hands. And that's when I get a crazy idea. It's probably totally stupid and I'm undoubtedly setting myself up for some Cathy-related abuse, but . . .

"Hey, Nessa."

Nessa stands in the doorway. "Yeah?"

"I was wondering . . ." My heart starts thumping the inside of my rib cage. "I mean . . . I don't know . . . You're so good at this." I wave the screenplay pages. "And I'm not and . . . Would you . . . ? Would you maybe want to help me out with writing this movie? I mean, me and my friends are actually going to try to film it and . . . Well, it might not go anywhere, but if it does . . . It could be a good credit to have. You know, to put on your résumé and stuff."

Nessa stares at me. I can see the cogs turning behind her cat-green eyes. She's either trying to figure out a polite way to turn me down or she's weighing which comeback will be the most cutting.

But then she smiles again. "Sure, all right. That might be fun."

I let out a relieved breath. With Nessa's help, I might actually be able to write a halfway decent screenplay.

"But we'll have to keep that a secret too, 'kay? Otherwise Cath might never speak to me again." Nessa grins. "We're still mortal enemies, you and I. At least as far as the outside world is concerned. No hellos or acknowledgment at school, either, understand? I have a reputation to uphold."

"Sure, no prob."

"Kewl," she says again, and then slips out of my room.

I'm staring at the open door—wondering what I've just gotten myself into—when my phone buzzes.

I tug it from my pocket and read the text from Evelyn: *6 pm dnt 4get.*

Forget? How could I? Sweet freedom is just a break-up away.

CHAPTER NINETEEN

THE LAST HOUSE ON THE LEFT

BREAK UP WITH HER IN PERSON. DO IT IN PRIVATE. CHOOSE WORDS CAREFULLY. DON'T POINT OUT FAULTS EVEN IF SHE ASKS. TRAP! TAKE ALL THE BLAME. LET HER FREAK OUT.

I'm reviewing the crib notes that I've scribbled on the palm of my left hand as I coast my bike up to Evelyn's house. I don't want to forget any of Val and Helen's advice. It's crucial I get this breakup right. My entire future with Leyna depends on it.

I get off my bike and lay it on the grass. My hands are trembling and I feel like I've got an ice pick jammed into my temple. I take a deep shaky breath and let it out. I can do this. No sweat.

I walk the stone path toward the porch steps. Evelyn's house looks totally normal. Just plain old boring beige aluminum siding with a faded blue porch. I'm not really sure what I expected. Something with red and yellow polka dots, maybe. An inflatable-arm-waving air dancer on the roof. A lawn littered with giant garden gnomes and a Sasquatch sculpture. Perhaps some circus music blaring out of the windows.

But no. It's just like anyone else's house. And why not? Evelyn hides her madness pretty well herself. Except when she doesn't.

I climb the porch steps and approach the front door, a thick sandy-colored mat "welcoming" me. Black iron letters spell out THE MOSSES under the brass knocker. It's all so nonthreatening. Meant to lure me into a false sense of security. Just like the girl who lives inside.

Another slow controlled breath before I announce my presence. Glance at the instructions on my palm one last time, then reach up and give a little rat-a-tat with the knocker.

A moment later and the door creaks open a few inches.

Evelyn pokes her head through the gap and smiles. "Hello, Jell-O," she says.

"Hi." My mouth is super pasty. I should have brought a bottle of water or something.

"Hold on one sec." She holds up a freckled fore-finger. "I'll be right out. I've got something I want to show you."

Evelyn shuts the door, leaving me standing there on the porch to stew in my anxiety a bit longer. All of a sudden, my hands feel like a couple of newly acquired appendages. I think about sniffing them, but instead I tuck them into my back pockets. Then untuck them again. I read over my palm notes once more and nearly levitate when the door opens again.

"Hey," Evelyn says, slipping out her front door with a large brown paper bag clenched in her hand. "Your hand smells good, does it?"

I suddenly realize I've got my right palm cupped over my nose. Jesus, how did that get there? I yank it away from my face and smile nervously. "I was . . . um . . . helping my mom make cookies." I waft my ink-free hand about. "I washed them but . . . they still smell like oatmeal."

"I can think of worse things," Evelyn says, laughing. "Come on, let's sit down." She makes her way over to a rickety old porch swing, brushes a thin layer of snow off it, and takes a seat.

"Oh, uh . . ." I glance over my shoulder. "I was wondering if we could . . . go for a walk?"

"Sure. Maybe after dinner." She places the bag on the ground between her legs.

"Dinner? What dinner? Aren't we just—?"

"I told you I had a surprise for you. You think you're going to come all the way over here for a study session and my mom's not going to feed you? Fat chance."

"I, um . . ." This is *not* going according to plan. The last thing I want to do is go into that house. "What about just a little jaunt around the block? You know, a relaxing premeal stroll."

"Sure, okay. But I want to show you something first." Her eyes flit to the front door like she's expecting someone to emerge.

"But . . ." I look over my shoulder again, feeling like my escape portal is rapidly closing behind me. "Can't you show it to me while we walk?" I swing my arms like I'm already ambling.

"*No.* I want to show it to you here. Why are you acting so weird?"

"Weird?" I look around like I'm trying to find this weirdness she's speaking of. "Am I acting weird?"

"Yes. Very. Now get over here. You'll be happy, I promise."

One last peek over my shoulder and I finally give up and make my way over to her.

"Okey-dokey." Evelyn wriggles with excitement as I sit. "Now, remember our conversation at lunch yesterday?"

"Yeah, sure, of course." How could I forget?

"Wellll . . ." She smiles big and unfolds the top of the paper bag. "I told you I was going to get you something for your movie"—she reaches into the bag and gently lifts out a fairly large, very professional-looking video camera—"and here it is."

"Holy crap!" I say, staring at it like it's an ultra-scarce

Pokémon Illustrator card. "These things are like three thousand dollars!" I can't believe she actually did it. She got us a professional video camera.

I'm pumped at first. The biggest hurdle in the way of moviemaking glory has suddenly been removed. But then the full impact of this surprise hits me: how the heck am I supposed to break up with her now?

"Wow," I say, blinking like a madman. "That's . . . wow. But . . . where did you get it?"

Evelyn smiles coyly. "Ah, you know. It was just lying around. Take a look." She holds up the camera by its handle, turning it this way and that, like she's some kind of hostess on the Home Shopping Network. "It's a pro model. High-definition and everything. Just like Coop asked for."

I stare at it suspiciously. "You just *happened* to have this video camera lying around?"

"Who cares where I got it?" she says testily. "*God.* The point is, I got it. Just like I told you I would. Don't you want to use it for the movie?"

"Yeah. No. I do, but . . ." I rub my aching forehead. "I'm just . . . a little confused." It seems too good to be true. And if it *is* too good to be true, then I don't have to accept the camera and I can still break up with her. Then we'll just have to figure out another way to shoot our movie.

Evelyn sighs, her shoulders deflating. "Okay, *fine.* You want to know where it came from? Would that make you feel better? All right, then. It was my dad's. He left it here when he went to live with his mistress and their secret love child. Are you happy now, Sean? That you have an explanation?"

"Jeez. I'm sorry. I had no idea—"

"Forget it," Evelyn says, stuffing the camera back in the paper bag. "What matters is we have a camera now, right? We might as well make something good out of something bad. Just"—she glances at the front door again—"don't mention it to my family, okay? They don't know that I'm lending this to you. And it'll only bring up bad memories."

"Yeah. For sure. Definitely." I reach for the camcorder, knowing that the moment I accept it, my fate will be sealed. But what choice do I have?

Just as my fingertips brush the paper bag, Evelyn suddenly pulls it back like Lucy yanking away Charlie Brown's football.

"There's one condition, though," she says, suddenly dead serious, all signs of the sad little abandoned-by-Daddy girl gone.

"I'm sorry?"

"You can use this camera. *But . . .*"

I sneak a quick sniff of my palm. "But what?"

"*I* get to be in the movie."

CHAPTER TWENTY

PREDATOR

ALL THE MUSCLES IN MY SHOULDERS and neck seize up. "Wait a second. I don't think—"

"And not just any part, either," she says. "I want to be the leading lady."

"Okay, first of all, I haven't even written the script yet, so I don't even know—"

"Perfect. Just make sure you write a major role for a cute, spunky, clever girl."

"Do you even know how to act, Evelyn?"

She shrugs. "How hard could it be? I'm really good at pretending."

"Okay, look," I say. "It's vital that we do this as professionally as possible. We're trying to win a film festival here. I don't really think that—"

"Fine." She hugs the brown-bagged camera. "Maybe I'll just make my *own* movie with *my* camera."

I try to rub some of the tension from my neck. I could *so* use this as an excuse to break things off with her. I mean, she is basically blackmailing me here. I can hear the words in my head. *I don't think things are going to work out with you and me, Evelyn. I don't appreciate being coerced. Thank you, but no, thank you.*

Except then where does that leave me? Much further away from getting my own room. And with no movie to shoot, what excuse will I have to spend some quality time with Leyna?

"Okay. Fine," I say through clenched teeth. "I'll . . . I'll see what I can do."

Evelyn smiles and hands over the precious camera. It feels like it weighs about a million pounds.

"Hey, is this your guy?" a deep manly voice calls from behind me.

I turn my head to see a seriously ripped dude— maybe nineteen or twenty—standing in the doorway in a wifebeater and gray-and-white khakis. Here is a person who could kick my ass six ways to Saturn and not even break a sweat.

Evelyn leaps up, causing me and the porch swing to sway. She bounds to the door and grabs the guy's burly left arm.

"This is my big brother, Nick," she says, beaming. "He's a Navy SEAL." She cups a hand around her mouth and stage-whispers, "He just got back from a secret mission in South America, but we're not supposed to tell anyone."

Oh.

Shit.

My stomach knots. Just when I thought things couldn't get any worse, enter Evelyn's killing-machine brother.

Nick holds out his massive right hand. "You must be Sean," he says, his voice all Clint Eastwoody.

I place the camera down, get to my feet, and reach out to take Nick's massive meat hook.

"Hi," I squeak.

I fully expect the bones in my fingers to be ground into powder by Nick's handshake, but he's surprisingly gentle with his grip. Not to mention his skin is oddly soft and smooth.

"You're all we've been hearing about for the past week," Nick says, letting go of my hand. "My sister's totally smitten with you." He smiles big. "And I can see why. You're a handsome fella." He smacks me lightly across the cheek. "And you've got a good energy. I can tell; I've got a sixth sense about these things."

"Thanks," I manage.

"Whatcha got there?" Nick gestures with his square chin toward the porch swing.

"That's Sean's new video camera," Evelyn says, furtively winking at me. "He's making a movie with his friends. And guess what? He just asked me to be his leading lady. How cool is that?"

Nick cocks a single eyebrow. "That so?"

Oh, crap. He knows she's lying about the video camera. My throat closes up. "Yeah, well. I mean . . . We're still writing the script and everything. . . . We haven't exactly worked out all of the characters yet. . . ."

Evelyn's jaw starts jumping. She glares at me, her eyes like dagger tips.

"I mean, yeah, though," I say. "Definitely. Evelyn's going to be in the film. For sure."

"Nice." Nick bobs his head. "Hey. What about me? Can I be in it too? I mean, I've got some free time on my hands. I was just put on stress leave." He leans in conspiratorially. "Apparently I have a tendency toward 'outbursts.'" He laughs. "Whatever *that* means."

Evelyn perks up. "What do you say, Sean? You think there's a role for my big brother?"

"Uhhh . . . I'm not . . . I mean, I'd have to see. . . ."

Nick stares at me without blinking. It's the most intimidating stare I've ever seen in my entire life.

"What am I saying? It's my script. Of course you can be in the movie . . . somewhere." I laugh nervously, waiting for the blow to fall. But after another insanely long second, Nick blinks.

"Sweet," Nick says, puffing up his chest. "I'm gonna be a movie star."

He and Evelyn practically do little happy dances. Meanwhile, my mind is racing, trying to figure out how I can work both crazy Evelyn and her roided-out brother into the film. Maybe Nick could be one of the humanzees. I wonder if we could get him to wear a monkey costume.

"Dinner!" a woman shouts from inside the house. "Everyone come and get their plates."

"Homemade pasta," Nick says. "You *must* be special. Ma only makes that once or twice a year. You're in for a real treat, guy."

Oh, I think I've had about as many treats as I can handle for one day.

☞ CHAPTER TWENTY-ONE ☞

FEAST

THESE ARE DELICIOUS, Mrs. Moss," I lie, cutting a tiny corner off one of the foot-size raviolis.

Evelyn's stick-thin bug-eyed mom smiles as she chews. "I'm so glad you like them."

I don't know if homemade pasta is supposed to taste this gummy and doughy, but somehow I doubt it. I stare down at the mountain range of raviolis Evelyn has heaped onto my plate and wonder how in the heck I am ever going to plow through them all.

"There's plenty more where that came from," Mrs. Moss adds.

"Oh. I think I'm good for now." I shift in my seat at the kitchen table, supremely aware of the tiny scratchy tag at the back of my boxer shorts.

"You have any brothers or sisters, Sean?" Nick asks, refilling his water glass.

"Twin sister," I say. "Not identical. Obviously." I laugh awkwardly but no one else even cracks a smile. "Oh, and, um, actually, it looks like I'm going to have another brother or sister in a few months. My mom's pregnant," I explain.

"Ohhhh, a little bundle of joy," Mrs. Moss coos. "You must be so excited."

"Mmm." I force a smile. "Yeah. Really thrilled."

Evelyn stares at me. "You didn't tell me that, Sean. I guess you forgot to mention it."

Uh-oh. Here we go again.

"Yeah. No. I mean . . ." I shift in my chair again. "We just found out. Today." The lies just keep flopping from my mouth. "So . . . That's why, you know, I'm telling you now."

"So you haven't told Matt or Coop yet?" she asks, all fake-casual. "Or Valerie and Helen?"

"What? Um. No." My dang underwear tag is slicing my lower back to bits. "When would I have done that?" Oh, God, I better text them all before she tries to verify this.

"Oh. Okay." Evelyn pats my arm. "Well, then, congratulations."

I start breathing again, my clenched-up shoulders relaxing.

We sit in silence for a bit. All the sounds of dinner — the clinking utensils, the slurping of water, the smacky chewing that must be a Moss family trait—seem intensely loud to me.

"So," Nick finally says, "tell me something. You have a test today?"

At first I'm not sure who he's talking to, since he seems to be focused on his third helping of ravioli. But then I realize that Evelyn and her mom are looking at me expectantly.

"A test?" I ask, confused.

"Yeah." He lifts his chin at me. "The writing on your hand. Is that some kind of . . . crib sheet? You're not a cheater are you, Sean?"

My entire body flushes hot and cold. I grip my left hand tightly around my fork so that nobody can read the breakup notes.

"No," I say, my voice cracking. "It's not . . . No . . . It's private . . . notes for stuff . . ."

Nick narrows his eyes. "You're not being honest with us, Sean. As a SEAL, I'm trained to tell when someone is being deceptive."

"What?" I say, clearing my throat. "I'm not . . . being deceptive. Why would I be deceptive?" I reach up and pretend to scratch my nose with my right hand, hoping to take a quick, reassuring sniff of my palm.

"Right there." Nick slaps the table. "You see that? Scratching his nose. Clearing his throat. Using *my* words to answer the question. It's textbook dishonesty."

"Just because I had an itchy nose?" I drop my hand, suddenly hyper-aware of all my movements. "That's ridiculous."

Nick glares at me. "We don't like cheaters in this family. And we like liars even less."

"That's enough, Nick," Mrs. Moss says. "He said it was private."

"Private stuff you write in a diary." Nick leans forward, staring at me. "Crib notes you write on your hand."

"I wasn't cheating on a test," I say, clenching my left fist. "If you really want to know, this is . . . advice my friends gave to me on how to deal with a very personal situation. Okay?"

The silence stretches on for eternity, my eyes darting around for an escape route. I am seriously debating bolting from the table and taking my chances out on the streets. Surely one of their neighbors would call the cops and report the sounds of a scrawny tenth-grader being beaten to death by a jacked Navy SEAL?

Nick suddenly bursts out in a loud cackle. "Buddy. Guy. Relax. I'm just yankin' your chain. No need to get all bent out of shape. I don't care what you've got scribbled on your hand."

Now Evelyn's cracking up too. "Sorry, sweetie. It's Nick's sense of humor. He likes to make people uncomfortable. Sometimes *I* don't even know when he's kidding."

"Oh," I say, my hunched-up shoulders relaxing a bit. "Yeah. Okay. Funny."

Nick points his knife at me. "Seriously, though. I meant what I said about liars and cheats. We don't tolerate that in this family."

"Jeez, Nick," Evelyn says. "Leave him alone already."

"What?" Nick shrugs. "This is important. You don't want to date a guy and then find out he's just like Dad."

"Nicky, please," Mrs. Moss says. "Can we have one meal where we don't bring up your deadbeat father?"

Oh, thank Gandalf, the spotlight's off me. I grab my cup of water with my left hand, hoping the beads of sweat on the glass will smear the ink on my palm.

"I *didn't* bring him up," Nick barks. "I was just making an analogy." He eviscerates one of the gigantic raviolis with his knife, spilling the spinach and cheese filling like entrails. "But since we're already talking about him, I might as well tell you, I think I've found a lead."

A lead? What the heck is he talking about?

Evelyn must be picking up on my confusion, because she reaches out and touches my forearm. "It's like I told you. Our dad walked out on us three years ago."

"He didn't *walk* out," Nick spits. "He left us for another family. A Post-it note on the fridge and that was that. Never heard from him again. No cards at Christmas, not a penny of child support." He leans over his plate, gesturing wildly with his fork. "How the *hell* is my mother supposed to support a family on a cashier's salary? You want to tell me that?"

I'm not sure if I'm supposed to answer this question or not, so I just gulp.

"She *can't.* That's how," Nick continues. "So she gets a second job. And she goes with less so that Evelyn and me can have more." He turns to Mrs. Moss and motions toward her plate. "Eat, Ma. Eat. You're wasting away."

"Okay, Nick." Mrs. Moss twists her lips into a partial smile. "I'll eat. But can we just drop it now?"

"No! We can't drop it. I'll never drop it. Not until I find him."

Evelyn looks at me. "Nick's been trying to track down our dad for the last five months."

"Asshole's hiding out somewhere." Nick shakes his head. "Every time I think I've got him, the trail goes cold. But I'll smoke him out eventually."

"Smo—Smoke him out?" I blink. "Wha—What for?"

"Pfff." Nick lets out a sarcastic laugh. "Oh, I don't know. Maybe jog his memory a little." He makes a gun with his finger and shoots me with it. "Remind him of his responsibilities."

Mrs. Moss sighs. "Now, Nicky. Let's not get crazy."

Nick slams his hand down on the table, sending all of our plates and utensils jumping. "Don't you stand up for him! He broke your heart and tossed it out like a used Kleenex. And I'm supposed to stand by and let him get away with it? No. He owes us. Family sticks up for family!"

"Okay, okay." A weary Mrs. Moss holds up her hands. "It's just that I don't think Sean needs to hear about all of our dirty laundry."

"Yeah, well." Nick wafts his utensils in the air. "He's going to hear about it eventually. I mean"—he stares at me across the table—"if he's planning on sticking around. You *are* planning on sticking around, aren't you? You're not the love-'em-and-leave type, are you, Sean?"

I grip the edge of the table, feeling a little woozy. "I . . . uh . . . I . . . uh—"

"Of course he's going to stick around." Evelyn beams at me. "Right, Sean?"

"Yeah," I say. "Absolutely."

Nick winks at me. "Good answer. Anything else and I might have had to kill you."

I think I might hurl.

Nick laughs. "Look at that face! This guy's too easy. I'm just tuggin' your tamale."

"Yeah. No. I knew that," I say, trying to force air into my constricted lungs.

Nick laughs again as he shoves a big forkful of ravioli into his mouth. "I like this guy," he says, chewing. "He's a good sport. Hey, how about after dinner you come up to my room and I'll show you some of my SEAL stuff? If you're good, I'll even let you hold my heater. You ever handle a real gun before? Nothing in the world like it, I'm telling you."

CHAPTER TWENTY-TWO

RETURN OF THE LIVING DEAD

I'M TOTALLY SERIOUS," I say to Matt and Coop. "Her brother is tracking down their deadbeat dad using his Navy SEAL skills. He's got an entire *WarGames* setup in his bedroom. Files, maps, video monitors. He showed me the whole thing. It's insane."

The three of us are setting up my family room for our casting session. We've corralled all of my pets into the other rooms, and now we're busy putting out snacks and drinks, picking up stray tufts of dog, cat, and ferret hair, and moving furniture around to create an audition space. Luckily, the house is all ours today. Cathy's working this afternoon, and I managed to convince Mom and Dad to go baby-clothes shopping by telling them we needed privacy to rehearse some stuff for Drama.

"That's fucked up, dawg," Coop says, unwrapping Twinkies and Ding Dongs and laying them out neatly on a plate. "The SEALS are like the ninjas of the military."

Matt lines up cans of soda on the coffee table. "What's he gonna do when he finds him?"

"He's a *Navy SEAL,* Matt," Coop says. "They're trained in torture. They like to hook guys' meats up to car batteries and then douse them with water." He grabs a Twinkie at one end and shakes it until it crumbles apart.

"Oh, God," I say, my own junk turtling up inside me.

"And that's not even the worst part," Coop continues. "They'll also tie a dude's hands to the arms of a chair and drive bamboo splints under his fingernails. Then they'll punch holes in his eyelids so he can never really close them. After that, they'll put a scorpion-filled potato sack over his head so that the bugs can sting the shit out of his eyeballs."

"Jesus Christ, would you shut the hell up?" My stomach bucks and lurches.

"What?" Coop shrugs. "I'm just trying to let you know what you're up against."

"I *know* what I'm up against, thank you very much." I pour some Cool Ranch Doritos into a plastic bowl. "The guy's a complete psycho. He showed me his gun, for shit's sake."

"Really?" Coop waggles his eyebrows. "Flashed you the old pants pistol, did he?"

"A *real* gun, douche bag. He took the clip out, handed it to me, and made me aim it at the eighty-by-ten of his father that he has tacked up on a dartboard."

"Sweet," Coop says. "I've always wanted to hold a real gun. How'd it feel?"

"How did it *feel*?" I can still sense the heft of the pistol in the palm of my hand. "Like he was sending me a message: 'Stay with Evelyn and we're bosom brothers. But break up with her and all bets are off.'"

Coop shrugs. "Personally, I think everything happens for a reason."

"What the hell is that supposed to mean?" I say.

"It *means* that if you broke up with Evelyn, then we wouldn't have use of her super-chillicious video camera. And then we'd have to blow Unc's entire grand on equipment instead of splashing all that cash up on the screen. Think of it as an opportunity presented. You play house with Evelyn for a couple of months while we make a kick-ass movie. Then, when we're all done, we figure out a way to get *her* to break up with *you.* It shouldn't be too hard. What'd you do to make Tianna dump your sorry ass?"

I glare at him but otherwise ignore his comment. "There's one other thing," I confess. "She wants to be in the film. And not just a cameo. She wants to be the lead."

Coop lip-farts. "Fine with me. If girlie wants to run around all topless, her chesticles splattered in fake blood, being chased everywhere by vampanzees, far be it from me to stop her. It's one less warm body we need to recruit."

"I seriously doubt she's going to agree to do nudity," I say.

"Please." Coop smirks. "Leave the directing to me." He turns the soda cans around, reading the labels. "Hey, didn't you get anything diet?"

Matt shrugs. "The girls'll just have to make do."

"Not for the babes, doinkle," Coop says. "For me."

Matt laughs. "Since when do you drink diet?"

"Since we decided to become multimillionaire moviemakers. Cameras add ten pounds, dawg. Everyone knows that. I don't want be on the cover of the *National Enquirer* as a 'Cellulite Nightmare' or a 'Sloppy Celebrity.'" Coop reaches into his backpack and takes out a pink bottle of something. "Good thing I brought along my own sensible shake."

"So, what, you've joined"—Matt tilts his head to read the label—"*Sally Gregg*? A little girly don'tcha think?"

"This from the talking vagina," Coop says. "If you must know, I borrowed this from Angela." He waves the shake in Matt's face. "She's paying for the diet program. I'm just benefiting from it." He turns and narrows his eyes at me. "Because *I* know how to take advantage of an opportunity when I see it. Which is what all the most successful people do." He uncaps the drink with a loud *pop.*

"Enjoy that." Matt stifles a laugh before grabbing a handful of chips.

"Chuckle away, dawgs," Coop says. "Just wait until

you catch sight of the sleeker, sexier Coopmeister on the cover of *Details*." He runs his hands down his rounded body. "Then we'll see who's all green and grudging." For emphasis, Coop takes a sip of his shake—leaving a decidedly *un*sexy pink mustache on his upper lip.

"Hello?" a female voice calls from the front door. "Is this where the casting session is?"

"In here, honey," Coop responds.

I look over at Matt and point at my lip but he shakes his head in response to my silent question.

A moment later, Prudence Nash rounds the corner, looking hotter than any girl should legally be allowed to. She's wearing high heels and a form-fitting charcoal-gray sweater dress that expertly hugs every curve of her bodacious body, magically highlighting her world-class, perfectly pert pooters.

"Oh . . . my," I hear myself mutter, my heart skipping a beat.

Matt's jaw hangs open as he backs himself into the couch and flops down onto it.

If it were actually true that excessive masturbation can lead to madness, then Prudence Nash would have sent me over the edge years ago. But as that's just a myth, all I can blame her for is the occasional sore wrist.

Well, that and being our toughest competition at the Battle of the Bands.

Oh, right, and single-handedly trying to destroy Helen's reputation at school.

It's odd how she can manage to make you forget how truly evil she is simply by flipping her long hair and canting her totem-pole-inducing hips.

Prudence's lusciously made-up face scrunches up in disgust. Clearly she's not quite as pleased by the sight of us. "Are you fucking kidding me? *You* wankjobs?"

"Nice to see you too, Prudence," Coop says.

Prudence narrows her eyes. "I thought this was a movie audition, not a retard convention."

"It *is* a movie audition," Coop says, checking his phone. "You're a little early, babe, but I suppose we can squeeze you in." He's acting all confident and producery, but his bravado is completely undermined by the strawberry milk shake mustache he's sporting.

"Thanks, but no, thanks." Prudence turns on her heel and starts to leave.

"Hey, hey, come on, now," Coop says. "No need to let the past get in the way of our possible future. You've come all this way. Why not show us what you've got?"

I can't believe Coop thinks this is a good idea. Prudence is Helen's mortal nemesis. The girl who started all the hot-dog rumors back in eighth grade. Matt and I look at him like he's nuts, but he doesn't even acknowledge us.

Prudence whips around and smirks, like she's just read my mind. "Audition? For you? Really? And how's your little girlfriend going to feel about that?"

Coop sits in the armchair and leans back, acting oh-so-chill. "Business is business, sweetheart. I think we can agree that we want to do what's best for the movie." He glances at us, the streak of pink pastel drying and cracking under his nose. "We're all professionals here."

Prudence laughs. "Yeah, you're looking like a real pro there, Milkstache." She taps her lip.

Coop quickly swipes at his mouth and stares down at the pink smear on his hand. He turns and glares at me and Matt accusingly. "Nice," he mutters. "I'll remember this." Coop's pissed-off expression shifts like smoke as he turns back and smiles at Prudence. "So, you've done some acting before?"

"Oh, sure." She gives him the slow burn. "In fact, I'm acting right now. Like I don't want to scratch your eyes out."

"Well, I can't say I'm buying your performance." Coop leans forward, pressing his palms together. "Still, we might be able to use you. Tell me this. What are your thoughts on nudity?"

"I wouldn't get naked for you for a million dollars," Prudence snaps.

"Fair enough." Coop nods. "How about for free, then?"

"Die, reject." Prudence flips us off and storms out of the room.

A second later, I hear my front door slam.

"That went well," Coop says.

I shake my head. "I can't believe you were actually considering giving her a part."

He laughs. "I wasn't, asscup. I was just playing with her." He shrugs. "Still, if she was willing to give us a little show before I turned her down, I wasn't going to stop her."

Matt rolls his eyes. "Real classy, there, Coop."

"Oh, yeah?" Coop stares at Matt. "I'll show you classy." He dives on Matt and pins him to the couch. Before Matt can squirm away, Coop sits right on his head. "Payback is a dirty little whore, Matthew."

Matt's face is all squished up and red, his lips puckered like a fish. "Get the hell off me," he gripes, his voice muffled by Coop's ass.

"Just one second." Coop scrunches up his eyes, then lets go with a surprisingly loud sputtering pants blaster, which makes me totally lose it.

"Goddamn it!" Matt heaves Coop off of him and leaps up, rubbing at his face like crazy. "You're such a dick. You're going to pay for that."

"Umm," Coop says, stumbling away, "I may have already paid for it." He grabs the back of his jeans. "I think there might have been some fudge in that fart." He laughs hysterically. "Which means you may have gotten a little extra sumpin'-sumpin', there, Mattie."

Matt looks totally pissed. He shoots Coop a sky-high finger salute, which just makes me crack up even more.

"Hold that thought," Coop says. "I'll be right back." He quickly shuffles off toward the bathroom, his hand clenching the back of his pants.

My stomach hurts, I'm laughing so hard. Tears trickle out of my squeezed-shut eyes.

Even Matt can't help himself as he starts busting up too.

A minute later, Coop emerges from the bathroom smiling. "False alarm, dawgs." He gives us two thumbs-up. "We're all clear on the launchpad."

"What's going on here?"

The three of us whip our heads around to see Helen and Valerie standing there, both of them looking seriously pissed, their arms crossed over their chests.

"Just getting ready for the casting session," Coop says, back in producer mode.

"Really?" Helen narrows her eyes. "So why did we just pass Prudence Nash in the driveway?"

Valerie glowers at Matt. "Was she helping you guys 'get ready'?"

There have been many times over the years when I have been seriously jealous of Coop and Matt.

But this is definitely *not* one of those times.

CHAPTER TWENTY-THREE

AUDITION

Coop has to do some major verbal gymnastics to convince the girls that we had no idea Prudence was going to show up, that we had no intention of ever casting her in the movie, and that we didn't even let her audition but ushered her right to the door as soon as she arrived.

"Okay," Helen finally says, her face relaxing. "But I'm watching you, Cooper Redmond."

"Watch away." Coop grins, gesturing down at his body. "It's why God made me."

"Hey, hey! Is this the home of the world-famous filmmaker Seanie O'Spielberg?" Uncle Doug, wearing a blue TEAM DOUG hockey jersey, steps into the family room. He has a cigar-size joint in one hand and a Diet Coke in the other.

"Val, Helen," I introduce. "This is my uncle Doug."

"Nice to meet you," the girls say.

"The pleasure's all mine." He flashes a smile then spins around. "Where's that filthy-mouthed parrot of yours?" He wafts his joint around, leaving long gray wisps in the air like a stoned skywriter.

"You asked me to put all of the animals away because of your *'allergies.'* Remember?"

"I know, I know. But she's in a cage, right? I just want to say hello. It's been so long since Uncle Doug's had anyone talk dirty to him."

"Ingrid's sleeping," I say, the harsh sticky-sweet smell of the pot smoke clawing at my sinuses. "Can you please get rid of that thing? You're going to get me in trouble."

Uncle Doug regards his Diet Coke with squinty-eyed confusion. "What? Your mom's got something against artificial sweeteners?"

Everyone but me laughs.

I glare at my friends then look back at Uncle Doug. "You know what I'm talking about. They'll think I was having a party or something."

"Please." Uncle Doug screws up his face. "Just say Uncle Doug dropped by to visit his knocked-up sis. She knows I have a prescription. It's for my gout." He takes another deep hit before unleashing a cumulonimbus from his mouth. "I mean, my glaucoma." Uncle Doug laughs hysterically at this, then catches my look. "Okay, okay, I won't take my medicine. Who cares if Uncle Doug's in pain? Not my nephew, apparently." With that, he makes a big show of licking his fingers and squeezing out the glowing tip. He takes a pack of cigarettes from his pocket and slips the joint inside. "Happy?"

I nod. "Thank you."

"Cool Ranch or Blazin' Jalapeño?" Uncle Doug asks, gesturing at the chips bowl as he plops down into one of the armchairs.

"Cool Ranch," I say.

"Excelente." He grabs a handful of Doritos and starts crunching away. Hey, so, you've got some pages for Uncle Doug to peruse, right, boy?"

"Right here." I grab a copy of the scenes Nessa helped me with yesterday and hand them to him. "It's only the beginning of the movie. I've got a lot more to write."

Uncle Doug flips through the pages. "Dr. Schmaloogan? Okay. Interesting."

"It's just a rough draft for the auditions," Coop explains. "There'll be changes, of course. We're going to have all the guys read for Jack and all the girls read for Stacy. We just need to see who can act. We'll figure out everyone's actual roles once we're ready to start shooting."

Uncle Doug slaps the scenes down on the coffee table. "It's a good start. You have Uncle Doug's seal of approval. Honestly, it's much better than I expected."

I force a smile. "Thanks."

"Sorry we're late," Evelyn calls from the front door.

There's a clatter and some hushed grousing before she appears in the family room with Nick and a red suitcase in tow. She waves and introduces her giant G.I. Joe brother to the group. "We took a minor detour. Nick thought he recognized someone he's been looking for in one of the passing cars."

Nick shrugs. "What can I say? It was a false alarm. No one was hurt . . . *too* badly."

"Anyway." Evelyn laughs loudly, waving it all aside. "We're here now."

Part of me wants to ask what he did to the poor guy he thought was their dad, but the smarter part of me doesn't want to know.

"Where do you want me to put this?" Nick motions toward the suitcase.

"What's in there?" I say, images of a chopped-up body flashing in my head.

"Your video camera." Evelyn beams. "And a few other things." She crouches down and unzips the bag. Camera equipment spills out like the guts of a disemboweled tauntaun.

"Holy crap." I stare at the mounds of electronics. "Where'd you get all that?"

"One of my friend's mom's cousins is a wedding photographer. He had a few small lights, a DSLR, a wireless lapel mic, some electrical cords, and a nice tripod he wasn't using. I thought it'd be a good idea to tape all of the auditions and, you know"—she grabs the still camera—"snap some pictures so we remember who everyone is."

Uncle Doug grins and wags his finger at her. "I like this girl. She's a forward thinker."

Evelyn giggles. "'Be prepared.' It's the Girl Scout motto."

"Sweet." Coop hoists himself out of the armchair. "Let's set this up. We'll look totally pro."

Everyone descends on the equipment and stakes a claim. Valerie calls videographer while Helen grabs the DSLR. Matt says he'll put up the lights. Coop agrees to be in charge of being in charge. And Uncle Doug volunteers to watch over the snacks.

And me, I just stand back, an uneasy queasiness in my stomach. Something doesn't feel quite right here. It just seems a little too convenient that Evelyn suddenly has access to all of this movie stuff. Except nobody seems terribly bothered by this but me.

CHAPTER TWENTY-FOUR

TREMORS

I. WISH THAT. SOME . . . THING. Exciting would. Happen around. Here. Once in. A while."

Good Gandalf, Nick is the worst actor I've ever seen in my life. He sounds like a malfunctioning robot. I don't know why he insisted on auditioning. We all agreed he could be the general who's investigating the humanzees. But no. He didn't want to just be handed a part because he was Evelyn's brother. He wanted to show us what he could do.

Which, it turns out, is not very much.

"So." Nick lowers the script pages, looking all shy and hopeful. "What do you think?"

The room is dead silent. Nobody looks at each other. Nobody speaks. We're all too terrified to say what we really think. Even Uncle Doug is at a loss for words.

Then Evelyn leaps to her feet, applauding like mad. "Bravo! *Bravissimo!* That was amazing, Nick." She looks back at us. "Didn't you think that was amazing?"

Crooked smiles abound as we all nod and say, "Yeah. Oh, yeah. Really great. Super."

"I had no idea you were so talented," Evelyn gushes.

Oh, my God, I think she's serious. She actually thought that was good acting. Which is terrifying on so many levels, I don't even want to consider it.

"Do I get the part?" Nick asks, his eyes wide.

"Well," Coop says, "I'm not gonna be the one who says no." He juts his hand out and Nick shakes it. "Welcome to the cast."

For the next three hours, a wide assortment of actors files through my family room. Some of them are from drama class—Kerosene Kelsey, Jacket Jake, Forehead Fortney—and others are people I've never seen before. Most are kids, but several of them are adults. A few who've done community theater, others who just always wanted to act.

I had no idea what kind of turnout to expect, but it certainly wasn't this many people. And all would be going just fine if not for the two giant horseflies in the soup.

The first is Evelyn, of course. She hates every single girl who auditions. Not that you would know this by the grin plastered on her face during the readings. Instead, she chooses to lean over and whisper her disgust into my ear as each one leaves.

And then there's Uncle Doug, who's acting like a cracked-out five-year-old with Tourette's. Scribbling his notes on the paper towels we put out to use as napkins. Fidgeting like he's got ants in his pants. Chain-smoking. And mumbling inappropriate things at inappropriate times: *"El stinko."* "Me no likey." *"Un fuego en mis pantalones."*

"Could you at least wait until they leave?" I say when the latest actress exits, her sobs ringing in my ears.

"Hm, what?" Uncle Doug looks up from his napkin notations. "Did you say something?"

"No, *you* did. While that woman was doing her audition. You said there's a fire in your pants. In Spanish."

"Oh." Uncle Doug looks genuinely surprised. "Did I say that out loud?"

I nod. "Yes. Yes, you did."

"Ah, well." He crushes out his fifteenth cigarette. "She probably didn't understand me."

"Her name was Feliz Jimenez," Valerie says.

"Right." Uncle Doug points his pen at her. "That'd be why the thought came to me *en español.*" He stretches his arms out wide and yawns. "All right, well, I think it's time old Uncle Doug calls it a day. I've got hockey to watch." He stands and collects his cigarettes and lighter. "Carry on without me. I'll catch the video replay."

We all say our good-byes and then the next actor walks in.

It's Mr. Nestman. Gripping one of the audition scenes. He smiles and holds up his hand. "I know what you're thinking. But hear me out."

Helen leans over and whispers, "Who's that?"

I stare at him, slack jawed. "My drama teacher." Only I forget to whisper.

"Jerome Nestman," Mr. Nestman says. "Professional actor and Bergby-nominated director of the Peebles Puppet Theater in the Park. Yes, *and* drama teacher." He says the last bit with reluctance. "I have thirty years of acting experience, *and* I've been in over a hundred local TV commercials. I know what you're thinking: why does someone of my caliber want to be in this movie?" He places his hand on his chest. "Well, because someone like me will raise the production to an entirely new level. Let me show you how the pros do it."

Mr. Nestman dives right in to Jack's lines without even waiting for Helen to read Stacy's intro line. He flounces and leaps around the room, emoting like crazy, his arms gesturing wildly like he's fending off a snowball attack.

"I thank you," Mr. Nestman declares when he's finished, bowing with a hand flourish. I open my mouth to speak, but he cuts me off with a raised palm. "Please. No praise. Save it for the others. Just let me know what part I'll be playing when you've got it all sorted out."

With that, he twirls around dramatically and exits.

"Finally," Evelyn declares. "Somebody who can actually act. I was getting worried we weren't going to find anyone good today."

Coop and Matt shoot me a pair of what-the-fuck looks. I try to send them a look that says, *See? See what I was saying about her being a total nutjob?*

Coop calls out to Nick, who's manning the kitchen/waiting room. "Send in the next one!"

Another hour passes and more actors audition. There are guys with too much cologne and girls with too much makeup. There's Douchebag Dan, who's even more of a ham than Mr. Nestman. There's Rectal Ryan, reciting a monologue instead of our audition scene. There's Hand Grenade Hunter, who turns out to be as good as I suspected he'd be.

And then there's Voluptuous Victoria, wearing a top cut so low that her volcanoes nearly spill out as she bounds into the room.

"What does *this* one think she's auditioning for?" Evelyn hisses in my ear. "A cathouse?"

"I know, right?" I say out of the corner of my mouth.

I purposefully avert my eyes—forcing myself to look anywhere but at Victoria's gazongas—as she giggles and bobbles her way through the audition.

"Floozy much?" Evelyn blurts when Victoria finally leaves.

"Horrible," I say, shaking my head in disgust. "Cross *her* off the list."

"Some girls are so shameless." Evelyn shivers like she couldn't be more repulsed. "I'm just glad *I* have a boyfriend who isn't impressed by things like that." Her eyes zero in on Matt and Coop. "*Some* people can't help themselves, I suppose, but it does reveal a person's character, don't you think? Anyway," Evelyn slaps her thighs and stands. "I've got to go wee. I'll be back in a jiffy, my gallant." And with that, she pinches my cheek and exits the room.

Evelyn's not gone two seconds when Helen backhands Coop in the chest. "What the hell were you staring at, mister?"

"Nobthings," Coop says, blinking. "Nothing. I wasn't staring at anything." He reaches out, grabs his empty diet shake, and pretends to take a sip, as if busying himself will make this all go away.

Helen crosses her arms. "You were gawking at her boobs."

"I was not," Coop insists.

"You were watching her pretty damn closely," Helen accuses.

"I'm watching *everyone* closely, so I can figure out who's the breast — *best* actor."

"You're lying." Helen's mouth is tight. "You know how I feel about lying."

"I'm not . . . I was just . . ." He sighs, his shoulders slumping. "Okay, fine. I was looking at them. But how could I not? They were jiggling. Like a couple of Jell-O molds. It was hypnotizing. I can't be blamed for that. Beside, they make up like one-quarter of her entire body, so logic dictates that twenty-five percent of the time I'd have to be staring at her wobblers."

"*Staring.* Exactly," Helen says. "There's a big difference between staring and noticing."

Valerie turns to Matt. "You were staring too, weren't you?"

"Yes," Matt says, not missing a beat. "But only because I felt sorry for her. I can't imagine that's comfortable. She must have a really bad back. Poor girl."

"Goddamn it," Coop grumbles. "Why didn't I think of that?"

"Consider yourself on probation, mister," Helen says. "I may or may not be speaking to you tomorrow."

"Okey-dokey." Evelyn springs back into the family room. "The natives are getting restless out there. Let's finish this up."

By the time five o'clock rolls around, I've got a screaming migraine. I'm just about to suggest we call it a day when I sense a shift in the air. It's like, all of a sudden, there's this warm, wonderful psychic ripple in the fabric of the universe or something.

My headache instantly eases, the tension in my shoulders subsiding. And when I turn around, I'm not at all surprised to see Leyna stepping into the room.

"Oh, great," Evelyn says under her breath. "Here we go again. Another hussy."

I don't let on that I know Leyna. I just meet her eyes and give her a furtive nod. A tiny smile pulls at the corner of her lips, but she keeps an otherwise straight face. Very professional.

Valerie starts the video camera, and Helen takes a few snapshots.

"Name?" Matt says, his pen poised over his notebook.

"Leyna Jansen," she states, looking poised, confident, and drop-dead gamer gorgeous.

"Acting experience?" Coop asks.

"I've been in over a dozen plays at school and at the Turning Point Theatre. My biggest role was last year when I played Helen Keller in *The Miracle Worker*."

Helen Keller! So *that's* what *The Miracle Worker* was about.

Evelyn whispers in my ear, "I wish *I* was Helen Keller. Then I wouldn't have to see or hear this braggart anymore."

I nod thoughtfully, my brain working like crazy to figure out how I'm going to be able to cast Leyna in this film without causing Evelyn to freak out and take back all the equipment—or worse.

"Matt." Coop turns to him. "Start Leyna off, please."

"Sure." Matt looks down at the scene and begins to read, *"I really wish something exciting would happen around here once in a while."*

Leyna takes a moment to set herself. Then her face shifts and suddenly, magically, she becomes Stacy. As soon as she starts to speak, it's obvious she's ten times better than anyone we've seen so far. There's a naturalness to her. A truth to her words. Like you can tell exactly what she's feeling even when she isn't talking.

Immediately I know that Leyna has to play the lead. It's obvious. With her playing Stacy, we might actually have a chance to win one of the prizes at the film festival. Even Evelyn must see that we're in the presence of a real actor here.

"Ehhhhh!" Evelyn voice-buzzes as soon as Leyna's gone. "Fail." She punctuates this with a thumbs-down and a loud, super-wet raspberry.

"Really?" Valerie says. "I thought she was pretty good."

"Me too," I add.

"Are you kidding? That wasn't acting. She didn't even *do* anything. She just stood there and talked. Frankly, I was bored out of my skull." She shakes her head. "Honestly, I don't think any of the girls we've seen today are even remotely castable. Maybe I'll just have to play all of the female roles in this movie myself." She nuzzles her sharp nose into my neck. "You wouldn't mind, would you, smoopykins? Not after I got you all this great equipment."

Over the top of Evelyn's stringy-haired head, I see four pairs of eyes widen in horror. Oh, crap. What have we just done?

CHAPTER TWENTY-FIVE

INTERVIEW WITH THE VAMPIRE

INT. HOME BASEMENT LABORATORY — NIGHT

Dr. Schmaloogan puts a slide labeled CHIMP-MAN under a microscope and looks into the eyepiece. He spins the dial, trying to focus the lens.

CLOSE-UP ON THE SLIDE

The slide comes into focus. A single cell splits into two cells. Then the two cells split into four. Then eight. Then sixteen!

Dr. Schmaloogan stumbles back from the microscope in excitement.

> DR. SCHMALOOGAN
> Yes! I've done it! A monkey-man virus!
> Soon I will alter the evolution of the

entire human race! Of the entire world!!!
Bwah-ha-ha-ha-ha-ha!

CUT TO:

INT. JACK'S HOUSE — NIGHT

Jack and Stacy are watching a zombie movie. Stacy buries her
face in Jack's chest.

STACY

Turn it off, Jack. It's horrible. I'm scared.

JACK

Relax, Stacy. It's just make-believe. Zombies
aren't real.

STACY

Yes, they are. Or could be. I read an article
about an airborne mutated rabies virus that
could cause everyone to go insane and start
killing each other.

JACK

Where did you read that?

STACY

On the Internet.

JACK
(laughing)
Haven't you learned yet? The Internet's
not always the most reliable source of
information.

I scroll through the script pages on my laptop feeling
worn out. This writing business is pretty grueling stuff.
I thought that with Nessa's help, things would be moving along a lot quicker, but actually it's made the whole
process even slower. Sure, the few scenes we've worked
on together are good—way better than what I could have
done on my own—but every time I e-mail her some
pages, she sends them back the next day marked up with
a ton of changes.

"What's *that*?"

I jump at the sound of Cathy's voice. She's leaning
down, reading the screenplay over my shoulder. I slam
my laptop screen shut and whip the desk chair around.
"Haven't you ever heard of knocking?"

She looks at me sideways. "Are you writing a gay
porn film, Sean?"

"Why are you even here?" I say.

Cathy plops a Winnie-the-Pooh lamp on my desk.
"Mom asked me to bring this up to the baby's room."

"It's not the baby's room yet," I snap.

"Oh, really?" Cathy laughs as she looks around at
all the baby crap—the crib, the collapsed playpen, the

folded-up changing table, the rocker—that Mom and Dad have been squirreling away in here. "Could have fooled me."

"It's mine until it isn't," I say, shaking my head. "And I'd appreciate you knocking before you just barge in here. Jeez, doesn't anyone in this stupid house have any respect for privacy?"

"Might as well get used to it, loser," Cathy says. "It's not like I'm gonna be knocking on my own bedroom door when you move in. Which reminds me. Since you'll be invading my space, you're considered an unwanted guest. Now, I've been giving this situation some thought, and I've decided that the only way I'm going to be able to tolerate it is by charging you rent."

I laugh. "Right. I'm going to pay you rent to live in my own house."

"Great. I'm glad we agree. I was afraid I'd have to threaten to out you to the entire school. And as much as I want you to be true to yourself, I don't imagine it's how you'd choose to have the world find out about your love of all things penis."

I stand up so that Cathy isn't towering over me, though she's still two inches taller than me when standing.

"Okay, let's get a few things straight," I say. "First of all, I'm *not* paying you rent."

"Twenty-five dollars a month should do." Cathy

studies her spiderweb-adorned fingernails. "That still leaves you with enough of your allowance to buy your homoerotic video games."

"And nextly," I say, "I'm not even going to respond to the gay thing again."

Cathy smirks. "You just did."

"No, I didn't."

"Methinks he doth protest too much." She makes like she's turning to leave my room, but at the last second she reaches over and plucks the movie folder off my desk. "What do we have here? A collection of love letters from your boyfriends?"

I lunge for the folder, but Cathy spins away. "That's private property," I say.

"What the hell is this?" Cathy laughs as she peeks inside and plucks out the TerrorFest entry form. "Oh, my God. A *horror movie*? You *can't* be serious. You guys are such morons."

"Yeah, well, for your information, that movie is what's going to save *me* from having to share a bedroom with *you*."

It takes about a second for me to realize what I've just said. Damn it. Why can't my stupid brain work faster?

"Oh, really?" Cathy crooks an eyebrow. "Do tell."

"Forget it." I make another try for the folder.

Cathy just smacks my forehead with it. "*Hello,* turdling? This concerns me as much as you, so spit it out." As she pulls back the folder, ten fifty-dollar bills—the first installment of Uncle Doug's investment—slide out and flutter to the floor.

I dive to the ground and snag most of the bills but Cathy's witch-boot-clad foot pins two of them to the rug before I can get there. I pinch the corners to try to free them, but my sister bears down with her full weight. If I tug any harder, they'll just rip. Checkmate.

"My, oh my." Cathy squats and plucks up the money. "This is getting interesting."

"That's *my* money!" I seize Cathy's wrist, but she just raises her arm like the Statue of Liberty, leaving me dangling on her limb like the "Hang in There!" kitty.

"You might as well just give it up, weasel," she says, peeling me off her arm. "Save yourself the heartache and tell me where you got all this cash."

"It's mine. I saved it up."

"Please." Cathy pulls a face. "You've never saved a penny of your allowance, *ever*. Spill it. Where'd you get this?" She waves the hundred dollars in my face. "Did you steal it?"

"No, I didn't *steal* it."

"Are you turning tricks? Now, *that*'d be cool. Having a gay gigolo in the family."

"We *raised* the money. From investors. We're using it to make our movie. Satisfied?"

Cathy stares at me dubiously. "Somebody gave you

hundreds of dollars to make a movie? *You* and your idiot friends?"

"Try a *thousand.* Once we get our second installment."

Ah, shit! Again with the slow brain! I sniff my palm and try to keep from hyperventilating.

"A grand? Someone gave *you* a *grand* to make a *movie*?" Her tone drips with disbelief. "Why would *anyone* be stupid enough to do that?"

"Because they *believe* in us!" My voice croaks with earnestness and I can feel my ears reddening. "Look, this is our Get Out of Jail Free card, Cath. When our movie wins TerrorFest, we'll have enough cash to build an extension on the house, okay? And then you and me won't have to share a room."

Cathy screams with laughter. "Oh, sweetie. That is *so* cute. But as your older sister—and future landlord—I feel it's my responsibility to protect your fragile little ego by letting you know that there's not a chance in *hell* you are going to be able to make a movie good enough to win any contest. But"—she plucks one of the fifty-dollar bills from her hand and starts folding it up—"since you're suddenly so flush, I *will* do you the favor of taking your first and last months' rent in advance." Cathy flicks the other fifty-dollar bill at my face.

"That only leaves me with four hundred and fifty bucks!"

"Excellent subtraction skills there, little brother." She tucks the folded-up money into her back pocket. "I don't know why you're not in AP math with me and Nessa."

I glower. "You know I'm just gonna tell Mom and Dad."

"Be my guest. I'm sure they'll be fascinated to learn that you've got hundreds of dollars stashed up here. But don't worry. They probably won't ask you where you got it. Of course, I *might* just have to let it slip that you're a gay male prostitute now." She shrugs. "I don't know. I'm thinking that fifty bucks is a pretty fair price to buy my silence. But that's just me."

"You are such a bi—"

Cathy places her long black fingernail on my lips. "Uh-uh. Mind your words, young man. We wouldn't want this to be an ongoing extortion thing, would we?"

I swat her hand away. "Oh, you mean like me having to pay rent every month to stop you from spreading lies about me?"

"That's just basic compensation for the inconvenience you pose. And believe me, it doesn't even come *close* to balancing things out. You'd never be able to afford that."

Just then, Nessa pokes her head into my room. "There you are," she says, completely ignoring me. She's wearing a blue Wal-Mart vest and pressed khakis that are such an odd contrast to her Gothness. "I knocked but nobody answered the front door. We better get going or we're going to be late again."

"I'm coming." Cathy saunters to the door. "Just give me a sec, okay? I have to go find my uniform." She looks back at me. "Hey, baby brother. Why don't you entertain Ness with the details of your brilliant plan? I'm sure she'll find it fascinating."

I flip Cathy off, but she just laughs as she exits the room.

As soon as Cathy's gone, Nessa reaches into her pocket and pulls out a folded-up piece of pink notebook paper. She glances over her shoulder, then steps into my room and presses it into my hand.

"Here are some more suggestions for the last few scenes," Nessa whispers.

"Why didn't you e-mail this to me? I just finished incorporating all of your other notes."

Nessa checks the doorway again. "These came to me on the bus ride over here."

I sigh, imagining all the new work Nessa has likely created for me. "We're supposed to start filming next week. Could we maybe meet up in person again instead of all this back-and-forth?"

"Tomorrow," she says, without missing a beat. "My house. Five o'clock. We'll order pizza. Cathy's working until closing, so we should have a nice long run at it."

"Wow, you've really worked this out," I say, running through my schedule in my head. "Yeah, okay. I've got to help out my uncle in the afternoon, but later should be fine."

"Kewl." Nessa leans in close. "Don't you love all this clandestine stuff? It feels like we're spies. Or like we're having an affair."

I gulp so loudly that even Cathy probably heard it. Jeez, when did it get so warm in here?

"Oh, and Sean?" she whispers, her breath tickling my neck. For a second I think she's going to try to kiss me again, and I remind myself why that would be a bad thing. "I was also thinking that maybe Dr. Schmaloogan should have an evil sidekick. Sort of like a Renfield or an Igor."

I blink and try to clear my head. "A who?"

"Someone to do his bidding. To steal the test chimps and spread the virus and stuff. It's a classic horror-movie character. Jesus, Sean, we're going to have to have a movie night and bring you up to speed on these things."

"A sidekick. Yeah. No, I get it. That could be good."

"Maybe." Nessa teeter-totters her head. "Maybe not. I don't know. Think about it. I'll see you tomorrow."

She flashes me a quick smile, and then she's gone.

I stare at the note in my hand for a second before bringing it to my nose. It smells a little like carnations. *An affair,* I think, a jolt of excitement running through my body.

But then my brain finally kicks in: pink, scented

stationery? This whole thing couldn't be more obviously a trap if her note actually said *This is a trap!*

Whatever she and Cathy are up to, as long as it keeps Nessa around long enough for us to finish this screenplay, I don't really give a flying Fearow. I just have to be on guard and make sure the ensign in my pants follows captain's orders.

CHAPTER TWENTY-SIX

DRESSED TO KILL

EXT. STREET — NIGHT

Jack and Stacy race down the street, out of breath and sweating. They keep looking back over their shoulders as if they are being chased.

STACY

Do you think we lost them?

JACK

I don't know. They seem to have a really good sense of smell. Let's just keep running.

Jack grabs Stacy's hand and pulls her down a back alley. The alley is lined with trash cans and dumpsters and doors to stores and restaurants.

Halfway down the lane, they notice that it dead-ends at a brick wall.

                    STACY
       It's a dead end. We have to get out of here.

Suddenly, they hear a GROWLING MOAN. They turn around to see a horde of humanzees shuffling into the back alley, blocking their escape.

                    JACK
       Try all the doors. Maybe one of them is open.

The humanzees shuffle toward them as Jack and Stacy try all the doorknobs.

                    STACY
       They're all locked! What are we going to do?

Jack slams his shoulder into one of the doors but it's not budging. He tries again and again, but the humanzees are rapidly closing in on them.

                    STACY
       Hurry! They're almost here!

All morning long, I've been pounding energy drinks— I think I've had six cans by now—as I make Nessa's changes to the script and try to write some new scenes.

Nessa keeps saying I have to build the tension. Build the tension before we see the monsters. Build the tension before someone gets killed. And so I've been trying to keep the screws turning on our main characters. I'll know if I'm doing what she wants when I meet with her later today.

In the meantime, I'm trying to get through as much of the script as I can before I have to head over to Uncle Doug's store and make good on his final condition of the loan. I drain the last drops of my Berry Beast and look over at the clock. Oh, crap! It's eleven forty. Where the hell did the last forty minutes go? Damn it damn it damn it!

I slam my laptop closed, grab my keys and phone, and bolt for the door. I have no idea what he's going to make me do at his shop—stocking, cleaning, or something equally unpleasant, I'm sure—but I've only got twenty minutes to get there and I know he's not going to be too pleased if I'm late.

"This costume is itchy," I say, looking down through a brown spandex mask at the life-size Persian rug I'm wearing.

"I told you you weren't going to like it," Uncle Doug says.

"And it smells like rotten eggs."

He laughs. "I don't doubt it."

"Why—?"

"Trust me, you don't want to know." He cackles as he raises a spliff to his chapped lips and takes a drag.

"Suffice it to say, it's one of the reasons the last guy quit. Not the *only* reason. But one of the reasons."

"I don't blame him." I try to stick my Lycra-covered face farther out of the tiny oval cutout in the rug suit. "It's disgusting."

"Aaaa." Uncle Doug releases a big plume of pot smoke and swats my comment away with the back of his hand. "Don't be such a pussy. You'll be fine once you're out in the fresh air." He starts walking toward the two-tone green Doug's Rugs van parked by the garage doors. "Besides, what you really need to worry about are the wind currents."

"The *what*?" I shuffle-turn my carpet-clad body to look at him. "What wind currents?"

"The wind currents. The gales out of the east." He waves his joint in the air as he steps up to the driver's-side door. "It gets pretty damn blustery up there on Newport Road. And that costume can act like a goddamn kite if it catches the breeze. That was the reason the guy *before* the last guy quit. A heavy gust blew him right into the street. Poor bastard was nearly plowed down by a semi. You think you can't move so well in that thing, but you'd be surprised how agile you get when you have to play dodge the traffic." Uncle Doug laughs as he scoots from left to right to left in a little sidestepping dance. "Come on," he says, checking his watch. "Let's get a move on. Time is money." He opens the van door and climbs inside.

I start to waddle over to the passenger side as fast as I can, my steps seriously hindered by the constraints of this stupid outfit. It's like I've been stuffed down a single pant leg of a fat man's jeans. I pump my unitard-sheathed arms as hard as I can to try and propel myself forward, the gold tassels at the top of the carpet costume slapping away off rhythm.

I finally get to the van, yank the door open, and struggle to clamber into the seat. It's a real battle against physics because as soon as I pull myself partially onto the seat I have to straighten out my legs, which then causes me to slide back down again.

By the time I manage to inchworm myself into the front seat I am completely exhausted.

"That was some show, Seanie boy." Uncle Doug chuckles. "I feel like I'm really starting to get my money's worth out of this investment."

"If I'd known this is what you meant"—I wheeze—"by helping you out at the store . . . I wouldn't have agreed to it."

"Oh, sure you would, Seanie. It's a means to an end. A means to an end." He turns the key, and the van coughs to life. "Besides, you haven't lived until you've dressed up like a carpet and waved signs at passing cars. It's how I started out thirty years ago. Now look at me. I own the place." One more puff on his joint, then he throws the car into reverse. "All right, here we go."

We back out of the warehouse garage, the tires

crunching through the hardened snow. A moment later, we're driving along an industrial street headed toward the main road.

Uncle Doug's got his left wrist draped over the steering wheel, his joint-holding hand stroking his giant gray-flecked beard. Little wisps of smoke fizzle into the air as the occasional whisker is singed. "Hey, so, I've been watching the audition tapes."

"Oh, yeah?"

He nods. "You've got a few winners there, I think. The buzz-cut kid. Harper? Hummer? Hunter? And the girl with the blunt-cut hair." He chops at his forehead with his hand. "Laney?"

"Leyna," I say.

"Right. Those two are our stars. No doubt about it."

"Hunter's no problem, but we've already promised Evelyn the female lead, so—"

"Absolutely not." Uncle Doug shakes his head. "I don't care if she's sleeping with the screenwriter. If she's anywhere near as bad as her brother, this film's dead in the water."

"Yeah, well, we don't have a choice. It's her camera we're using. So, it's either her in the lead or we have nothing to film with." I shrug. "Unless . . . you want to up your investment so we can rent something."

Uncle Doug laughs. "Give 'em a grand and they want two. Sorry, but it's not gonna happen, Seanie. You use what you've got and figure it out. That's what all good businessmen do. I don't care what you have to do, but Handler and Lorna are going to be in the film we show at the festival or Uncle Doug's going to be plenty PO'd. Are we clear about this?"

It's hard to argue when I actually agree with him. "Sure. Fine. Whatever. I'll figure something out."

"Good man. That's what I like to hear."

I turn and gaze out the window, watching the industrial landscape go by. I don't know if it's the sound of the tires going through puddles or the motion of the van, but suddenly I realize that I have to pee. Bad. "Hey, so, what do I do if I have to go the bathroom?" I ask as casually as I can. "You know, while I'm out here?"

Uncle Doug looks over at me, his eyebrows raised. "Oh. You should have taken care of that back at the store."

"No, I mean, I'm okay now," I lie, "but if I'm supposed to be out there for four hours, I might have to go at some point." Like in the next few minutes. "Is there a Starbucks nearby?"

Uncle Doug snorts. "First of all, there's no way for you to get out of that costume without help. Remember how I had to zip you up in the back? Secondly, we're on a major commercial thoroughfare here lined with autobody shops and self-storage facilities. The nearest public toilet is over a mile away. So, I suggest you just hold on tight and, uh . . . don't think about waterfalls."

My horror must be pretty apparent if Uncle Doug can see it through my spandex mask.

"Look, worse comes to worst," he continues, "just pee in the suit. It sure as shit won't make it smell any worse. Hell, it might even warm you up. For a little while." He throws his head back and howls.

A couple of thigh-clenched minutes later, Uncle Doug pulls the van up to the curb at the corner of Newport and Millburn. Cars and trucks whoosh by at top speed on the six-lane road.

"Here we be," Uncle Doug says as he gets out of the van.

I shove open my door, swing my legs to the side, and slowly slide out of the passenger seat to the curb below. A quick scan of the landscape reveals a whole lot of nothing. The large plot of snow-laden grass slopes pretty dramatically from the sidewalk where I'm standing to the parking lot of a busy lumberyard below. No big trees or bushes in sight. A great spot to do some sledding but certainly not an ideal place to take a whiz.

"All right, then." Uncle Doug pulls several large signs from the back of his van and drags them over to me. "I've got three ads here. I want you to cycle through them periodically."

He holds up the first board, which reads BE AS SNUG AS A BUG IN DOUG'S RUGS! 30% OFF EVERY DAY! He shifts the front sign to the back so I can read the next one: DON'T

BE A THUG: BUY YOUR GAL A NEW RUG AND GET 30% OFF! He flips the signs once more and shows me the last one: 30% OFF EVERYTHING! DOUG'S GONE MAD! COME TAKE ADVANTAGE OF HIS INSANITY!

Uncle Doug hands me the signs and checks his watch again. "All right. I'll leave you to it. Oh, and, uh, be sure to stay alert and keep your eyes peeled."

"For what?"

Uncle Doug drags his hand down his face and beard. "I probably should have mentioned this before but . . . the Doug's Rug mascot has a tendency to . . ." He swirls his hand in the air like he's trying to grasp the words.

"To *what*? A tendency to *what*?"

"To get attacked. Jumped. Roughed up a little. Nothing serious. Just . . . knocked down occasionally. By hoodlums. And . . . sometimes egged. Or shaving creamed. You know. For fun."

"Wait a second." I take a wobbly step toward him. "Are you saying I'm going to be ambushed?" I look down at myself. "Dressed like this? With no chance for self-defense?"

"Look." Uncle Doug starts to walk backward. "It's probably not going to happen. I mean, they've done it already. These guys. Several times. I'm sure, whoever they are, they've moved on to something else. You know how it is."

"No. I don't." I take another step forward. "Because

I've never assaulted a store mascot before. You can't leave me here."

"It's going to be fine." Uncle Doug continues to back away. "I wouldn't put you in any *actual* danger. I need you out here. This kind of thing pays real dividends in increased store traffic. Besides, the last attack made the evening news. You can't buy that kind of publicity." He chuckles nervously, then checks his watch again. "Oh, hey, listen, I've got to get back to the store. But don't worry, I'll be out here to pick you up around four o'clock."

"Uncle Doug, please." I reach toward him with my brown-stockinged arm.

"Don't forget to move around. You know, writhe a bit, like you're a wavy carpet." He undulates his torso and arms. "You want to make sure you're noticed."

"I don't think I do. Not if I'm going to be beaten up. I want to lie down and disappear."

"Hey, I'm not paying you to lie there like a rug." Uncle Doug laughs a great big belly laugh.

"You're not paying me at all!" I remind him.

"Now, now. Did I or did I not advance you five hundred dollars against my one-thousand-dollar investment? The least you can do to repay your uncle Doug's generosity is generate a bit of traffic for his store." He winks at me. "You're a good kid, Seanie. See you in a bit."

🎥 CHAPTER TWENTY-SEVEN 🎥

MISERY

I'M DANCING AROUND in the snow on the side of the road in my carpet costume. Not because I want to attract attention to myself—certainly not, after finding out about the mascot assailants—but because I still have three and a half hours before Uncle Doug is coming back to get me and I have to take the mother of all whizzes.

I spin around desperately, searching for somewhere I can pull off this stupid outfit and drain the dragon.

But there is not a single solitary tree, bush, or abandoned building to crouch behind.

Ow, ow, ow, ow, ow. Jesus.

A little pee devil on my shoulder is trying to convince me to "just let go." To open the floodgates inside my costume like Uncle Doug said to.

Sure, it's disgusting, but I am in some serious pain here. And I don't want to die. Because it can totally happen. I know. I heard about this one dude who was "holding his water" to try and win a water scooter on some radio show and his bladder totally exploded.

Oh, God, it hurts so bad. From my belly all the way to the very tip of the tap.

All right. All right. Forget it. I'm done. If I don't go right now I'm going to pass out. It's fine. It's no big deal. Astronauts pee in their space suits. Scuba divers pee in their wet suits.

And I can pee in my carpet costume.

I have my change of clothes back at the store. Everything'll be mostly dry by the time I get picked up anyway. And this costume definitely can't smell any worse than it already does. Nobody'll know the difference.

I just have to relax and let nature take its course. I take a deep breath, exhale slowly, loosen my grip on things, roll my eyes back into my head, and . . .

and . . .

Nothing. Not even a pressure-relieving dribble. Not a single goddamn drop.

I can't believe this. I actually get myself to the point where I'm ready to whiz all over myself and my stupid, pee-shy bladder won't even let me go?

Okay. Okay. Calm down. Maybe it's like in public bathrooms when people are waiting behind me and I can't get things flowing. I'll just make a deal. That's it. I'll make a deal with my dingle. It's my go-to strategy in desperate times.

I close my eyes and tell myself, *If you pee right now,*

you will win the film festival and you will not have to share a room with your evil sister. But only if you pee right now. By the count of five.

One . . . Mm-hmm. Okay. I can feel the tension starting to ease. *Two* . . . Oh, yes. That's right. Here we go. All I needed was some incentive. *Three* . . . Almost there . . . Almost there . . .

"Incoming!" some guy shouts.

My eyes fly open, everything inside me clenching back up. A giant red truck is screeching to a halt right in front of me. Two ski-masked kids hang out the windows and start rifling eggs, tomatoes, and—zucchini?—at me.

"Go shag yourself!" one of them hollers.

I undulate like Uncle Doug showed me to try and ward off the onslaught, but it's pointless. I am pelted from tassels to toes. Eggs exploding all over my costume. Zucchini battering me like dozens of tiny green baseball bats.

A giant juicy beefsteak tomato catches me in the face, erupting on impact and saturating my spandex mask with gloppy pulp.

I try to spin away from the assault, but my sneaker catches a patch of ice, sending my feet flying into the air. I flop onto the sidewalk with a muffled thud.

"Woo-hoo!" the guys whoop. "Fifty points! Did you get that on your phone?"

"Sure did."

"Sweet. Let's go YouTube it!"

The truck peels off and I lie there for a minute,

stunned. A few self-pitying moments later, I realize that the trauma of the attack has totally scared away my pee urge. Well, thank Lord Vader for small favors.

Finally I roll over, hoist myself to my feet, and waddle back over to the signs. I might as well carry on until Uncle Doug comes back. What else am I going to do dressed as a giant rug and stranded in the middle of a suburban wasteland?

But as I bend over to retrieve the boards — which looks about as awkward as you can imagine — Uncle Doug's two-tone green van coasts up to the curb. And just like that, my desperate need to whiz comes back with a vengeance. It's like now that my bladder knows a toilet is only a quick van ride away, it can stop playing possum and start making noise again. *Major* noise.

I start to waddle like mad toward the van. The sliding back door flies open, the dark cabin ready to take me in and whisk me to indoor plumbing.

And then, all of a sudden, three humongous hairy things spill out of the van all at once and begin stampeding toward me. It's like something out of a nightmare. And I wonder, did I hit my head on the sidewalk? Am I in a coma? Am I dreaming this? Or did the mascot thugs go costume up and hijack Uncle Doug's van so they could come back and attack me again?

The beasts growl and howl as they charge. My heart thuds in my chest as I shamble backward as fast as my leg-constricting carpet suit will let me.

That's when I catch sight of the video-camera lens furtively poking out from the van's open back door.

And suddenly it all makes sense.

These are our humanzees and I am meant to be one of their unwitting victims. I barely have time to wonder how we're going to work a human-size rug into our script before the first creature is upon me. I get a glimpse of the fangs and the blood dripping from the corners of the flying vampanzee's mouth—a pretty realistic effect, I must say—just as I turn to run. But it's too late. The monster slams into me, ramming my lower back like I'm a football-tackling dummy. The creature's hairy arms squeeze my midsection and I lose my balance once again.

We both hit the ground hard and the wind—together with a sizable gush of pee—is knocked right out of me. An odd mix of pain, relief, and humiliation swirls through my body as the wet warmth spreads over my thighs. I bear down, attempting to close off the tap, but there's no way the flow is gonna stop before the tank's been emptied.

I'm lying there on my stomach, clinging to the desperate hope that my carpet costume will soak up the embarrassing leak like a sponge, when I suddenly realize that me and the monkey-man have begun to slide down the snow-slicked slope.

And fast.

He is kneeling on top of me, riding me like a toboggan. I hear howls of laughter coming from the hilltop and console myself with the fact that at least the zombie-monkey costumes look pretty dope.

We finally come to a thumping halt against a mound of snow that's been cleared from the lumberyard parking lot.

"Are you okay, there, buddy?" the monkey-man asks as he climbs off of me. His voice is familiar but since it's muffled through the monkey mask, I can't exactly place it.

"Yeah." I sit up, coughing. "I think so."

He turns his chimp-head and looks back at the hill we just sledded down. "What the—?" He starts to laugh. "Jeez, kid, did we *actually* scare the piss out of you?"

My body tingles with horror as I brush the snow and tomato guts out of my spandex-covered eyes and see what it is that he—and everyone on top of the hill—sees: a long, wide, Berry-Beast-bright-yellow swath cut through the snow.

He busts up, grabbing his hairy stomach. "Oh, buddy. Guy. I'm sorry. That's . . . That's . . . Wow." But he doesn't sound sorry at all. He reaches around his neck and starts to pull off the mask. I cringe, wondering which of our acquaintances just rode me down a hill while I pissed my tights.

The mask comes off and Nick smiles a huge psycho smile at me, his large teeth still stained red from the blood dye. "Now you know how I'll be coming after you if you ever break my sister's heart." He cracks up like this is the funniest thing in the world.

To add insult to injury, Nick has to practically drag me back up the hill, as it's impossible for me to do any climbing in my soggy restrictive rug suit. Everyone— Coop, Matt, Valerie, Helen, Evelyn, Uncle Doug, and the other two vampanzees—gathers around us once we reach the top.

"Oh, my God," Evelyn shrieks, squeezing through the crowd to stand beside me. "Are you okay, sweetie pie? We didn't know you were going to slip down the hill. I wouldn't have let them do it if I'd known. I swear."

"It's okay," I lie. "I'm fine." Just clammy, achy, and pee scented.

"That was epic!" Coop hoots. "The kind of happy accident filmmakers dream about."

"Were you scared?" Evelyn asks.

Nick chuckles. "Oh, he was scared all right." He looks back at the yellow path I've left in the snow.

"What *is* that, anyway?" Helen asks, snapping a million photos of the scene.

"Nothing," I say, my cheeks burning up behind the spandex.

"Probably just some dye from the cheap-ass rug costume." Coop winks at me. "Don't sweat it. We'll make it work for us. We can recolor it in post. Make it red so it looks like blood. Your unc wanted product placement, and, boy, we got it! Zombie-vampire-chimps attack Rug Boy! I can't wait to see the footage. I bet it looks spectac!"

CHAPTER TWENTY-EIGHT

ARMY OF DARKNESS

ANOTHER ROUND OF JALAPEÑO poppers," Uncle Doug calls out over the loud mariachi music from our long table at Los Muchachos. A sombrero-clad waiter hustles over with his order pad in hand. "And some more of these tasty fried Mexi-cchini sticks." Uncle Doug pops one in his mouth. "Mmm-*mmm*. Who knew veggies could ever taste so good?"

Uncle Doug felt so bad about my traumatic time as his rug mascot that he offered to take the whole cast and crew out to lunch—me, Matt, Coop, Valerie, Helen, Evelyn, Nick, and the two other primates: Matt's older brother, Pete, and Tony "the Gorilla" Grillo.

I couldn't believe it when Tony took off his mask. But not even the girls' best makeup efforts could create a lip scar that scary, or a sneer that smarmy.

"Don't you think we have enough food?" I say, staring at the dozen plates of deep-fried appetizers spread out before us.

"What are you talking about?" Uncle Doug laughs. "We've got some big boys to feed."

Which is true enough. I crane forward and glance down to see Nick, Pete, and Tony at the far end of the table. Pawing at the food and yukking it up with each other like a bunch of bodybuilder buddies after a hard workout.

I lean over to Matt and keep my voice low. "So, how'd you manage to get the three *gigantes* to dress up like monkeys for us?"

"Nick was easy," Matt says, taking a bite of a Tex-Mex egg roll. "He'll play as many parts in the movie as we want. As long as he also gets to play the head of the military."

I nod. "Okay. And your brother and Tony?"

"That took a bit more negotiating. Originally they wanted fifty bucks a day. But I talked them down to twenty-five."

"Twenty-five dollars?" I splutter. "A *day*? That's . . ." I do some quick mental math. "Seven hundred bucks if we have to shoot with both of them for the whole two weeks!"

"We didn't really have a choice. They're the only guys we know who even come close to filling out the costumes. We'll just have to pick and choose which days we need to shoot full-on chimp suits. Don't worry about it. It's like Coop said, a lot of stuff can be done with just the paws and mouths."

I press my fingers into my temples as a six-Berry-Beast headache thrums its way through my skull. All right, so, that's fifty bucks for Tony and Pete today. And another hundred for the monkey costumes and makeup the girls bought. Plus the fifty Cathy stole. That still leaves us with three hundred of the original five. With another five hundred to come. I guess we're still okay. As long as nothing else unexpected comes along.

"Hey, could you move over a little?" Matt asks, scrunching up his nose. "No offense or anything, but you still kinda smell like piss."

"Sorry." I scoot my chair toward the corner of the table. We made a pit stop at Uncle Doug's store so I could wash up in his bathroom sink and change back into my street clothes, but until I take a long hot shower, I won't be completely pee-free.

I'm hoping that this lunch ends soon so I can get home and really scrub down before I have to head over to Nessa's.

But lunch does *not* end soon. And as it stretches into its second hour—the three muscleheads having started a full-out eating contest, with Uncle Doug taking bets from the other customers in the restaurant—I start to worry I'll miss my meeting with Nessa entirely.

I glance at my cell phone. Four fifteen. Okay, so,

showering is out of the question. But I can still make it to Nessa's—maybe just a little late—if I can get back to Uncle Doug's shop, grab my bike, and go straight to her house. Hopefully the ride over will sufficiently air me out.

I look over to see Evelyn pounding the table and cheering her brother on as Nick tilts his head back and swallows an entire burrito like a python gulleting a rabbit.

Here's my chance. While everyone is preoccupied.

I tap Matt on the shoulder. He turns around, looking slightly annoyed that I've interrupted his viewing of the freak show.

"What do you want?" he asks.

"I have to get out of here. Can you cover for me?"

"What? Why?"

"I don't feel well," I say, which isn't a complete lie. I do feel a little nauseous after eating all that grease. "I just want to slip out without making a big deal out of it. Otherwise Evelyn might want to come with and I really don't want that right now. Just tell everyone I went home to get some rest and that I didn't want to ruin their good time."

Matt keeps glancing over his shoulder, trying to keep track of who's eating what. "Okay, fine, sure, whatever," he says, then turns back to watch the festivities.

I crouch down and skulk out of the restaurant. With all the whoops and hollering, no one notices, which is just how I want it. I'll send Evelyn a text in a little while saying I'm going to take a nap and I'll see her tomorrow. That way she won't decide to swing by my house to see if I'm okay.

A little less than an hour later, I hop the curb and ride up Nessa's driveway. I've only been here once before, three years ago. Nessa's mom had passed away and there was a get-together where they served crustless tuna-salad sandwiches with relish, a shrimp plate with way-too-hot cocktail sauce, a soggy lasagna, and three different brands of cola.

Mrs. Caldwell was the first parent I ever knew who had died, and I spent most of my time in the kitchen, trying to stay out of the way. Vacillating between being grateful that it wasn't my mom who was dead and feeling really guilty for being so grateful.

I ride my bike around to the back of the house. Nessa gave me explicit instructions not to leave my bicycle in front and to be careful not to be seen by anyone who might narc us out. I lay my bike against the tree with the tire swing and walk across the frozen lawn, lugging my backpack up to the patio. The sliding glass door is cold on the knuckles as I give a light knock. A minute later, Nessa appears, all pale skinned and violet lipped — dressed in tight black jeans, a spiked choker, and a low-cut black shirt with a blue-jeweled cross dangling hypnotically just above her cleavage.

She looks pretty hot, I have to admit, but all I keep thinking about is what Leyna would look like in this very same outfit. It'd take her *Final Fantasy* persona to a whole new level.

"Hey there, stranger," Nessa says, sliding the door open.

I smile awkwardly. "Hey."

"No one saw you, right?" She cranes her neck, searching behind me for potential spies.

"Not that I could see."

"Good." She steps aside. "Come on in."

She leads me through the dining room, where nearly all of the surfaces—the table, the sideboard, the chairs—are stacked several feet high with overflowing orange file folders, old newspapers, and unopened mail.

"Don't mind the mess," Nessa says. "My dad's an accountant." As if this explains everything. "Come on. We'll work in my room. It's the neatest place in the house."

We make our way up the green-carpeted stairs, hang a left, and head down a short hallway. We stop at an ornate blood-red wooden door. Carvings of vines, tree branches, and leaves decorate the six inset panels. This is not a door to a bedroom. More like an entryway to some enchanted castle.

"Sweet," I say.

"My dad found it by the curb with someone's gar-bage. They were just throwing it out. Can you believe that? We had to sand it, and cut it down, and paint it. But it was worth it."

"For sure," I say. "That's the coolest bedroom door I've ever seen."

Nessa smiles. "I think my dad secretly likes the fact that I'm into dark and weird shit. It gives him an excuse to hunt for cool stuff at antique shops and garage sales and flea markets. He's always coming home with some new thing he thinks I'll like."

"That's nice. You know, that he's supportive and all."

"Yeah. He's pretty cool. When he's not totally embarrassing me." Nessa grasps the brass knob, then turns back. "All right, so. This is my inner sanctum. I don't let just anyone in here. You are being afforded an honor, and I expect you to show courtesy and decorum. But most of all, I expect you to keep your mouth shut."

"Yeah," I say. "Sure. Of course."

"If I find out you've breathed a word about my room to anyone—and that includes your drooling, emotionally stunted friends—not only will I no longer help you with your script, but I will happily place the world's worst acne curse on you, which will make your face break out so badly that even your mother won't be able to recognize you. Are we clear on this?"

I blink. "You . . . you know curses?"

"Screw with me and you can find out." Nessa pushes open the door and steps inside.

My nostrils are filled with the sweet scent of smoky

spices as I follow her into the darkened space of her bedroom. The heavy incense works in my favor as it should mask any lingering scent of pee. It takes a second for my eyes to adjust to the dim candlelight, but as soon as they do, my jaw drops. Everything is lush purple and deep crimson and dark wood. Her four-poster bed is canopied with sheer white drapery. The walls are decorated with all sorts of crosses, daggers, and knives; sketches of wolves and demons; old horror-movie posters; and dried boughs of red roses. The dressers and tabletops are covered with flickering candles, dragon statues, incense burners, chalices, and skulls.

It's like we've entered someplace medieval and haunted and otherworldly.

"Holy crap," I say, gawking at all the badass stuff. "This is hands down the coolest bedroom I have ever seen. Way cooler than Cathy's gargoyles and red drapes. "

"Thanks." Nessa smiles. "Glad you like it."

"Like it?" I circle around, taking in the old beat-up leather-bound books lining her bookshelves, the crystal ball on her nightstand, the small flat-screen TV and PS3 on her desk, the fake tombstone hanging on the wall over her bed. "It's like a movie set or something." I turn to look at her. "Are you telling me your dad actually helps you decorate your room like this?"

Nessa shrugs. "At first he wasn't too pleased by the whole 'dark' thing. I think he thought I was getting obsessed with death or something after my mom passed away. Which was kind of true. I mean, for a while I was really sad. But then I got really interested in dying."

"Interested?" I say. "Like, wanting to?"

She rolls her eyes. "No. It was more like intense curiosity. Wondering about the process."

"Of *dying*?"

"Yeah. Like, how it feels, you know? Is it like falling asleep? Does it hurt? And what happens afterward? Once you're gone? Are we just here one day and then poof? Nothing? Or is there something else?" She laughs at my blank stare. "Don't you ever wonder about that?"

"I try not to."

"Well, you should. It makes you appreciate your life more when you know you only have a finite amount of time on this planet."

"I think it would just make me depressed."

"Actually, it's just the opposite. Thinking about death gives you perspective on all the things that are fleeting in the world. The fact that we're going to die gives life more significance. That's why vampires are so bummed. They're immortal and everything, but it's meaningless because nothing matters. And speaking of meaning"— she moves to her desk and opens her laptop—"we need to talk about the theme of this movie of yours."

"Theme?" I say. "What theme?"

"Exactly." Nessa sits in the antique desk chair, which lets out a little creaking groan as she settles in. The light from the computer screen casts a blue glow on her white face, making her seem fairy-like. "What are you trying to say with this film?"

I move to the desk and look over Nessa's shoulder, forcing myself *not* to look at her cleavage. "I don't want to *say* anything. I just want to scare people."

She shakes her head. "Writing something just for the sake of scaring someone is pointless. And not particularly scary, to be honest."

"I don't understand. Isn't that the whole point of a horror movie?"

"Yes and no." Nessa looks up at me. "The great thing about horror, any horror, is that it forces you to confront the dark side of life. To make you think about things you might not want to think about."

"Why would you want to be forced to think about things you don't want to think about?"

Nessa smiles. "Because, Sean. It's like I said. It makes you feel more alive. Seriously, how would you know what was good in your life if you had nothing bad to compare it to?"

"I guess. But how can seeing zombie-vampire-chimps make people feel more alive?"

"That's what we need to figure out," Nessa says. "What do you want to say to the world? About what's important in life?"

"I don't know." I shrug. "Don't experiment with human and chimpanzee DNA?"

Nessa gives me that frown that teachers and parents

give you when they don't feel you're trying your hardest. "All right, let's do a little thought exercise, see if we can uncover something. Tell me, what's been on your mind lately? What concerns do you have?"

My mind flips around like a broken television searching for channels. The baby, the movie, moving into Cathy's room, trying to ditch Evelyn so I can actually have a shot with Leyna.

And then of course there's Nessa's cleavage, which I *really* don't want to focus on.

Her porcelain. White. Cleavage.

"Well?" Nessa asks. "I can see the wheels turning. What are you thinking about?"

"Nothing." I chew on my tongue. "Everything. It's hard to focus on one thing, I guess."

"All right, then." Nessa pops up from her chair. "Let's do your tarot cards. That should focus things." She walks over to her nightstand and grabs a black satin pouch. "And once we get the personal, we can transform it into the universal." She dangles the pouch in the air and grins. "Are you ready for me to probe your inner-most psychic secrets, Sean?"

Suddenly I'm very aware of the closed door, the candles, the incense, and Nessa's low-cut shirt. Oh, God. What have I gotten myself into?

CHAPTER TWENTY-NINE

THE SIXTH SENSE

GRAB THAT CHAIR and bring it over here." Nessa lays a square of purple velvet on her desk and slides the tarot cards and a small clear crystal from their pouch.

I drag the antique wooden throne from the corner of the room and take a seat beside her.

"Come on, now, don't be scared." Nessa reaches over and pulls my chair really close to hers. I shift my legs to keep our knees from touching. "I don't bite." She grins. "Unless you want me to."

"Um . . . I . . ." My eyes dart around, trying to look at anything but her on-display dirigibles.

"Okay, now." She takes my left hand and places the tarot deck in my palm. "Hold the cards and clear your mind. Try not to think of anything. Just breathe and let your thoughts float away. We want the tarot to reveal what you need to know. When you're ready, cut the deck three times, then place the cards at the bottom of the square here." She taps the velvet at the bottom edge opposite the crystal. "Any questions?"

"No," I squeak.

The cards are slippery and a little clumsy in my hands. They're bigger than regular playing cards. And there are more of them. The backs are black with a framed gold weave pattern all around and a squiggly ruby-red sunburst at the center. Kind of mesmerizing, in a way.

I have to say I'm a little nervous. Most people don't believe in this kind of stuff. But I believe in pretty much everything. Ghosts, UFOs, alien abductions, psychic abilities, curses, Bigfeet, the Bermuda Triangle, the Loch Ness monster. You name it. Coop makes fun of me all the time. Says I'm way too gullible. But I don't care. There are too many strange things in the world to discount it all.

I take a deep breath and close my eyes. Try to clear my mind, to let all of my thoughts and feelings drift off. Which is harder than you might imagine. Especially when there are very specific thoughts that are insisting on your attention—like Nessa's plunging neckline. Or the bejeweled cross that's bobbing ever so gently between her breasts.

My eyes fly open. "I can't do it. I can't stop thinking."

Nessa smiles, her dark lips full and glistening. "You don't have to stop thinking. Just don't focus on any one thing. That's all."

"Yeah, I can't do that either." I squeeze my legs together, my Stormtrooper starting to stand at attention. All of a sudden I feel guilty. Like I'm cheating on Leyna or something. Which is ridiculous because we're not even dating yet.

Nessa reaches over and places her warm hands over mine. And that doesn't help matters.

At all.

"It's okay," she says. "The cards will tell us what the cards want to tell us. Just cut them three times and put them on the desk."

My eyes are drawn to Nessa's breast-indicating cross like a magnet. I've been trying so hard *not* to think about this very thing that it's now all I can think about. And I realize too late that I'm staring. Staring at her boobs. Drawn to them like Gollum toward the One Ring.

I blink hard and point at the necklace to try and salvage this one. "That's pretty," I say dumbly. "I didn't know you were religious."

Nessa looks down and takes hold of the pendant. "You like it? It isn't a Christian cross. It's a way older symbol than that. I wear it to remind me that we are constantly at crossroads in our lives. And that you are always being asked to make choices."

"Wow," I say. "Coolish."

"Maybe that's why you're attracted to it," Nessa says, her expression totally open and sincere. "Why your eyes were drawn to it. Maybe you're at a crossroads and you have to make a decision."

I shift uncomfortably in my seat. "Uh, yeah, could be, I guess."

"Well. Let's find out, shall we?" Nessa gestures at the tarot cards in my hands.

"Sure. Okay." I cut the cards three times, feeling a little helium headed and jangly inside. "But then we should really get to work. We're starting to film next week, and I need to have—"

"This'll only take a few minutes," Nessa says. "Once we discover what you're struggling with in your own life, we can weave that theme into the movie. It'll make the whole thing more meaningful. Trust me." She closes her eyes and hovers her hands over the deck. "We'll do a simple three-card spread. First position will tell us what the situation is. Second position will inform us of the problem. And the third card will explain the solution." Eyes still closed, Nessa deals out three cards and places them facedown in a row. Then she opens her eyes and smiles. "And here we go."

It's bizarre, but just looking at those three cards lying there on that purple velvet, the candlelight flickering and dancing over them, makes me feel a little nauseous. It's like when I go to the doctor and she tells me she's going to take blood and I get an all-over-body queasiness.

"I don't feel so good."

"Just relax and breathe into it. It's normal to resist self-discovery, Sean. Don't worry. It'll pass. Okay, now. The situation is . . ." Nessa reaches out and turns over the first card. "The Ace of Wands. Oh, that's a powerful one. If I remember correctly."

I stare at the picture of a hand bursting out of the earth and holding a flaming wand topped with glowing jewels. It certainly *looks* powerful. "What's it mean?"

"Let's see." Nessa opens her desk drawer and takes out a *Tarot for Newbies* book. She flips through the pages and finds what she's looking for. "Here we are. 'Beginnings. A moment of great opportunity. A time for action. For decision. A new way of life. Transition.'" She looks up from the book. "Does that make any sense to you? Do you feel like something new is coming into your life? Something that maybe you're afraid to fully embrace? Or to take action on?"

The flipping TV channels again: baby, movie, Cathy's room, Evelyn. Leyna. Cleavage. "There are lots of new things in my life right now. Can you be more specific?"

"Hold on." Nessa flips the page and runs her finger down it. "Aha, okay. 'The Ace of Wands is filled with active *male* energy.'" She looks at me knowingly, then returns her gaze to the book. "It's associated with 'procreation and the seed of life.'" Nessa raises her eyebrows. "What do you think *that* could be referring to?"

Masturbation. Cleavage. Oh, God. My upper lip starts to sweat. "I don't know. My mom's pregnancy, maybe?"

"Really?" Nessa scrunches up her face skeptically. "Are you sure?"

Don't look at her boobs. Don't look at her boobs. "Could be."

"Does that feel right to you? Do you have conflicting feelings about that?"

"No. I mean, yes. Sort of. I think so. I don't know. Sometimes. Yes."

"Orrrr"—Nessa points to something else in the book—"it also could have to do with relationships. *New* relationships. Perhaps something different for you. One you might be resisting. Something recent. Or something that might be just around the corner. Are you conflicted or concerned about your relationships at the moment?"

I cast my eyes around her room for something else to focus on. There, on the wall! A dagger! Think of daggers. And weapons. And armor. Bows and arrows. Staffs. Helmets. Chest plates. No. No. Not chest plates! Back to daggers! Just daggers!

"That card could mean anything, Nessa. I don't think this is really helping. Maybe we should just get back to—"

"Ah." Nessa holds up her hand. "We've only looked at one card. The other two should clarify things." She flips the center card over. The head of a blindfolded woman floats over an ocean with two broadswords crossed beneath her. Weapons. Yes. Thank goodness.

"The problem: Two of Swords." Nessa thumbs through her book. "Okay, now. The Two of Swords. It means a stalemate situation. A conflict between what your heart wants and what your brain is telling you. Between female energy and *male* energy. This is your problem. You find yourself paralyzed and unable to act. Even though your situation"—Nessa taps the first card—"demands that you take action on a new opportunity." She lowers her tarot guide. "Isn't that interesting? Are you finding yourself stuck right now? Like you can't make up your mind about something? Or *someone*?"

But I have made up my mind. Leyna. I like Leyna. So what if my divining rod seems to say otherwise? A guy can't help what happens to his body around a pretty, half-naked girl. "No, I'm not feeling stuck," I say. Then I remember Evelyn. Ew. Talk about salt on a slug. "Well, I guess *maybe*..."

Nessa smiles sympathetically. "I thought as much. Unfortunately, this card cannot say how long the problem will last. Or which side will win. Female or male. Heart or brain." She places the book aside and gazes at me. "So tell me, Sean, what's your mind saying that your heart doesn't agree with?"

It's not my mind I'm worried about. "Look, I don't think this is really helping," I say again. "Can we stop, please?"

"Come on, now. Don't turn away. What comes to mind?"

"Nothing," I lie. "Nothing comes to mind."

The disappointed-teacher frown again. "Okay. You don't have to tell me. That's fine. But let's at least take a look at the solution." Nessa flips the last card over, revealing . . . *Death.*

A Grim Reaper wearing purple robes sits on top of a large skull. In the background, a single white rose sprouts from the scorched landscape.

"Great," I say. Whatever this card is referring to—my horny thoughts about Nessa, my love for Leyna, my desperate desire to break things off with Evelyn—it can't be good.

"Don't worry," Nessa cautions. "This card rarely means an actual physical death." She quickly searches for the page in her guide for an explanation. "Except when it *does.* All right. Here we are. Death. You are facing a major change in your life, Sean. But you'll have to let go of your old self first. And it might be very challenging. Even painful. A tearing away. But"—she turns the page—"if you manage to get past all of this and allow the end to come, however horribly agonizing and excruciating it might be, there is a new and better you waiting on the other side."

I gulp. "It actually says that—'agonizing and excruciating'?"

"It's a rebirth, Sean." Nessa snaps the tarot guide shut and smiles. "*Your* rebirth. And that's never easy. But it's your path right now. And *that's* what you want your movie to be about: death and rebirth. The world is being overrun by lifeless, soulless creatures that must be defeated so that a new and better world can rise from the ashes. It all makes perfect sense." She leans forward, giving me an even closer look down her shirt. Sweet mother of Thor. "Don't you see?"

My eyes bounce between her amazing cleavage and the Grim Reaper. Boobs or death? Boobs or death? What'll it be, Seanie boy?

"Can we . . . ? Can we get back to the screenplay now?"

Nessa smiles. "Sure, Sean. Now that we know what it is we're writing about, there's nothing standing in our way. Is there?"

I do my best to smile, but the specter of the Grim Reaper looms large.

CHAPTER THIRTY

DON'T LOOK NOW

WE'RE NEXT!" LEYNA CALLS OUT, taking my hand and pulling me up to the front of the room.

"All right." Mr. Nestman looks at his Mickey Mouse watch. "But you guys are the last ones. I've got a commercial audition at eleven thirty, which means I need to be out that door the second the bell rings. The Discount Meat Warehouse waits for no one."

Ever since the auditions last week, Leyna has wanted to partner up with me on almost every exercise we do in Drama. And since she's one of Mr. Nestman's star students, I've had to embarrass myself in front of the entire class on an almost daily basis.

Leyna plucks the black blindfold off Mr. Nestman's desk. "You'll be the blind man, okay? And I'll lead."

"Sure," I say.

If this were anyone but Leyna, I would be making every excuse in the book to beg off. But I am her devoted

Jedi, and I would battle the entire evil Empire for her. Besides, I did betray her honor with Nessa—if only in my mind—and so I feel like I need to make amends.

I take a glance at the obstacles—chairs, tables, traffic cones, broomsticks, boxes—that have been laid out around the room. Of course, they'll all be moved around once I'm blindfolded, but still, it's good to have a general idea of the sizes and shapes of things.

Leyna is going to have to try and guide me safely through the course with only the tips of her ten fingers touching the tips of mine. Mr. Nestman has offered a prize—a ten-dollar gift card to DeLuca's Coffee Corner—to the first team that can successfully navigate the entire path without touching a single object. Five teams have tried so far and only one of them—the surprising tandem of Douchebag Dan and Voluptuous Victoria—has made it even halfway through.

"We can do this," Leyna says, drawing me in with her intense gaze. "But you have to trust me. Just focus on how my hands are moving. Forget everything else. Can you do that?"

I nod.

"Good," she says, gently sliding the blindfold over my eyes. And then I feel her warm breath on me as she whispers in my right ear. "Use the Force, Sean."

Oh, my God. A Star Wars reference. From Princess Leyna. Forget tarot—this is a *real* sign.

I breathe deep to try and calm the nervous flutter in

my lungs. There's a wonderful toasted-almondy-sweet-honey scent coming off of Leyna. It's subtle and delicious and intoxicating and I find myself teetering toward her. It takes all of my willpower not to bury my nose in the nape of Leyna's neck and fill up on her wonderful smell.

It's not until I hear the scraping and shuffling of the obstacles being moved around the room that I'm startled from my scent-induced trance. I need to focus here. Leyna seems so sure that we can do this, and I really want to do well for her. I can already picture her excitedly jumping up and down. Giving me a victory embrace. Maybe even a congratulatory kiss as we're caught up in the moment.

I can sense Leyna moving toward me even before she's there. I hold up my hands and feel her tenderly pressing her fingertips into the soft pads of mine.

Oh, jeez. That's nice. That's *really* nice. Her touch is so light and tingly. Like she's emitting these minuscule sparks. She lightly swirls her fingers against mine, waking up every last nerve in my fingertips.

Holy moly. That's crazy. My head starts to spin. My breath catches in my throat and . . .

Whoa, Nelly!

Easy, boy. I do *not* need that response right now.

I shift my weight and start imagining Klaus, our one-hundred-fifty-pound Rottweiler, squatting and squeezing off a ginormous mound of duke. Me having to bag that monster. The soft squishy warmth of it in my fist. The heft of it in my palm.

And the foul beefy stench of it wafting up to my nostrils.

Gugg. I nearly make myself yak. But at least it does the trick.

"You've got three minutes," I hear Mr. Nestman call out. "Starting . . . now!"

Leyna begins to pull away ever so slightly. I slide my feet along the floor toward her, trying not to break the connection between us. It's such a bizarre feeling having to put your total trust in someone like this, but with Leyna it feels perfectly natural. I bet she really *was* a great Helen Keller.

She leads me this way and that, raising her hands in the air when she wants me to step over something, closing her fingers when she wants me to move toward her, spreading them out when she needs me to back away. I don't know how I figured out her silent sign language, but it seems to be working, because I haven't knocked into any of the objects yet.

And then, of course, there's my secret weapon. My nose. I'm following the scent of Leyna's honey-nut aroma as much as anything else. I'm still not sure if it's a subtle perfume or her lip balm or just her natural scent, but it's attracting me like a hummingbird to nectar.

"One minute!" Mr. Nestman shouts.

Leyna guides me to the left, and I hear the entire class gasp. Uh-oh. Must have just missed something. Leyna presses on my fingers to stop me from moving forward.

She has me step a little to the right and then we're moving forward again.

I take a few more steps this way and another turn to the left, and then I hear Leyna scream with joy just as the class breaks into whoops and cheers.

"We did it!" She whips my blindfold off and gives me a big hug. It. Feels. *Amazing*. "Oh, my God! You're such a good follower! It's like you were inside my head, listening to everything I was thinking."

"Congratulations." Mr. Nestman claps loudly, and Leyna pulls away.

I instantly miss her. Her warmth stolen from me. Like someone's just opened the door to Alaska.

Mr. Nestman takes his well-worn brown leather wallet from his back pocket, plucks a DeLuca's gift card out, and hands it to Leyna. "Don't spend it all in one place. Well, actually, scratch that. You *have* to spend it all in one place. Enjoy." He turns to me. "So, how's the casting come along? Have we made any decisions yet?"

"Oh, um . . ." I glance over at the clock, praying for the bell to save me. "Not just yet. We're still sorting it out. Going through all the tapes, you know. By next Monday for sure."

Mr. Nestman smiles and nods. "Well, don't give me *too* big a part. Third or fourth lead should be fine. I want to keep myself available to help with the directing and rewrites. But don't take too long. I am a professional actor, and I do have other irons in the fire."

"Yeah. Okay. We'll keep that in mind."

"Excellent." He claps me on the shoulder. "Just let me know when you have some scenes you'd like to workshop in class and I'll make it happen."

And on that, the bell rings, sending everyone scrambling for their shoes.

I turn back to Leyna, who waves our DeLuca's gift card at me.

"Yay!" she squeals. "Are you free tomorrow? We should totally go to the mall and get a mocha. Enjoy the spoils of our victory. And maybe talk about your movie? What do you say? Is it a date?"

"Yeah. Absolutely. Definitely." The affirmative words tumble out of my mouth like wash from an overflowing dryer. A date with Leyna? Are you kidding? I'd stand up Slave Leia herself if it meant going on a date with Princess Leyna.

"Great," she says. "How about four o'clock? Does that work for you?"

"Yes, it does. Four o'clock tomorrow works for me. It does. Yes." Jesus, I sound like someone who's been kicked in the head by a horse.

"Awesome," Leyna says. "Well, see you there." She glances over her shoulder as she goes, flashing me a melt-my-heart smile just before she pushes through the door that leads out to the courtyard.

I'm grinning so big that my cheeks hurt. I feel like

Jigglypuff leveled up with high happiness and Aprijuice. Man alive, things could not be any sweeter.

"Hello, *Sean*. Are you about ready to go?" *Bzzz!* Game over. I'd know that strained, nasal, disapproving voice anywhere. Evelyn.

I turn around to see her standing stiffly, strangling her books to her chest, a pinched look on her face like someone just forced her to swallow a mouthful of sour milk. Oh, crap. This is *not* going to be pleasant.

CHAPTER THIRTY-ONE

HELLRAISER

I *KNEW* I SHOULD HAVE switched into Drama," Evelyn says, shaking her head violently as we walk down the hallway. "I'm so stupid. I should have trusted my instincts." If her textbooks had lungs, they'd be gasping for air.

"What are you talking about?" I say, calling on all of my drama skills to try to sound completely ignorant.

Evelyn stops dead in her tracks and turns on me. "You *know* what I'm talking about. Miss Hotsy-Totsy you were chatting with. Don't think I don't recognize her. She was that terrible actress at the auditions. What's she trying to do? Seduce you so she can glom on to our movie?"

"What? No. I mean, maybe she auditioned, I don't remember. A lot of kids in Drama did, but . . . We just did an acting exercise together. That's what we were discussing—"

"*I'm* leading lady, mister." She jabs me in the chest with her finger. "Don't you forget it. You aren't even filming this movie without me and my video camera."

"Okay, just calm down, Ev—"

"Who the heck does she think she is, anyway? Looking at you like that. I'm gonna scratch her eyes out so she can never ogle someone else's boyfriend like that ever again."

"She wasn't"—my mouth has gone cottony, making it hard to get my words out—"ogling anybody."

"Oh, right." Evelyn juts her chin out, her eyes narrowing to slits. "Tell me you didn't see her slowly unzipping your pants with her gaze."

I blink. "No, I did not see that."

"What's her name? I'm gonna have Nick do some digging. Tail her a bit. See what kind of home wrecker she is."

I take a deep breath to try and bring my heart rate back from the stratosphere. "Don't you think maybe you're overreacting a bit?"

"Overreacting?" Evelyn grabs my arm and glares at me, a furious purple vein pulsing in her forehead. "What am I supposed to do? Sit by and watch as she steals you away?" She gets right up in my grill, releasing her Swiss-cheesy smell like an angered skunk. "Should I just let her snatch the love of my life away? I don't *think* so."

Love of her life? My junk shrivels. "She's not snatching anything. We were just talking. That's all. Just like I talk to people every day. Girls. Guys. Teachers. It means nothing. Less than nothing, even."

Evelyn glances away, biting her lower lip. Then she looks back at me, her eyes starting to fill up. "Do you swear?"

"Yes. Absolutely. Totally."

"On your"—her gaze falls to my crotch—"'down there'?"

I blink hard. "I'm sorry, what?"

"Do you swear on your 'down there'? It's the only way I'll know if you're telling the truth. No guy wants his . . . thingamabob to stop working."

She can't be serious.

Oh, but I can see she's as serious as a .44 Magnum pointed at my head. If she wanted me to swear on anything else—my arm, my nose, my brain—I'd just go ahead and do it. No question. But some things you don't want to screw with. Just in case anyone is listening.

But then—as if God knows this chick is bonkers and wants to throw me a life preserver—a memory pops into my head.

"Yes," I say, trying to keep my expression earnest. "I swear. On my . . . thingamabob." In my mind I am picturing the thingamabob I made in kindergarten out of clay, rocks, twigs, and pipe cleaners. The very thingamabob that my mother still has on top of one of our bookcases. It's a thingamabob that I'm sure would be more than happy to take a bullet for me.

"Oh, snuggy bear! I'm so relieved!" Evelyn crumples into my arms and breaks into heaving sobs, trembling and snuffling against me. It's a more dramatic personality switch than anything I've seen in drama class. "I'm so sorry. I totally schmucked up. Can you ever forgive me?"

I pat her back tentatively, as the clammy warmth of her snot and tears soaks through my shirt. "It's fine. There's nothing to forgive."

Evelyn drags her nose across my shoulder, then lifts her head to look at me. "Really?"

I force myself to hold her rheumy red-eyed gaze. "Of course. It was an honest mistake. No big deal."

She leans in and administers one of her patented Miss Universe death-grip hugs. "You are the greatest boyfriend *ever*. I don't deserve you." She cranes her head back and sniffs up the gooey gelatinous drip that hangs precariously from her nostril. All I can think is, *Surely I don't deserve* this. "I am *never* going to let you go," she adds, and smiles big, a large mucusy saliva bubble inflating on her teeth.

I force a laugh. "That's . . . great."

Evelyn's mouth bubble pops, sending a mist of spittle onto my cheek.

"I want to make it up to you," she says. "For being a jealous Nelly. Seriously."

I casually lift my hand to my face to wipe away the wet. "That's really okay. There's nothing to make up for."

She grabs my forearms, cutting off the circulation to

my hands. "I insist," Evelyn demands, her voice deadly serious. "I won't feel better until you let me do something nice for you."

I can't imagine what Evelyn's idea of being nice entails. Surprising me with a ticket to go run with the bulls? Signing us up for couples cliff diving? Or a tour of Arkham Asylum?

Just then the late bell rings, which means if I'm not in math class in thirty seconds Mrs. Buckeen is going to make me sit in the Throne of Shame at the front of the room.

"Sure," I blurt. "Okay."

"Thank you!" Evelyn shrieks, bouncing up and down. "Thank you, thank you, thank you. You will *not* regret this."

But, of course, I already do.

"I've got a great idea." She shakes my arms like she's trying to straighten out a particularly wrinkled bedspread. "Let's go to the mall tomorrow afternoon. You and me. We can pick out your Valentine's Day present. I want to get you something really special."

The mall. That doesn't sound so bad. Better than Arkham Asylum, anyway. "All right," I say. "The mall. Tomorrow. Let's do it."

"Oh, you're the bestest, snuggle bunny." Evelyn grabs my head and practically gives me a tonsillectomy with her tongue before pulling away with a sloppy *smack.*

"Four o'clock by the H&M," she says. "And don't be late! Toodle-oo, kangaroo."

Then she's gone and I can finally breathe again.

I turn and hurry down the hall, shaking off the ickiness that lingers.

It's not until I've taken the two flights of stairs down to the math wing—feeling almost normal again—that I am punched in the face with the realization of how completely and royally I've just screwed myself.

CHAPTER THIRTY-TWO

WRONG TURN

Just tell Evelyn you forgot that you had a doctor's appointment," Matt offers, unwrapping his tuna sandwich, the fishy smell wafting through the Hole—our secret storage-room hideout in the basement of the school—where me, Matt, and Coop have gathered for an emergency meeting. "Then you'll be free to meet up with this Leyna girl."

I shake my head. "Evelyn's already super suspicious. Forget it. I have to find Leyna and cancel. I just wish I had her number so I could just text her."

Coop tsk-tsks, like he's disappointed in me. "I don't understand why you don't just keep your dates with both babes. You can shuttle back and forth between them. One at the coffee shop, the other at the food court. How dope would that be? You'll be the super-stud of the Rockville Mall."

"Yeah, *right*. Like that doesn't have disaster written all over it." I take a bite of my baloney and cheese on Wonder bread. "I'm just going to have to wait until after we finish the movie, dump Evelyn, and ask Leyna out then."

Coop screws up half his face. "That is complete lame sauce, dawg. This kind of sweet sitch only comes around once in a lifetime. You're the man with the gland, dude. Two babes wanting to paw you to pieces? You owe it to your fellow brethren to make this happen." Coop pulls a squashed Sally Gregg Diet Meal Bar from his back pocket and starts to unwrap it. "Besides, boss. You blow this girl off now, and she's gonna take it as disinterest. She'll go scouting for another dude, stat. Trust me."

"I am *not* going on two dates with two girls at the same time," I protest. "Even if I could pull it off—which I *can't*—it wouldn't be fair to either one of them."

"Don't be such a yam bag," Coop says. "It's their own fault. Babes always want what they can't have."

Matt raises one eyebrow skeptically. "What the hell are you talking about?"

"Mattie, my son. Must I always have to be your guide to all things vagina? It's how the female brain is hard-wired. When a guy isn't hooked up with anyone, he's radioactive. Girls are all, 'Eek, stay away from me.' But when same-said dude is unavail, every girl wants him. It's Babeology 101."

Matt turns to me. "Just ignore him. He's full of shit."

Coop shrugs and takes a bite of his diet bar. "Who're you going to listen to? Valerie's bitch or the man with subscriptions to *Maxim* and *FHM*? I'm telling you, dawg, the whole thing's biochem. It's the scent you're giving off. Before it was *eau de* desperation. Which is why you attracted Her Nuttiness to begin with. But once you were bound and tied, you started emanating fondle-me phero-mones." He pulls a second flattened diet bar—this one a Sumptuous S'more Snack—from his other back pocket. "Look, this isn't a big ish, dawg. You can have your steak and eat it too. It's a simple matter of time-and-place management."

"No way." Matt shakes his head. "Don't listen to him, Sean. You don't want to risk your life on one of Coop's whacked-out plans. Trust me on this one. I almost lost a perfectly good appendix thanks to him."

"Matt's right," I say, looking at Coop. "I don't want any part of it. Maybe *you* could pull off going on two dates at once, but I'm not you."

"You're not me, that's very true." Coop stands and starts to pace. "But what if you had *me* backing you up? That would almost be as good as being me. Not only that, what if you had Matt backing me up backing you up? That's double backage, dude. It's like wearing two con-doms at once. Protection on top of protection. You think you could pull it off then?"

Matt laughs. "Didn't you learn anything from your safe-sex presentation with Helen?"

Coop waves this away. "Whaddya say, Sean-o? Are you ready to step into the big leagues?"

"I don't understand how this would be any better than going it alone," I say suspiciously. "What, exactly, are you and Matt going to do to make this possible?"

"We'll be the ultimate wingmen," Coop explains. "Here's the deal. We'll all go a little early and meet up with Leyna at DeLuca's first. Just so she knows you didn't bail. Then you and Matt excuse yourselves. For whatever. Matt can pretend to get a text from the lost and found saying they've located Sean's phone or something. Then you both head over to H&M to greet Evelyn while I stick around the coffee shop and occupy hottie. After a few minutes, you excuse yourself from Evelyn and Matt'll run some interference with her for a while. Easy."

"Whoa, whoa, whoa," Matt says. "Why do *I* have to deal with Wacky Slacks?"

"Sorry, dawg." Coop shrugs. "You're the only one for the job. You're levelheaded and no-nonsense. I swear, the cops should hire you to talk jumpers down from buildings."

"Look," I interject. "I appreciate the offer. Really. But I don't think I'm up to it."

"Oh, come on," Coop says, gesturing with his crumbling snack bar. "You can't afford *not* to do this. If you ditch Leyna, that will be that. You don't get second chances with a honeypot like her."

"How would you know?" I ask. "You met her for, like, five minutes at the auditions."

"That's right, and I pegged her right away. She's the insecure hottie. If a guy rebuffs her, then it's cold-shoulder time. Look, you already said you can't get out of going to the mall with Evelyn. My way keeps everyone happy. Including *Mr.* Happy." He waggles his eyebrows at me. "What do you say?"

This is a really bad idea. I know this. And yet the thought of letting Leyna slip through my fingers fills me with dread. I take a deep head-clearing sniff of my palm.

Coop sits down next to me on the squeaky bench and rests a hand on my back. "It's gonna be a piece of pie, boss. Trust me. You won't even have to break a sweat. You're in capable hands. Me and Matt will take care of everything."

☛ CHAPTER THIRTY-THREE ☚

NEAR DARK

EXT. STREET — NIGHT

Jack and Stacy are being chased by a pack of hairy blood-drooling humanzees. They race up to an old house and BANG ON THE DOOR.

> JACK
>
> Open up! Help! Please!

> STACY
>
> Jack! Hurry! They're going to get us!

Jack pounds on the door again, but nobody answers. He looks back to see the humanzees gaining ground. He pulls a Swiss Army Knife from his pants pocket and quickly unlocks the door.

INT. HOUSE — NIGHT

Jack and Stacy stumble into the house and slam the door behind them. Jack slides the dead bolt shut. The two of them start moving furniture in front of the door and windows.

The humanzees begin beating on the doors and windows. Stacy starts to freak out.

> STACY
>
> They're going to get in, Jack! They're banging on the door! What are we going to do? They're going to infect us. I don't want to be a vampire-zombie-monkey like all those other people! Please don't let them make me one!

Jack grabs Stacy by the shoulders and plants a deep, hard kiss on her.

> JACK
>
> I won't let that happen, Stacy. I promise. Trust me. Do you trust me?

> STACY
>
> Yes. I trust you, Jack.

Stacy leans in and kisses Jack heavily and passionately. They are interrupted by the SOUND OF BREAKING GLASS.

A humanzee's arm reaches in the broken window and unlatches the lock.

Stacy SCREAMS. Jack grabs Stacy's hand.

Come on. Let's go. Follow me.

Jack and Stacy head for the stairs just as the humanzees start climbing in the window.

Coop finishes reading the last line out loud, then looks up from the screenplay pages, a big grin on his face. "This is totally brill, dawg," he says, hopping up on my bed. "I am über-impressed. It just keeps getting better and better. Seriously."

"I agree." Matt nods. "I think you've found a hidden talent, Sean."

We've gathered at my house prior to my double date at the mall. If I had any balls, I'd just bail. Call the whole thing off and save myself the misery. Instead I'm just trying to pretend it'll all go away. Which is why I've given the guys the latest script pages. So we can talk about the movie instead of going over Coop's way-too-complicated game plan.

"There's one thing about the script that keeps bugging me, though," Coop says. "The main characters' names. I think we need to change them before we start the real filming."

"You don't like Jack and Stacy?" I ask.

Coop wrinkles up his nose. "They don't grab me by the meat pouch—know what I'm saying? We should make something up. Something cool and video-game-esque.

What about—and maybe this isn't it—but what do you think of"—he marquees his hands—"Rogart and Nashira?"

"Really?" I say, looking over at Matt, who's sitting on the floor, petting my ferret. "I don't know. I kind of like Jack and Stacy."

Coop gives a dismissive wave. "You gotta trust me on this one. We need heroic names. Jack makes me think of jacking off."

Matt laughs. "Everything makes you think of jacking off."

"True," Coop says. "But that's not the ish. Jack-off is not the guy you picture when you think about the dude who's going to save the world from a zombie-vampire-chimpanzee apocalypse. Let's call him Rogart instead. And let's make him less of a pussy, okay? Ya gotta give dude some balls. Right now he's just like a limp schween."

I look down at the script. "He's got some balls. He's just—"

"A wimp. But that's okay. It's an easy fix. You'll work on it. And then there's Stacy. We can't use that name because it rhymes with *lazy.*"

"No, it doesn't," I say.

"Close enough. It's what came to *my* mind and if I thought of it other people will too. We want this girl to be badass. Like Lara Croft or Selene from *Underworld.* Let's call her Nashira Axe. Rogart Crush and Nashira

Axe. Those are names that will kick zombie ass and also look good on T-shirts, collector cups, and lunch boxes. What do you say?"

To be honest, Coop's names sound kind of cheesy to me. But he does know how to sell things to people, so I cave. "Sure, okay, I guess."

"Great." Coop waves the script pages. "Everything else is spectac." He flashes a quick smile, then looks all serious again. "I mean, yeah, there's a thing here or there we can tweak as we're shooting, but nothing major." He turns to Matt. "What about you? Anything you don't think works?"

"I don't know," Matt says, the ferret curled up and sleeping on his leg. "It seems like you added a lot of kissing. Jack and Stacy—"

"Rogart and Nashira," Coop corrects him.

"Right. Whatever." Matt shakes his head. "They seem to kiss, like, two or three times in every scene. It just feels a little excessive."

"Yes." Coop points at me. "The kissing. I wanted to talk to you about that too."

My neck and ears suddenly get hot. Sure, maybe I added a bit more making out after Leyna auditioned—fantasizing as I wrote that it was me and her playing the leads, even though I had no clue how I'd make that happen—but I didn't realize it would seem so obvious.

"I don't know," I say. "I just . . . That's their relationship, I guess. It's how Jack—I mean Rogart—calms

Nashira down. And . . . they're not sure how much longer they have to live and stuff. They're taking advantage of what little time they have."

"Hey, I'm not complaining, dude," Coop says. "I'm all about sexing this puppy up as much as possible. I'm just thinking you might want to make it part of the plot. Like, okay, what about this? What if Rogart has zombie antidote in his glands—I don't know, maybe he got a little of the virus in him in a fight with one of the human-zees and it acted like a flu vaccination or something—doesn't really matter, however you do it—and the only way to administer this vaccine or antidote or whatever is by Frenching Nashira all the time. Or, you know, maybe later on, his saliva isn't strong enough and he has to give her the antidote intravaginally." He waggles his eyebrows. "Which actually addresses another problem I had with the script. I wasn't going to bring it up, but there seems to be a distinct lack of gratuitous nudity. We need to show major boobalas if we want to bag the serious coin. You should think about having Nashira take a bath at some point, or maybe she gets her shirt torn off by one of the monsters. Or, you know, she could do a sexy webcam show before the outbreak. Things like that."

My mind flashes to an image of Leyna taking off her clothes in front of my friends and I get a serious pang of jealousy. I need to divert this train before it heads farther down that track.

"I don't think we have to stoop to that level just to

sell tickets," I say. "I mean . . . I don't know . . . As the writer of this film, I just don't see how nudity adds to the story. I don't think it makes it any better."

Coop cracks up. "Are you jockin' my taters, dawg? Everything is made better with nudity. Movies, car washes, skydiving, horseback riding, pizza delivery. I can't think of a single thing that doesn't become infinitely superior when you add nakedness into the mix."

"Football," Matt says.

Coop does a double take. "I'm sorry, what?"

"Football wouldn't be better naked," Matt answers. "Not on TV *or* playing it in Gym."

"Especially flag football," I add. " 'Cause, where are you tuckin' the flags?"

"We're not talking about dudes, dudes. Why would you even go there?"

Matt shrugs. "Because you said everything is better with nudity. And I don't agree."

"Oh, really?" Coop smirks. "Ask some ladies if they wouldn't prefer football if it was a bunch of buff naked dudes flip-flopping around the field. And what if it was guys versus girls in gym class? Now naked doesn't sound so bad anymore, does it?"

I glance at my Death Star clock and see that it's two forty-five. My stomach drops. "It's, um . . . It's . . . time." I try to swallow but my throat is suddenly pasty and dry.

Coop looks at his cell phone. "Oh, shit. It is." He hops off my bed. "Let's rock and roll, dawgs."

I force a smile. "Or, you know, we could just call the whole thing off."

"Forget it," Coop says. "This is going to be the best thing that's ever happened to you. You have my word on that."

CHAPTER THIRTY-FOUR

THE MOST DANGEROUS GAME

A LITTLE OVER AN HOUR LATER, we reach the doors to the Rockville Mall. I stop dead and stare at the HOURS OF OPERATION stenciled there.

"Yeah, I can't do this," I say, my heart vibrating in my chest like a cell phone on steroids. "This is a stupid, stupid idea. Why the hell did I let you talk me into this?"

"Chillax. We've got everything timed out perfectly," Coop assures. "Just stick to the plan, dude."

"I've already forgotten the plan." I'm starting to pit out the underarms of the fancy green button-up I put on especially for Leyna. "All I've got is radio static in my head. I need to end this." I pull my phone from my pocket. "I'm just gonna call DeLuca's and ask them to tell Leyna I got sick. And then I'll text Evelyn the same thing."

"Uh, I think it might be a little late for that," Matt says.

"No, it isn't." I point to the time display on my phone. "It's only three fifty. I've got ten minutes before—"

"Hey there, koala bear!"

I whip around to see Evelyn leaning out of the window of a beat-to-shit matte-black Mustang—with what look like bullet holes in the side—that's parked in the passenger loading area.

Oh, crap.

She heaves open the creaky door and is out of the car and on me like a straitjacket before I know what's happening.

"Look at you!" she squeals, stepping back and yanking open my winter coat. "Love the shirt! God! It's like you get sexier every day."

"You're early," I croak.

Evelyn laughs her hyena laugh. "By, like, ten minutes. But you're early too, cuddle bear! Is that kismet or *what*?"

"Yeah," I say. "Kismet."

Nick, dressed in gray, black, and white urban camo, leans over from the driver's side and waves through the open passenger-side window. "Hey, buddy. How's it hangin'?"

"Uhhhh . . . good?" I say.

"Wish I could stick around and chat, but I've got a hot lead on the old man. Gotta check it out before the trail grows cold. I think I might have hit the jackpot this time."

"Great." I force a smile, remembering the heft of the Glock in my hand.

Nick points at me like the Uncle Sam I WANT YOU poster. "Don't you keep our girl out too late, now, you hear, soldier? Don't want to have to add you to the list of people I'm hunting down." Nick laughs like this is hysterical.

"I won't," I say. "Keep her out late, I mean. You don't have to . . . add me to your list . . . for hunting." It's like Niagara Falls in my armpits now.

"Good to hear. You keep it real, now." He gives me a wave, then ducks back to the driver's seat. The tires screech and smoke as he floors the gas.

Suddenly the car backfires and I hit the pavement, my jangled nerves reacting to the report.

"Just . . . testing my reflexes," I say, slowly peeling myself off the ground and wiping the pebbles from my palms.

Evelyn laughs as she watches the Mustang go. "Nick's rigged the car to do that on purpose. He thinks it's funny."

"Yeah, hilarious," I say, my heart still lodged in my throat.

Evelyn turns to me, beaming. Then she looks over at Coop and Matt as if she's only just noticed them. Her expression goes from thrilled to pissed in point-zero-five seconds. "Oh. I didn't know we were having company."

"They were just . . ." My stomach flip-flops. "I mean, we were just—"

"Matt's been jonesin' for a Wetzel's Pretzel all week," Coop says, throwing his arm around Matt. "He practically wetzels himself over the Sinful Cinnamon. Isn't that right, Mattie?"

"Yeah." Matt narrows his eyes at Coop. "I'm getting all moist thinking about where I'm going to shove that pretzel once I get my hands on it."

"Anyway," Coop says, "Sean-o told us he was meeting you at the mall and we thought we'd tag along. I mean, if that's chill."

"*Actually*"—Evelyn squints up her left eye in a most unattractive way—"if you wouldn't mind, this is sort of a date. I acted like a real jerksicle yesterday, and I want to make it up to Sean."

"Well, you know what they say." Coop waggles his eyebrows. "Nothing screams 'I'm sorry' quite like a dressing-room blow—"

"Whoa-kaaaay!" I grab the door and yank it open. "We better get inside before, you know, it starts to, uh, snow."

"Or *something*," Matt adds under his breath.

The four of us enter the stale warmth of the mall. The nearby food court swaddles us in its Subway-sandwich-meets-sweet-and-sour-pork smell.

"Seriously," Evelyn says as we take a left toward Sears, "I was really hoping it could just be Sean and me."

Coop smacks this idea out of the air. "Don't sweat it. You won't even notice us. We'll be like ghosts. Besides, Matt'll probably want to ditch you guys once we find the Body Shop. He's run out of his Jolly Orange Body Butter, and he can't live a day without it."

"You think you're dissing me," Matt says, "but the fact that you even know what they sell at the Body Shop just shows what a girl you are."

"*Au contraire, mon frère,*" Coop says. "The only reason I know the stuff exists is because you won't shut your yap about it. How it smoothes out your pimply butt skin. How it makes you smell like an Oran-*gyna*. It's pathetic, dude."

"Hey, didn't you want a pretzel, Matt?" Evelyn points to the Wetzel's Pretzels at the far end of the food court. "Maybe you guys could go get one and we could meet up with you later."

I stare at Matt, silently begging him not to bail on me.

"I *do* want one," he says, "but I think I'll get it on the way out. The longer I wait, the more sinful the cinnamon tastes."

Aw, man, I've never loved him more than right now.

Evelyn sighs. She weaves her arm into mine and leans into me as we walk. "Can't you ask them to leave us alone?" she whispers.

"They're my friends," I whisper back. "I don't want to hurt their feelings."

I take a furtive glance at the clock above the mall directory. I've got one minute to somehow ditch Evelyn and get over to DeLuca's to meet up with Leyna.

How the hell am I going to pull *that* one off?

CHAPTER THIRTY-FIVE

THE BIRDS

Anything you want." Evelyn's right hand sweeps out toward the mall like Willy Wonka presenting his scrumdiddlyumptious chocolate room. "My treat. Money's no object."

"Seriously, Evelyn," I say, "this isn't necessary."

"You promised you'd let me do this for you."

"But there's nothing I want."

"You haven't even looked. Come on, let's go in here." Evelyn peels off and goes into Banana Republic.

I turn and glare at Coop. "What now, Einstein?"

"Dude, take a pill." He glances at Evelyn, who's pawing the sweaters on a display table in the store. "We just need to rejig a little. Let me think a minute."

"I don't *have* a minute." My jaw is clenched so tight I feel like my teeth might shatter. "I'm supposed to be at DeLuca's *right now*. How am I supposed to get away?"

"Okay, okay." Coop scrubs his hand over his face. "Matt. You need to keep Evelyn here for, like, twenty minutes while we go to the coffee shop."

Matt's eyes nearly flop from their sockets. "What? How? What am I supposed to say?"

"Tell her Sean wants the gift to be a surprise." Coop grabs my arm and starts pulling me away. "And that you'll help her pick out the perfect thing."

"But . . . What . . . I don't . . ." Matt stammers, his head on a swivel, looking from us to the store and then back to us again. "Don't do this to me!"

"It'll be fine," Coop calls over his shoulder, shoving me toward the nearest exit. "We have complete faith in you. Meet you back here in twenty!"

"I hate you!" Matt calls, defeated.

Coop flashes him a smile just as he yanks me out the door.

"Where are we going?" I say. "DeLuca's is in the mall."

"We're taking the outside route," Coop explains. "Just in case Evelyn decides she wants to come after us. She'll look in nearby stores, not outside."

"Good idea."

Coop grins, a twinkle in his eye. "It's the only kind I have."

We start jogging down the sidewalk. The outside air is crisp and frosty. Tiny puffs of steam escape our lips as we dodge the winter-coat-clad shoppers with their bags and carts.

The perimeter of the mall is hunormous. We run for what seems like forever, passing the Gap, Toys"R" Us, the movie theater, and T. J. O'Halligans before we make the turn around the corner of Wal-Mart. My legs and lungs are burning, and I've actually started perspiring.

I'm so hot that I have to take off my coat and tie it around my waist so that I don't drench my fancy shirt in sweat. The cold air feels good on my body, cooling me down, drying my skin.

We're jogging by a graffiti-tagged dumpster when Coop reaches into his pants pocket and takes out his phone.

"Text from Matt," he says, slowing down to a walk so he can read it. "Evelyn loves the idea of surprising you." He's huffing and puffing and trying to catch his breath. "She's got him imprisoned in the changing room right now trying on a whole whack of shirts." Coop snaps his phone shut and slides it back into his coat pocket. "What'd I tell you? We're golden, dawg."

For the first time, I start to believe that this crazy plan just might work. "How close are we to DeLuca's?" I ask.

"Not sure," he says, starting to jog again. "Let's duck in the next set of doors."

I break into a trot right behind him, my feet lifting

from the pavement in a rhythmic ease. Your Jedi Master is on his way, Princess Leyna!

As we pass the loading docks and round the corner, I see the SOUTH ENTRANCE sign up ahead.

"There," Coop says. "Let's go."

We pick up our pace, making a beeline toward the doors. I can almost make out the writing on the glass when I hear a loud feathery fluttering overhead followed immediately by a heavy, wet, rain-patter sound on the sidewalk all around me.

In the same instant, I feel a splatter of something warm and gloppy on my head.

And shoulders.

And all over my torso.

I skid to a halt, my stunned brain struggling to compute the meaning of the thick gobs of white and purple that spackle the pavement in front of me. It's not until the shitty-sweet smell assaults my nose that I am struck with the full realization of what's just happened.

"Coop!" I shout, holding my drenched arms out to the sides, not wanting to look down at myself.

"Dude," he calls out over his shoulder, "come on! Stop screwing around."

"Oh, God." I stand there stiff as a scarecrow, feeling the wet leaching through my clothes. Trying not to breathe in the thick bird-crappy stench that envelopes me. "We have a problem here!"

Coop whips around. "Would you stop your—? Oh,

Jesus!" He starts walking toward me in slow motion, his horrified expression almost more than I can bear.

"Is it that bad? Please tell me it's not that bad."

He bursts out laughing. "Christ, dawg! What the hell *is* that?"

"It's shit, Coop. A bird shat on me." My splattered clothes feel heavy and clammy against my skin.

"Bird? More like a pterodactyl." Coop snorts. He cups his hand over his nose. "*Fuuuck* me. It reeks!"

"Does it, Coop? Does it really? I hadn't noticed." Tiny globs of guano fly off me as I shake with rage. "We need to wash it off. Like, *now.*"

"Dude, you're head to foot," he says, cracking up. "There's no washing this off."

"But . . . I have to meet Leyna. You said so yourself! If I stand her up, she'll never forgive me."

"Yeah, well, she's not gonna be too pleased if you show up smelling like ostrich anus, either." He busts up once again.

"So then what? What are we gonna do about it? There has to be something. Think. You're the guy with all the plans."

"Dude," Coop says, trying to compose himself. He sniffles and wipes the tears from the corners of his eyes. "I don't think you understand the severity of the sitch here. Not even the Coopster can work the kind of miracle you'd need. I'm sorry, but this mission is over and out."

CHAPTER THIRTY-SIX

SHIVERS

No," I SAY, LOWERING MY ARMS slowly as my muscles quit on me at last. "I refuse to accept that. You got me into this. You need to help figure something out."

"Okay, okay, just hold on a sec. Let me think." Coop studies the heavens as though praying for inspiration. "All right," he says at last. "Take off your clothes."

"What? No. Why?"

"Look, dawg, you wanted a plan. Here is a plan. Your current togs are totally tainted, unsalvageable. I'm gonna pool our resources and get you some new threads. But in the meantime, you need to shuck off the shit-shirt before that bird crap soaks into your skin and completely contaminates you. If that happens, it won't matter what new duds I scrounge up because the stink will leak right through them."

I glance down at myself for the first time, surveying the damage. It's even worse than I thought. My entire shirt, most of my jacket, and even my pants are saturated. But I shake my head. "I don't care. There's no way I'm taking my clothes off out here."

Coop swivels his head. "Look, we'll head back to that dumpster," he says, nodding toward the Wal-Mart. "You can hide behind it till I'm back. It'll be three minutes, tops."

"My hair's completely covered in crap too, so what's it matter if I take off my clothes?"

"It *matters*. We can wash your hair in the bathroom sink. We can't give you a full sponge bath. We're wasting time here, boss. Leyna's not going to wait for you forever. I'd say we've got around fifteen minutes before 'casually late' becomes a big F-you."

"Just go tell her I can't make it. Say I came down with the flu or something."

"Bird flu," Coop says with a laugh. "Sorry." He sobers his expression. "Look, if you really want to blow your only shot with your dream girl, that's fine."

"Isn't there any other—?"

"Dude!" Coop roars. "With every second you bitch and moan, the shit particles are seeping deeper and deeper into your pores."

"Can't we at least go into the mall bathroom so I can hide in a stall?"

"Right. Sure. And risk running into Leyna? Or Evelyn? Or anyone else from our school? Looking like you were just shot from a whale's vagina?" He sweeps his hand up and down. "You really want to take that chance?"

I throw my head back and groan in frustration. "Cripes. Okay. Fine."

We trudge back behind Wal-Mart and duck behind the dumpster.

I unbutton my shirt with the tips of my fingers, careful not to touch the gloppy guano. It really does reek to holy hell. I slip the shirt off and let it slop to the pavement. The cold air stings my bare chest as I reach for my coat, which is balled up on the ground.

Coop steps on it. "No, sir. That's slathered too."

I wrap my arms around my naked shivering torso. "It's cold."

"Tough testicli. Deal with it."

"Give me yours, then."

"Uh, yeah, I don't think so." He runs his hand down the sleeve of his bomber jacket. "This is genuine leatherette, dawg. I just got this bad boy for Christmas. I'm not about to have it contaminated with bird squat. Go huddle in that doorway over there. It'll be warmer."

I glance over at the blue WAL-MART EMPLOYEES ONLY door just a few yards away.

"No way. Someone might drive by and see me. Or come out for a smoke."

"Don't be such a wet tampon. Have you seen a single car drive by? And who the hell's going to take their cigarette break by a dumpster? Get real. You're safe and sound. Besides, I'm only going to be a minute. I'll grab the first thing I see."

"Fine," I say. "But if I freeze to death, you'll be the one who'll have to explain it to my mother."

He sighs loudly. "Okay, you infant. You can have my coat. But not before you remove those beshitted jeans. I don't want you getting any splooge on my brand-new hide."

"Thank you." I gingerly pinch my wallet and phone from my front pockets, then unbutton my jeans and let them drop to my ankles. Finally, I kick them off over my sneakers. "There," I say. "Happy?"

Coop laughs, pointing at my four-leaf-clover boxers. "Those your lucky underpants?"

"And what if they are?"

"How they working out for you?"

"Eat me, okay?"

Coop squats down and pinches up my crappy clothes. "You owe me for this, boss. Big-time." He flings the whole bird-shitty mess into the dumpster, then slips out of his bomber.

I snatch the jacket from him and quickly pull it on, hugging myself to try and get warm.

"All right." Coop thrusts his hand out. "How much cash do you have?"

I open my wallet and pluck out the lone bill that's there.

"Ten bucks?" He grimaces. "For a pair of pants

and a shirt? They don't have a Salvation Army in the mall, dude."

"It's all I brought," I say, through chattering teeth. "Don't you have some money? I can pay you back later."

"Unfortunately I'm a little light right now." He plucks the ten from my fingers. "I'll see how far I can stretch this. Maybe Wal-Mart's having a sale. What's your size? Dwarf?"

"Short jokes? Now?" I crouch down, rubbing my bare legs. "Like I'm not humiliated enough here already?"

"Fine, I'll guesstimate," he says, turning to go.

"Hurry," I say.

"No prob," he calls over his shoulder as he jogs away. "Be back ASAP. You won't even have time to miss me."

I turn and lean my head against the dumpster. I guess if you have to be half-naked in public, this is the place to do it. With nobody around to see you and a nice big dumpster to hide behind.

Five minutes go by. Ten. Twelve. What the hell's taking him so long? I just hope we make it in time to catch Leyna. And that she's not too pissed that I'm so late. Maybe Coop can help me concoct a brilliant excuse— something that makes me seem selfless and maybe even a little heroic. Maybe I was resuscitating a cat that was hit by a car. Or maybe I should just tell her about the birds. She might find it funny. And feel sorry for me. And offer me a consoling, passionate kiss.

I'm so lost in this fantasy that I almost don't hear my phone ping with a text message.

I slip my cell from Coop's jacket and look down, fully expecting to see another update from Matt.

But what I read on the screen is like a wrecking ball to the gut. It's a text from Coop:

n trbl w/ mall cops. srry dawg. cnt get 2 u :(

CHAPTER THIRTY-SEVEN

DRAG ME TO HELL

My HEART NEARLY BURSTS from my chest like an *Alien* fetus. Mall cops? Holy *crap*! He must have tried to jack some clothes, the idiot. Jesus Christ! What the hell am I supposed to do now?

I cup a hand over my nose and start whiffing like mad. Think, Sean, think. I can't go anywhere like this— half-nude, wearing clover boxers and a crap hat. I'll be the laughingstock of Lower Rockville. Forget Leyna. Forget Evelyn. This would be the end of *everything*!

Goddamn it, why do I always listen to Coop? Why do I let him talk me into these things? I should have just canceled with Leyna like I wanted to. Gone to the mall by myself with Evelyn. Maybe even worked up the courage to end things once and for all. Forget what Valerie and Helen said about doing it somewhere private. This totally needs to happen somewhere public, where there are too many witnesses for Evelyn to go all *Exorcist* on me. Somewhere like the Rockville freakin' Mall.

But *noooo.* This was "too much of an opportunity." This was "too good to pass up." This was "every guy's dream." I "owed it to my brethren" to take advantage of the situation.

God*damn* it! Every time. Every single *freakin'* time it's the same with Coop and his lamebrain plans. They *always* end in disaster. And yet he convinces me. Over and over again.

Oh, Christ, what am I going to do? What are my choices here?

And what in God's name is that stink?

I look down at my turd-slicked palms.

Aw, man! Seriously? Did I just run my hands through my crappy hair? Son of a blaster, it's on my face too. I feel it on my face. I wiped the bird shit on my face. How the *hell* did I not notice I was doing that?

"Fuuuuck!" I scream, wiping my hands all over Coop's jacket. I yank the bomber off my body and use it to swab all the guano from my face and hair. "There! How do you like your leatherette now, *buddy*?" I cock my arm back and hurl the soiled jacket into the dumpster. "Screw you, Coop! Screw you and your dumbass plans straight to Hoth!"

A gust of frigid wind snaps me back to sanity. Super. I just threw away the one thing keeping me semiwarm.

Now I'm down to sneakers, socks, and my stupid unlucky boxers. Brilliant. Just brilliant.

I take a deep breath, the chilly air numbing my lungs.

All right. It's okay. I'm fine. I don't need Coop. Or his stupid jacket. I'll just call Matt. Explain the situation. Have him duck away from Evelyn for a few minutes, get me some clothes, and meet me back here. No problem.

I reach for my cell phone. And that's when I realize: My cell phone was in the pocket of Coop's jacket. Right along with my wallet.

Shittidy shit shitting shitter! I can't believe it! Why don't I just take off my boxers and run around the mall with my dingus flopping around and be done with it?

Come on, Sean. Gain control here. I can work this out. I'll just climb into the dumpster and get all the crappy clothes back. Because crappy clothes are better than no clothes. Then I'll call Matt and he'll—

All of sudden I hear the roaring *whoosh* of a big truck pulling around near the loading docks. I quickly duck behind the dumpster. Looks like I'll have to wait it out before I can go on my recovery mission. That's okay. I can hold on for a few more minutes as they dump off whatever cargo they're hauling. I crouch into a little ball, hugging my knees to try and keep warm.

The truck engine gets louder.

And louder.

And louder still, until finally I hear the clunk of

metal on metal and see the dumpster rocking a bit, just before it starts to rise in the air.

Oh, no.

Oh, no, no, no!

The dumpster swings high in the sky and is tipped over, sending the contents — including Coop's jacket, my clothes, my cell phone, and my wallet — rattling and clanking down into the big garbage truck.

And here's me. Completely exposed. Squatting on the ground in my lucky clover boxers, frozen like Han Solo in carbonite.

The only ray of sunshine in this entire shit storm is that the dude operating the truck is too busy rocking out to his iPod to notice me. The hydraulics puff and wheeze as the now-empty dumpster is lowered, hitting the ground beside me with a loud hollow mocking *thunk*.

Now what, Sean? Now what?

CHAPTER THIRTY-EIGHT

BASKET CASE

I AM IN TOTAL PANIC MODE, desperately searching for something that could substitute for clothing. A cardboard box? A rolled-up carpet? A paper bag I can put over my head? Anything I could use to get me home.

But there's nothing.

And just when I think things couldn't possibly get any worse . . .

There are voices in the distance. Muffled, echoing, *girls'* voices.

I have to hide. Anyone who walks by will see me crouched here behind this dumpster. Where? Where can I hide? I'll never make it to the fence in time. Even if I did, I wouldn't be able to scale it. I could dash out into the parking lot, pray that I get lucky, and hide between parked cars before anyone spots me.

But before I can take off, I hear the girls' voices getting closer. *Much* closer. Like they're just on the other side of the WAL-MART EMPLOYEES ONLY door.

Crap!

Desperately I leap up, grab the ledge of the empty dumpster, and clamber up the side, scraping the hell out of my knees as I go. I manage to drop inside just in time to hear the *snick* of the push bar on the door followed by girls' laughter spilling out into the open air.

"So, what are you guys up to tonight?" One of the girls asks.

"Kyle's parents are out of town," another girl says. "He was supposed to have a party, but he totally pussied out."

There's the *skritch* of lighters being lit and soon the pungent smell of cigarettes mixes with the nasty wet-dog-farts-and-blue-cheese dumpster stink around me.

Who the hell's going to take their cigarette break by a dumpster? Oh, man, I could strangle Coop. It's okay. It's okay. I'll just wait them out. A cigarette break is what, fifteen minutes? Surely I can make it that long.

"We're going to try and scalp tickets for Angel's Womb," a third girl says. "They're playing Nocturnal Submissions over in Dowling."

That voice.

I *know* that voice. Know it as well as my own.

Cathy.

"They're completely sold out," I hear another familiar voice add. Nessa! "But there's always someone on the corner selling tickets."

Good Gandalf! How could I have forgotten that they both work at Wal-Mart? It didn't even cross my mind. Not with everything else I've been dealing with.

All right. All right. No need to panic. They don't know I'm in here. They're going to smoke their cigarettes and then leave. There's no reason for them to look in the dumpster.

"No matter what, though," Cathy says, "I am *not* staying home tonight. My mom is driving me fucking nuts. I don't know if it's all the baby hormones or what, but suddenly she's become a complete psycho bitch from hell."

"Oh, my God." One of the other girls laughs. "My mom was a major train wreck when she was pregnant with my little brother. One minute she was crying because she spilled something on the counter, and the next she was screaming at my dad for leaving his socks on the coffee table."

"Yup." I hear Cathy take a drag on a cigarette. "That about sums it up."

"Do you guys know if it's a boy or a girl yet?"

"Like I even care," Cathy answers. "I don't even want the stupid thing in the first place, right? I mean, I know that sounds totally bratty, but it's true." She takes another puff on her smoke. "Who knows? Maybe I'll feel different when it's finally here, but right now? It's like everything is *'the baby, the baby, the baby.'* It makes me want to puke. And don't get me started on the freakin' room situation. I'm still trying to pretend *that's* not actually going to happen."

It's weird listening to my sister say all this. On one hand, it sounds so horrible and mean. On the other hand, I know *exactly* how she feels.

"Speaking of your brother." One of them giggles. "Has he . . . you know . . . come out yet?"

Jesus Christ. She's gone public with that? I grip my knees even tighter, feeling my entire body flush with heat.

"Not yet," Cathy says. "But I'm working on it." I hear the unmistakable sound of Cathy-Nessa laughter.

If I needed proof that they are conspiring against me, their evil cackling certainly seems like a smoking gun.

I clench my eyes shut. Just go away. Just go back inside so I can get out of this reeking dumpster and cling to my last shred of dignity.

"Goddamn it! What a freakin' rip-off!" one of their coworkers grouses. "This latte's not even hot."

A millisecond later, I feel something lukewarm and liquid hit my stomach. My eyes spring open and a surprised squeal escapes my lips before I can stop it. I lose my balance and fall back, my shoulder hitting the side of the dumpster. I look down to see a brown puddle spreading across my stomach and soaking my boxers, making it look like I just squirshed my shorts.

I hold my breath. The girls are silent and there's a brief hopeful moment where I think that maybe they didn't hear me. Maybe my lucky boxer shorts are finally starting to kick in.

And then I hear Cathy: "What the hell was that?"

🎥 CHAPTER THIRTY-NINE 🎥

THE HOWLING

A PAIR OF HANDS grasps the side of the dumpster.

I cover my drenched junk with my hands and curl into a tight little ball in the corner of the empty bin, like if I make myself small enough, maybe I won't be seen.

A mop of black hair starts to peek over the ledge in torturous slow motion.

Oh, God. I can*not* believe this is happening to me. I will *never* be able to live this down. Not ever. Not in a million years.

I watch as the hair becomes a forehead, becomes eyes, and then becomes an entire face.

It's Nessa, and as soon as she catches sight of me, her eyes bug. "Holy shit!" she blurts.

"What?" I hear Cathy ask. "What is it?"

I lock eyes with Nessa and press my hands together. *"Please,"* I mouth. *"Don't."*

Nessa hops down from the dumpster and I hold my breath, waiting for the worst. There'll be laughter and finger pointing and shooting of cell-phone videos for sure.

I'll have to go into hiding. Join an ashram or something.

But then I hear Nessa say, "It's just a raccoon. It scared me at first, but he's really just a pathetic little guy."

I don't even mind the slight dig. I'm far too grateful.

"Seriously?" one of the other girls says. "I want to see."

"Oh, I don't think you do," Nessa warns her quickly. "You nailed it with your latte and it looks pretty pissed. It's all red-eyed and frothing at the mouth. I think it might be rabid, actually."

Oh, Nessa. Oh, my God. Thank you, thank you, thank you.

I take the cue and make what I imagine to be a loud rabid raccoon sound, kind of a hiss-howl thing.

"Jesus," the coffee hurler says. "You think it'd attack us from the bottom of a dumpster?"

"Are you kidding?" Nessa argues. "They've got back legs like a kangaroo. He'll launch himself at you and bite the shit out of your face."

"Reeeeeeek!" I screech, scraping the side of the metal of the bin with my fingernails.

The girls shriek. "Let's get the fuck out of here!" Cathy says. "We can call animal control from the break room."

The girls' shoes crunch through the snow as they stampede away. I listen for the sound of the EMPLOY-EES ONLY door clinking shut. It does, and after waiting another few just-to-be-safe minutes, I finally brave getting to my feet. I grab the ledge of the dumpster and pull myself up to have a look.

There's no one around.

I can't believe it. Nessa totally saved me. I don't get it. One minute I think she's in cahoots with Cathy, and the next she's bailing me out of the most embarrassing situation of my life.

I swing my leg up, climb over the side, and jump to the ground.

Only to see the Wal-Mart door start to push open again.

Goddamn it, here they come. Probably armed with cameras or harpoons or something. I knew Nessa's turn-around seemed too good to be true.

I dive behind the dumpster, flop to the ground, and try to shimmy underneath. Gravel pokes into my naked chest, arms, and thighs. But there's no way I'll fit. It's too low. Too tight.

I'm screwed.

A second later, I hear laughter. This time it's of just the Nessa-only variety.

"What the hell are you doing down there?"

I look up from the ground to see Nessa standing

there, partially silhouetted against the sun, with something wadded up in her right hand. She appears to be alone.

"I was just . . . I thought . . ." I mutter. "I dropped something."

"*Really?*" Nessa says. "Like, all of your clothes?"

"It's a long story." I get to my feet, covering the front of my clinging, clammy coffee-browned boxers with one hand and brushing the embedded pebbles from my skin with the other.

"No kidding," she says. She glances down at my crotch. "You need medical attention there?"

"Uh . . . no. I'll be okay." My neck and ears burn. "It wasn't that hot."

Nessa takes a step closer. "You sure you don't want me to take a look? You know, just to make sure?"

"No." I stumble backward, visions of every porno nurse I've ever seen on the Internet popping up in my mind. And they're not the only thing popping up. Damn it. Change the film, change the film. Hairy men's butts. Ms. Luntz's gazongas. Maggot-infested wampa guts. "I'm good, thanks. I, uh . . . I don't think you want to get much closer. I kind of stink."

Nessa sniffs the air. "Is that you? I thought it was the dumpster."

"The rotten food is the dumpster. The bird shit and coffee, that's me."

She chuckles. "Okay, I'll keep my distance." Then she holds out the balled-up thing she's been holding. "I got you an old uniform. I thought you could use it."

I've never been so psyched about khakis and a polo in my entire life. "Wow, Nessa, thank you. That's . . . that's really nice of you. I guess I'm going to owe you."

She smiles. "I guess so."

I glance at the EMPLOYEES ONLY door. "Are you sure this is okay? I don't want to get you into trouble."

"Nobody's going to miss it. Just give it back to me the next time I see you."

"Great. Thanks again." I quickly tug on the khakis and pull the polo over my head. It's all a bit big, but it feels so damn good to be covered up again.

Nessa glances at her cell phone. "I've gotta go. But I want to hear all the details about this at our next writing session. I bet it ties in nicely with your tarot reading."

"I don't know about that," I say. "I didn't actually *die* of humiliation—though I came pretty close."

Sure, it's a lame joke. But Nessa doesn't even crack a smile. "Tarot isn't a science, Sean. It's an art. You can't expect it to be so literal."

I worry that I've upset her by not taking it seriously enough, but after a second Nessa's expression softens. "Anyway, I'd be willing to put good money on the fact that this whole disaster has something to do with that thing you've been so conflicted about."

I can't help it—my gaze immediately goes to her boobs. But then I clench my eyes shut and force myself to think of the *real* conflict in my life: Leyna and Evelyn. And I wonder how much worse this little bird-shit-tastrophy has made things with them.

CHAPTER FORTY

PSYCHO

I'D ONLY GOTTEN HALFWAY through explaining how I'd just f-f-f-f-*forgotten* to p-p-p-p-*pay*," Coop says, demonstrating the horrible stutter he pretended to have to get out of being prosecuted for shoplifting, "and the rent-a-cop got so frustrated with me that he finally just let me off."

"You don't even feel bad about it, do you?" I ask. "Exploiting a disability like that?"

Coop makes a face. "Please. If anyone should feel bad it's Paul Blart. He's the one who didn't have the patience to wait for a poor stutterer to f-f-f-*finish* t-t-t-*telling* his s-s-s-*story*."

Just then, my bedroom door bursts opens and Matt rushes in. "Holy crap," he says, looking all bleary eyed, like he didn't sleep a wink last night. "Evelyn is totally insane. You were right. I'm sorry I ever doubted you."

Coop, Matt, and me have convened at my house today to finalize the casting for the movie and to organize our filming schedule for this week.

Well, that, and to debrief each other on what went down at the mall yesterday.

"So what the hell happened?" Coop laughs. "Your texts last night were incoherent."

"Oh, my God, okay, so listen to this." Matt hops up on my bed and leans forward. "*After* Evelyn tried calling Sean's phone a billion times. And *after* we tried calling your phone, Coop."

"I was being detained," he explains.

"Yeah, well, when we couldn't get in touch with you guys, Evelyn started getting more and more panicky, until at last she's convinced something terrible's happened to you. So we search every freakin' store in the mall, including both restrooms, then she badgers security to announce your names over the PA system. And we wait and wait, and when I finally say that maybe we should just give up and go home, Evelyn goes absolutely ballistic. I might as well have suggested we strangle a couple of babies. She started screaming and wailing and blubbering that I was a terrible friend and that you both could be dead in a ditch somewhere."

"Oh, man. It sounds like a total nightmare." Coop bites his lower lip, trying not to crack up as he leans back in my desk chair. "You're a real hero, there, Mattie."

Matt gives Coop a death stare. "Thanks for nothing, dipshit. But I'm *still* not finished." Matt shakes his head like he can't believe he actually survived this train wreck. "So we're searching all the stores. *Again.* And Evelyn's darting in and out asking all the employees— *again*—if maybe they'd seen you two. All this time, I'm trying to talk her down, but everything I say keeps making her madder and madder until finally, I swear to God, I see her jack a shirt from GUESS. Right after the store clerk blows her off. Evelyn's totally steamed, ranting and raving, and she grabs this fancy blue guy's shirt off the shelf and stuffs it into her purse."

"What?" Coop says. "She doesn't get caught and I do? That's bullshit!"

"Yeah, well," Matt goes on, "at this point I don't know what the hell to do. I'm thinking maybe she was just so crazed she didn't realize that she was stealing. So, when I try to casually ask her about it, Evelyn goes apocalyptic. She rips the arm off a sweater mannequin at H&M and starts clubbing me with it."

That's when Coop completely loses it. He doubles over, howling with laughter, tears rolling down his cheeks. And I can't help it, I start cracking up too. The image of Evelyn whaling on Matt with a mannequin arm is just too priceless.

"Laugh it up, boys," Matt says. "You weren't the ones who got chased down an up escalator by an arm-wielding klepto psychopath."

"Oh, man." Coop is laughing so hard he can barely speak. "I would have paid good money to see that." He sniffles, wiping the corners of his eyes.

"I'm so sorry, Matt," I say, catching my breath. "God, she sure didn't seem too concerned about me when I tried getting in touch with her last night. She wouldn't even take my call."

Matt grimaces. "Yeah, well, she *was* concerned. Until we were leaving the mall. We're heading toward the bus stop, Evelyn's blowing her nose, apologizing for wigging out on me, when suddenly she stops dead in her tracks. And her eyes narrow. Then she starts running after this bus and screaming at the top of her lungs, 'Stop! Stop! Stop that bus!'"

Coop and I stare at Matt with identical you've-got-to-be-shitting-me faces.

Matt holds up his hand. "I swear to God, I had no freakin' clue what the hell she was flipping out about until the bus pulled away and she came back. It was like she'd flicked a switch. She was totally calm. *Eerily* calm, especially after everything I'd just witnessed. She said that she'd just seen the girl you were flirting with in drama class. Then she told me to have a good night and marched off."

"Leyna?" I say, my lungs feeling like punctured balloons. "She saw Leyna? Holy shit!" I stand and start to pace the room. "You should have led with that information, Matt. It would have given me more time to go into hiding."

Matt screws up his face. "What are you talking about?"

"Evelyn's brother! Nick? Giant guy? Navy SEAL? Remember him? I'm sure she's told him by now. Oh, God. I'm a dead man. That's it. Forget the movie. Forget everything. I have to get out of here." I bolt to my closet, grab a duffel bag, and start shoving clothes into it.

"What the hell, dawg?" Coop says. "Chillax. It's not like she saw you two together. So she saw Leyna at the mall? Big whoop. That's hardly incriminating. I seriously doubt Nick will do anything just based on that."

As if on cue, there's a pounding on the front door. The entire houseful of animals erupts into barks, hisses, and squawks.

I freeze. My eyes go wide. I look at Matt. At Coop. My hands start to shake.

Coop lets out a nervous laugh. "Come on. That's *so* not him."

Another set of bangs on the door. The sound of a massive fist beating on wood.

I gulp. "You guys, what the hell should I do?"

But Coop's still in denial. "There's no way. What are the chances of that? It's like he followed Matt here and then waited for him to fill you in before—"

"I know you're in there, Sean! You and your pals!"

There's no doubt about it. That's Nick's voice.

He shouts again, and we have no trouble hearing him all the way up in my room: "You and me need to talk, guy, so get your ass down here right now!"

CHAPTER FORTY-ONE

THE HILLS HAVE EYES

ALONE, IF YOU DON'T MIND," Nick says when I show up at the front door flanked by Matt and Coop.

"Whatever you need to say to Sean you can say to us," Coop replies. He's armed with a baseball bat. Matt wields my replica *wakizashi* sword. And I'm clutching my shillelagh like my life depends on it.

Which maybe it does.

Nick laughs. "You guys are cute." He chin-gestures to the weapons. "I'm not going to hurt you, Sean. It's true, my sister's very upset, but I'm here as peacemaker. I swear."

I don't know why I believe him, but I do. Something about the tone of his voice. The look in his eyes. The lack of any visible firearms.

I turn back to Matt and Coop. "It's okay. I've got this."

"You sure?" Matt asks.

"Yeah. It's fine."

"Okay." Coop nods. "But we'll be in the family room watching TV if you need us. Just give a shout." He narrows his eyes at Nick as if warning him, then motions to Matt with his head. "Come on. Let's go."

Once they've gone, Nick shoots me a smile from the doorway. "May I come in?"

"Sure," I say, moving back to let him enter. I rest my shillelagh against the wall.

Nick steps inside. "Cute dogs." He squats as the pups jostle one another to get a cuddle, all of them in total suck-up mode. Not even Klaus is acting like the watchdog he's supposed to be. Once Nick has given each of the animals some attention, he stands and faces me. "So. Let's cut right to the chase. Yes?"

"All right." I gulp.

Nick jams his hands into his coat pockets. "You fucked up. You know that, right?"

I shake my head. "It wasn't my fault. I don't know what Evelyn told you but—"

"She told me you ditched her to meet up with a girl in your drama class."

"I didn't meet up with Leyna. I swear."

"Yeah, yeah, I know."

"You do?"

"Sure," Nick says. "Because I happened to have been tailing her."

My mouth goes dry. My heart starts pounding in my head. "I'm sorry, *what*? *Tailing*? As in . . . following her?"

He shrugs. "Evelyn asked if I would do a little investigating. Find out what I could about this drama-class girl. So, I got her name. Her address. And her cell-phone number." He laughs, shaking his head. "GPS makes it so easy to follow people these days. Anyway, when I saw she was headed to the mall, I debated with myself whether or not to tell Evelyn. But I decided it was best to wait and see how things played out. I mean, I didn't really think you'd be stupid enough to cheat on my sister right under her nose."

"Ha. Yeah. That would have been really stupid. Can you imagine? I mean, who would even think to . . . Ha." I take the most massive of massive palm whiffs. That flock of shitting gulls may have saved my life. Lucky boxers, indeed!

"Anyways," Nick says, "I laid it all out for Evelyn last night—how this girl had some coffee by herself at DeLuca's and then did a little shopping before heading off. And while Evelyn was extremely relieved to hear this, she's still very hurt that you abandoned her. It was shades of our father all over again."

"Right. No. I understand that." I'm chewing the hell out of my tongue. "And I was trying to apologize when I called last night."

Nick jabs me in the shoulder with his Navy SEAL

finger, punctuating each sentence with a fresh poke. "Apologies don't mean dick, Sean. You need to *do* something. To make it up to her. Something romantic. Something that says you value her."

I resist the urge to rub the spot. "Okay, sure. Romantic. I can do that. Do you, uh . . . ? Do you have any suggestions?"

Nick smiles. "Funny you should ask." He pulls a hand from one of his pockets and holds out a little red jewelry box.

I stare at it suspiciously. "What's that?"

Nick thrusts his hand out to me. "Go on. Open it."

I take the box and slowly lift the hinged cover, like whatever's inside might spring out and bite me. Lying on a tiny cushion is a pair of sparkling blue sapphire earrings. "Wow. Those look . . . expensive."

"Not too bad," Nick says. "I know a guy who knows a guy. They only set you back a hundred and fifty bucks. But Evelyn's worth it. She's had her eyes on those babies for a while now. Of course, you wouldn't know that, so I thought I'd help you out. Plus I've made a reservation at Le Chat Noir for the two of you for Valentine's Day."

"Valentine's Day?" I squeak, my brain whirring. "Le Chat Noir? That sounds . . . fancy."

"*Super* fancy. It's a little overpriced, but Evelyn will love it. You bring her to that restaurant and then surprise her with those earrings, and I guarantee you all will be forgiven."

I stare down at the earrings, feeling sweaty all over. "That's . . . really nice of you, Nick. Seriously. But I don't know how I could ever—"

"Thank me?" He holds up his hand like a traffic cop. "No thanks necessary, buddy. All I want is for my baby sis to be happy." Before I can breathe a sigh of relief, he adds, "Just give me the hundred and fifty and we'll call it even." He holds out his hand.

The floor tilts under my feet. Where am I going to get a hundred and fifty—?

But then I remember: the movie money. There's not a ton of it left; if I give a hundred and fifty to Nick, it'll mean we probably can't afford some of the special effects we've been planning on. But I don't see that I have much of a choice here.

"Sure. Just a sec." I slog up to my room, grab three fifty-dollar bills from the budget envelope, and hand them over to Nick.

He tucks the bills in his wallet. "Pleasure doing business with you, Sean." He salutes me, then turns to the door. But just as he's stepping over the threshold, he stops and turns back. "Oh, I almost forgot. What an idiot." He laughs, shaking his head. He reaches into his jacket pocket and holds out his hand again. "I believe this is yours."

It's my cell phone.

My eyes nearly flop from their sockets. "Wha . . . ? How . . . ? Where'd you find that?"

He shrugs. "Dump truck. You must have accidentally thrown your phone away, huh?"

I reach out with a shaky hand and grab my cell phone. Oh, shit, did he see me? Stripped down to nothing but my sneakers and lucky boxers? He must have been trailing me too. "I guess so."

"I will say, I was a little worried when I finally tracked it down. I thought I might find it on your dead body. I was very relieved to find just the phone. And no calls, e-mails, or texts to the drama-class girl either. How about that?"

"Yeah," I say, feeling like I can't breathe. "How about that?"

CHAPTER FORTY-TWO

PLANET TERROR

YOU DID *WHAT?*" Coop shouts at me from the sofa. "We're supposed to be using that money on our film. Not to pay your sister rent and to buy fancy Valentine's Day presents for your girlfriend! That only leaves us with a hundred and fifty bucks!"

"What the hell was I supposed to do, Coop?"

"Tell him thanks but no thanks." He grabs the remote and shuts off the TV.

"That *wasn't* an option."

"Okay, then, fine." Coop settles himself. "We'll just return the earrings to the store. Recoup some of our losses."

"Yeah, right. You think Nick's not going to wonder why the hell Evelyn isn't wearing them after Valentine's Day? Forget it. The guy's a freakin' psychopath." I toss my cell phone on the floor at our feet. "He's tracking me, for fuck's sake. Leyna too. And God knows who else. This is a total nightmare."

"He got your phone back for you," Matt says. "That's kind of cool."

"No. It's not cool. At all. I'd rather not *have* a phone than know he can find me wherever I am. I can't believe this. All my hopes of breaking up with Evelyn when we're finished with this movie are trashed. I'm never getting out of this relationship. Ever." I flop down into the armchair, feeling sick to my stomach.

"All right, don't have a zonkey," Coop says. "Let's just take things one step at a time. We'll get this movie in the can as fast as possible, then we'll deal with the Evelyn situation."

"Yeah, well, I hate to tell you this," I say, chewing the heck out of my tongue, "but getting this movie done isn't going to be as easy as you think."

Matt looks at me sideways. "What do you mean?"

"Uncle Doug watched the audition tapes. He wants Leyna and Hunter to play the leads."

Coop laughs. "That's your big problem? I have to say, I'm surprised at you, Sean. And a little disappointed. Hunter and Leyna were obviously the best out of the bunch. I'm with Uncle Doug: I say we cast them."

I let my head fall forward, too exhausted to explain it all again. But Matt mans up. "We can't do that," he tells Coop. "I mean, sure, Hunter, fine. But Sean already promised Evelyn she could be the female lead. And if we don't cast Evelyn, we don't have a camera."

I lift my head. "But if we don't cast Leyna, then my uncle's pulling the rest of the financing. See? Screwed."

"Fuuuck me." Coop stands and starts to pace. "Okay. Okay. Let me think about this for a second." He runs his hand through his hair and mumbles to himself. "What if we . . . ? Or maybe . . . No . . . That wouldn't work . . . I mean . . . if we were dealing with sane people, but . . ." He continues pacing around the family room, shaking his head, scrunching up his face, and looking skyward until . . . "Holy crap, I think I've got it." Coop whips back around, a strange look on his face. "All right, this is going to sound totally insane. But sometimes you have to fight crazy with crazy."

Me and Matt share a look. Because if *Coop* thinks it's crazy, then it's bound to be Green Goblin crazy.

"What if—and I know it's going to be a pain in the ass, but bear with me—what if we shoot *two* movies? A real one, with Leyna and Hunter as Nashira and Rogart. And a pretend one with Evelyn and Nick playing *all* the parts."

Somehow my hand has worked its way over my nose and mouth and I am sniffing like a madman. "Oh. Oh, my God," I say into my palm, the wheels spinning into overdrive. "That . . . That could actually work."

Matt laughs, obviously relieved. "Evelyn *did* say she wasn't a fan of any of the other actresses."

"That's right." Coop nods. "She wants to play all the female parts. Let's let her do that."

"And Nick can be all the guys," Matt adds.

"Yes, he can." Coop's got an excited gleam in his eyes. "It solves all our problems. We're shooting on video, so it's not like it's going to cost us anything but a little extra time."

"We'll have to be sneaky about it," I say. "We'd have to leave all our cell phones at home whenever we're filming with Leyna and Hunter, in case Nick is tracking us." A collective shudder runs through our bodies. "And I'll have to rewrite the script a bit. Make Rogart and Nashira brother and sister."

"Only for the Nick and Evelyn version," Coop corrects.

"No," I say. "Because I don't want Hunter making out with Leyna. That's a deal breaker for me. In fact, I think I should be the love-interest sidekick character. The one with the antidote in his saliva."

"OK, sure," Coop agrees. But before I can get too excited, he continues. "But you'll have to make out with Hunter as well. We can't have you giving antidote to Nashira and not to Rogart."

I wince. "All right, fine. Forget it. We won't have a love interest. They'll just be brother and sister. We'll leave it at that."

Matt's complexion suddenly goes pale. "You do realize, though: if Nick and Evelyn find out what we're doing . . ."

We all stare at my cell phone, resting innocuously on the carpet.

"We're dead meat," I say.

☛ CHAPTER FORTY-THREE ☚

THE OMEN

EVELYN'S AT HER LOCKER, her back to me as I approach. My mouth is bone-dry and I am dizzy with fear. If this were a scene in a movie, there'd be a loud thumping heartbeat on the soundtrack, underscored by creepy tension-building music.

I have two pieces of news I need to impart here. The first is about our dinner date. I have no idea how she's going to react to the Valentine's Day plan. Presumably, she should be happy and accept it as an olive branch. But you can't presume anything where Evelyn is concerned. Maybe she'll be over the moon, or maybe she knows Nick arranged it all and will come at me like a honey badger after a cobra.

The second thing I need to talk to her about is the movie. And I need to tell her about it without seeming nervous. Otherwise she might suspect that something is up. And I don't even want to consider what might happen after that.

"Hey, there," I croak. I clear my throat. "How's it going?"

Evelyn slowly turns around but says nothing.

"I wanted to—" I start, then shake my head. "I'm sorry. About Saturday. I know you probably don't want to hear my excuses but . . . it was just a series of unfortunate things. One right after the other."

"Go on," Evelyn says coldly.

I tell her everything. Well, everything except why Coop and I were running along the perimeter of the mall in the first place. But I tell her all about the birds, the crap, my clothes, my cell phone, even my sister's friend coming to my rescue with a Wal-Mart uniform. Though I do lie a tiny bit there and turn Nessa into a dude named Omar. Anyway, it all sounds totally true because it *is* all true, and with Nick corroborating the cell-phone part, I've even got Evelyn laughing by the time I'm all through.

Thank Gandalf.

And so, when I get around to asking her if she'll come to dinner with me at Le Chat Noir on Valentine's Day, Evelyn is beaming.

"Really?" she squeals. "That's so romantic, pooky." She leaps at me and grabs me in a lung-crushing hug. "I can't believe I ever doubted you."

"There's one more thing," I choke out.

Evelyn releases me and smiles. "More surprises. This is the best day ever!"

"Yeah, well . . ." I cough as my lungs slowly reinflate. "I wanted to let you know . . . Well, *we* wanted to let you know . . . Coop, Matt, and me . . . that . . ." Oh, God, can't breathe. Going to pass out. Did Evelyn just collapse one of my lungs or am I having a panic attack?

"What is it, cuddle bear?"

"It's, um . . ." I swallow. "The movie. You and Nick. We just . . ." Deep breath. It's okay. I'm okay. "We want to film it. With . . . just the two of you. Playing all the parts." Oh, God, I said it. I can't believe I just said it. It sounds so fishy. Better add something else. "Well, and, you know, Uncle Doug and the humanzees, of course."

"Of course." Evelyn's nodding. Her eyes narrowed. Is she mad? Suspicious? "I *knew* it," she says. Oh, shit. But then she smiles. "It's just like I said. None of those people were any good, right?"

"That's right," I say, my breath returning. "So, are you okay with that? And do you think Nick will be? I mean, it's going to be a lot of work."

"Okay with it?" Evelyn lip farts. "I'm the one who suggested it, silly cakes. And Nick will be thrilled. He's dreamed of being an actor ever since the auditions, when he realized how much talent he has." She dives in for another death hug. "We're going to make the best movie ever! You just wait and see."

• • •

As soon as I step foot into drama class, I head right over to Leyna, who's searching in her messenger bag for something.

"Leyna, hi," I say. She glances up at me, and it's impossible to read her expression behind her red shutter shades. "Listen, about Saturday—I am so, so sorry that I stood you up. I really didn't mean to. I was looking forward to our date. Really looking forward to it. You have no idea how much . . . Anyway. But something came up. Something awful. I—" My bird crap saga went over so well with Evelyn that I am actually ready to launch in to the same gory details with Leyna, only as I'm about to say it I realize that the last thing I want is for her to have any of those images of me in her mind.

"You what?" she asks, and again I can't read her. Is she pissed? Bored? Can she tell I'm about to launch into a massive lie?

My brain scrambles for a partial truth, something I can say with authority, the way I told Evelyn about the beshitting. "I . . . had to take one of our foster dogs to the vet. Chester. He's a cocker spaniel," I explain. "He swallowed one of my toy—er, figurines. A Klingon. And he started projectile vomiting. We had to rush him to the animal hospital to have emergency surgery."

This is all true. Chester really did eat one of my Klingons and he did have to be operated on. Two years ago. But still.

"Is he okay?" Leyna asks, raising her shutter shades and sounding genuinely concerned.

"Oh, yeah. They were able to get it out of him, thank God. It was close, though, because it could have ruptured his intestines. I knew once he started vomiting that he must have a blockage somewhere. I'd been worried for a few days, because he seemed a little dehydrated and looked like he was losing weight."

She smiles. "Wow. You seem to know a lot about animals, Sean."

"I should. We've been fostering them ever since I was a baby. My mom says I should go to veterinarian school."

"I thought you wanted to go to acting school."

"Oh, yeah. I do. Definitely. It's my mom's idea. Vet school, I mean. She's the one who says I should go. But I told her, 'No way, Mom. I'm going to be an actor.'"

"Sorry." Leyna laughs. "I didn't mean to put you on the spot."

"No, it's fine. I mean, it's nice to have a backup plan, though, right? You know, if the acting thing doesn't work out. And I am good with animals, so . . ."

"That's great. I'll have to ask you about my corgi sometime, then. She's had this rash for a while now, but my mom doesn't want to take her to the vet because it's so expensive. She says it'll go away on its own."

"It might," I say. "Depends on what it is."

Leyna frowns. "It just looks rashy to me, but what do I know? Maybe you could come over and have a look at it sometime."

I nod, perhaps a little too enthusiastically. "Sure. Absolutely."

"Well, I'm glad your dog's okay." Leyna reaches out and touches my arm. An electric current shoots through my body. "Most of all, though, I'm glad *you're* okay. I was getting a little worried. I tried looking up your number but you're not listed. I almost came by your house, but then I thought, what if you were just standing me up? Then I'd be all embarrassed."

"No, no. I wasn't. I would never. I tried looking you up too. But you're not listed either."

"Yeah, my dad's pretty paranoid about stuff like that. He won't even use a cell phone because he's afraid someone might be able to track him." Leyna laughs. "I mean, seriously. Like people don't have anything better to do than track other people."

"Yeah. That's ridiculous." My gaze slides off to the side. "So, anyway. What I was going to tell you Saturday when we met was that we're casting you as the lead in our movie. Nashira Axe."

Leyna's eyes go wide. "Really? Are you kidding?"

I smile. "Nope. I'm dead serious. You and Hunter are going to be our stars."

"That's amazing!" Leyna pulls me in for a hug. Oh, man, I could never get tired of this. Such a stark contrast to Evelyn's strangling. "I really appreciate it, Sean. I'll work super hard. I promise."

Just then Mr. Nestman claps his hands, quieting the room. "All right, thespians. Today we are going to start on an exciting new project. As you already know, one of your classmates, our very own Sean Hance, is making a film to be shown at New York's world-famous TerrorFest. And so, in the interest of giving you all some real-world experience, I've decided to dedicate a portion of our class to helping Mr. Hance accomplish this goal." Mr. Nestman holds up a copy of the script pages I e-mailed him last night. I can see very clearly that he's marked the hell out of them with red pen. "The first thing we'll do is have Sean announce his lead casting choices, which he's informed me were finalized this weekend. I know we're all *very* interested to find out who made the cut." He looks at me as he says that part and it sounds very much like a threat. "Then we'll do a complete read-through of these early scenes." He turns to me, placing his hand solemnly on his chest. "Now, Sean, just so you know, I've taken the liberty of making a few . . . mmm, *minor* corrections. Improvements, if you will. To add some depth and texture, that's all. As I am a twenty-year professional in this business of show, I didn't think you'd mind."

I smile tightly, worrying less about the "improvements" to my script and more about just how professional Mr. Nestman will be when he finds out he didn't land one of the leading roles.

⚞ CHAPTER FORTY-FOUR ⚟

VILLAGE OF THE DAMNED

I FLOAT ALL THE WAY HOME from school on my bike, tak-ing my time as I weave along the streets, intermittently glancing down at the back of my hand and the phone number that Leyna's written there in red-raspberry ink. I love how she writes her fives. And don't get me started on how sexy her eights look. All curvy and round.

To be honest, I didn't think today would turn out as well as it has. Though, despite Leyna's accepting my apology, drama class was torture. Mr. Nestman acted like it was *his* movie we were rehearsing instead of mine. Changing everything that Nessa and I worked so hard on. And that was *before* I read the cast list and he real-ized I've only got him playing an army sergeant.

And then, after school, we tried to film the first scene with Evelyn and Nick. That was pretty much a two-hour nightmare. Not only are Nick and Evelyn horrendous actors—I mean really, truly terrible—but they both move in slow motion. And take ten times longer to say their lines than they should. If we were actually going to use their scenes, our movie would be twenty hours long.

The good thing is, I'm more convinced now than ever that we are doing the right thing by shooting the decoy film. And so are Val and Helen, who were dubious at first. But once we met up with Leyna and Hunter—sans cell phones, of course—and shot the very same scene in one-quarter the amount of time, and with infinitely better acting, there was no one who wasn't on board with the plan.

And that's not even the best part. As soon as we wrapped, Leyna came up to me, all excited and full of ideas for her character. She took my hand and wrote her phone number down on the soft pad between my thumb and forefinger—"So we can always get in touch with each other"—and everything felt right again. Better than right.

I turn up my driveway, lifting my hand to my nose and breathing in the raspberry aroma of the ink. I hop off my bike, lift the garage door, and tuck my ride right in beside Mom's old black Volvo. Even this, putting my bicycle away, feels effortless and fluid. It sounds totally weird, I know, but taking control of things and putting our movie plan into action has made me feel taller. And lighter. Like I'm half helium. Like if someone were to hand me a basketball right now, I could dribble it across the street to the Goldsteins' and slam-dunk it in their crappy old basketball hoop.

I'm in my house and bounding up the stairs—thinking about how great it's going to be to continue filming with Leyna this week—when I step into my room and see that it's nearly empty except for all the baby stuff and a few scattered Pokémon cards on the floor.

I stand there in the doorway. Blinking at the void. My stomach taking a nosedive. Trying to work out how this pitch-black puzzle piece fits in to the sunny brightness of my day. But it's like in those shows where an alien ship suddenly appears over Manhattan and everyone's brain short-circuits because they simply can't handle the enormity of the situation.

"Hey, there, mister." It's Dad, clapping me on the shoulder, a big isn't-life-grand smile on his face. "How was your day?"

"What are you doing?"

"You're home earlier than we thought," Dad chirps. "Another half hour and your mother and I would have had the entire move completed."

"We wanted to surprise you," Mom says, waddling up behind me, a half-eaten Ding Dong in her hand. Jeez, I can't believe how much her belly has inflated in just the last month. "Don't worry, though. Your father isn't letting me do any of the heavy lifting." She takes a big bite of the chocolate hockey puck, which leaves icing smears on her lips.

"Wait." I shake my head, unable to process anything they're saying. "I thought . . ." I clench my eyes shut, trying to ward off the killer migraine that's blossoming in my skull. "I thought I wasn't going to have to move until right before the baby was born."

"Sorry, kiddo," Dad says, pushing past me and stepping into my bedroom. "We had to accelerate the schedule a bit. The doctor said the baby's trending faster than she expected. We thought we'd better get started on painting the room." He begins pulling my swords down from the wall. "It's better this way, anyway, I think. Yank the Band-Aid off quick and clean, right? Interesting factoid about change: they actually did a scientific study where they found that people acclimate to new situations much faster when—"

"I don't care," I snap. "You guys said I had until May."

"Um, no," Mom says. "We said the baby was due in May, but now it looks like—"

"This isn't fair." I feel my eyes starting to well up. "I'm not ready yet. You should have told me." I march into the room and start gathering up the Pokémon cards from the floor. "These are valuable. You could have damaged them. You should have let me organize my stuff first."

"Sorry, guy. We thought it would be easier for you this way." Dad leans the swords gently against the wall. "Not to have to move the stuff over yourself. That was the other thing they discovered in this study. People who were thrust into new situations were more likely to—"

"Whatever." I look around at the near-empty space that used to be my room. "I don't care about your stupid study." I glare at Mom's swelling stomach. "Or the dumb baby."

Mom tilts her head, acting all sympathetic. "Look, hon. We know how hard this is—"

"No." I shift my glare from Mom to Dad to Mom. I hate them both so much right now. It's just like Cathy said: it's all *baby, baby, baby.* "You have no clue how hard it is. If you did, you wouldn't be making me do this. I know you think this baby's some kind of *miracle.* But for me it's a curse. You've cursed my life."

"Sean!" Mom gasps, her eyes starting to leak. "That was uncalled for." She sniffles as she takes another bite of her Ding Dong. "So much for gay sons being more kind to their mothers."

"What?" I screech. "You can't be serious! How many times do I—?"

"Look, mister." Dad levels his gaze at me. "We didn't just spring this move on you, okay? We told you it was going to happen weeks ago. You're not the only one having to make sacrifices here. The whole family is pitching in. Because that's what families do. They work as a team. And if you expect us to be accepting of who you are, then we expect the same courtesy."

"Oh, my God!" I throw my head back. "How did this get turned into a conversation about me being gay? I'm *not* gay. You don't have to accept anything! We're talking about *you* making me move out of *my* room."

"You mean the 'curse's' room." Mom is now full-on sobbing. She takes a Kleenex from the pocket of her paisley maternity dress and blows her nose. "I'm sorry. I can't deal with this."

Mom turns and waddles off down the hall.

Dad glowers at me. "I hope you're happy, mister. Now I'm going to have to spend the next hour talking her down from this." He glances over his shoulder at the bedroom. "Finish moving your stuff and then you can come downstairs and apologize."

And with that, Dad goes after Mom, leaving me standing there alone.

I take a closer look around the room. There's an indentation in the carpet where my bed used to be. My books are gone from the bookcase. The closet door is open, a row of empty hangers on the rod.

My throat tightens and my eyes start to tear up again. A miserable ache settles in the center of my chest. I can't believe this is actually happening. A thousand different memories of my room flicker in my head. Hanging out with my friends, listening to music, reading my books in bed, sneaking out the window onto the roof, practicing my lightsaber moves.

Everything I've ever done in my life is somehow connected to this place.

I wipe the tears from the corners of my eyes. Damn it. I knew it was going to suck having to move into Cathy's room. I just didn't realize how much I was going to miss my own.

A little while later, I slog into Cathy's bedroom, carrying my replica swords wrapped carefully in the brown Jedi cloak I wore for Halloween a few years ago—and for a few imagined lightsaber battles after that.

My parents have split the place in two, stringing a heavy curtain down the middle and rearranging things so that my bed is positioned on one side, with my Lord of the Rings poster hung on the wall and all my Star Wars books arranged in a tall bookcase. It's like they've shrunk down my old bedroom and tucked it into the corner of this one.

I flop on my bed, my anger at this sucky situation still boiling over. I can't believe how a day that was turning out so well could just spin on a dime and end up being so miserable. It's an about-face that would even make Evelyn proud.

📽 CHAPTER FORTY-FIVE 📽

NIGHTMARE ON ELM STREET

INT. HOUSE ATTIC — NIGHT

Rogart and Nashira are huddled close under a blanket. SCREAMS can be heard outside.

>   NASHIRA
> Shouldn't we go try to help those people?

>   ROGART
> We can't help them. It's too late. If we go
> out there, the vampanzees will eat us just like
> they're eating them.

>   NASHIRA
> Are we just supposed to hide forever?

>   ROGART
> I don't know what else to do.

Nashira pulls a cross necklace out from under her shirt.

NASHIRA

You know what this is, Rogart?

ROGART

It's a cross. They don't work against these
monsters. Believe me, I've tried.

NASHIRA

I know. This cross was Grandma's. She gave it
to me before she died. She said it symbolized
a crossroads. Life is filled with them, brother.
We have to make a choice here. We either run
and hide, maybe live for a few more days. Or
we fight these things and maybe save the
human race. What's it gonna be, Rogart?

Cathy stomps into our bedroom without saying a word
to me, slams the door behind her—like she's been doing
the entire last week—then goes to her side of the room
behind the heavy curtain, turns on Joy Division at full
volume, and opens the window to let in the cold air.
These are her battle tactics, meant to torment me till I
move out of the house and in with one of my friends.

I'd hurl some salvos back at her—blast a few of my
own songs, maybe some Arnold Murphy's Bologna Dare
for her listening pleasure, or perhaps ask her if the crank-
ing whiny death music means that she doesn't have a

date for Valentine's Day—but I am far too swamped keeping all my movie and girlfriend balls in the air to be bothered.

At this very moment, I'm on my bed, e-mailing Nessa the changes to the latest few pages we've been working on. We haven't been able to get together recently because of Cathy's work schedule, which is making things really difficult. It wouldn't be so bad if we were actually going to use Evelyn and Nick's takes because it's taking forever to film anything with them. But since Leyna and Hunter are amazingly efficient—not to mention really good— there's a chance we'll be caught up with everything I've gotten written in less than a week.

My e-mail bings. It's Nessa again. *Nice detail with Nashira's cross, but Rogart is too passive in this scene. He needs to take charge of the situation from the start. Keep up the good work. Hey, just ate a candy heart that said I'M HORNY. What are the odds? :)*

Ugh. I don't know what I'm more annoyed with: having to rewrite this scene *again* or Nessa's incessant pretend come-ons.

Actually, Cathy's pounding music trumps both of those things in the irritation department.

I glance at the Death Star. Six thirty. Nick's picking me up for my dinner with Evelyn in fifteen. I better get dressed. It shouldn't take me too long. I've only got one suit that I wore to my cousin's wedding two years ago.

I shut my computer down and grab my phone off the

bed. I flip it off vibrate and glance at the screen to see I've got a message. It's from Leyna. Or, as she's entered in my phone, Leon, for security's sake.

Hppy <3 dA. hOp ur hving fn. Wtnd u 2 c ths. hEr's my lttl mffn. wht do u thnk?

There's a picture attached. I click on it to get a better look.

It's slightly out of focus. And it's dark. And hairy. And . . .

Whoa, hey, now. Is that . . . Is that what I think it is? Nooo. It can't be, can it? I squint hard at the photo. Trying to will it into focus.

Oh, my God. I think . . . I think Leyna just sexted me for Valentine's Day.

☛ CHAPTER FORTY-SIX ☚

MY BLOODY VALENTINE

Le CHAT NOIR is the fanciest restaurant I've ever been to. There are dimly lit chandeliers all around, white tablecloths, candles, wineglasses, soft almost-inaudible classical music playing in the background. And waiters wearing tuxedos and white gloves.

Evelyn and I are the only kids in the entire place. All the other couples are old. Like, my grandparents old. And it's so hushed in here. Like a church or something. Like you're afraid to even lift your silverware for fear of making any kind of clatter.

The whole atmosphere makes me feel as uncomfortable as a Trekkie at a cotillion.

Well, the atmosphere, along with my waist-strangling floodsies and my motion-constricting suit jacket, which makes it impossible for me to reach out for the bread basket. I should have tried on these clothes as soon as I knew I was going to have to wear them. Now all I can do is hold in my stomach and lean down anytime I want to take a sip of water.

"I can't believe you set this all up," Evelyn says, smiling at me from across the table. "It's the most romantic thing anyone has ever done for me."

"Yeah, well." I try a humble shrug, but my shoulders are pinned in. "I just thought, you know, Valentine's Day and all."

As soon as the words are out of my mouth, I'm thinking of Leyna's picture again. Her Valentine's present to me. I dart my eyes to the side to see if I can locate the bathroom. Maybe I can sneak off and have another peek. Just to make sure I'm seeing what I think I'm seeing.

Just then our waiter appears at the table and hands us our leather-bound menus. "*Bonjour, monsieur. Mademoiselle.* Will we be having a virgin cocktail before we eat? Perhaps a glass of sparkling cider?"

Evelyn smiles at me. "Ooh, let's, okay? So we can toast to our undying devotion."

I look up at the waiter, who looms over me, his nose in the air, his mouth turned down, like I'm some sort of dirty cretin. "Two sparkling ciders. Yes. Thank you."

"*C'est bon.*" The waiter gives a curt little bow and marches off.

"I'm so excited." Evelyn's vibrating in her chair as she lifts the towering menu. "I've never been to such a fine restaurant. I wonder what they have."

"Yeah," I say, hefting my own menu and cracking it open, wondering if I'll be able to make sense of any of the French.

Holy shit! I may not know many of the words, but the numbers I recognize. Eighteen dollars for . . . onion soup? Thirteen dollars for what I think might be salad? And . . . And . . . Fuuuck me! Steak and French fries—I'm sorry, *frites*—for forty-three bucks! My stomach churns. This whole night is going to cost me a fortune.

I take a deep breath, trying to calm myself down without resorting to sniffing my palm. But it only makes my jacket tighter, which makes it harder to breathe, in part because the stupid earrings box that's jammed in my inside jacket pocket feels like it's digging in to my heart. Okay. Don't panic. Maybe Evelyn will see the prices and take mercy on me.

"I'm ravenous," she says. "I haven't eaten all day in anticipation of tonight. It all looks so good. I want *everything.*"

"Really?" I laugh nervously behind the cover of my menu. "I don't know. I'm actually having a hard time deciding. And I had a big lunch—a *really* big lunch—so . . ."

"Well, *I'm* ordering the five-course tasting menu. And since the whole table has to order it, I guess that's what you're having too. It'll be fun. We'll get to try a little bit of a lot of things." She snaps her menu shut like it's already a done deal.

I glance over at the tasting menu and nearly fall off my chair. Sixty dollars per person. That's . . . *a hundred and twenty bucks*! Plus tax. Plus tip. Holy cannoli, there goes the rest of our movie budget. I think I'm going to cry.

"I . . . I don't know, Evelyn," I squeak. "That's . . . It's . . . maybe too much food."

"Oh, poo on you." She paddles my words out of the air with the back of her hand. "This is a special night. It's our first Valentine's Day together. We're going to remember this for the rest of our lives."

Our waiter returns with our flutes of sparkling apple juice. He places them carefully on the table, then stands tall. "*Monsieur. Mademoiselle.* Have we decided on dinner?"

"Yes," Evelyn blurts. "We're having the tasting menu, please." She holds up her menu and the waiter takes it from her. "Both of us."

The waiter turns and smiles at me, suddenly much happier than he was a moment ago. He nods and removes my menu from the table. "I will get that started for you, *tout de suite.*"

As soon as the waiter is gone, Evelyn hoists her glass in the air. "To us."

"Right," I say, clinking her glass with mine.

I'm about to take a sip of my cider when Evelyn continues, "To trust. To honesty. To seventy-six more Valentine's Days spent together. To best friends, partners, and soul mates."

"Okay." I raise my glass again, thinking, *Yes, it'll be great to find all that someday. With someone. Someone who's not at this table.* I bring my glass to my lips but apparently Evelyn's not finished yet.

"To being there for each other. In thick and thin." She stares at me over her glass. Her eyes wide and intense. "To never *ever* cheating on each other. To being true and faithful. To listening to each other. And respecting each other. And being supportive in every way possible."

Jesus Christ, it's like wedding vows from hell.

"Mm-hm." I quickly bend forward and take a sip of my juice before she can say anything else. I set my glass down and try to think of a way to change the subject. "So, um, yeah. I guess . . . I sort of . . . have something for you." I reach for my inside jacket pocket, but I'm so sausaged into my suit that it's nearly impossible. "It's . . . a gift." I have to swivel my entire body around, and even then I can only just grasp the top edge of the pocket. The threads on my sleeves make a straining sound as the tips of my fingers just graze the top of the box wedged inside the pocket.

"What is it? What is it?" Evelyn's bouncing up and down. Clapping her hands like one of those insane wind-up cymbal monkeys.

"Just . . . Almost . . ." Finally I've got a grip on the jewelry box and tug it from my jacket. "Here you go," I say, out of breath. "It's just . . . a little something . . . I thought you might like."

She leaps up and snatches it from my hand. "I know what these are!" she squeals. "Nick told you, didn't he?"

"Yeah. He was a big help," I say, my smile strained.

"They're beautiful!" Evelyn beams at the earrings. "I can't believe you spent this much money on me." Big swollen tears start to form in her eyes. She sniffs. "You must really, really love me. I can't believe I ever doubted it." She stands up, walks around the table, and strangles me in a hug. "I love you too, Sean," she declares.

"Wow," I say, blinking hard. Confused how the *L* word got thrown in the mix here. "That's . . . Wow." I should have seen that reaction coming. *Damn you, Nick!* "I'm just . . . glad you like them."

"They're perfect. And so are you." Evelyn returns to her seat and grabs her giant purse. "I got you something too, snuggle boo." She pulls out a large gift-wrapped present and hands it to me.

I shake my head. "You didn't have to do that."

"It's nothing compared to what you got me. But just because I don't have as much money as you doesn't mean I love you any less." She motions at the gift. "Go on. Open it up."

I force a smile and start to tear away the paper. As soon as I see the blue fabric of the shirt, the GUESS label in the collar, my stomach lurches. "Oh. Thanks," I choke out, afraid to even touch the stolen goods. "It's . . . nice."

"You really like it?"

"Sure. It's . . . great." My belly is in so many knots I

think I might hurl. I glance back over my shoulder, thinking this would be a good time to go to the bathroom. Splash some water on my face, have a quick look at my Leyna photo to help calm me down. "Excuse me for a moment," I say, placing my napkin on the table. "I'll be right back."

I push my chair back, start to stand, and hear a low ripping sound. The cool draft I feel on my butt is all the evidence I need that tonight is going to be the longest night of my life.

"On second thought," I say, dropping back into my seat, "maybe I'll wait until after the appetizer."

CHAPTER FORTY-SEVEN

ONE HOUR PHOTO

OH, MY GOD, VALENTINE'S DAY is forever ruined for me." I step off the bus followed closely by Coop and Matt. We make the left turn and head toward Uncle Doug's house. I lost the coin toss, so I'm lugging Evelyn's red suitcase while Coop and Matt are each hauling two small animal crates. "Not only did I go on the world's most expensive and torturous date—where the tiny bits of undercooked food were served to us over the course of *three hours*—but then I get home, ready to pass out, and guess who's snoring like a grizzly bear with a couple of kazoos shoved up its nose? I didn't freakin' sleep one minute last night."

Matt can barely contain his laughter. "You should have done what Val and me did. Ordered a pizza and watched a movie at home."

"Yeah." Coop glares at me. "It would have saved you a lot of embarrassment and us a shitload of money.

Speaking of which, we're completely tapped, so you're gonna have to ask your uncle for the other five hundred bucks he promised us. We still need to buy more props, and costumes, and the editing software."

"I know. I know," I say. "I'll do it today. There'll be plenty of time since we're getting there so early."

"Actually, we don't have much time at all," Coop says.

"What are you talking about?"

"You didn't tell him?" Matt asks.

"He would have just freaked," Coop says.

"Freaked?" My head's on a swivel, looking from Coop to Matt to Coop. "About what?"

Coop sighs. "I told Leyna and Hunter to meet us at your uncle's house at eleven. We're going to shoot a scene with them and Uncle Doug first before Evelyn and Nick arrive for lunch at around one."

"What?" I stop dead on the sidewalk. "Are you insane? You just totally screwed us. Why would you do that? We have to keep everything separate. Oh, my God. I'm a dead man."

"Take a pill," Coop says. "I left plenty of wiggle room. Leyna and Hunter will be long gone before everyone else shows up to film the humanzee rampage scene."

"That's not the point." I grab my phone and shove it in his face. "Nick's tracking us, remember? He'll see our cell-phone signals in the same location."

"No, he won't," Coop mocks. "I told Hunter and

Leyna that your uncle was all paranoid about microwaves and they had to leave their phones at home. So chillax. The Coopster has it all covered."

"Oh." My tensed-up shoulders relax.

"Yeah. 'Oh.'" Coop shakes his head. "Sometimes you lack faith, boss."

I take a deep breath. "It's still risky, though. I don't see the point."

"We're on a schedule here, dawg. We have to be efficient about these things. When we're at a location, we need to film as many scenes as we can at that location."

"Yeah, I guess." I start walking again. Despite my initial panic, I'm excited to see Leyna. I want to ask her about the picture she sent me. All night long, I kept going back and forth on it. Did she? Didn't she? I call the photo up on my phone and stare at it again. If it is what I think it is, I'd prefer to keep it to myself. But just in case I'm way off base about this, I'd rather know for sure.

"Okay, question. What do you guys think this is?" I hold my phone out for Matt to see as we make the turn onto Uncle Doug's street. "Leyna sent it to me last night. I can't figure it out."

Matt squints at the screen. "A blurry photo of something hairy."

Coop leans over to take a look. His eyes go wide as soon as he sees it. "Holy crap, dude." He bursts out laughing. "Are you serious? You guys don't know what this is?"

"No," I say.

Coop shakes his head. "Oh, you poor, naive little boys. That's a shot of her squish mitten."

Matt looks at it again. "No way."

"Yes way," Coop insists. "What was the message that came with it?"

I click back and read, " 'Happy Valentine's Day. Hope you're having fun. Wanted you to see this. Here's my little muffin. What do you think?' "

Coop is in hysterics. "Jesus Christ, dawg! Could it be any clearer? That's her *muff*-in. She's totally sexting you."

"That's what I thought at first." I pull the phone back and stare at the picture again. "But now I don't know. . . ."

"How could you think that was anything else?" Coop hoots. "It's dark, and hairy, and mysterious. Look up *growler* in the dictionary and *that's* what you'll see. I mean, come on, now. 'Here's my little muffin. What do you think?' No lines to read between there."

"I know, but . . ." I shake my head. "She doesn't really seem like the sexting type. And even if she was, why would she send me something like this? We're not even dating."

"She's probably bored waiting for you to make the first move, dude. It's her way of thanking you for giving her the lead in the movie."

I look at Matt for some confirmation here. "What do you think?"

He just shrugs. "I have no idea. It could be anything. Maybe it's her bran muffin."

Coop rolls his eyes. "Why the hell would she ask his opinion about her goddamn bran muffin? Get a clue, dude. Oh, wait, I'm sorry, I forgot who I was talking to. You haven't actually seen a Batcave up close and personal, have you?"

Matt lifts one of the cat carriers so he can brandish an upside-down middle finger at Coop.

"Mm-hmm. Just as I thought." Coop turns to me. "What did you write back to her?"

"Nothing. I didn't know what it was, so I didn't know what to say."

Coop reels back like he's been shot. "Dude, this girl went out on a limb for you. And you just left her hanging? That's totally malicious. You better thank her when you see her. First off."

I feel my insides curdling. "But what if it isn't her—?"

"I'm telling you, it *is*," Coop says. "Believe me. I've seen enough close-up shots of the wizard's sleeve to know one when I'm looking at one. And if you don't acknowledge receipt of this wonderful gift, you'll be insulting her." He turns to Matt. "Come on, Mattie. Back me up."

"Sorry." Matt shakes his head. "I'm staying out of it."

"Do you think she actually *could* be sexting me?" I ask Matt. "Come on, man. You're the voice of reason here. I'm begging you."

"*Could* she be?" Matt shrugs. "Anything's possible, I suppose. But do I *think* she is? I guess I don't know her well enough to make that call."

We turn up Uncle Doug's driveway, my stomach in complete knots. Oh, God. What the hell am I going to say to Leyna when I see her?

☛ CHAPTER FORTY-EIGHT ☚

THE ISLAND OF DR. MOREAU

WE FOLLOW UNCLE DOUG into his kitchen, and my nostrils are filled with the spicy-greasy smell of chili and frying bratwurst. Uncle Doug snatches up a long wooden spoon and gives the bubbling cauldron on the stove a quick stir.

"I hope you boys brought your appetites." Uncle Doug sips some of the chili from the spoon, his eyes going instantly wide. "Whoa! Hello! That'll put some hair on your taste-icles."

Matt, Coop, and me share a nervous look as Uncle Doug leans down and peers through the oven window.

"Ah, yes, my little sweltering wieners," he says. "Roasting nice and leisurely in there." Uncle Doug stands and pulls off his apron. "You're in for a treat. I only make this meal for my loved ones. Slow-cooked chorizo slathered in chili, chicory, and Cheez Whiz. Let me tell you something: you haven't lived until you've chowed down on a Doug's Dirty Dog."

"I know Sean's excited." Coop waggles his eyebrows. "It's all he could talk about on the way over here. Filling his mouth with your dirty dog. Isn't that right, Matt?"

"Yup," Matt responds. "We couldn't get him to shut up about it."

Uncle Doug smiles proudly. "I bet *you'll* be the ones talking about it on the way home."

"Oh, you can count on it," Coop says, suppressing a laugh.

"So." Uncle Doug glances nervously at the animal carriers in the corner. "Shall we, uh . . . get things set up down in the basement so we're all ready when the cast arrives?"

"Good idea," I say, leaping to my feet.

The plan is to shoot the scene where Rogart and Nashira happen upon Dr. Schmaloogan's lab and learn all about his evil plan. Unfortunately for us, Uncle Doug is terrified of animals. He says it's because he's highly allergic but Mom's told me it's really because he was bitten on the penis by a hamster when he was a kid. Honestly, though, I've never delved too far into it because I'm afraid to find out why there was a hamster anywhere near his penis to begin with.

For that reason, and the fact that we have to get

Leyna and Hunter out of here by noon, we're going to have to film this section as fast as we can.

"Hey, so, Uncle Doug," I say as we descend the stairs into the cellar. "We were wondering if we could get the second half of the thousand dollars you said you'd give us."

"Oh, really?" Uncle Doug doesn't look back. Just keeps focused on the steps ahead of him. "I'd like an expense sheet first. See what you've spent the first five hundred on."

I shoot the guys a panicked look.

"You've seen what we have so far," Coop responds. "Monkey costumes. Blood makeup. And . . . other stuff. It goes a lot faster than you think."

The four of us get to the bottom of the stairs and make our way into the unfinished basement. Uncle Doug has already set up a "lab table" in the middle of the room.

"Yeah, well." Uncle Doug runs his hand down his beard. "Unfortunately, Uncle Doug's a little strapped for cash right now. What with the stock market shitting the bed and . . . other losses. So, I'm afraid I'm going to have to change our business arrangement. Five hundred's all you'll be getting. I do apologize, but that's the way of things in the business world."

Coop turns and shoots me a wave of fury. And I don't blame him. I'm pretty pissed myself. Our super-low-budget movie's just become a no-budget movie.

I'm just about to open my mouth to protest when

there's a knock at the front door. "I'll get it!" I offer, already scrambling up the stairs.

I hustle to the door and yank it open. It's Leyna and Hunter. Together. Which annoys me a little bit, though it'll annoy me a whole lot less if I find out Leyna sent me a picture of her Bermuda Triangle.

I send Hunter down to the basement, tell him they need his help setting up. And ask Leyna if I can speak with her for a second.

We go into the family room and sit on my uncle's ratty old dust-billowing sofa.

"What's up?" Leyna asks, not looking anxious or embarrassed at all.

I take out my phone and call up the picture of her Fur-tress of Solitude. I need to do this quick before I lose my nerve.

"Oh, hey, you got it," she says, smiling and sounding relieved. "I wasn't sure it went through, when I didn't hear anything from you."

"Um, no. Yeah. I got it," I choke out, feeling sweaty all over. "It's just . . ."

Oh, jeez, Leyna looks adorable. And she smells spectacular. Her almondy-sweetness. God, it's like a drug or something. The scent of her makes me light-headed and tingly all over. I just want to nestle into her and never leave.

"So." She gestures at my phone. "Have you had a chance to look at it?"

"Oh, yeah. For sure. I've been looking at it a lot." Oh, come on. Just ask her what it is and be done with it.

"Well, what's your diagnosis?" Leyna giggles and gives me a nudge. "Doctor."

Doctor? Is that what we're playing here? So this *is* what I think it is? Holy crap.

My heart takes off like a jackrabbit, my breath all shaky.

"Well, um, it's, uh." I gulp. "I mean, I'm glad you sent it to me and everything. . . ."

Leyna places her hand on my thigh, which sends a rush of excitement right into my lap. "Do you want to see it in person?" she asks. "I know the picture's not very clear. It wasn't the easiest thing to get that shot."

"No," I say. "I imagine it wouldn't be."

"Maybe you could come over to my house to have a look? I don't want to impose or anything, but I seriously think it needs some attention."

My leg begins to bounce, and I find I'm chewing my tongue like a maniac. "Yes," I say. "Of course I'll come over. Just tell me when and I'll be there."

"Oh, you're so sweet. What about next weekend? Would that be okay?"

"*Okay?* Absolutely. Yes. That would be very okay."

"Thank you, Sean." Leyna leans over and hugs me. "And my little Muff-Muff thanks you too. I mean, she *would.*" Leyna laughs. "If she could talk."

"Hope I'm not interrupting anything," Coop says,

sticking his head in the door. "But we're on a bit of a time crunch here." He looks at me knowingly. "I think we should get started."

Forty-five minutes later and we're *still* down in Uncle Doug's dimly lit basement trying to get him to hold Buttons on the "lab table" so he can use the fake needle and pretend to draw some blood from her. She's the most docile cat you've ever met, but Uncle Doug's acting like we're asking him to handle a Siberian tiger.

"These things carry all sorts of diseases," he says, holding his hands up high and close to his lab coat. "There's a reason they don't want pregnant women going anywhere near kitty litter."

"Well"—I take a furtive whiff of my palm—"It's a good thing you're not a pregnant woman."

"*Anyone* can get sick from cat feces," Uncle Doug argues.

Coop sighs. "We're not asking you to stick your finger up its ass. We just want you to hold it. Like a billion people do a billion times a day."

Leyna and Hunter are crouched outside, looking in the open basement window and laughing. They're supposed to be catching Dr. Schmaloogan in the act of doing evil experiments. But the only thing they're witnessing is my uncle's breakdown.

"It's not just their excrement." Uncle Doug tugs on his bushy beard. "It's their saliva too. These things bite.

They carry all kinds of pathogens. Staph. Meningitis. The plague. Not to mention, cats are one of the main transmitters of rabies. Believe me, I've done the research."

"Buttons doesn't have rabies." I start to chew my tongue nervously. "Look at her. She's a sweetie. Besides, I have her trained. She won't move unless I tell her to."

"Be that as it may." Uncle Doug steps back from the table, looking flustered and sweaty. "Cats are unpredictable. I'd just as soon do the scene with some kind of replica. I'll put up with having the animals in cages in the background for verisimilitude. And I'll deal with the aftereffects of all the fluff and dander. But I am *not* about to have my penis bitten off by a venomous disease-ridden feline, thank you very much."

"Your *what*?" Hunter calls from the window.

"I just don't want to be bitten. Or scratched. *Anywhere.* Okay? So"—Uncle Doug wafts his hands at Buttons—"take this thing away from me. Immediately." He grabs his pack of American Spirits and taps one out. The cigarette's in his mouth and lit before I even have a chance to move.

"We don't have any animal models." Coop checks his cell phone. "And we're running out time. You don't like cats? What about the ferret?"

Uncle Doug sneers and puffs on his cigarette. "I think I'll pass. The last thing I need is a feral weasel wriggling out of my hands and sneaking down my pants. Thanks, but no thanks."

"The dog then," Matt offers. "I'm not even a dog person and I think it's cute. And you'd have to work *really* hard to get it down your pants."

Uncle Doug picks a fleck of tobacco off his tongue. He studies it while seeming to consider this latest proposition. "What kind of dog is it?"

"A Maltipoo." I slide Buttons back into her cat carrier. "He's around six pounds."

"Dogs *are* much more obedient than cats," Uncle Doug says. "You have a muzzle for it?"

"A muzzle?" I move over to Jo-Jo's kennel and take him out. He's a gray fluff ball barely bigger than my hand. "I don't think they make muzzles small enough."

"Come on, Uncle Doug," Coop pleads from behind the video camera.

"It's pretty cold just squatting out here," Leyna says from outside.

Uncle Doug gestures at me with his cigarette. "How well you got that thing trained?"

I place Jo-Jo on the floor and show my uncle all his tricks. Ballerina, play dead, flip, lie down, roll over. By the time we're done, his tiny little tongue hangs from his mouth as he pants.

Finally Uncle Doug sighs and crushes out his cigarette. "Okay. But I want that beast to lie stock-still. In total submission. If he even flinches, I'm gonna hurl him across the room."

"You will not," I say.

"Okay, then, I'll hurl *you* across the room. How's that?"

"Fine." I scoop Jo-Jo up and put him on the table. I get him to lie down and roll over. "Stay, Jo-Jo. Stay."

"Look how adorable," Matt coos.

Uncle Doug shuffles cautiously up to the table. "Yeah, that's how they get you. Kill you with cuteness. Sucker you in and then go right for your nuts."

I laugh. "I can guarantee you he's not going to go anywhere near your balls."

"You think it's funny, but go ask any emergency-room physician how often she sees pet-incurred testicular injuries. You'd be mighty surprised how common it is."

"Yes," I say. "I would be incredibly surprised. Now, can we get on with this?"

We have to do at least a dozen takes of the scene because Uncle Doug is simply not believable as an evil mad veterinarian who experiments on animals. Sure, he looks the part. Big and gruff, hairy, rubber gloved, lab coated, and red eyed. But he's barely touching the dog with the tips of his fingers, and his scrunched-up face completely betrays his absolute revulsion.

For twenty minutes straight, Jo-Jo doesn't move a muscle. He is being such a good boy. There's no biting. No scratching. No ball-sack lunging. Not even a whimper. Just a frozen little Ewok-faced puppy with his tiny furry paws stuck in the air.

"Look," Coop finally says, his face red from frustration, "grab the dog like you mean it. You're a vet, for fuck's sake. You're not scared of animals. Just jab it with the needle and take the goddamn blood. You wanted to be in the movie. So be in it."

Uncle Doug takes a deep breath. "Okay. Fine. I'll do it. Once. But you better make sure you've got that camera rolling, because it's the last time you're going to see this."

"Thank you." Coop nods to Leyna and Hunter at the window, then hits the record button and points at my uncle.

Uncle Doug quickly grasps Jo-Jo by the belly and raises the collapsible hypodermic. "All right, you mutt," he grumbles his dialogue. "Time to do your part in my grand experiment." Uncle Doug cackles evilly, then leans over the dog and prepares to stick him with the needle. "I'm going to need a nice hefty sample from you."

And, as if on cue, Jo-Jo sends a streaming spout of whiz straight into Uncle Doug's face. Dog pee soaks his mountain-man beard and cascades down the front of his lab coat.

Leyna and Hunter bust into hysterics.

Matt and Coop's jaws drop in sync as Uncle Doug leaps away from the lab table and unleashes the longest string of curses I think I've ever heard. He grabs a soiled rag from the workbench—which, truth be told, is probably way more bacteria laden than Jo-Jo's pee—and swabs at his face and neck like a madman.

"YOU!" Uncle Doug points at me with the dirty cloth.

My eyes dart to Jo-Jo, still frozen in place on the table. He looks at me for some sort of guidance. *Can I move yet? Sorry about the pee, dude, but he squeezed me like a sponge.*

I have several options here. Run away and leave my dog to the mercy of my foaming-at-the-mouth uncle. Dart in to save him and risk being beaten to death with any of the numerous blunt objects—baseball bat, pipe wrench, bong—that are in grabbing distance.

Or try to reason with a raging zoophobe who's just been whizzed on by a dog.

"It was an accident," I try. "He didn't mean it. You just spooked him. When you grabbed him so suddenly. He's a little dog. He's got a little bladder."

"Not. So. Little." Uncle Doug swipes at his face again with the rag, glaring at me, breathing heavily and loudly through his nose, like a speared bull that's getting ready to charge.

"I'm s-sorry," I stammer. "At least he didn't bite you." I catch Matt's and Coop's looks. At any other time, with any other person, we'd be screaming with laughter right now. Just like Hunter and Leyna are doing at the window.

But this is Uncle Doug we're talking about. And he is royally steamed. And he is three times my size. And he could snap us all in half in the blink of an eye.

Uncle Doug closes his eyes. He takes a deep, deep breath, his hand strangling the filthy rag. "Okay," he says. "I need a smoke. And I need it now."

"Your cigarettes." I dart over to the workbench and grab his pack of American Spirits. "They're fine. They're not wet. See? You put them down over here. They're safe."

Uncle Doug slowly opens his eyes. "I don't think you understand. A cigarette is not going to be strong enough. Not by a moon shot. Uncle Doug needs to forget this little . . . incident. In fact, we're *all* going to forget this." He waves his hand in the air. "Wipe it from our hard drives, so to speak. Understand?"

We all nod vigorously, though I can tell by the expression on Leyna's and Hunter's faces that they're never going to forget this.

"If Uncle Doug ever finds out that anyone *else* has found out about this"—he laughs, but in a really scary way—"well, let's just say the person who leaked it will regret they were ever placed on this little planet we call Earth. Are we crystal on this point?"

Suddenly Leyna and Hunter don't look quite as amused anymore. And Coop totally ignores the "leaked it" bait. The five of us nod like bobblehead dolls in an earthquake.

Uncle Doug takes another deep breath. "All right. Good. Now, you guys go upstairs and take my sausages out of the oven. I'm going to take fifteen in my trailer."

And just as I'm starting to relax, feeling like we dodged a major laser blast . . .

There's a loud thumping at the front door.

Matt, Coop, and me whip our heads around toward the stairs.

My stomach plunges hard. Because there's only one person in the world I know who knocks like that.

CHAPTER FORTY-NINE

RISE OF THE PLANET
OF THE APES

HEY, HO," I SAY AS I OPEN the door to see Nick and Evelyn standing there. "You guys are early. That's . . . great. Excellent. Come on in." I quickly usher them inside and close the door just as Leyna and Hunter are walking by behind them. Coop stalled them just long enough, thank God.

"I saw you were already here." Nick laughs. "Not that I'm keeping watch or anything. But we figured, might as well join you, right? You know, in case you needed help setting up."

"No, that's . . ." My chest feels like it's going to cave in. "It's all good. We were just . . . shooting a scene with Uncle Doug. By himself. You know. Alone. And, uh . . . But . . . Anyway. It's good you're here because lunch is just about ready. The others should be here in around twenty."

A short while later and we're all crammed into Uncle Doug's tiny dining room—Nick, Evelyn, Val, Helen, Matt, Coop, and me. We're still waiting on Pete and Tony, but Uncle Doug said we should just eat and they can join us when they get here.

"Start. Start," Uncle Doug calls from the kitchen. "I'll be there in a second."

Nick grabs hold of the sloppy bun with two hands and somehow manages to shove half of the sausage into his mouth, the chili spilling all over his hands and pitter-pattering onto his plate.

"Guess I'm off my diet today." Coop follows Nick's lead and goes for the hand-to-mouth method while Matt, Val, Helen, Evelyn, and me opt for our forks and knives.

I don't know if it's the stress of this whole situation or what, but I am absolutely ravenous. Still, I'm a bit wary of my uncle's gloppy concoction. Beyond the fact that he keeps calling them his Dirty Dogs, there's something about them—the shriveled sausages, the dark chili sauce, the Day-Glo Cheez Whiz—that looks . . . unappetizing.

I cautiously cut off a small bite, give it a quick sniff—lots of spice, pork, tomatoes, a hint of coffee—and then slide the goopy mess into my mouth.

It tastes pretty good, actually, and before I know it I'm eating way too fast and washing down mouthful after mouthful with generous gulps of tropical punch Kool-Aid, which, oddly enough, is the only drink—besides beer and whiskey—that Uncle Doug has in the house.

"Guess who we saw at Starbucks?" Helen asks out of the blue.

"Who's that?" Coop says through a mouthful of chili-cheese chorizo.

"Miss Boobalas." Valerie pushes a kidney bean around the plate with her fork. "Remember her? Bursting out of her dress at the auditions."

Evelyn sits up like a meerkat that's heard a hawk. "Oh, yeah. The sloppy strumpet."

Coop forces a smile. "I don't know who you're talking about."

"Oh, sure you do," Helen says. "You couldn't take your eyes off her."

"Or, a certain *part* of her," Valerie adds.

Matt just starts shoveling food in his mouth like it's his job.

Coop, on the other hand, rolls his eyes. "Okay, look. We've apologized for that. Matt and I even took you girls out for ice cream as a show of our deepest regret for our appallingly caveman-like behavior. So do we never get to hear the end of this?"

Nick lets out a snort. "You guys obviously don't know women very well." He takes the last bite of his first chili dog and talks while he chews. "I have no idea what you did, but I can assure you, you'll be punished for it for the rest of your lives. Or as long as you're going out, anyway. Girls sheathe that shit and then pull it out to jab you with at random odd moments."

Helen laughs. "We have to keep our cavemen in line somehow."

"*Santé.*" Valerie raises her glass in a cheers-to-that gesture.

Just then Uncle Doug tromps into the room, carrying a massive plate of food and an NFL souvenir cup filled to the brim with Kool-Aid. "So, what did I miss?" He plops down in his chair, the neon-pink liquid sloshing over the rim of his cup.

"Nothing." Coop smirks at Helen. "We were waiting for you before we started talking about anything *worthwhile.*"

"*Excelente.*" Uncle Doug hefts his loaded chili dog off his plate. "That's how I like it. When the king arrives, the conversation thrives."

Matt's phone buzzes. He checks the screen, and his eyes go wide. "Oh, crap," he says. "We've got a problem."

It doesn't take nearly as long as I'd hoped to get into the oversize monkey costumes. In fact, it could have taken the rest of the day and it wouldn't have been long enough for me.

As it turns out, thirty-four minutes after we find out that Tony and Pete have bailed on us for a pickup basketball game, Nick, Matt, and me are dressed in the ill-fitting humanzee outfits and the whole crew is driving to the Elk Hills Country Club in Uncle Doug's green rattletrap of a van.

"Everyone okay back there?" My uncle glances in the rearview mirror. He's smoking his third joint since lunch, and I can't believe he can still see straight, never mind pilot a car. But he's driving just fine, which only means he's probably got the pot tolerance of a Colombian drug lord.

"Sure," I lie, from the second set of backseats. "It's all good."

I actually feel pretty carsick. I don't know if it's nerves, or the fact that I'm sitting in the very back of the van and breathing in wafts of smoke through the rubbery stench of this monkey mask, but the chili-cheese sausages are starting to seriously complain to the tropical punch Kool-Aid about their current accommodations.

Not to mention I feel totally claustrophobic in this costume. I try to casually tug at my monkey-crotch, which is riding up and cutting in to my mansack.

"Hey." Coop swats my furry leg. "Don't play with your chimp-choad, dawg. Those costumes have to last for the whole shoot. We don't need your simian semen gumming them up."

"I'm not *playing* with anything. The costume's a little big, okay? I'm adjusting."

"Yeah, well, don't adjust too vigorously." Coop

chuckles. "Someone else might have to wear that thing at some point."

"Be my guest," I say.

Coop throws up his hands. "Hey, we've already discussed this. I need to be behind the scenes to direct. This whole operation has to be perfectly timed or we're screwed."

"These costumes are hotter than an oven," Matt says from the first set of backseats, his voice muffled by the mask.

"Yeah, but they smother your buck snorts pretty good." Nick lifts his shaggy left butt cheek and rips a meaty rumbler. "Okay, well, maybe not that good." He doubles over laughing.

The warm-wet-manure stench hijacks the interior of the van almost immediately.

"Oh, man. Come *on*." As if I wasn't feeling nauseous enough already. I shove my ape nose out the minuscule air slit afforded by the latched windows back here and sniff away, trying to replace the poo particles in my nostrils with the clean outside air.

Evelyn smacks Nick's hairy head. "Real classy."

"What? I'm just getting into character. Chimps are disgusting creatures. They fart just like truckers and hurl their own dukers. Isn't that right, guy?" Nick grabs Matt's neck and shakes him violently.

"Could you not, please?" Matt complains. "I'm hot enough in this thing."

Valerie leans over and examines the seam between Matt's mask and body. "Maybe we should have added some ventilation. We'll have to see about that when we get home later."

"All right," Coop says, glancing down at his notebook. "Let's go over the game plan. The Elk Hills' website says the Rico Petrelli party is taking place in the Amethyst Room. That's in the east wing of the club. It's the only thing going on this afternoon, so it'll be easy to find."

"Are you sure this is such a good idea?" I ask. "I mean, it's the poor guy's sixtieth birthday celebration. Couldn't we do this somewhere else?"

Coop cants his head. "Don't be a schween. This is the perfect opportunity to get some real fear on tape. It's exactly what we need to make our film stand out. Besides, my dad's worked on this Rico dude's Rolls-Royce and he says he's a royal dingus. Getting mechanics fired for no reason, hitting on the young receptionists, throwing garbage out his window as he drives away. Basically, he's a pig, so he deserves whatever he gets. But be careful. Apparently dawg's got a bad temper. So we're going to want to get in and get out as fast as we can."

"Hey," Nick says, "I had just had a great idea. Wouldn't it be cool if the monkeys could talk? That way they could threaten the party guests. Write us some dialogue, Sean."

"No. Absolutely not. Humanzees don't talk." Coop shakes his head.

"What about me?" Evelyn asks. "Shouldn't I have some dialogue in this scene? Why am I at this party to begin with? What's my motivation? Should I attempt to thwart the humanzee attack?"

"No. No. No." Coop is looking panicky. "Don't say anything. Nobody say *anything*. This is a key scene in the movie. It's the very first outbreak. Nashira is there as a witness. So she can go back and report it to her brother. That's all. Your motivation is to just take it in and be terrified." He flips through his notebook. "Okay, now. I'm going to slip in the front door and head straight to the party. Acting all cazh. Like I'm there to partake in the festivities. Monkeys, I want you to sneak in the service entrance. Let's hope you don't run into anyone. It's Sunday, so it shouldn't be too busy. But anybody stops you, just say you're a surprise for Rico Petrelli's party." He flips a page in the book. "Once you're inside, don't think, don't hesitate, don't waste any time. Just find the party and rush right in, roaring as loud as you can, waving your hairy arms in the air. If you can manage it, try and chase the people toward the emergency exits."

"And what are we doing while all this is going on?" Helen asks.

"You take a whack of still photos as the guests run outside," Coop says. "As many as possible. Try to get people's horrified expressions. We can edit those into the movie. It'll make a cool effect. Like a running photographer's record of the first outbreak or something. Evelyn and Val, you'll come with me. Val will run camera while I direct. And Evelyn, we'll get you to mingle in the party. Sit at one of the tables at the front if you can. Try to stay inconspicuous. We don't want anyone to be suspicious. And Uncle Doug, you keep the getaway vehicle running in the parking lot with all the doors open, ready for us to make our escape."

Uncle Doug raises his smoky joint. "Righty-oh."

"Once we've got our shots," Coop continues, "everyone get the hell back into the van, stat. No screwing around. We'll have maybe a minute, two minutes max, where everyone'll be too confused to know what the hell's going on. But eventually someone's going to call the cops, and we want to be long gone by the time they arrive."

"You're damn straight," Uncle Doug chimes in. "I've got a pillowcase full of yerba maté in the boot of this bad boy. And I definitely don't need the fuzz finding that."

CHAPTER FIFTY

THE UNINVITED

HERE WE BE," UNCLE DOUG SAYS, turning the van into the parking lot of the Elk Hills Country Club. The building looks sort of like a squat, elongated White House. It's definitely high-class, for sure. And absolutely no place we should be going dressed up like feral monkey-men.

Uncle Doug drives around back to the service entrance, parks between two trucks, and lets the engine idle. I can't stay in this smoke-and-fart-filled sardine can any longer, so I push past Coop, yank open the side door, and am the first to leap out.

I breathe as deep as I can through the golf ball–size hole at the back of my monkey-mouth. The fresh air—as fresh as it can be, filtered through the plastic of my mask—eases the nauseous feeling that churns my gut. Thank God. I thought I was going to lose it there for a moment. But I'm okay now. My head's still swimming a bit, but I'm no longer at code orange.

I quickly scan the area. There doesn't seem to be anyone around outside, so that's good.

Coop, Matt, and Nick hop down from the van and huddle around me.

"Remember," Coop says. "The louder and scarier you are, the more crazed the people will be and the more realistic it will seem. Really get into the roles you're playing. Keep in mind the situation you're in. You guys are pissed off because you've been turned into zombie-vampire-chimpanzees. And these people are having a freakin' *party*. They don't care. But you want to *make* them care. You want to infect the world so that everyone can feel your pain."

Val, Helen, and Evelyn step out onto the pavement. Helen checks the settings on the DSLR while Evelyn slips on a chain-draped jacket.

"I just got this the other day," Evelyn says. "I thought it looked like Nashira. What do you think?"

"It looks . . . great," I say, wondering where she lifted it from. "Definitely Nashira-esque."

Coop grabs the video camera and hands it to Valerie. "We've only got one shot at this, so let's get it right."

"As long as there are no big-boobed girls in the room to distract me"—Val smirks as she hoists the camera onto her shoulder—"I should be fine."

Coop flashes her a screw-you smile, then turns to us. "Okay, humanzees." He points to the service door. "Get going. Before someone sees you."

"Wait a second. I almost forgot." Helen grabs her purse from the backseat. She removes three dark-red capsules and hands one to each of us monkeys. "They're filled with stage blood. You just bite down on them and the blood will spill from your mouth."

"Cool." Matt holds the little pill between his thumb and forefinger, examining it.

"That's brill, Helen. Great work." Coop grabs my furry shoulder and pulls me aside. "Just to warn you," he whispers in my ear. "If you see Leyna and Hunter in there, don't freak. I asked them to mingle at the back of the party."

I nearly drop a load in my monkey suit. "Are you fucking kidding me?"

"Don't make a scene," Coop hushes. "It's chill. I'll have Evelyn hang at the front of the room and once the rumpus begins, Leyna and Hunter will be the first ones out. We need to get them on tape for this scene. It's too big a part of the movie."

"It's like you want to get caught or something."

"It's all good. You'll see."

I start to turn and go, but he pulls me back. "One more thing. Now that you've got the blood, if you get a chance, try and grab someone in the party and pretend to bite their neck. It'll be totally epic."

"Right," I say, wanting to scream. "I'll keep it in mind."

Matt, Nick, and me take off like three raggedy-ass

Bigfeet, crouching and skulking toward the peeling brown service-entrance door.

"This is gonna be fun," Nick says. "I feel like a SEAL again. Sneaking up on the unwitting. I can't wait to see the expressions on people's faces."

Christ, is that what he looked forward to as a SEAL?

I just want this to be over already. My heart's fluttering like a spooked parakeet in a too-small cage. And I'm still not feeling so good in the stomach department.

I grab the door and hold it open. As Nick and Matt jostle inside I press on my diaphragm, pushing up a little burp to help ease the seasickness in my belly. I get that thick orangey-acid taste at the back of my throat, but it makes me feel quite a bit better.

Just as I'm about to duck into the country club, I see Coop, Val, and Evelyn jogging toward the front of the building. Coop looks my way and gives me a raised solidarity fist.

Fucker. I can't believe he asked Leyna and Hunter to come. If Evelyn or Nick sees them . . . I'm one dead chimpanzee.

I take another full breath and then slip inside.

"Which way?" Matt whispers, his chimp-head on a swivel.

We seem to be in some sort of vestibule or foyer or something. There are three tinted glass doors: one leading to the left, one directly in front of us, and a third to the right. I cock my head and listen for some sort of audible clue—music, talking, laughing—but there's nothing.

"Let's go straight," I say, pointing to the door directly in front of us.

"Decisive. I like it." Nick grabs the handle with his mangy paw and pulls it open.

We step through the doorway and tiptoe down a long fluorescent-lit deserted hallway. There's a musty brussels-sprout smell back here, and it's hard to get air deep into my lungs. The world starts to swirl and I have to brace myself, reaching out for the wall with my right hand.

"You okay?" Matt asks.

"Yeah." I'm trying not to hyperventilate. "I'm just . . . Lunch isn't sitting so well."

"It's the gas," Nick explains, launching a little squeaker for emphasis. "Let it breathe."

"You want to go back?" Matt says to me, his voice hopeful.

It's tempting, for sure. More than tempting. But then I remember why I'm here. The baby. The sister. The room. The snoring.

And Leyna, of course.

"Let's just get this over with," I say, pushing myself away from the wall.

We continue on, passing a large storage room and a few empty offices, until finally we come upon the bustling kitchen. The three of us duck into a doorway, out of sight, and wait as trolleys of food are wheeled from the kitchen and down another hall.

"What do we do now?" Matt whispers.

"We wait," Nick instructs. "Until they're done bringing the carts out."

"Coop said to head straight for the party," I say desperately. The longer we wait here, the more time Evelyn has to notice Leyna. "So that's what we should do. Just act like you belong."

I suck in as much air as I can and lead my fellow monkeys ahead.

We're just about to follow the latest food cart down the hall when I see another waiter balancing a tray of appetizers push through the double kitchen doors.

"*Nein!*" A buff dude in a formfitting tux bursts through the doors and grabs the waiter's arm. "Where do you think you are going?" His German accent is right out of *Call of Duty*, his spiked bleached-blond hair and black nail polish straight from *Dragon Ball Z*.

"T-To serve the a-appetizers?" the waiter stammers.

I wave Nick and Matt back, and we make ourselves thin in the doorway.

"Appetizers are over, *dummkopf*!" The spiky-haired guy slaps the tray out of the waiter's hand, sending little puff pastry squares flying into the air and the silver platter clanking to the floor. "If you cannot cut the mustache, then you should get out of the kitchen."

"Oh, shit," Matt whispers. "That's Ulf."

"Who the hell's Ulf?" Nick asks, keeping his voice low. "A Nazi?"

"No. He was my lifesaving coach last summer. I snuck into this country club when I was trying to learn how to swim the fly and got roped in to his course." He looks at me. "Remember?"

"Yeah. I also remember you telling us he was a sadistic bastard."

Matt scratches his hairy arm. "He wasn't *so* bad. We ended up getting along okay, but he won't think twice about beating the piss out of us if he finds out what we're up to."

"I could probably take him," Nick says, looking down at his hairy self. "Although the costume might make things interesting."

"Why is he here now?" I ask.

"I don't know." Matt shrugs. "I guess he has to do something during the off-season."

"Perhaps you have chewed off more than your head," Ulf says.

The waiter trembles. "I'm s-sorry. I just thought—"

"This is your first mistake. Stop thinking. And start listening." With that, Ulf shoves the waiter back into the kitchen through the saloon doors and follows right on his heels.

"Here's our chance," I say, pushing away from the door.

I quickly skulk past the kitchen and turn down the

hall. Matt and Nick shadow me as we creep toward Rico's birthday party. The doors to the reception room are only fifty yards away.

And just as I'm thinking we're going to make it, someone clears his throat behind me.

"May I help you?"

Matt, Nick, and me freeze.

I turn around slowly to see Ulf looming there, his hands tucked behind his back.

"We're, um . . ." I try to clear the thick clump in my throat. "We're here for the . . . Rico Petrelli party? We're the . . . entertainment? The . . . Singing . . . Zombie . . . Monkey Brothers."

"No one mentioned any"—Ulf looks us up and down, his eyes narrowed—"singing monkeys to me." His suit is so tight on him that it'd take just one hard flex for him to rip through the fabric like the Incredible Hulk.

"That's because," Matt says, lowering his voice a couple of octaves, "it's a surprise. We're Rico's grandkids. He thinks we aren't going to be able to come. But we're here now."

"Monkeys are Great-grandpa's favorite animals," Nick adds.

If I wasn't so terrified that he'd kill me, I'd smack Nick. *Great-grandpa?* The dude's only sixty years old!

But just like that Ulf's shoulders relax. "Well, thank you, my lucky charms," he says. "Why did you not mention this in the very first place? Finally, we will have some family members at this celebration. Perhaps you can increase the mood. It is like someone died and went to heaven in there." He snaps to attention again. "Follow me. I will show you the way."

☛ CHAPTER FIFTY-ONE ☚

SCREAM

WOULD YOU LIKE FOR ME that I introduce your entrance?" Ulf asks when we arrive at the door to the Amethyst Room.

"No," I say, my breath shaky. "We don't want to ruin the element of surprise." My temples start to throb, and my left eye begins to twitch. If I had a communicator, I would *so* call Scotty on the *Enterprise* to have him beam me up right now.

"Okay. If that is how you wish." Ulf cracks open the door and peeks inside. "Someone is giving a speech right now. You will go in after the man is finished."

Through the opening, I can see that the room is packed with hundreds of miserable-looking people. Old and young alike. Everyone dressed in party clothes, their eyes glazed over as they watch a cauliflower-nosed man standing on a riser with a glass of red wine in his hand give a speech.

I scan the crowd and see Evelyn, sitting at a table near the front of the room. Chatting to an elderly couple. Stuffing her face with food. Her Nashira-jacket chains jangling. Hardly inconspicuous.

And there's Val and Coop standing in the corner, videotaping the whole affair.

And—oh, God—there's Hunter and Leyna, loitering near the back. Jesus Christ.

"Well, Rico," the speaker drones, "as everyone in this room can attest, you and I have not always seen eye to eye over the years. In fact—if we're being perfectly honest—it's safe to say that I am *not* your biggest fan. But, as your employees—I mean, *guests*—would likely agree, if you had to choose between making friends and making money, you'd take money every time."

"Damn straight!" a grumpy, Mr. Clean look-alike in a tuxedo calls out, raising a tall glass of whiskey. "Friends might *kiss* your ass, but cash will clothe it!"

"Ah, yes." The speaker forces a smile. "Another witty Rico-ism. Because we haven't heard enough of *those* over the decades. Anyway." He sighs. "There really isn't much more I have to say, and I see our food is being served, so I'll just sign off." He raises his glass of wine and nods. "Happy birthday, Rico."

"Fuck you very much, Larry!" Rico hollers. "I should have fired you when I fired your whore wife."

There's a scattering of uncomfortable laughter. A few people clap awkwardly.

And then everyone starts to eat.

Ulf turns to us. "If you are all ready." He thrusts his hand toward the room. "The show must go on the road."

"Right," I say, looking over at Matt and Nick, my hurly belly gurgling. "On three?"

They nod.

I gulp. "One." Oh, jeez, I can't believe we're really going to do this. "Two." There's no going back now. "Three!"

I slip the blood capsule into my mouth and lead the charge through the double doors.

Nick, Matt, and me burst into the Amethyst Room, screeching like anally probed lab chimps, waving our furry arms in the air, and rushing straight toward the first set of tables.

"You're all going to die!" Nick screams, exactly like he's not supposed to. "We've come to drink your blood!"

People shriek in terror. Suit- and dress-clad bodies fly from their seats and stumble over each other, trying to get away from our rabid monkey menace.

"Nein! Nein! Stoppen!" I hear Ulf holler behind us. *"Hör auf, verdammt!"*

The pushing and shouting at the front of the reception causes a chain reaction as table after table of partygoers leap up and bolt toward the exit doors.

It's immediate and complete mayhem at the Elk Hills Country Club.

Which is exactly how we planned it.

Well, almost.

Evelyn—in her leather chain jacket—hops up on one of the tables, wielding a chair. "Oh, my God! It's humanzees!" she barks. "Vampire-zombie human chimpanzees! Don't let them take over the world!"

Nick springs onto the now-empty riser and howls into the abandoned microphone. "You cannot stop us! We are humanzees! Hear us roar!" His deep guttural growl echoes in the high-ceilinged reception room, evoking a new ripple of cries from the fleeing flock.

Oh, crap, they're totally ruining this scene! I have to save it somehow. Give Coop something to splice in that matches our original vision for the film.

Without thinking, I charge a group of younger guys in suits who scream and clutch at each other like little girls and launch myself at the smallest of them—a large-headed, wispy-haired dude with no chin and bug eyes. I grab him in a tight bear hug, bite down on my blood capsule—which tastes almost like real blood, warm and metallic and nauseating—and pretend to sink my teeth into his neck.

"Help!" he squeals. "It's biting me! I'm bleeding! Get it off! Get it off!"

It's the perfect line of dialogue, actually. Way better than Nick's and Evelyn's, for sure.

Suddenly I'm slammed in the lower back with

something. My kidneys scream in pain. I fall to the floor, releasing the howling guy, letting him run off with the rest of the crowd.

I hoist myself up and turn over to see Evelyn standing above me, brandishing her chair.

"Take that, you filthy humanzee!" she shouts, then tosses the chair away and runs off.

I stumble to my feet, my paw pressed into the bruise on my back. I turn around, and there's Ulf—all two hundred muscly pounds of him—barreling straight toward me.

Oh, shit.

Every atom of me wants to bolt, but I am frozen to this spot, feeling the trickle of fake blood dribbling down my throat, watching Ulf charge me like the Rhino in a Spider-Man comic.

And then it's too late.

Ulf's powerful hands are on me. Clenching my shoulders. Shaking me violently.

Jostling my already queasy stomach.

"Just hold your handbag right there, mister!" Spittle flies from his thin lips. "You are in some very hot potatoes! The authorities have been summoned and you are—"

YAAAAAAARRRRRK!

A ferocious scarlet stew of half-digested sausage, chili, Cheez Whiz, and tropical punch Kool-Aid spews straight from my monkey-mouth right into Ulf's face and streams down the front of his expensive suit, covering his torso like a vomit vest.

Part of me is mortified by the sudden uncontrollable blast of sick that is shooting out of me, while another part of me is completely fascinated by the sheer amount of hurl I am producing. I just hope that Coop and Val are getting this all on tape.

When the discharge is finally over, my stomach feels a million times better.

The same can't be said of Ulf, who staggers backward, coughing, sputtering, and wiping the thick scarlet chum from his eyes.

And while it's not usually polite to barf and bail, I take this opportunity to hightail it.

If I'd been thinking at all, I would have beelined it straight for the doors leading to the hallway. But instead I'm leaping over capsized tables and chairs, following the mob toward the exits at the back of the Amethyst Room.

And here's Cauliflower Nose wading through the mob scene, trying to get his hands on one of us. He lunges for me and I barely dodge his grasp as I hop over another upturned chair.

By the time I'm halfway to the exits, I'm huffing and puffing, my vomitty mask smelling like a terrible casserole of spoiled milk and rancid Fancy Feast cat food.

But I don't let that stop me. I just breathe through my mouth and charge on.

Finally there's a clearing and I jam it toward the exit. I can hardly believe it when I'm outside, sucking in the sweet scent of fresh air. There are people everywhere — some laughing, some crying, some just shaking their heads.

But I don't stick around to take in the scene. I pound it down the concrete path toward Uncle Doug's van in the parking lot.

Helen and me are the first ones to make it to the getaway vehicle, but for some reason the engine isn't running.

I leap into the front passenger seat and see Uncle Doug with his head tipped back, snoring away as a string of drool hangs precariously from the corner of his mouth.

"Oh, my God," Helen shouts from the backseat. "Is he sleeping?"

I reach out and shake Uncle Doug's shoulder. "Wake up! Wake up! Start the van!"

"What? Huh?" Uncle Doug jolts upright. "What's going on? Where am I?" He looks around, blinking like crazy. "Goddamn it. I was just having bacon cheeseburgers with the Dalai Lama at the Beefery, and he was about to tell me the meaning of life. Nice going, Seanie."

I glare at him. "There isn't going to *be* a life to have any meaning if we don't get the hell out of here right now!"

"Okay, okay," Uncle Doug says. "Don't get your

dander up—we're going." He reaches down toward the ignition but finds no keys. "Hmm. That's odd. Where'd my keys go?"

Oh, crap.

I glance out the window and see Matt and Nick barreling toward the van, a lynch mob of guests closing in on them. "Oh, man, we are totally screwed," I say.

"We're fine," Uncle Doug scoffs as he runs the tips of his fingers all over the gritty floor mat. "They have to be here somewhere. Keys don't just up and walk off on their own."

Then, all of a sudden, there's the wail of a police siren in the distance. And it's getting louder. Very quickly.

Uncle Doug bolts upright. "Oh, shit. Okay. Um. You two get out. And, uh . . . check the surrounding area for the keys. Hurry! Before it's too late."

Without thinking, Helen and I obey, leaping outside to search the ground.

Suddenly, and without warning, Uncle Doug's van roars to life and tears out of the parking lot.

Leaving Helen and me standing there. Completely dumbstruck.

"Holy crap!" Coop shouts as he, Val, and Evelyn skid up to us. "Did Uncle Doug just bail on us? What the hell?"

We all watch as the van pulls an illegal U-turn and takes off down the street.

"It was the pillowcase full of pot," I say.

"Goddamn it!" Coop yells. "Everything was going so well."

And just as Matt and Nick arrive at our side—the pursuing partygoers clopping toward us in their fancy dress shoes—a cop car screams into the parking lot and skids to a halt right by the curb.

CHAPTER FIFTY-TWO

THE EXORCIST

POLICE!" ONE OF THE COPS shouts as he bounds from the car. "Nobody move!"

Everyone freezes, including the posse that was chasing Nick and Matt.

"We got a call of a possible disturbance," the second officer says, staring at the seven of us huddled together. He looks like a chubbier, angrier Will Smith. "Something about people dressed up in ape suits and causing havoc?" He points at Nick, Matt, and me. "I'm assuming that's you three."

"Oh, crap," Nick mutters, his voice low and hollow in the monkey mask. "There goes my probation."

I turn to him. "Your *what*?"

"Just clamp it," Nick spits. "Play it cool. Don't take off your mask until they make us."

"All right." The first cop circles us. He's got acne-scarred cheeks that make him look like a James Bond villain. "Who wants to do the talking?"

"We're shooting a movie," Coop leaps in. "We were told we could film here."

"Is that so?" the bloated Will Smith says.

"That is *not* so." Ulf tromps over to us, still wiping at his bepuked face with a napkin. "No permission was given. That is a bald-headed lie."

"May I?" The first cop motions to the video camera in Val's hand. She hands it over, and the officer examines it. "Hey, Trent. Didn't we get a report of a bunch of stolen camera equipment recently?"

"Sure did, Jay. I think it was Leo's Cameras." Trent steps up to Helen and holds his hand out to her. She passes off the DSLR to him and he turns it over, inspecting the bottom. "We better run the serial numbers on these."

"That's not stolen." Helen turns to Evelyn. "Tell them where you got it."

"*You* tell them," Evelyn snaps. "It's your camera."

Helen jerks back. "No, it isn't. You said—"

"I didn't say *anything*." Evelyn stares daggers into Helen. "Just shut your mouth."

"Okay, okay." Officer Trent holds up his hands. "Let's take this down to the station, and we'll get everyone's statements." He turns to his partner. "Better get the wagon down here. We've got a horde to transport."

"Oh, my God! What the hell is *she* doing here?" Evelyn's arm shoots out like a switchblade.

Everyone turns to see what she's pointing at. And there's Leyna and Hunter standing on the periphery of the crowd.

Oh, shit. As if things weren't bad enough.

I give them a quick shake of my head, psychically telling them to leave.

Evelyn spins on me. "*You*! You invited that tramp? To our movie set? I *knew* it. You cheating bastard. I *never* should have trusted you."

"Just hold on a second," Officer Jay says. "Are those two somehow involved in this?"

"No," I say. "They're not. I don't know what she's talking about. I've never seen those people in my life."

"You lying sack of crap!" Evelyn pounces on me like a possessed puma, knocking me to the ground. She tries—but thankfully fails—to rip the mask from my face. So she goes to town on the mask itself, hitting and scratching it while cursing at me, all of the crazy bursting out of her like a volcano. "You toasted to trust, you jerk! How could you toast to that when it wasn't true? I hate you! I hate you! I hate you!"

The police officers try to pull her off of me, but Evelyn is raging.

"Holy Jesus, she's strong," one of the cops says.

She is screaming and crying and flipping out. The monkey mask absorbs most of the blows, though my eyes are sprayed with the occasional fleck of flying spittle. I turn my head to try to catch my breath.

"I can't believe I stole that equipment for you. For *you*! So that you would love me. You used me like a piece of meat. All this time. Lying and sneaking around. How dare you? *How dare you*?"

She takes another swipe at my face, just as I turn toward her, and her fist connects with my nose. *Hard.* The police officers finally manage to pull her off of me. But it's too late for my nose.

Matt and Coop are at my side in an instant, hoisting me to my feet and asking if I'm okay.

"Fine, fine," I say, grabbing my nose, the pain shooting through my head. I think it might be broken.

And maybe I deserve at least that. Because as nutty as Evelyn is, she isn't completely off base. I was sneaking around and lying. And I was using her. It just . . . seemed like I didn't really have a choice. But of course I did. I just didn't want to do what was hard. What was right.

I shake my head, feeling like a royal tool for letting things get this far out of control.

And then Officer Jay stands and looks around. "Hey," he calls out, "I thought there were three monkeys. Where the hell did the other one go?"

☛ CHAPTER FIFTY-THREE ☚

NIGHT OF THE
LIVING DEAD

I FLIP OVER ON MY BED, lying on my left shoulder, turned away from Cathy's side of the room, where her snoring has kicked into high gear. I've tried everything to block out the sound: balled-up tissue, earplugs, my iPod earbuds. But nothing can match Cathy's vicious log sawing.

I pull the pillow up over my head, but I can *still* hear her rasping and wheezing.

In. *Zzzzzzzzzz!* Out. *Zaaaaaaaah!* In. *Zzzzzzzzzz!* And out. *Zaaaaaaaah!*

Ugh. It's no use. I let the pillow flop back onto the bed. It's too claustrophobic to sleep like that anyway. What I can't understand is how Cathy isn't waking *herself* up. I mean, if I shouted as loud as she's snoring, she'd be awake in a second.

I close my eyes. Try to imagine her breathing as the loud hum of a boat engine. Which might actually lull me into a slumber . . . if the stupid engine didn't backfire every five seconds.

BRRRRRUCKUCKUCK!

I roll onto my back and stare up at the ceiling. Four weeks I've been grounded. Twenty-eight days to think about my actions at the country club. Six hundred and seventy-two interminable hours with no computer, no television, no video games, and no guests.

One solid month of sleepless nights to curse my miserable life and anguish over the fact that there is absolutely no way we'll be able to finish the movie in time now.

No way I'll ever escape this room.

Or this torture.

Zzzzzzzzz! Zaaaaaaaah! Zzzzzzzzzz! Zaaaaaaaah!

Ultimately, Rico decided not to press charges. And he convinced the country club to do the same. He said he hadn't had that much fun for a long time. That it made his sixtieth birthday "a celebration that people won't soon forget." And that his guests thoroughly deserved to have the crap scared out of them.

Of course, it would have been nice to have found this out *before* my parents came down to the station and begged the police for leniency. Saying how I was under enormous stress after having just come out of the closet.

Zzzzzzzzz! Zaaaaaaaah! Zzzzzzzzzz! Zaaaaaaaah!

I swear I'm going to go insane if I can't get some sleep

soon. Yesterday I spent half an hour looking all over the house for my coat when I was wearing the stupid thing the whole time. The day before that, I got into the shower wearing my pajamas.

Speaking of insane, since Evelyn confessed to stealing the camera equipment, we were off the hook on that one. She tried to convince the cops that this was a one-time offense, that she'd only taken the electronics because she was trying to help out the love of her life. And that she fully intended to return everything when the movie was done shooting. She even tried pinning that on me, saying I coerced her into jacking the equipment by telling her I'd break up with her if she didn't. She put on a pretty good act, I have to say, and I could see some of the cops softening toward her. But that all changed when her mom showed up at the precinct with two duffel bags full of stolen merchandise she'd found in her daughter's closet—clothing, jewelry, perfume. None of it remotely related to our movie.

No one's seen her since her meltdown. There was talk that she was put on probation. And that she has to go to a special school now with therapists who deal with things like kleptomania. But nobody knows for sure.

If it *is* true, that'd make two Moss kids on probation. Although it seems like Nick has broken his by disappearing—along with our humanzee suit. Coop says he's probably using it to his advantage. Going undercover at the zoo. Or hiding out in some South American rain forest. I've heard all sorts of rumors about why he was in trouble to begin with—from illegal surveillance to assault to DUI—but whatever the reason, he's not likely to be coming back anytime soon. Which works out just fine for me.

Zzzzzzzzz! Zaaaaaaaah! Zzzzzzzzz! Zaaaaaaaah!

I flip over to my other side. When you lie in bed too long without sleeping, your whole body starts to ache. I never knew that until now. That you could actually get sore just lying down. Also, you start hallucinating. There have been several nights where I swear I saw General Grievous's face on the ceiling. Or Uncle Doug's giant hairy beard crawling up the walls.

He apologized. My uncle. For bailing on us. He came by when the dust finally settled, said he was sorry for hanging us out to dry but that a pillowcase full of marijuana trumps a disturbing-the-peace charge every time.

Zzzzzzzzz! Zaaaaaaaah!

The one saving grace in all of this is that Leyna's asked me over to her house to "examine her little muffin" once I'm not grounded anymore. Which is this Saturday. She actually seemed pretty upset that I wouldn't be able to come over any sooner, which is both thrilling and terrifying. I feel like all this extra time has only heightened her expectations. Still, the thought of actually seeing her—seeing *that*—is the one thing that's kept me going. The carrot I dangle in front of myself every day.

Zzzzzzzzz! Zaaa—

Oh, my God. It's stopped. Cathy must have rolled over onto her side or something. Here's my opportunity. If I can fall asleep before she starts up again, I might be able to coast through the rest of the night.

I shut my eyes tight. Sleep. Sleep. Must sleep.

I count Angry Birds being slingshot through the air. One red bird. Two blue birds. Three black birds. Four yellow birds. Five toucans. One red bird. Two blue birds. Three black birds . . .

Damn it! It's not working. I lift my head and smack it back down into the pillow. Take a deep breath and try to nestle my body deeper into the bed.

The room is eerily quiet. *Too* quiet, maybe.

I strain to try and hear Cathy breathing at all. But there's nothing.

A thought, both scary and slightly satisfying, occurs to me.

What if she suddenly died? Choking on her own flapping tonsils? Sure, I'd be upset. I mean, Cathy *is* my twin sister after all. But haven't I—in my most desperate, panicky, sleep-deprived hours—silently prayed for this very thing?

It's true. I've wished my sister dead. But I didn't really mean it. Not *really* really. It's just that extreme sleepiness can make you antsy and frustrated and desperate—did I mention desperate?—and—

Zzzzzzzzz! Zaaaaaaaah! Zzzzzzzzz! Zaaaaaaaah!

Well, there you go. Apparently she's still alive. That's a . . . relief.

I sigh loudly and try to adjust to the rhythm of her snores. But it's no use. My mind is too wide-awake. I can't shut it off. It just wants to keep thinking and thinking and thinking.

About Evelyn, of all things. And how I finally got thrown a bone in that whole hurricane of heinousness. Except my brain refuses to let go of how dumb-lucky I got.

You don't deserve this, it keeps whispering to me. *You aren't blameless here, buddy. You could have stopped it all before it got out of control. If you'd had any balls.*

Yeah, yeah, brain, whatever. It's not like I got off entirely scot-free. I got a busted nose out of the deal, remember? And my movie is an epic fail. Besides that, I haven't been able to see Leyna outside the confines of drama class. And maybe worst of all, I'm going to spend the rest of my high school life sharing a bedroom with Darth Vader until eventually I graduate or I totally crack and start cackling like the Joker and begin plotting world domination.

These little arguments have become part of my nightly ritual, which makes me worry that the Joker scenario is the likelier of the two.

There is only one thing I've found that gets me through these dark and troubling times. I only use it when things are really bad, because to be honest, I feel a tiny bit guilty about it.

But tonight is definitely one of those nights.

I slip out from under the covers, grab my phone, and tiptoe into the bathroom.

☚ CHAPTER FIFTY-FOUR ☚

CUJO

"WE HAVE *NO* MONEY. We have *no* camera equipment. We have *no* time. I thought we already discussed all this." I'm talking to Coop on my cell phone as I pedal like crazy toward Leyna's house—finally free to roam the world outside of school again.

"Just hear me out, dawg," Coop insists. "It came to me in a flash last night. I don't know why the hell I didn't think of this sooner. We shoot the rest of the film on our cell phones."

"Oh, yeah," I say. "That'll look real professional."

"No, it won't. That's the point. We don't want it to look professional. It'll make it seem more realistic. Like the outbreak is actually happening and Rogart and Nashira are capturing some of it on their phones. It's totally brill. And it's never been done before."

"Uhhh, yeah, for a reason. Nobody's going to sit through a film shot on someone's cell phone."

"It's not going to be *all* cell-phone footage," Coop argues. "I've got our old scenes on my computer. So we can still use those. We'll edit the phone footage in between. It'll be dope. It adds a voyeuristic element. Makes it more personal. And intense. Seriously. I'm actually glad that this happened because it's going to make the film even better. Maybe we start the movie with someone in the future finding a buried cell phone. They plug it in and this is what they see: the destruction of the human race."

"I don't know, Coop."

"You don't have to know. Because I know. You just make sure that Leyna is still on board. And then leave everything else to me."

We hang up, and while I should know better by now—boy, should I know better!—Coop's enthusiasm and conviction have started to infect me. Or maybe it's the thought of getting to tell Leyna that the film's still on, that she's still my leading lady.

Or possibly it's just the sleep deprivation.

Whatever the cause, I stroll up to Leyna's house—a cute yellow-and-white two-story that looks like it should be on a TV show—with a big grin on my face. Give a light *rat-a-tat-tat* on the front door, and a few moments later, a tall hollow-cheeked woman with long bleached-blond hair—Leyna forty years from now?—is standing in the entryway.

"You must be Shane," the woman says, extending her bony hand.

"Sean," I correct her as we awkwardly shake. Weird that her mom would be home. I'd think we'd need some privacy for the unveiling.

"Of course. Sorry. I'm terrible with names. Forgive me. I'm Claudia."

"Hi," I say.

Claudia steps to one side. "Leyna will be right down."

I enter the house, which smells vaguely of lemons and is as picture-perfect inside as out. I'm shown to a formal room—with uninviting ornate floral couches and armchairs—and am told to make myself comfortable.

I glance around at the museum-ness of it all and think that it isn't exactly the living room of a girl who wants to show you her "little muffin." But then I guess growing up in such an uptight environment might make you want to be a bit more wild and free.

I stroll over to the window and stare outside at the well-manicured bushes just starting to regain their leaves. I need to think about what I'm going to say when she shows it to me. I have to be easygoing about it. Happy and grateful but not overly enthusiastic. I don't want to come across as some noob who's never seen a naked girl up close and personal.

Even though it's true.

Yes, I saw Ms. Luntz on the nude beach last year. But I don't count that. A grossed-out chill rockets up my spine as the image escapes its lockbox. Besides, while that may have been in person, it was hardly up close, thank Gandalf.

I pace around the living room, being careful not to bump into anything. Shake my arms out, roll my head around my neck like I'm about to do the fifty-yard dash.

Have to stay chill, Sean. Be all casual when she shows you. Just observe, and smile, and say something like, "Yes, that's lovely. One of the prettiest I've seen. Quite impressive."

Quite impressive? What are you, an art critic? Jesus.

I crane my neck to see if Leyna's coming down the hall.

Okay. Deep breath.

Claudia told me to make myself comfortable and so that is what I will do. I sit down on the fancy couch facing the window and casually cross my right foot over my left leg. I toss an arm up over the back, glance over to the seat next to me, wink and point, and say, "Hey, there. Nice vagina. Thanks for showing it to me."

Oh, come on, Sean. You can do better than that. I hunch over, press my palms into my eyes. Think, man. Think. How would Captain Kirk respond to seeing a woman's Mystical Coif of Elements?

"I'm not going to . . . *lie* to you, Leyna. . . . Your genitalia . . . is ravishing. . . . Perhaps the . . . most *exquisite* specimen in the known universe. . . . Of all the females in all the races that I have had the . . . *privilege* . . . of encountering . . . your Omega Nebula . . . is unrivaled."

"Who are you talking to, Sean?"

Oh, crud. It's Leyna.

I pull my hands from my eyes and look up to see her backlit form standing over me.

"I was, um"—I swallow—"just going over some dialogue. For a new scene. That I wrote. Just now. In my head."

"Oh," Leyna says doubtfully. "But I thought the movie was dead."

"Oh, my God, no . . . That's . . . what I was going to tell you . . . now . . . Coop just had this great idea for filming the movie. On our cell phones. I know it sounds crazy, but we think it might actually work. Anyway, I was hoping . . . uh . . . I mean, if you're not doing any other movies at the moment"—I laugh way too loud at my own lame joke—"if you're free, maybe you could go back to being Nashira?"

"Are you kidding? I'd love to!" she says, sitting next to me on the couch and putting her hand on my leg. "I'm so glad to hear you haven't given up on your dreams."

"No, no, still got those dreams," I say.

"Well, I want to talk all about it. But first, the reason I asked you over." She gives my knee a squeeze. My leg jumps like it's been stun-gunned. "Would you like something to drink first?"

My mouth is pretty parched, but I shake my head. "Nah. I'm good. Thanks."

"Okay, then." Leyna slaps her knees. "Should we get

right to it? I mean, I don't want to rush things, but I have been waiting quite a while for you to have a peek at this." She laughs. "Time to put your doctor's hat on."

I gulp. "Uh . . . I . . ." My eyes dart around, all my grand plans gone up in smoke. "Where do you want to . . . ?"

"My room, don't you think? It's quieter and more private. That way you can take your time and get a good look."

"Sure." My voice is all shaky. My head dizzy with excitement. "Sounds good."

"My little Muff-Muff's looking pretty cute." She smiles proudly. "I spent the last hour doing some primping and trimming."

"Oh, yeah?"

"Got her all gussied up for your visit. I even clipped on a little pink bow." Leyna laughs. "I know, cheesy, right?"

"No," I say. "It's nice." My jeans feel like they've shrunk two sizes. Lord Vader, I can't believe this is about to happen. Just stay chill. Just stay chill. Forget Captain Kirk. Think Han Solo all the way. I cock my head, try on a bit of swagger, and say, "All righty, then. Let's see this little muffin of yours."

Just then a tiny brown-and-white corgi with a pink bow in its hair trots into the room.

"She must have heard you." Leyna pats her leg. "Up, Muffin."

The dog leaps into Leyna's lap and starts to pant.

"Muffin?" My stomach plunges. "Your dog's name . . . is Muffin?"

"Muffin, Muff-Muff, Muffy. And all the variations of." Leyna giggles. "Sometimes my brother calls her the Muffinator." She laughs and scrubs at the dog's neck.

"And the picture you sent me?" I point at Muffin. "Was that of her?"

"Well. Of her butt." Leyna turns the dog around and lifts her tail stump. "The rash I was telling you about. Way back when. Remember? It seems to get better for a while and then just comes back again. See?"

I blink hard, my entire fantasy world melting away. The dog looks back at me over its shoulder. "Yeah. I see."

Leyna furrows her brow. "Why, what did you think the picture was?"

"Nothing." I turn away. "I just . . . I didn't know what . . . part of her it was. That's all." Oh, my God. I feel nauseous. "It's probably mites." I gesture at the dog, unable to look it in the eyes. "The rash. You were right. You should take her to a vet. She can prescribe some ointment. It'll be gone in a week."

A rash. A rash on a dog's butt. Son of a Sith.

"So that's all this ever was?" I attempt to clarify. "You just wanted my . . . veterinary expertise?"

"I hope you don't mind," Leyna says, a small shy smile dimpling her cheeks. "You just seem to know so much about animals, and I was really worried about little Muffy here."

"No, yeah, of course," I say, shaking the disappointment from my head. "I definitely don't mind. It's just that . . . I guess what I mean is . . . I've been thinking . . . about you and me, right? . . . And how we have such a strong connection and everything. In drama class. And when we talk and stuff . . ."

"Yeah." She smiles and gives my knee another squeeze. "It's great, huh?"

"For sure." I nod. "Really great. Which is why . . . I—I thought maybe . . . when you texted me . . . on Valentine's Day . . ." My face flames as I see the words in front of me, just waiting to be blurted out. All ready to make a bad situation infinitely more awkward. But my brain's right. I need to grow some balls. So it's either say what I want to say or skulk off with my tail between my legs. Yet again. "I thought maybe you might want to go out? With me? You and me? Going out."

Leyna smiles again, but this time it seems kind of forced. Like acting. Bad acting. "You mean, like, out to coffee?"

"Uhh." I gulp. She's gonna make me say it. "No . . . Not like that. Like, you know, something . . . *more* than coffee."

"Like coffee and a donut?" she says. Is it just me, or is that a hint of hopefulness I detect in her voice?

"No, I mean, like *going* out. Like, dating."

"Oh, Sean." She leans away. Not a good sign. "I'm really confused. I thought . . . God, this is . . . I mean . . . I thought . . . I thought you were . . . gay."

I jerk backward like she's just smacked me in the face with a sock full of oranges. "What? Why would you . . . Did my sister tell you that?"

"You have a sister?"

"A twin sister. Cathy. Yes. She thinks I'm gay too." Every muscle in my body has tensed.

"Yeah, well, aren't you?" Leyna asks. "I mean, you're sweet. You're sensitive. You're in drama. I don't know. You *seem* gay. I guess I just sort of . . . assumed."

"Well, you assumed wrong. Way wrong. Like . . . completely wrong. I'm not gay. I mean, I'm a guy and I can barely tolerate being around myself. I like girls. A lot. I like *you*. A lot. Okay?"

"Yeah. No. I get it." She cocks her head. "I like you a lot too. But . . ." And there it is. The *but* we've both been waiting for. "Just . . . not in that way. I'm really sorry, Sean, I didn't mean—"

"Sorry? Why would you be sorry? There's no need for that . . . for you to be sorry. It's not—" I give a loud lip fart. "Sorry. I mean, what's that about?"

Leyna laughs nervously. "So you're not . . . You're not upset?"

"What? Upset? No, definitely not. I knew it was a long shot. I mean, we're nothing alike, really, when you think about it. You want to be an actor and I . . ." told her

I wanted to be an actor too. "Uh, I have to focus on my screenwriting, you know? It's just . . . not a good time. For me, I mean. But thanks anyway."

Jeez Louise, did I just thank her? Like she was the one asking *me* out? Time to abort this mission, Seanie boy. Way *past* time. I hoist myself to my feet.

"Well, I'm glad I could help with . . . uh . . . Muffin," I say, gesturing at the dog, still not able to comfortably look at it. "Enjoy the rest of your Saturday. And, uh, I guess I'll be in touch soon . . . about the movie? If you're still in, I mean?"

"Yeah, for sure. Listen, Sean, I really am so—"

"No, no. No need for that. I'll just . . . let myself out. I remember the way." I laugh loudly, pointing at the front door, which is about ten feet from the couch. "See you . . . See you Monday. Bye, Muffin."

"Bye, Sean."

I book it out of there, my face and ears red-hot. Good God, I don't know what's worse: the fact that I've just been totally blown off by Leyna, the fact that she thought I was gay, or the fact that the only thing that has given me comfort lately turns out to be a picture of a little dog's anus.

As I hop on my bike and pedal like mad for home, I try to think of what the hell I can tell the guys—other than the truth, obviously. Because even though I know they'd both take a bullet for me if asked, there's no way they're ever going to let me live this one down.

🎥 CHAPTER FIFTY-FIVE 🎥

SHAUN OF THE DEAD

WAIT A SECOND," COOP SAYS as we ride our bikes to school on Monday. "I don't get something. If Leyna thought you were gay"—he nearly chokes with laughter just saying it, just like he's done the last three hundred times he's said it—"then why would she send you a picture of her hobgoblin?"

"Because she *didn't,* nosebag." I sigh. I spent most of Sunday coming up with cover stories, each one getting more and more elaborate and dramatic until I was the one turning Leyna down, telling her that she obviously had some deep-seated issues regarding her self-respect and that I was too much of a gentleman to take advantage of that fact. But I've never been very good at lying. And especially not to my friends.

And so I finally decide it'll be less painful in the long run if I just get this over with now.

"It wasn't her . . . hobgoblin," I repeat. "Muffin is the name of her dog. It was a shot of Muffin the dog, of its rash. Leyna wanted me to diagnose it." No need to mention where the rash was, exactly.

"Seriously?" Coop looks mystified. "I could have sworn it was a shot of her gravy boat."

"So"—Matt raises his eyebrows at Coop—"*obviously* you don't know the female anatomy as well as you thought."

"Please," Coop says. "It's an honest mistake. Anyone could make it. Are you sure it was the dog, dude?" Coop asks me. "I mean, I've seen dogs before. Lots of times. And none of them ever looked like—"

"It was definitely the dog," I assure him, starting to sweat. "I mean, I saw the rash in person when I got there. Trust me, it was the dog."

"I believe you, Sean-o. I mean, why would you tell us it was a picture of a dog's rash if it was actually Leyna's love gully? Still, I find it hard to believe. It totally looked like a—"

"It was the anus, okay?" I blurt. "The rash was on Muffin's anus. Happy now?"

Coop and Matt both skid to a halt.

Look at each other.

And then kill themselves laughing.

"Oh, no," Coop splutters. "Oh, Seanster, no. You can't be serious? That is odious, dude."

"Man, Sean, that's . . . wow." Matt's trying his best

to control his laughter and sound sympathetic, but he's failing. Big-time.

Coop is still bent over with laughter. But suddenly he straightens. "Shit, dude. Tell me you didn't . . . Oh, Sean-o, please tell me you didn't scratch Yoda behind the ears looking at that picture?" He holds his breath waiting for my response.

"Pfff, right." I look off into the distance. "I was never convinced in the first place."

"Oh, my *God.*" Coop turns to Matt. "Our best bud mangled his midget gawking at a shot of a dog's anus. *That* is absolutely grievous!"

He leans over and fist-bumps Matt as they double over with laughter again.

"Okay, okay, wait," Matt says, trying to catch his breath. "Is Muffin a boy or a girl?"

I glare at him. "Are you done?" I hop up on my bike seat and start pedaling.

The guys follow.

"That's a good question you pose there, Mattie," Coop sputters. "Because if it was a girl dog, well, that's bad enough. But if he used a shot of a *guy* dog—"

"She's a girl," I snap. "And it doesn't matter because I didn't 'use' that picture for anything, okay?"

The guys are still going on about it as we turn into the school parking lot and coast our bikes up to the racks. I jump off and start locking up my front wheel.

The sun is glaring in the sky this morning. So much

so that it hurts my eyes. It's like someone removed a layer of the atmosphere or something.

"Don't worry, Sean-o." Coop snorts. "Your dirty little secret's safe with us."

"Right, whatever. You guys can get your jollies thinking whatever twisted things you want." My phone buzzes in my pocket. I pull it out and read the text from Leyna. "Perfect. Things just keep getting better and better."

"What's up?" Matt asks, clicking his bike lock shut.

"Leyna just quit the movie." I wave my phone at them. "She just texted."

"Did she send along another shot of her dog's sphinc?" Coop asks.

"No." I sigh. "She just said she's 'thought it over' and she's 'uncomfortable working with me' now that she knows I like her."

Coop raises his eyebrows. "Think how uncomfortable she'd be if she knew what you were doing with that picture of her dog's butthole."

I flip Coop the bird, then say, "Well, that's it. It's really over now."

"What's over?" Helen asks, strolling up with Val.

"Our movie." I stare off at all the trees and flowers that are blooming. Green, yellow, red, blue. Bright colors everywhere. Mocking me and my miserable life.

"I thought we decided to shoot it on our cell phones," Valerie says.

"We did," Matt explains. "But now Leyna's just dropped out."

"Which is terribly unfortunate." Coop reaches into his backpack and pulls out a Three Musketeers bar. "But here's the silver lining. I no longer have to worry about how I'm going to look on the cover of *Entertainment Weekly*." He unwraps the candy bar and takes a big bite. "Oh, you sweet nougaty goodness, how I missed ye."

"It doesn't have to be over," Helen says. "I could do it. Play Nashira, I mean."

"Yeah, I don't think so." Coop gestures with his candy. "I'm not about to have you spending all that QT with Hunter. No way, no how."

"I'm not like you, sweetie. I can remain professional while in the presence of someone of the opposite sex who also happens to be very attractive."

"Aha!" Coop says. "So you admit that you find Hunter attractive?"

Helen looks anything but flustered. "The very fact that you have to ask me that means that you haven't noticed if I found him attractive. Which means that I can behave myself around hot guys. Unlike you with Chesty McBreastington during the auditions."

Coop sighs, knowing when he's been beaten. "Do you need me to blind myself? Is that what it's going to take for you to get over this?" He wields the Three Musketeers in front of his eyes. " 'Cause I'll do it."

"Aw, honey." Helen reaches over and pinches Coop's

cheek. "I'm *way* over it. I just like to torment you every once in a while."

"Seriously," Valerie says. "You didn't think we were actually bothered by that, did you?"

Matt laughs. "No. Of course not. And we didn't buy you ice cream because we thought you were bothered by our behavior. We're just really thoughtful guys."

Valerie slips her arm around Matt's waist and snuggles up against him.

"Seriously, though," Helen says, "I'd be happy to act in the movie. It'd be fun."

"Thanks," I say. "But to be honest, I doubt Hunter's going to want to be in the movie now that Leyna's bailed. I mean, we'd have to start all over again. And it's not like we're paying Hunter for his time. Or that we can even afford to." I sigh. "Let's face it: the movie's dead."

As is my shot of ever finding a cool girlfriend.

Someone who teases me about my own wandering eyes.

God. Who knew I'd even be jealous of *that*?

CHAPTER FIFTY-SIX

PICNIC AT HANGING ROCK

H_EY, SO, WHAT'S THE DEAL?_" Nessa's voice sounds slightly irritated over the phone.

"What's the deal with what?" I ask.

"Why haven't you called me?" she says.

"I was grounded for a month. Didn't Cathy tell you?" I adjust myself on my bed and click through my Facebook page for the first time in weeks.

"Of course she told me." Nessa laughs. "Are you kidding me? She was counting down the days. It was driving her nuts that you were always in her room."

"*Our* room," I clarify. Whoa, Aaron Altman ate a whole box of Raspberry Zingers without hurling. I'm, like, the last person to "Like" that. Sean Hance, always late to the party.

"Yeah, but you've been free for a week. So, what, you hate me now?"

"I don't hate you, Nessa." I close the screen on my laptop. "It's just . . . We're not doing the movie anymore, so I guess I didn't—"

"Wait, what? Why not?"

"Oh, God. It's a long story."

"And one I deserve to hear, don't you think? I've put a lot of work into this screenplay, and I've spent the last five weeks jotting down new scenes. I think I've got a pretty good ending written here, if I do say so myself."

"Wow, I had no idea you were still working on it. Sorry . . . I guess I should have told you sooner."

"Ya *think*? Well, I guess that's two things you owe me: an explanation and the Wal-Mart uniform you still haven't returned. What are you doing right now? Maybe you can swing by and kill both bats with one bone."

I look around my empty room. Cathy's at work, and Matt and Coop are off with their girlfriends somewhere. I was maybe going to play a couple of hours of *World of Warcraft,* but I guess I could go by Nessa's first. "Okay," I say. "Sure. Sounds good."

"Kewl," Nessa says. "Bring some snacks. We're going on a picnic."

It's weird how you can know someone for so many years but not really *know* anything about them. My sister and Nessa have been best friends since third grade— when Cathy's first best friend, Aubrey, moved to San Francisco—but beyond the fact that her mom died, and that she works at Wal-Mart, and that she used to have brown hair and a lot fewer piercings before she went all Goth, there isn't much more I could have told you about Nessa prior to our picnic at Cypress Lawn Cemetery.

I certainly had no idea that she was such an expert on graveyards. She knows all about the different kinds of materials they use for coffins and tombstones. How long it takes for a person's body to decompose. How deep a person is usually buried (apparently it doesn't have to be six feet, like everyone thinks). That graves used to have footstones as well as headstones. And that people have been having picnics in cemeteries since Victorian times, when it was considered a lovely relaxing Sunday-afternoon activity to commune with nature and the deceased.

I also didn't know that she was so funny. She likes to read the names on the tombstones and make up bizarre stories about the people who are buried there.

And I definitely had no clue that she was such a good cook.

I take a second bite of the grilled-chicken-and-pesto sandwich Nessa claims to have made and am amazed all over again at how good it tastes.

"Seriously, you made this from scratch?" I ask, holding up the sandwich. "The chicken, the sauce, everything?"

"Of course." Nessa laughs, her legs tucked up on the purple blanket she's spread out in front of an old weather-stained headstone. She dabs at the corner of her mouth with a paper napkin. "I don't see what the big deal is. You just grill a couple of chicken breasts, mash up some pesto, slice up some tomato and lettuce, and chuck it all on a baguette. It's not brain surgery."

"Might as well be. At least to me. I can't even make toast without burning it."

"Cooking's all about measurements. Measuring your ingredients. Measuring your time. That's what my mom used to tell me whenever she let me help bake cookies."

"Do you miss her?" The question is out of my mouth before I can stop it. Instantly I wish I could take it back. My scalp tightens and my chewing sounds exponentially louder in my ears. "I'm sorry. Never mind. You don't have to answer that."

"No, it's okay." Nessa forces a smile. "We can visit her later. She's buried here. Her grave's in the newer part of the cemetery." She points off to the right. "But it's a lot prettier here in the older section. For a picnic, anyway." She takes a sip of her coconut water, like she has to think about how to answer my question. "It's strange, you know. I *do* miss her. A lot. But I can only remember little moments of her. Like short YouTube clips. I can still hear how she used to read *Goodnight Moon* to me when I was little. The way she'd read it so slowly and reverentially. I mean, it's a pretty dull book, but she used to make it sound so magical. And then there was this one Thanksgiving where she was lifting the turkey from the pan and it exploded all over the place. She just started laughing hysterically. Like it was the funniest thing ever. I have no idea why those are the things that stuck. But I play them over in my mind sometimes late at night when the missing really hits hard."

"Yeah." I say. "That's exactly how it is with my grandparents. They died a few years ago. I used to love going over to their house on holidays and stuff. And it's, like, now all I have are a few collected memories— washing the dishes together, playing gin rummy with my grandpa—that I take out and look at once in a while. Almost like Pokémon cards in a shoe box." D'oh! Coop would make me turn in my testicles for saying that.

But Nessa doesn't seem weirded out. "Yeah, it's sort of sad, really," Nessa says. "Unless you're famous or something, most of us are just a couple of generations from being totally forgotten about."

"Wow. That's pretty depressing."

"Or inspiring." Nessa takes another sip of her drink. "Depending on how you look at it." She lifts her chin toward the weather-stained headstone with the angel baby on top. "Take Maggie Stillman, for example."

I read the words on the gravestone.

MAGGIE STILLMAN

AUGUST 16, 1901 – OCTOBER 24, 1909

BELOVED DAUGHTER

"God, she died so young," I say.

"I know, right? She had her whole life ahead of her and so many things she didn't get to experience. But we're going to die someday too. And there's nothing we can do about that. But knowing that, I don't know. It's, like, freeing or something."

"Freeing? Like we should all go out and take whatever we want? Steal stuff? Kill people?"

"No, that's not the point at all." She shakes her head. "It's more like, if our time here is limited—which it is, only we don't know by how much—then why would you let other people tell you what you should and shouldn't be doing? Make your own choices, and who cares if you fall flat on your face? 'Cause if you don't, it's an insult to people like Maggie Stillman, who never had the chance to make those choices."

"Yeah." I nod. "That's true, I guess. Makes sense."

She tilts her head, considering me. "You know, most people get annoyed when I go off on my philosophical ramblings. But you don't seem bothered or creeped out or anything."

I shrug. "No. I mean, it's a little gloomy, for sure. But interesting. And important."

"All right, so," Nessa says, sitting up, "since we're on the topic of making choices—and death and all that— why don't you tell me why you decided to kill your movie?"

"I was hoping we might just avoid that topic alto-gether." I look around at the cemetery. The long stretch of lawn. The trees sprouting their leaves. The flowers that have started to bloom. "I'm having such a good time. I don't want to ruin it."

"All right, then." Nessa smiles. "You can tell me how you ended up nearly naked inside a dumpster at the back of the mall instead."

"Okay, so, about the movie . . ."

Nessa cracks up. For some reason, she just makes me feel comfortable. And so I go on to tell her all the gory details. About everything. First about the trip to the mall and getting spackled with bird crap. Then about how the movie thing pretty much blew up in our faces. I skip the part about the dog-butt picture because it's an unnecessary detail that really has nothing to do with the film. But everything else—with Evelyn, and Leyna, and the camera, and Uncle Doug—I lay it all out for her.

When I'm done, Nessa stares at me shaking her head. "And after all of that, you're just giving up?" she says.

"Giving up? That's like . . . that's like saying the people who got into the lifeboats on the *Titanic* were giving up. At some point, you've got to know when to jump ship."

"No. Sorry." Nessa crosses her arms. "It's nothing like that. This isn't a disaster, Sean. It's just a hiccup."

"Uhhh, the film festival is in less than a week and I

have no camera, no budget, no leading actors, a drama teacher who'd like to take over my movie, and a stoned-out-of-his-gourd uncle who thinks every animal wants to bite off his penis. Whatever you want to call it—a hiccup, a disaster, a screwed-up mess—I've run out of options."

"That's one perspective on things. Would you like to hear how I see it?"

"Sure." I laugh. "I don't know how else you *can* see things. But sure."

"Okay." Nessa stands and brushes off her pants. "Here's my take. You know that saying, 'If you want something done right, you have to do it yourself'?"

"Yeah. So?"

"Well, you're the exact opposite of that."

"Huh?"

"Think about it. You let everyone make choices for you. Your friends. This Evelyn girl. Your uncle. Your drama teacher. They all bulldoze their way over you and you just stand there and take it. You're just like Rogart— well, Rogart before I got my hands on him, anyway. You're too passive, Sean."

"That's not true," I say, a sourness blooming in the pit of my stomach.

"It *is* true. You know it is. But it doesn't have to be. You don't have let people drag you around like a rag doll. Come on. Get up." She grabs my hands and pulls me up, dragging me over to the headstone.

"I thought I wasn't supposed to let people drag me around."

"Ha, ha," Nessa says. "Be serious for a minute." She points at Maggie Stillman's name. "Someday that'll be your name on a gravestone: Sean Jebediah Hance."

"Jebediah?"

"Lucky guess," Nessa teases. "But this is where we all end up, mister. Now, are you going to be the guy in the cemetery who lived his life the way *he* wanted to live it, or the way *other* people wanted him to live it?"

I stare at the grave, transfixed. "I get what you're saying. And sure, I'd rather be the first guy. You know, the one who lived for himself. I just . . . I don't understand how it pertains to the movie."

Nessa takes my hands. Her fingers are incredibly soft and smooth. "Today it's the movie. Tomorrow it's what college you go to. After that it's what job you're willing to settle for. Where you live. Who you get married to. It spirals out. Thing after thing after thing."

I shake my head. "I wouldn't even know where to begin. I mean, there's so many things. Where am I supposed to get another leading lady who can shoot the entire script in a week?"

Nessa smiles. "Maybe she's standing right in front of you, Sean. I mean, seriously, you're not going to find anyone who knows the screenplay better than the person who helped write it."

"Wow, that's . . . really generous of you, Nessa . . . and

you *would* make a pretty kick-ass Nashira," I say, wondering how on earth I didn't see that before. "But we still don't have a leading man. There's no way Hunter will—"

"Haven't you heard a single thing I've said?" Nessa asks. I wait for her to continue, to tell me what obvious answer I've missed, but she just looks at me expectantly.

"What?" I ask. "Do you know another guy who would be willing to—Ohhh. It's me. I'm the guy."

"You'll be great," Nessa insists. "You know this character like nobody else. *We* know these characters like nobody else. And if you're in charge of the characters, then I know this movie will be in good hands."

"What about Cathy? We won't be able to hide this from her."

Nessa smiles. "Don't worry. I'll deal with Cathy. Just say you'll do it."

My stomach is all clenched up as I think of all the confrontations I'll have to have to make this work—with Coop, and Matt, and Mr. Nestman, and Uncle Doug. "I don't know if I can. I mean . . . I don't know."

"Yes, you can." Nessa reaches behind her neck and unclasps the chain with the cross pendant. "You just have to believe you can do it." She drapes the necklace over my head and fastens it. "And make the choice."

CHAPTER FIFTY-SEVEN

IT'S ALIVE

IT SEEMS ALMOST IMPOSSIBLE but we've nearly done it. Five days after Nessa convinced me to take charge of the film—and with a small advance on my allowance—we are just a single sequence away from finishing it.

And just under the gun too, because in less than twenty-four hours, we will be screening our movie at TerrorFest. If all goes well, we'll get this final scene in the can, onto the computer, edited, and burned onto a disc before we have to head into the city tomorrow afternoon to turn in our submission by the deadline.

"Quiet on the set," I say as I adjust the padding under my shirt. I decided to give myself some fake Hunter-like muscles so I look more Rogart-esque in the movie. If I'd had a few months to buff up, I would have done it naturally, like most actors do. But as we're on such a tight schedule, I had to make do with some special-effects magic.

Coop and Helen are standing by with their cell phones, ready to get the shot from two different angles. Matt and Valerie are upstairs editing everything together on my computer. The two of them have done a masterful job, I have to say. They've managed to salvage some of the old scenes—especially the humanzee ones—and cobble them together with the new Nessa-and-me stuff. With the addition of some close-up shots of mottled monkey paws and chomping mouths, and Helen's kick-ass soundtrack, Matt and Val have put together something I think we can all be proud of.

"Can I just say one thing before we start?" Mr. Nestman asks, buttoning up his military jacket with one hand and looking down at the script pages in his other.

I point at him. "No, you cannot. Sorry, Mr. Nestman. There's no time."

"But it's just this one line here." He gestures at the script. "Where I say—"

"Nope. Don't even want to hear it."

"But it's only—"

"Zip it. Now. Or I will take away your single-card billing and bury your name in the end credits. Are we clear?"

I can tell by his scrunched-up face that he is not happy about this, but he backs off.

Nessa smiles and waggles her eyebrows at me as I walk by. "Very sexy," she says.

I head over to Coop and Uncle Doug, who are

standing by the "lab table." We've lined the surface with a variety of colorful smoking beakers and test tubes. The rest of Uncle Doug's basement is filled with kennels holding my foster dogs, cats, and ferret, which Helen has made up to look like zombie-beasts, with matted-down hair and blood makeup and everything.

"Okay," I say. "It's the grand finale. Nashira and Rogart have led Colonel Ballcock to Dr. Schmaloogan's basement hideout." I pick up a glass jar filled with orange Gatorade. "This is the vampanzee antidote. It's the only thing that can stop the zombie-vampire-chimpanzee virus from continuing to spread." I motion to Uncle Doug. "But now that you know you've been found, you want to destroy it."

"Got it." Uncle Doug slips on his long blue doctor's coat. *"No problema."*

"And you know your lines?"

He taps his temple. "All up here, Seanie. Don't you worry about Uncle Doug."

"Great." I turn to Coop and Helen. "This is going to be a frantic scene, so I need you two to keep each other out of the frame. Okay?"

Coop nods. "We're on it, boss."

"And at the very end, Rogart and Nashira have their final kiss. I want you to linger on that shot because that's how we'll end the movie."

Nessa was the one who insisted on changing Rogart and Nashira back into lovers. She said she always felt that the brother-sister angle was weak and that a romantic connection upped the stakes. Hey, I wasn't gonna argue. It gave me an excuse to make out with Nessa all week. And make out we did. Some of those kisses. Man, oh man. They felt really real. Especially as the days went on.

I know it's probably way more likely that she and Cathy are still trying to orchestrate some sort of epic plot to humiliate me but . . . I don't know. Haven't they already had plenty of opportunities to pull the rug out from under me? And even though Nessa is a pretty decent actress, is she really good enough to fake the kind of passion she's been putting into her kisses?

"All right!" I shout. "Let's get this rolling. With any luck, we can get this in one or two takes and get the heck out of here."

Two hours, fifteen takes, and countless screwups later, we finally make it all the way through the scene.

"He's dead," Mr. Nestman emotes as he wrenches the jar of Gatorade from the "deceased" hand of Uncle Doug. "We've done it. We've saved the human race!" He stands and raises the jar into the air. "Our future is secured!"

Goddamn it. He changed the line anyway. And now there's nothing to segue to my final kiss with Nessa. Crap. I'd slap him upside the head if we weren't so pressed for time.

"Aaaaand cut!" I shout, on my knees beside Nessa

and Uncle Doug. "That's good enough. Get your phones up to Val and Matt and have them slap it on the ending."

"You got it, dawg," Coop says.

He and Helen take off and bolt upstairs.

Nessa helps me to my feet and gives me a big hug. "Congratulations." She pulls back and smiles at me. "Did I tell you or did I tell you?"

"You told me." I smile at her. "Thanks for helping out. You didn't have to."

"Are you kidding me? It was a blast. I can't wait to see it up on the big screen."

I should be just as excited as she is. I mean, I really do think we have a solid chance at TerrorFest—maybe not winning, but at least not totally embarrassing ourselves, either. But as I look into Nessa's deep brown eyes, I feel . . . sad.

This whole week, working so closely with her, has been great. Really great. She's so easy to be around. But now that the film is wrapping up, I no longer have an excuse to hang out with her.

Unless . . .

"Hi," Nessa says, her cheeks flushing. We've just been staring at each other awkwardly for the last minute or so.

"Hi." I'm blushing now too. But she hasn't moved away. And a ray of hope shoots through me. I step a little closer. Lean in. Her lips curl up in the tiniest of smiles.

I close my eyes and—

"Well, Seanie." Uncle Doug claps me on the back and Nessa and I jump apart. "I have to admit that I doubted you could pull this off. But I am duly impressed. You showed *muchos testículos, mi amigo.* I'm proud of you."

"Thanks," I say, turning toward him. "You did a great job. Even with the animals."

"Thank you kindly, and I do concur." He cackles loudly. "And now I believe it is time for Uncle Doug to raise a nice big Fatty Boombalatty in celebration." He squeezes my neck a little too hard and then takes off.

Nessa turns to go too.

"Nessa, wait," I start to say. But just then Mr. Nestman accosts me.

"Sorry about that last line," he says, taking a slug from the jar of antidote. "It just came out, you know. I think I changed it in my head and then I changed it back to your line and, I don't know, I got them mixed up, I guess. Anyway, I think it works okay, don't you?"

"Sure." I force a smile. "It's fine. Thanks for your help with everything."

He winks at me. "My pleasure. Oh, one more thing. I don't know if we have time to shoot this little extra bit, but I was thinking—"

"Hey, Sean," Nessa says, suddenly across the room and waving at me. "I've got to get home. But I'll see you here tomorrow, right? One o'clock."

"Yeah," I say, my heart sinking. "Tomorrow. See you then."

☛ CHAPTER FIFTY-EIGHT ☚

FRIGHT NIGHT

CATHY ISN'T SNORING TONIGHT. It figures. The one night I know I'm never going to get any shut-eye and she's lying on the other side of the curtain quiet as a clam.

My sheets feel like they're strangling me. Clinging to my neck and my shoulders. Swallowing my feet.

Ugh. I yank all my covers off.

My mind spins a million miles an hour. My thoughts on full volume. Thinking about the movie. And the film festival. And how we managed to get the whole thing finished just in time. It was almost miraculous, the way it all came together.

I wonder if we have one more miracle coming to us. If we might actually have a shot at winning this thing. I think of all of Coop's other harebrained ideas over the years, and how they sort of ended up working out even though they didn't seem like they would at the time: sneaking onto a nude beach to try to see a naked girl, sabotaging Tony "the Gorilla" Grillo's Speedo to give Matt a fighting shot at winning the fly, transforming us from the lamer-than-lame Arnold Murphy's Bologna Dare into a semidecent rock band with Helen's amazing lead vocals and The Doctor, Coop Daddy, and *El Mariachi* backing her up.

I remember all of the adventures we've been through together ever since kindergarten, and how those days may be coming to an end. I mean, both Matt and Coop are paired off, and while they're all pretty great about including me, they're not going to want to put up with Fifth Wheel Sean forever.

For some reason, this makes me think of Nessa. And that look in her eyes this afternoon. The one I could swear was drawing me in for a kiss right before we got interrupted. I wonder what would have happened if we'd had just a couple seconds longer. Would we have—?

"Hey." Cathy's sleepy voice is low and raspy. "You awake?"

"Yeah," I say impatiently. "I'm awake. Why?"

"I can't sleep."

"Me neither."

"What are you thinking about?" Cathy asks.

"I don't know. Nothing. Everything." Certainly not kissing your best friend. Not pushing Uncle Doug aside and sweeping Nessa into my arms and giving her a finale kiss she wouldn't soon forget. "Uh, how about you?"

"The baby," she says. "I keep wondering what it's going to be like. You know. When it's finally here."

"Different. That's for sure." I feel kind of guilty for how little I've actually thought about this baby. Aside from brooding over how much it sucks that I've had to give up my room. And how much worse it sucks that I have to share Cathy's room. But beyond that, I haven't really given the actual *baby* baby much thought at all.

"Are you hoping for a boy or a girl?" she asks.

"A boy, definitely," I say, surprised at my own answer, given that I haven't really considered it much before now. But it's like the answer was there all along. "I don't know if I can deal with two sisters."

Cathy laughs, then she's quiet for a minute. "You think Mom and Dad'll love it more than us?"

My instinct is to say, "No, of course not. Don't be ridiculous." But then it hits me how focused they've been on the baby. How they didn't even know that me and my friends were making a movie until I invited them to the festival, let alone that I'm trying to win enough money for the extension on the house. And how they don't seem to have a clue just how miserable Cathy has been lately— even more miserable than her usual miserable self.

"They say that the youngest child is usually the most adored," Cathy continues. "That's why Mom loves you more than me."

"Right. Because I'm nine minutes younger. Makes total sense."

"I can't think of any other reason," Cathy says. "I mean, I'm the smart one. And the talented one. And the good-looking one. And the one with all the cool friends."

"You forgot that you're also the creepy weird freaky one," I reply. "Besides, Mom doesn't love me more than you. I just don't argue with her as much."

She laughs again. "Yeah, I guess that's true."

A still silence infuses the room. It lasts so long that I think Cathy might have fallen asleep. I listen for the first signs of snoring, but I can't hear anything.

"Can I ask you something?" Cathy finally says, startling me a little.

"Sure. I guess. I might not answer, but you can ask."

"Fair enough." I hear her shifting on her bed. "Would you . . . ? Would you like me any less if you found out I was gay?"

"Pfff," I say. "I don't like you now. How could I like you any less?"

"You know what I mean. As your sister. Would you look at me differently?"

I should have known there was a reason she wanted to get me talking. "Listen," I say. "If you think lulling me in to some pseudo-cozy brother-and-sister late-night chat is going to get me to say that I'm gay, you're out of your mind. It's not going to happen, Cathy. Good night. It was great talking with you." I huff and pull my covers back on. Fluff up my pillow and drop my head down into it.

"I know you're not gay, Sean," Cathy says.

"You do?" I don't trust this. There's got to be a catch.

"Yes, little brother. Regrettable as it may be, I now believe you are not of the homosexual persuasion."

"Why?"

"Why what?"

"Why all of a sudden do you think I'm not gay?"

Cathy laughs. "You sound disappointed."

"No. Just suspicious."

"Some things have come to my attention lately that lead me to believe that you are not as cool and interesting as I'd hoped you were. Okay? Let's leave it at that."

"Well. Good," I say, snuggling down into bed. "Now maybe you can convince Mom and Dad I'm not gay."

"Sure," Cathy offers. "Just as soon as I tell them that I am."

I sit bolt upright. "Excuse me? Tell them you're *what*?"

"Gay. Although, technically," she explains, "I guess I'd be considered a lesbian."

Okay, so what the hell am I supposed to say to that? This could easily be another trick. If I start being all sympathetic and understanding, she might crack up and make fun of me for being so gullible—and gay.

"Hell-*oooo*?" Cathy says. "Did you hear what I just said? I'm trying to tell you something important here, turdlet. I'm confiding in you. Are you just going to sit there and not say anything?"

"No," I croak out. "I just . . . It's not . . . I mean, I don't even know if I should believe you."

"What *possible* motive could I have for telling you I'm a lesbian if I'm not?"

"How should I know? You screw with me all the time. I mean, for months you've been insisting it was me who was gay. Now all of a sudden, it's you."

"I *did* think you were gay, Sean. Or at least I wanted you to be. I mean, we're twins, you know. Not identical, but still. And they say lots of times when one twin is gay, the other one is too. I guess I was hoping that if I could get *you* to tell Mom and Dad first, then I could see how they'd react. Since you're the golden child, I figured they'd accept it and then, when they found out about me, they'd already be used to the idea and it wouldn't be such a shocker."

I ignore the parts about her basically wanting to use me as a guinea pig, because that's pretty much textbook Cathy, and go right to the important part: "So . . . It's really true, then?"

"Yup. Your big sister's a girl's girl. Through and through."

"So, then," I say. "*Are* you going to tell Mom and Dad? You know, about you being a lesbian?"

"Eventually. I suppose. But after the baby's born. That way they'll be so preoccupied that they won't have time to worry much about it. So don't go blabbing to them. Or anyone else, for that matter. If I find out you've told your dweeb friends, I'll break every one of your appendages. Including the appendage you shake hands with every night before you go to bed. Are we clear?"

"Yeah, sure," I say, deciding to take it easy on her and not point out her hypocrisy where privacy is concerned because again, it's typical Cath. "How did you . . . ? I mean . . . When did you—?"

"Figure it out? I guess I kind of always knew. If I really think about it. Even though I've had boyfriends. But I was absolutely positive about it last year. When I met this really hot Israeli girl at a party." She laughs. If Cathy's lying, then she's an even better actress than Leyna.

"And what about Nessa?" I ask, bracing myself. "Is she . . . ?"

Cathy howls with laughter. "*Nessa*? Uhh, *no*. She tried. I mean, Nessa will try anything once. But she likes guys."

"Oh, good," I blurt, and clap my hand over my mouth. Crap. Maybe Cathy didn't pick up on that.

A painfully awkward silence swallows up the room.

Or maybe she did. . . .

"Okay, Sean," Cathy finally says. "I need to tell you something else."

The way-too-serious confessional tone of her voice makes my belly grip up.

"Tell me something about what?"

"I feel sort of bad about it." She coughs awkwardly.

"I asked Nessa to do a little . . . investigating for me. You know, to find out if you really liked girls or not."

"You *what*?" My skin flushes hot and cold.

"I'm sorry! I had to know for sure, okay? I just asked her to flirt with you a little, see how you responded. We figured out you weren't gay once she caught you staring down her shirt. So there it is. My confession."

"Goddamn it, I knew it." I'm chewing the hell out of my tongue. "You're sick, you know that? You need help. Seriously. Both of you. *God.*" I shake my head. "And just so you know, I wasn't ever interested in Nessa, and I certainly never looked down her shirt." I should probably have limited myself to just the one lie, but I'm practically vibrating with righteous indignation here. "I only let her hang around with me so she'd help me with my movie."

"You were definitely interested," Cathy says. "At least, according to Nessa."

"Screw you, Cathy." I slam my head back into my pillow. "Lesbian or not, you're still an asshole."

"I said I was sorry, okay? Jesus. Chill out. It's not like you didn't get anything out of it. I bet your movie's a million times better because of Nessa."

"Yup. You're right. It is. And when we win the film festival tomorrow—which you're *not* invited to, by the way—I'll be able to build my own room and I'll never have to see either of your stupid faces ever again."

CHAPTER FIFTY-NINE

DUEL

I CAN BARELY KEEP MY EYES open in the backseat of Angela's car. Normally a ride with Coop's sister wouldn't be worth the hassle—taking off your shoes, not being allowed to roll down the windows, having to listen to her sleep-inducing elevator music—but Matt, Coop, and me missed our bus and we're supposed to be meeting everyone at Uncle Doug's by one o'clock.

I've got that overtired cotton-headed nauseous feeling going on right now. I was wide awake and steaming over the whole Nessa situation all night long—well, that and Cathy's snores, which picked up like clockwork once she'd gotten her confessions out. I can't believe I let myself get suckered in by them. Especially after I'd told myself they were up to something. I'm such an idiot. Of *course* there was no way that someone like Nessa would have even the slightest interest in a total loser like me.

All that stuff about what a great writer I was and how I needed to be more assertive and stand up for myself. Ugh. All of it just to butter me up, to make me think she actually cared. And that stuff with the tarot—a conflict between *male* and *female,* needing to be reborn. God, how did I not see right through that? Pathetic.

Angela has slowed to a crawl as she leans forward and squints out the window. "Where the hell is this place, anyway?" she says. "I thought you said it was on Genesee."

"It is," Coop insists. "It's just up here on the right."

"Finally." Angela huffs as she coasts her pristine car up to Uncle Doug's house. "If I'd known it was *all* the way down Genesee, I would have charged you twenty bucks. You're lucky we prenegotiated."

"You're much too kind." Coop pulls a ten and a five from his jeans pocket, leans over the front seat, and hands the cash to his sister. "Keep the change."

Angela flips Coop off before popping the trunk. "And be careful taking your crap out. If I find a single scratch, you're paying for a whole new paint job." Just then Angela's phone rings. She grabs it as I reach for the door handle. "Hello? . . . It's about time someone from your stupid company called me back. Sally Gregg is a total rip-off, okay? I'm missing, like, half my diet stuff."

Coop's eyes go wide as he quickly shoos Matt and me out of the car. He slams the door shut as the three of us pull on our shoes.

Matt laughs. "I thought you said you were off your diet."

"I was," Coop says as we move to the rear of the car and take out our suit bags. "But that's when I thought we weren't going to get this movie made. Now it's going to be paparazzi city, dawg."

We trudge up the drive, and Coop turns to me. "You okay, dude? You're awfully quiet."

"I didn't sleep well," I say, knocking on the front door. "I guess I'm just anxious."

And pissed off. And embarrassed. And depressed.

I called Nessa this morning to tell her how I felt about what she did to me. But I got her machine. So I just left a message. Explaining how Cathy had told me all about their little scheme and how neither one of them was welcome at the screening this afternoon.

I wanted to sound angry and mean and nasty, but I'm pretty sure I just came across as stammering and nervous and pitiful.

Anyway, whatever. At least I won't have to see her today.

"Hi."

I look up to see Nessa standing in my uncle's doorway. There's a brief flicker of excitement followed immediately by a tidal wave of anger. "What are *you* doing here?"

"Can we talk? Please?" Nessa shoots an apologetic smile at Matt and Coop. "Alone?"

"I have nothing to say to you. I told you not to come."

"What's going on?" Matt asks.

"Nothing. She just . . ." I clench my jaw, my head and heart pounding. "She shouldn't be here. That's all."

"What are you talking about?" Coop says. "She helped save our movie."

I turn on him and snap, "She doesn't *care* about our movie. She doesn't *care* about me. Or you. Or any of us. Don't you get it? She and Cathy were just playing me. Having a little game. A big old laugh at my expense."

"I'm so sorry, Sean," Nessa says. "You're right: at first that's exactly what we were doing. But—"

"I don't want to hear it! Whatever you have to say, Nessa, can't possibly make a difference." I shove past her and into Uncle Doug's house. My stupid throat is closing up. If she doesn't get out of here now, I'm afraid I'm going to burst into some very un-Rogart-like tears. "Just leave, okay? You're not welcome."

"Sean," Nessa says. "Please, let me just—"

"I said *go*!"

"What do you mean there's no popcorn?" Matt's grandpa grouses. "I thought we were seeing a movie. How can they show a movie without any goddamn popcorn?"

"It's a fancy affair, Arlo," Mrs. Hoogenboom says, shuffling him along. "It's not like your regular showings."

The Trail Blazer Theater is decked out with balloons and flowers and posters everywhere. Practically everyone we know is here—my dad, my hugely pregnant mother, and Uncle Doug; Matt's mom, his brother, Pete, and Pete's girlfriend, Melissa; Matt's grandpa Arlo and Grandpa Arlo's lady friend, Mrs. Hoogenboom; Coop's parents, Helen's mom, Valerie's parents and little brother, George, and even Tony Grillo— who's apparently dating Kelly West again. Everybody all spiffed up in suits and dresses.

It's like a red-carpet film premiere and family reunion all wrapped up in one. The only people miss-ing are Cathy and Nessa. It's kind of weird not to have them here. I mean, Cathy is my twin and Nessa was my leading lady and cowriter. But it's not like I actually *want* them here. Not after what they did. Still, I float through the crowd feeling untethered, my emotions mixed up and swirling around inside me.

"Wait, wait, wait." Coop's dad has him and Helen cornered by a potted tree. "Explain the premise of this to me again. They're monkeys. But they're also human. And vampires. *And* zombies?"

"You'll understand when you see it," Coop says.

"I sure as shit hope so. Otherwise I want my twenty bucks back."

"You didn't *pay* twenty bucks, Dad."

"Yeah, but my time is money, mister."

Coop catches my look and rolls his eyes. I flash him a knowing smile and move along. Brush some lint off the lapel of my jacket. Luckily, Dad had an old suit he let me borrow. It's sort of plaid and a bit dated, but it sure beats the hell out of my split dress pants and straitjacket-tight sport coat.

Just then my phone buzzes with a text. I get a jolt of excitement, like maybe it's Nessa and she's decided to come anyway and . . . but no. When I look at the screen, I see that it's a good luck and congratulatory message from Leyna. Which is sweet, I suppose, though disappointing. And as a further bit of mockery—though certainly unintentional—Leyna's attached a picture of her corgi's rashless ass with a big THANK YOU Photoshopped in an arch over its tail stump. Lovely.

"So," Mom says, waddling up to me, leading with her basketball belly. "This isn't *too* too scary, is it?" She places her hand on her stomach. "We don't want to induce labor here."

"I told you you didn't have to come," I say, my tone more prickly than I want. "It's a horror film. It's going to be scary."

"All right. I'll just hide my eyes in your father's shoulder." She reaches out and squeezes my arm. "I'm very proud of you."

"Thanks."

"And I think you picked a great business to go into," Mom says, leaning in and whispering conspiratorially. "The movie industry is rife with gays. You'll feel right at home."

I should just tell her about Cathy. It would serve my

evil twin right. But instead I just sigh. "Thanks, Mom. That's great. I'll see you after the show."

I head over to Matt and Valerie, who are hanging around a standee for some film called *Crib Death 2: Baby's Back*.

"You doing okay?" Valerie asks.

I shrug. "I guess." I glance over my shoulder at the crowded lobby. "I wish they'd just start this thing already."

"I'm sorry about Nessa," Matt says. "That's too bad."

"Whatever. It is what it is. At least we got our movie made, right?"

Suddenly there's a loud crash by the front of the door, followed by shrieks and screams. The crowd parts, and I am afforded a full-on view of what all the ruckus is.

Nick! In his humanzee costume. Matted and muddied with half of the monkey mask torn off his face.

"You!" He points a filthy mangy chimp-finger at me. "I'm going to kill you!"

Holy crap! It's just like the end of every bad horror film when the supposedly dead creature comes back for one last attack.

Nick hurtles toward me, dragging his back leg slightly. I grab the nearest thing to me—the *Crib Death 2* standee—and swing it out wildly at him. By some miracle the corner of it makes contact with his eye and Nick goes reeling backward. Just as he's about to recover, Tony and

Pete leap into the fray. They grab both his arms and drag him, kicking and growling, out of the theater.

There is a moment of dead silence. And then the entire lobby erupts in applause. There's a chorus of "Bravos" and "Wonderfuls" and "Brilliants." Like everyone thinks the whole thing was staged. Like some ridiculous publicity stunt or something.

My friends—the only ones who know for real what just happened—are by my side in an instant. My heart's beating a million miles an hour, and I'm sweating right through my suit jacket.

"Holy crap, are you all right?" Matt says.

"Yeah." I reach out to steady myself on his arm. "I think. Jesus. That was . . . unexpected, huh?"

"You totally clocked him," Coop praises. "That was epic."

And then the lobby lights flick on and off several times just as we hear police sirens wailing outside.

"Guess that's our cue," I say.

Matt holds up his crossed fingers. "Here's to taking home the big prize. You freakin' deserve it after that."

We shuffle down the aisles, those of us in the cast and crew sitting in the prime reserved rows. I notice two empty seats—one next to Mom and Dad, a few rows back, where Cathy should be. And one next to me, in the VIP row, where Nessa should be.

Just as the lights in the theater dim, I glance over and see Helen grab Coop's hand.

And Matt put his arm around Valerie.

I sink into my seat and try to focus on the movie rather than the lump that seems to be caught in my throat.

The first thing I realize is that, while video shot on a cell phone doesn't look too bad on a laptop, it looks absolutely horrible when blown up to movie-screen proportions. Fuzzy and blurry and shaky and pretty almost impossible to look at.

The next thing I notice is Nessa.

And how even blurry and fuzzy and shaky, she still looks amazing. She's got a face made for the big screen; even when shot in super-lo-res, her eyes find you and are totally expressive, and her cheekbones are killer. And those lips . . . wow! How did I ever think Leyna was the girl of my gamer dreams? She couldn't hold a candle to Nessa.

I'm so transfixed by her that it takes me a minute to realize that almost everyone in the theater is laughing hysterically. Uncle Doug just came on screen, and while I'll grant you that he's no Ian McKellen, I didn't think he was *that* laughable as Dr. Schmaloogan. But when the scene shifts and it's me and Nessa up on the screen, acting our little hearts out, and they're *still* laughing, I finally get it: they think it's a farce. The scare-your-pants-off horror film that we've all been slaving over for months is getting bigger laughs from this crowd than *The Hangover.*

Of course, I immediately turn to look at Nessa, to share in this bizarre but kind of awesome twist with her. Only she's not there. Because I yelled at her. And told her she didn't care about the movie. That she wasn't welcome here.

And before I know it, I'm up and out of my seat.

Running toward the exits.

Charging through the theater doors. Into the lobby. Then out on the street. Searching for the nearest subway station.

🎥 CHAPTER SIXTY 🎥

THE LAST MAN ON EARTH

My body was on the subway. And then the train. And the bus. And finally on my bike pedaling like crazy through the streets of Lower Rockville. But my mind was on Nessa the whole time. Thinking about what I want to say to her. Questions I want to ask. Things I hope she says to me.

And now here I am. In front of her house. Having built up this elaborate end-of-the-movie fall-into-each-other's-arms finale in my imagination. And I'm suddenly wondering if showing up unannounced like this—after having publicly told Nessa off—is a cool Han Solo move or just another one of my Jar Jar Binks-isms.

I mean, sure, *maybe* she was going to apologize profusely and confess her undying love for me when I cut her off.

But maybe she was just going to apologize. And give me the old "Can't we please just be friends" speech.

My stomach sours. Oh, good Gandalf. Of course that's what she was going to say. Just like it was with Leyna. What the hell was I thinking? I'm such an idiot.

Forget it. I'll just go home. Hop into bed. Tell everyone I was feeling sick and that's why I ran out of the theater. Nobody has to know. If I get out of here now I can save myself bucketfuls of humiliation.

I look around to make sure nobody's seen me. Hop on my bike. Set my foot on the pedal. And am just about to make my escape when I feel Nessa's necklace thump against my chest.

I stop, remembering what she said about crossroads and choosing our paths. Do I really want to be the guy lying in the cemetery who let everyone else make his choices for him? Or do I want to take charge of my life, do what *I* want to do? Okay, sure, maybe I'll be humiliated. Maybe Nessa will shoot me down and I'll cringe every time I see her for the next couple of months.

But at least I'll know I tried. That I took a chance — a chance Maggie Stillman never got to take.

I muster my courage, my heart slamming so hard in my chest it feels like I might actually die, and force myself to swing my leg off the bike.

As I do, my phone buzzes in my pocket. I slide it out and see a text from Nessa: *gt the hll n here alrdy, wld ya!*

I look up and see Nessa staring down at me from her

window. How long as she been standing there, watching me choose my fate?

I don't know why this makes me smile, but it does. I quickly text her back: *b rIt thr.*

I start to jog my bike toward the back of her house.

"Drop it on the front lawn," Nessa calls out her window. "I think we're past all the clandestine stuff, don't you? Just come in. The door's open."

I do as I'm told and am standing in front of Nessa's mystical magical fairy-tale bedroom door in under thirty seconds, my stomach all twisted in pretzels. Does she want me in here so she can yell at me for totally losing it earlier and barring her from the screening? Or could she actually be as excited to see me as I am to be standing here, a door's width away from each other?

Nessa opens the heavy wooden door and ushers me in. "I have to say, I'm kind of surprised to see you. Isn't your movie screening at this very moment?"

"*Our* movie," I say quickly. "Look, Nessa, I'm really sorr—"

"Don't," she says, looking pained. I flash back to Leyna's living room, to my awkward confession of love—well, lust, really—and how horribly I misread that whole situation. Nessa's screwed-up face hits me harder than any rejection from Leyna ever could. The tears that I'd suppressed earlier come screaming back. If I don't get the hell out of here *right now,* I'm afraid I'll give

Nessa all the ammunition she and Cathy need to mock me for the rest of my life.

I reach behind me, fumbling for the doorknob. "I should go," I say quickly. "I don't know why I—"

"Sean, wait."

I look up and finally meet Nessa's gaze. That pained expression that I thought was revulsion actually looks more like . . . regret. "You still haven't let me apologize," she says. "I never meant to hurt you. Cathy and I . . . we just thought we'd have a little fun, that you'd show zero interest in me and Cathy would know that she wasn't alone, you know? That you were just like her. But it was pretty clear from the start that you weren't gay. I should have stopped as soon as I realized it, but I kind of *liked* hanging around you. I thought your movie was awesome, and I was flattered that you seemed to think my ideas were helpful. And I was also flattered that you . . . seemed to find me attractive." Her pale neck blots pink as she admits this, and as amazing and adorable and hot as I've found Nessa in the past, seeing her neck flush with pleasure and embarrassment totally does me in. I'm but a humble Padawan to her Jedi Masteress.

"I like you, Sean," she says. "And I'm so sorry that I hurt you."

So, here it is: time for me to put all my cards on the table. I stand up straight and try to take a deep breath, though I can't seem to get much air. "I like you too,

Nessa. And . . . not just as a friend. Or my sister's friend. I *like you* like you. Like, *really* like you."

And just like that, it's as though I've shrugged a three-hundred-pound wampa off my shoulders. I blink, feeling like I can breathe again. The rest comes easily. "I was in the theater, watching you up on screen, and you were *amazing*. Like, truly, truly amazing. And I started thinking about this past week and how much fun we had. And kissing you. But even before that, when we were writing the script together. I mean, sure, sometimes you were a total pain in my ass and you made me work *way* harder than I'd wanted to. But the movie wouldn't have been half as good as it is without you pushing me and adding your own ideas to the script."

Nessa smiles shyly. "We did have fun, didn't we?"

"Are you kidding? Being with you has been the most fun I've ever had in my life. Hands down."

Nessa laughs, and there's a hint of her old teasing self when she says, "Come on, even more fun than when you and Matt and Coop dressed in drag? You know, we still have those pictures saved on Cathy's comp—"

"You do not," I say, a pleased tingling surging through my body despite the very heinous threat in her words.

"If you're nice to me, I might just go in and delete it once and for all."

I smile, and soon we're both standing there smiling at each other just like we were yesterday, when we were

wrapping up shooting. "Hey, can I ask you something?"
I say at last.

"Anything."

"When did it change? I mean, when did it . . . you
know . . . stop being a game?"

She winces at the word *game.* "It's hard to say. I
think it sort of started when I found you in the dumpster.
You looked so . . . I don't know . . . vulnerable. And not
entirely bad in just your boxer shorts," she adds with a
wicked grin. Now it's my turn to blush. "But maybe it
was before then. Hanging out and getting to know each
other. You're really sweet, Sean. I never really noticed
that side of you before."

I take a step toward her, my heart thumping in my
chest. But I stop a few inches from her.

"It's funny," I say, glancing around. "I still half expect
Cathy to come out of your closet, laughing hysterically
and snapping pictures that she can post on Facebook."

"Cathy coming out of the closet? Are we making gay
jokes, now, Sean? Just when I thought you were so sweet
and sensitive."

"What? No. No, that's not what I—"

Nessa laughs and the sound fills me. "Man, you're
cute when you're flustered."

Nessa closes the space between us, reaching up and
touching my cheek. Her intense green eyes lock onto
mine in a way that is desperately hot.

And before I know what's happening, I'm kissing

her beautiful soft lips again. But for real this time. And if I thought those movie kisses were good, well, forget about it. Because this is the most amazing thing I've ever experienced in my life. Her licorice smell, the taste of her tongue, the gentle sound of her breathing, the metallic brush of her lip ring, the heavy warmth of her cross pendant against my chest. All my senses wonderfully amplified.

Minutes pass. Or maybe it's hours. Anything seems possible when you're kissing Nessa in her fairy-tale bedroom.

But at some point, the real world intrudes.

"Whoa, Sean." Nessa pulls back, her cheeks pink. "Maybe we need to slow down."

"Oh. No. That's my cell phone," I say, reaching into my pocket to try to shut off the vibrations.

"And here I thought it was me," Nessa teases. "You'd better answer it, though. Maybe they're calling from the theater to tell you who won."

"Tell *us*," I remind her. "And given how hard people were laughing when I left, I highly doubt that." But I pull the phone from my pocket and squint at the screen. "It's my dad." I frown and click the answer button. "Hello?"

"Sean, where are you?" Dad shouts, sounding like he's out of breath. "Everybody was looking for you."

"I'm with Nessa," I say. "It's . . . a long story."

"Well, I don't even have time for a short story. We're headed to Walker Medical Center. Your mom was laughing so hard at your movie that her water broke. She's in labor. Can you take a taxi and meet us there?"

Suddenly my knees go weak. "Yeah, okay, sure. No problem," I ramble. "Is she . . . ? Is everything okay?"

"She's fine. She's good." Dad sounds like he might start crying. "Keep breathing, hon," he calls away from the phone, then says to me, "I've got to go. We're having a baby, Sean! You're going to be a big brother!"

And then the line goes dead.

Nessa's looking at me with these big wide what's-going-on eyes. "So?" she says.

"It's my mom. We've got to go to the hospital. She's having the baby."

CHAPTER SIXTY-ONE

WHAT EVER HAPPENED TO BABY JANE?

Do you want to hold her?" Mom asks me as I stand by the side of her bed, staring in awe at the tiny little baby girl she has nestled on her chest.

Mom—who looks both sweaty-exhausted and happy-glowing at the same time—has asked that only one person visit her at a time. And since Dad and Cathy were actually in the delivery room for the birth—I didn't think I could handle seeing what I thought I might see— I get to be the first one to visit with the cleaned-up and swaddled baby.

"I . . . um . . . I don't know if I . . ." I swallow the thick lump that's congealed in my throat. A thousand different emotions are careening through me. They've been slamming up against one another like a multicar pileup on the freeway ever since I stepped into the room.

First there was surprise at how small and beautiful the baby is.

Then there was shame for ever thinking this baby was a curse on my life.

Excitement, joy, nervousness, wonder, amazement all followed in quick succession.

And now I'm terrified, because I *would* like to hold my new little sister, but I'm also afraid I might hurt her.

"I don't know how to hold a baby," I finally say. "What if . . . I drop her?"

Mom smiles. "You're not going to drop her, sweetie. Just cradle her in your arms carefully. Like this." She shows me the proper carrying position, then holds out the small bundle of snow-white blankets to me. "Go on. It's okay."

I gingerly take the baby from Mom's hands, bring her close to my body, and cradle her like a super-rare vinyl-caped Jawa action figure.

Her adorable pinched-up pink face peeks out from under a minuscule pink stocking cap. She's heavier than I thought she would be. And she smells incredible. Like a fresh blueberry muffin and warm milk.

"She's beautiful," I say, suddenly feeling this enormous wave of love for her. "Hello, little Gracie. I'm Sean."

"So," Mom asks, "how does it feel being a big brother?"

"It feels good." I beam at Mom. "Really good." And then that pang of shame again. "I'm really sorry. About what I said. About the baby being . . . I didn't mean it." And of course I realize instantly that this is a lie. "What

I mean is, I *thought* I meant it. At the time. But now . . ." I stare down at my new baby sister in my arms. "I don't know what I was thinking." I snuffle back tears, wondering what kind of sappy-gas they pump into these hospital rooms to make you feel like you're constantly on the verge of sobbing.

Mom laughs and snuffles too. "It's all right, honey. I understand."

And, okay, I know it sounds corny and all, but holding my little sister, I'm proud that she's going to be sleeping in my old room. With all my old memories. Making new memories for herself. It feels good to be able to share that with her.

It's too bad my parents didn't wait until this moment to ask me to give up my room, because right now, I'd do pretty much anything for this little baby.

"She's amazing," I say. "It's like, I can't stop smiling at her."

"I know," Mom says, dabbing at her nose. "It's exactly how I felt when you and Cathy were born."

I start to lightly rock Gracie in my arms. She makes a tiny squeak noise, which causes me to smile even bigger.

"Welcome to the world, Gracie," I whisper to my brand-new sister. "You're in for one heck of a ride."

CHAPTER SIXTY-TWO

28 DAYS LATER

IT'S BEEN ALMOST A MONTH since Gracie was born.

Almost a month since our film totally tanked at TerrorFest. Apparently it was the funniest film they've ever screened. Unfortunately for us, though, they only award prizes to actual *scary* movies. And only our "publicity stunt" was terrifying. Well, before he was carted off by the cops.

But even though our movie didn't do what we'd hoped it would do, Nessa and I are kind of proud of the response our film got. I mean, who couldn't use a laugh with all the crazy crap going on in the world? And how many films—scary or otherwise—can claim they put a pregnant woman into labor?

Don't get me wrong. It still totally and royally sucks having to share a room with Cathy. For some reason her snoring has only gotten worse with the approach of summer. Call it allergies. Call it the effects of humidity. Call it whatever the hell you want, she continues to sound like a flock of tortured phlegm-afflicted geese.

And do not even get me started at how pissed off she is that I've "somehow managed to trick" Nessa into dating me. Cathy's taking *that* out on me in a big way.

Some things never change.

Still, the joys of having an adorable little sister far outweigh the pains of having a cranky nine-minutes-older one. Gracie has just started responding to the sound of my voice. Smiling and cooing when I make silly noises or when I quote her lines from *Zonkey!* in my best Rogart voice. She's a pretty great audience.

And all those months of work on the film haven't exactly gone to waste: because of the response we got at TerrorFest, we decided to upload parts of our film as weekly webisodes on YouTube. We've gotten several thousand views and quite a few comments on the movie so far, which is pretty cool. And since it seems to be so popular, Nessa and me have even been batting around ideas for a spin-off, featuring Nashira and Rogart and their adorable but genetically altered baby, Lazarus.

"Sean-o, your opinion on this, please," Coop says, hunkered over my laptop, Buttons curled up on his lap. "Should we end this episode with the scene where Rogart gets his arm scratched by one of the humanzees? Or when the zombie horde is trying to bust into the house?"

"The house," I say, nodding at the screen, where four floppy ape-hands are smacking into the front door over and over like giant hairy oven mitts. Jeez Louise, how did we ever think that scene was scary? "Definitely. It's funnier. Best to leave them laughing so they'll want to come back next week."

"I'll second that," Matt says, gesturing with my replica Gladius from the beanbag chair on the floor.

Coop nods. "Consider it done, then."

Just then the bedroom door bursts open. "You dweeblets just about done? I've got to get ready for work."

"You're supposed to knock, Cathy," I remind her for, like, the thousandth time. "When the sock's on the door? We agreed on that, remember?"

"Yeah, and you're supposed to pony up twenty-five bucks a month in rent. We agreed on that too, *remember?*"

"*You* agreed on it. When you stole fifty bucks from us!" I cry. "I still have to pay Uncle Doug back all of his money *and* the cost of the amp we busted at the Battle of the Bands. You'll get your money right after he gets his. *Not.*"

Cathy stalks over to her side of the room and yanks open her closet. "Any person with half a brain knows they should pay their rent before paying their creditors. Otherwise you might come home one day to find you and all your shit *evicted.*"

I'm just about to respond when there's a loud

elongated braying blare—like a giant wheezing clown's horn—coming from outside.

"What the hell was that?" Coop asks, setting the computer aside.

"I have no idea," I say.

It sounds again. A whiny fog horn that's annoyed it's being made to blow.

Matt hoists himself from the beanbag. "I believe this bears investigating."

The three of us head out into the hallway. "Later, masturbators," Cathy calls after us and slams the door. Obviously she lacks our inquisitive natures.

Me, Coop, and Matt make our way downstairs and out the front door.

And there, in our driveway, is a hunormous rickety old RV painted like the Milky Way with the words HAVE YOU BEEN SAVED? BETTER MAKE IT QUICK! THE END OF THE WORLD IS NIGH! printed across the top.

"Howdy ho!" Uncle Doug calls from the driver's seat, wafting a zeppelin-size doobie out the window.

The three of us approach the RV cautiously.

"So," Uncle Doug calls from his perch, "what do you think?"

"It's big," I say.

"Damn straight." Uncle Doug toasts this sentiment with his joint. "It's a thirty-foot Class C model. She's got about fifteen years on her, but she's not in bad shape.

Won her from some disgruntled Holy Roller in a sperm-count contest. Turns out all that bunk about the happy leaf affecting your spermatozoa is all a big myth." He takes a long drag on his hand cannon.

"Why'd you bring it here?" I ask, glad that Mom and Dad are at the pediatrician with Gracie and aren't around to see this monstrosity parked in their driveway.

"Why do you think?" Uncle Doug opens his door and climbs down. He gestures at the camper like a game-show hostess. "It's your new bedroom, Seanie."

I stare at Uncle Doug. My eyes strain from their sockets. "Are you serious?"

"As syphilis, my friend." He grins.

"Score," Coop says. "Your own place, dawg. How dope is that?"

Uncle Doug takes a generous drag on his joint. "I suppose you'll have to arm-wrestle your sister for it, though. Either way, you guys'll have your privacy back. Consider it Uncle Doug's own personal prize package for having the fortitude to finish your film." He lunges for me and grabs me in a headlock, giving me a skull-bruising noogie. "Of course, this doesn't excuse you from your carpet-mascot duties, Seanie. I'm still expecting payback for my outlay of cash, my friend."

"Okay, okay!" I shout.

"What are the magic words?"

"Uncle Doug! Uncle Doug! Uncle Doug!"

"That's my boy."

He releases me and I stumble backward, rubbing my scalp.

Uncle Doug nods toward the RV. "Go on. Take a look inside. I'm gonna go bury an elf in your john. I'd do it in the RV, but the commode's not exactly reliable at the moment."

Uncle Doug makes his way to the house as Matt, Coop, and me head into the motor home.

"This is spectac," Coop says when we get inside. "Your own kitchen. Bathroom. And lounge area." He flops down on the beige couch, props his feet up on the cushions, and laces his fingers behind his head. "You and Nessa are gonna have some good times in here."

"That's assuming, of course"—Matt turns the kitchen faucet on and off—"that you can beat your sister in an arm-wrestle."

"Pfff," I lip fart. "There isn't going to be any arm-wrestling. This puppy's mine." I take a seat at the steering wheel and pretend I'm driving. "I'm staking my claim."

"Is that so?"

I whip around to see Cathy, decked out in her Wal-Mart uniform, stepping up into the RV.

"Uncle Doug brought it over for me," I argue. "So take a hike."

"Tsk, tsk, little brother," Cathy says. "Being older than you, *I* should get the best room." She starts to stroll around, running her fingers over the counters.

"You're going to get your old room back," I say. "Isn't that enough for you?"

Behind Cathy's back, I can see Coop and Matt whispering conspiratorially. Then Coop readjusts his position on the couch, looking like he can't quite get comfortable.

Suddenly Cathy's nose starts to twitch. "Actually. You know what? This place smells like sweaty ass. I bet it was owned by some old skanky bedbug-ridden couple who never washed and sat around naked all the time." She wipes her fingers on her khakis. "You enjoy your new home, Sean. I think I'll stick with my nice, clean, uncontaminated, climate-controlled bedroom in the house. Buh-bye."

And with that, Cathy trots out of the camper.

Matt waves his hand in front of his nose. "Coop, dude, that was grisly. Way to bring out the big guns."

"Don't thank me," Coop says, getting up from the couch and opening a window. "Thank Sally Gregg. God only knows what they put into those bars and shakes, but Helen has banned me from consuming them for a twenty-four-hour period before I see her."

I look over at Matt and Coop, busting their guts, and feel a swell of emotion rising up in me. A guy couldn't ask for two more amazing friends.

I clear my throat. "I can't believe this thing's really mine. Just think how cool it will look once I put my stuff up on the walls, maybe repaint the outside. I bet we could even set up my Xbox in here."

"Speaking of summer," Coop says, leaping over and snagging the passenger seat beside me.

"Who was speaking of summer?" Matt asks. He walks over and perches on the console between me and Coop, his knees straddling the stick shift.

"I was. Just now." Coop leans back and places his feet up on the dash. "We gotta get planning, dawgs. Summer vacation's only a few weeks away. Don't you doinklettes think it might be prudent to start talking potential goals?"

Me and Matt exchange a look.

"Maybe our goal should be to *not* have a goal this summer," I offer.

"Yeah," Matt adds. "Leave things to chance for once."

Coop rolls his eyes. "Booooring. No." He sits up. "I say we take a page from Nessa's *Necronomicon*. We're all going to die someday, right? And there's no knowing when. So what's the one thing everyone should experience at least once in their lives?"

I eye Coop warily, expecting his filthy dirty worst. After all, the goals do seem to be getting raunchier and raunchier with each passing year. What does he want us to do now—combine all our recent schemes into some sort of homemade, cell-phone-shot porno, staged in my swinging new rock-and-roll Magic Bus?

But I should have given him more credit. Because Coop's got that gleam in his eye. The one he used to get back when our goals were simpler. Like collecting a thousand golf balls off the golf course or eating our weight in Funyuns over the course of the summer.

"I think you know what I'm talking about." Coop smiles wide and spreads his arms even wider, encompassing more than just the RV—encompassing the whole world. "Road trip!"

ACKNOWLEDGMENTS

I come to the end of the Swim the Fly series with a mixture of elation and melancholy. Although I am happy that I've been able to finish the series on such a high note, I am also saddened to have to say good-bye to these boys (at least for now).

Mostly, though, I am excited to have been able to tell a story from Matt's, Coop's, and now Sean's point of view. And I am extremely proud to have my name on the cover of these books.

But to pretend that I was singularly responsible for these novels would be a crime. *So* many people have been involved with these stories along the way—from the very first scribble that launched this series all the way through to the final chapter of this book.

And so, on that note, I would like to offer my deepest gratitude to:

Kaylan Adair—my very own Miracle Worker—for working her editorial magic (once again) on my manuscript. Kaylan has such an incredible sense of story and character, and I am eternally grateful that I've gotten to work with her. Simply put, she makes me a better writer, and you can't ask for much more than that.

Everyone at Candlewick Press. I feel so very fortunate to be published by such a wonderful house and so thankful that they employ such amazing people.

Jodi Reamer, agent extraordinaire, for her guidance and advice.

Ken Freeman and James Fant, whose assistance with these books has been epic.

Kelly Miller and her amazing students at Platte City Middle School for all their enthusiastic support.

To all the teachers, librarians, and booksellers on a mission to get boys to read more and who have taken my books into their hearts.

The Surrey International Writers Conference for introducing me to Kaylan and for their encouragement of writers all over the world.

My mom and dad for their love and for buying up all my books in their neighborhood.

Emily, David, and Will for their encouragement and inspiration.

And of course, my wife, without whom none of these books would have ever seen the light of day. I love you.